D1414389

RHODESIAN DOLL HUNT

RHODESIAN DOLL HUNT

A Backpack, a Doll, and Genetic Espionage in Africa

C.L. Manning

CAPER CREW PUBLISHING

West Africa map: amended by author to include places of interest in novel from public domain resource, *Macky Portable Atlas Maps,* Western Africa, Copyright © 2010, 2013 Ian Macky. PAT maps are public domain. https://ian.macky.net/pat/map/wafr/wafrblu2.gif

Botswana, South Africa, Rhodesia map: amended by author to include places of interest in the novel from the public domain resource, *The World Factbook, 2021.* Washington, DC: Central Intelligence Agency, 2021 https://www.cia.gov

Cover Illustration (the doll) by Nancy Griffin.

Cover model: Brian Manning

ISBN: 979-8-9893800-1-5

For Marie, who buys dolls for little girls she'll never know

West Africa

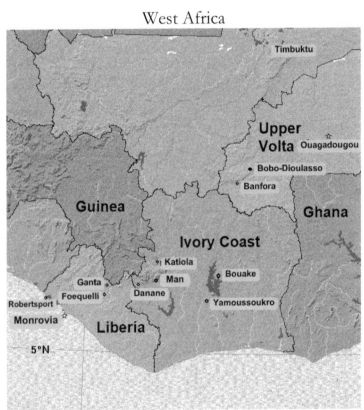

Botswana, South Africa, Rhodesia

The World Factbook, 2021. Washington, DC: Central Intelligence Agency, 2021

Kasane, Kazungula, Victoria Falls area

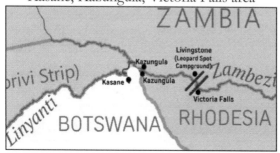

Part I
Bubba

Mad Dog, Bubba, and Craze on beach in Liberia

CHAPTER 1

"Will you marry me when you get back?"

Alex teetered, heels on the edge of the curb, eyes level with mine, palms pressed into her thighs. I was surprised, not so much by the question but by the timing of it. Hank had just pulled up in his Plymouth Valiant to give Mad Dog and me a ride to the airport. I'd spent the night at Alex's apartment, and it was time to go. It wasn't my first extended trip—I thought this goodbye would be like the others.

My mind had been in disarray all morning. Micro-tremors coursed through my legs and chest, aware I'd soon be setting foot in Africa for the first time. Had I packed everything—passport, malaria pills, international immunization record? Would Bubba be there to meet us at the airport in Liberia? Would Mad Dog and I get along on such a long trip? I balked, dry mouthed, my careless rectitude in the crosshairs of Alex's question. I hated leaving her, but the appeal of another junket had overwhelmed my travel addiction.

A previous trip to Israel popped into my head. I was living at Moshav Idan, picking tomatoes and eggplant in the Negev Desert. Four months of hard work, cutthroat games of Scrabble, and nightly talks of love, life, and politics had drawn me close to my Israeli family. Yet, my heart grew cold. Or was it indifferent? Worse. I'd been on the road for fifteen months by then, and goodbyes had become too easy. A quick shalom and a hug was all I could summon. I hitchhiked to London and caught the next Laker Airways flight back to Boston.

DanAndAlex. AlexAndDan. After eight years, our names were one word. We still exchanged gifts, flowers, and cards without occasion, and intimacy remained random in place and time. We were happy. Untroubled. Never spoke of marriage. One time she suggested I move in with her. Or was it twice? Between travel, work, and graduate studies, I couldn't find a reason to change things. In the back of my Catholic mind, even at the age of twenty-seven, I was sensitive to the thoughts of my father. Would he approve? The question forced my subconscious to seek refuge—evasion. I'd garble something like, "Not now," or, "It's not the right time." I loved her dearly but also loved life as it was.

Alex asked again, "Will you marry me when you get back?" With Mad Dog going bongo on the dashboard and "Light My Fire" blaring on WBCN, she was forcing me to focus.

Mad Dog stuck his head out the window, yelled at me. "C'mon Craze. Let's go."

My bottom eyelids squeezed upward. *This isn't how it should happen. In front of people. As I'm leaving. No roses, no ring, no down on one knee.* I was unnerved by my inability to form an appropriate response. *How about yes, you jackass?* I checked my watch—to buy an additional three seconds of thought. Five seconds passed. Nothing. I picked at the rubber seal on the car door, went in for another hug. Alex put her thumbs through my belt loops and pulled me closer, her cinnamon clove breath frozen in the quiet air. Josie, her roommate, locked her eyes on mine as I cradled Alex in the small of her back.

"I love you, Alex. We can talk about it when I get home."

Her yellow turtleneck parted from my breast. A burr on my shirt clung to hers, pulled, and released. Her shirt snapped and she let go a soft version of her legendary laugh. She twisted the edge of her mouth and peered at me, brown eyes chipping at my bedrock. She said, "Okay."

CHAPTER 2

Travis surged through the door, eyes squinted more than usual, vocals direct but calm. "Feds are swarmin' Curtis and Peg's house. Three minutes."

"I heard." Norah was already finalizing things. "Peggy called from the phone booth at the A&P. Got home and FBI blue jackets were all over the place."

Curtis and Peg, experts in diversionary tactics, were already on the road. Latex-gloved agents with black bags ducked under yellow crime scene tape at their house, dusting, writing on clipboards, pointing at handrails and tire tracks.

Travis tugged at the tip of his brown chevron mustache. "Where's Jaxon?"

"Little League."

"Shit."

Norah snatched their preassembled go-bags, each with a set of clothes, sneakers, layered coat, toiletries, chocolate, and nuts. Jaxon's included a new birth certificate with corresponding report cards, asthma inhalers, and his fourteen Willie Mays baseball cards. The family bag had a tool kit, first aid kit, license plates from Illinois and Florida, a book of contacts, passports, propaganda, and cash—US dollars, British pounds, and Deutschmarks. Guns and ammunition were locked beneath the dual facing rear seats of their Ford Country Squire. Travis changed the plates. Norah tossed bonus items into the car. They eased out of the driveway toward the baseball field—away from the chaos, away from their temporarily construed lives.

Jaxon was on deck. Travis saw his eyes flicker when he and Norah approached the chain-link fence behind the plate. Jaxon would understand the pursed lips and sharp nod of his father, the single-sided smile of his mother—looks he hadn't seen for two years. Travis confirmed his fears by reaching across his body and grasping Norah's left hand with his left hand. Jaxon recognized the cue. He dropped his head, pulled on the visor of his cap, and scuffed past the dugout, told the coach, "Don't feel good." Dust billows puffed beneath his cleats.

As a leader of the United Freedom Front, Travis had earned a seat on the FBI's Ten Most Wanted list and was still there in 1979. Each escape had been closer than the previous, and pursuit was now white hot. Logistics were nearly impossible with a ten-year-old and a pregnant wife.

Norah found the phone number of a sympathetic friend in the Weather Underground, a group formed in 1969 and led by Bernardine Dohrn. Their anti-imperialism ideology was in harmony with the UFF, subversives linked by an enemy of my enemy alliance.

"Did the Weathermen really name themselves after a Bob Dylan song?" Jaxon asked,

Travis smirked, unsettled by his son's remark but secretly feeling a sense of pride. "Yeah. At first, they called themselves the Weathermen. Changed it to the Weather Underground. Comes from "Subterranean Homesick Blues," Somethin' about a weatherman knowing how the wind blows. Or doesn't blow."

They found a phone booth. The contact filled Travis in on the principles and goals of a branch of the Underground called Weathermen Africa, whose recruiting arm was in London. Ninety minutes later, hands clasped, spines straight, the fugitive and his family strode through the airport as if they owned it.

CHAPTER 3

Alex: Why?

Alex sat in front of the TV and stared, folding laundry, hands angry, cheeks flushed with embarrassment.

"Where'd that come from, girl?" Josie asked, voice razor pitched.

"Don't know. Just came out."

"Hm."

"He froze. Do you believe it?" Craze's response rattled around her diaphragm and fluttered up to her mouth. 'We can talk about it when I get back.' Am I that pathetic?"

"No. But . . ."

A CBS news bulletin interrupted.

> "The FBI raided three houses in Deerfield, Ohio, this morning, suspected havens for members of the United Freedom Front, a revolutionary group committed to fighting inequities in the United States, apartheid in South Africa, and US imperialism in Latin America. They are implicated in a series of bombings targeting South African Airways, Mobil Oil, Honeywell, Motorola, IBM, and military facilities in Colorado, the Bronx, and Queens."

"You swore you'd never ask him, Alex. Said if he wants to marry you, *he* had to ask."

"Well, he's going away for what—six months. Nine? I never know with him. If I'm going to wait, I want to know where we stand. I'm ashamed I even asked."

```
"Its members are wanted for sedition,
defined as two or more people conspiring
to oppose, by force, the government's
authority, or to delay the execution of
any law of the United States. Their
stated goal is the violent overthrow of
the United States government, yet they
are known for warning their targets in
advance."
```

Alex gestured to the TV. "Do you hear this? The world is screwed up. I'm screwed up. You're screwed up."

Josie's flattened her lips. "Me? Straighten that out, girl."

Alex paused, dropped her forehead to her fingers, and laughed.

"You put a shock into Craze, girl. That was abrupt. Looked like he stepped on an oyster shell in Cape Cod Bay. Your timing was weird, but he deserved it."

```
"This is the same group that demanded
that Oscar Collazo be released from
prison, a man who tried to assassinate
Harry Truman at the Blair House in Wash-
ington. They also detonated a bomb when
Jimmy Carter campaigned in Clinton,
Massachusetts."
```

"Time to come to Jesus, Alex. If Craze can't answer that question by now, why you staying with him?"

Alex's fingers combed through her bangs. She could barely breathe. Head still, her brown eyes flowed to Josie's. "I still love him."

CHAPTER 4

Craze: Liberia

Hank screeched to a halt at Terminal E at Logan Airport in Boston, swearing he'd never drive again. Gas had gone from 65¢ to 72¢ a gallon in three weeks.

"There's a revolution brewing in Iran," I said. "Could hit a dollar by the end of '79." Hank and I looked at each other hard. I felt for him. He'd be joining us if he hadn't gotten his girlfriend pregnant when they were seventeen. He reached across the seat, interlocked his right thumb with mine and squeezed, web to web, in solidarity.

He said, "You get gored by a rhino, I get your Frampton album."

Mad Dog shook his head, unfond of drippy sentiment. He said farewell with a nod. The bitter scent of peeling rubber was Hank's signature goodbye.

Ten hours later, the Pan Am 747 bellied through a gray haze that followed the coastline of Liberia and glided onto the tarmac of Robertsfield, the international airport in Monrovia, the capital. Spinach and emerald shades of vegetation blended into the horizon like an impossible jigsaw puzzle. After stepping through the gray gasket that rimmed the exit door, it was a count of three before the tropical envelope that comes with being six degrees north of the equator declared its residence. Flak jacket heat, clam box humidity, skin turned to oatmeal.

A seamy, semi-rotten smell hovered over the entrance hall. Pass Control was lineless, a blotch of humans with snare drum faces fighting for position—victims of misplaced bureaucracy. Once through customs, I felt a reach and touch at my back pocket, an eleven-year-old boy testing his craft. A battalion of helpers encircled us like a noose. Men grabbed at Mad Dog's backpack offering to carry for cash. "Taxi, come. Taxi, come," rang from every direction. Instinct kicked in. Protect your things, protect your wallet, walk, keep moving. My preconceived notions of exotic Africa withered. Never had I felt so visible. Never had I felt so White.

I'd thought about what it would feel like to be a minority. We grew up in a one traffic light town halfway between Boston and Cape Cod—Norwell, home to a whopping three Black families. Anne was in our class—smart, flower child, wore ankle-length printed dresses when miniskirts were the rage. Her brother registered high on the nerd meter. The second Black family was all boys, athletes. I wasn't close to anyone in the third family.

I'd never thought about what it was like for them—apathy on my part, a mindless disposition of comfort, but one that nurtures disregard. Most in town would deem themselves enlightened, yet, as a kid, I heard the word *nigger* used without hesitation. Youth has its merits in that you get to choose what to embrace from the meshwork of parents, teachers, and friends; but still, you must choose to challenge or just go along. Our teachers preached inclusiveness while Walter Cronkite reported on deadly riots in Newark, Detroit, Chicago, and Omaha that were aimed at combating racism and cultivating rights for all. We discussed this in class, but there was one thing missing from most discussions: Black people.

Mad Dog spotted Bubba's red hair, which was closely cropped, a departure from the briar patch he wore in high school and at UMass, where he studied forestry. His freckled smirk said, "I can't believe you came to this fucking country." I'd forgotten how much I missed him. I hardly saw him after college when he moved to Oregon to be with the trees.

He was sided by his Peace Corps compadre, Mike, who oozed Tom Selleck confidence with his black, wavy hair and mustache, even tan, square jaw, and a shirt spun from cotton cloth he bought at a market in Kano, Nigeria. They both had the "lean Liberian look," a phrase they'd weave into our vocabulary. "Gotta kill some time," he said.

"You're staying at Mike's," Bubba said. We had riots over the price of rice last week, near my apartment in Monrovia. You don't want to be there. Besides, Mike's place is on the beach."

"My roommate and my girlfriend are still in my house," Mike said. "Leaving later this morning. Once they're out, you can move in." He turned to me. "Bubba told me about your background, Craze. We've got a place to show you while we're waiting."

They hailed a cab and took us to a biomedical research campus called ACORN. It was run by friends they'd become close with during the past two years. We walked along a canopy-covered path and came to a colossal, caged, environment set within a simple perimeter fence made of kino tree branches. The fence was there to keep humans at bay. Within the cage, chimpanzees swung, preened, and screeched at a pitch that could loosen the mercury in your teeth. Metal barrels with bottoms cut out were wedged horizontally into the crotches of tall tree branches, creating tunnels for the chimps to hide and play.

I protested. "We need down time."

"Just meet our friends at ACORN, especially Winston and Betsy," Bubba said. "They run the place. Have recruited highbrow scientists from all over the world."

Mad Dog surveyed the layout. He has an eye for detail, is good at remembering the trail, a string of events, or a rock that looks like a turtle. Friends since the fourth grade, we knew each other's idiosyncrasies and mainstays. If we agreed to something, it was good as done. One year we agreed to run the Boston Marathon, barely spoke of it all year, shook hands at the starting line. He tapped his front teeth twice with the knuckle of his thumb and said, "Let's go."

We followed the path to the entrance, absorbing the musk of the rainforest and a cocktail of odors spawn from tropical pollination, unaddressed deadfall, stale beetle dung, and uneaten fruit. A woman stood at the entrance beneath a red sign with a sprouting oak tree and raised black letters that read, "ACORN, Artful Conceptions in Organic Research and Nature." Hello, Bubba. These must be the friends you've chatted up," she said.

Bubba nodded. "Mad Dog. Craze. This is Betsy. CEO of this joint. Head honcho."

Betsy winked at me. "I don't suppose Craze is the name your mother gave you."

I laughed. "No, it's Dan, but nobody calls me that anymore. It's a holdover from our high school gang, the Caper Crew."

"He was a fan of Crazy Luke Graham, a wrestler known for a violent twitch he'd muster before making a big move," Bubba said.

"Ah. The Caper Crew. The master pranksters."

Mike laughed. "Are these the guys that started calling you Bubba?"

"Mm," I said. "We were in Bubba's car at the Wareham Drive-In. In the movie, the driver of the car was a goofball named Bubba."

Betsy grinned. "I never thought you looked like . . . a Bubba," she said in a dainty manner.

"The beauty of it," I said. Bubba's pale skin and Irish genes didn't advertise a scrapper.

Betsy carried a diminutive five-feet, one-inch frame that seemed to camouflage a brilliant mind. Her voice was thin but rang poised and knowing. "Welcome, Crazy Luke. Welcome, Mad Dog. Let's go say hi to Winston."

We stepped through a set of doors into a locked vestibule—some kind of security zone between two sets of doors. Betsy stepped into a phone-booth-sized box to the right of the door. Attached to the wall was a metallic half orb the size of a small beach ball with a circular window. She stared into the window and the door buzzed open.

Mad Dog's eyes widened. "Wha . . .?"

Betsy smiled. "It's a retinal scanner. Every retina has an intricate network of capillaries that are unique to the individual. Infrared light reflects off my capillaries, and the variation in the pattern is registered and stored digitally in our computer."

"You have a computer?" I was impressed.

Betsy clasped her hands behind her tiny waist. "We have funding sources that enable us to invest in the best equipment and attract top scientists. Our hepatitis research is driven by grants from the New York Center for Blood Research. And Winston. Winston has the cache to woo philanthropists that support our most prodigious efforts, ones that will bear life-changing technologies."

Mike, arms crossed, gave a hard nod. I thought, *This would be a remarkable place to work.*

Betsy led us down a hall, past doors with labels like, "Hepatitis A Sequencing Lab," "Hepatitis B Sequencing Lab," "Non A Non B Molecular." We passed an elevator with a sign labeled, "Skyway to Genetics." At the end of the hall, we stopped at the office plaque of Winston Walsh, Chief Research Officer & Director of Technical Operations. We were about to make the most consequential handshake of our lives.

CHAPTER 5

Betsy knocked and entered without waiting for an answer. The man with the long title was also long in stature: six feet three, thin, and fit, sandy mustache, with Gregg Allman hair spun into a ponytail. He finished stirring honey into his tea and rose from his desk, parading a Delphic smile and a Camel cigarette that hung from its corner. Winston greeted Bubba with a snappy local handshake.

"These are my buds, Craze and Mad Dog."

Winston's grip, firm but unchallenging, lingered while his charcoal eyes angled down, fixating on my left eye only, intense, almost flirtatious, like a best friend that might steal your lunch. Mad Dog offered him a sturdy hand that imparted integrity.

"Have a seat. Bubba has chewed my ear off about you." His inflections were mostly American, but I sniffed a shred of the British Commonwealth.

A sawn-off chimpanzee skull, inverted on his desk, served as an ashtray. It was full. The back desk, which ran the length of the far wall, sagged in the middle from the cortical mayhem of scientific papers and charts. I'd seen this before—no time to waste tinkering with organization.

Three of the walls were an unremarkable white. The fourth, accented by a layer of thinly laced rattan, was covered with diplomas. Bachelor's degree in biochemical engineering from Rice University; masters in molecular biology *and* a PhD in protein and cellular engineering from MIT; and a DPhil in genetics from Oxford. Flanking his diplomas were awards from the International Ligand Society, the Scandinavian Committee on Enzymes, and the

UK's Colworth Medal for outstanding biochemical research by someone under the age of thirty-five.

Winston's thumb clicked his pen with the regularity of a train on the rails. "They're just pieces of paper. Some would say products of a misspent youth." His graphite eyes made me feel like he knew my secrets. "I understand Bubba is taking you on a tour of Liberia and other parts of West Africa. Bravo. It will open your eyes and clean out your bowels. If you get up . . ."

Bubba snapped, "Jesus, Winston—they just got here."

"Well, your itinerary sounds exceptional. You'll experience sadness, joy . . . and women if you have a few dollars and your penis doesn't mind keeping company with gonorrhea for a week or two. Your first time in Africa and you boys come to Liberia. Moxie. Everyone else goes to Kenya or Tanzania for the big game. No elephants or rhinos around here."

"Where Bubba goes, we go," Mad Dog assured him.

"If I recall, Mad Dog, you're an environmental scientist. Cornell?"

"Dual major. Environmental sciences and football. Great school, but Ithaca is sheet of arctic hell in the winter."

"He was all-scholastic defensive end in Massachusetts," Bubba said. "Got a full ride to Cornell. A few of us went up there for the Syracuse game. On one play, he karate-chopped the offensive tackle, picked up the quarterback, slammed him to the ground, and added a forearm to the head. They carried him off—put in the backup QB. His teammates branded him Mad Dog."

"I like it. Do what it takes."

"Mm. And a great friend. When he commits, he's all in."

Winston shifted his attention to me. "Bubba told me you're a medical technologist. Are you board certified by the American Society for Clinical Pathology?"

I laughed. *Nobody knows what Medical Technologists do. We're a forgotten breed. Maybe this guy is okay.* "Yes. Certified by the ASCP for clinical chemistry, hematology, microbiology, and immunohematology. Been working at the teaching hospitals for Harvard Medical School and BU. Did some lipid research in Lund, Sweden—fractionating HDL into sub-components."

13

Winston's pupils bore in on me. His pen click clicked.

"Uh—used various concentrations of dextran sulfate and magnesium chloride to isolate the lipoproteins . . . then fractionated with electrophoresis across an agarose gel."

"Pleased. And now you're off to the wilds of Africa." He paused, took a pull on his Camel. "What will you do when you return from your ramble? Head back home?"

Pleased? "Already have tickets to fly from Monrovia to South Africa. We signed up with an overland rig run by an outfit called Trindell Travel. Doing a three-thousand-mile stretch from Johannesburg to Nairobi. Will see the big game in Botswana, Tanzania, Kenya. Going to Victoria Falls too."

Winston put out his cigarette and spent a few seconds staring at the corner of the ceiling. "When are you flying to Jo'burg?"

"April 10th. The Trindell trip leaves from Johannesburg a couple of days later."

A signed photo of Winston posing with Richard Feynman was propped on his desk. It was positioned in a way that made it hard not to ask about it. I did, delighting Winston. "I met him at a conference," he said. "He's brilliant. Leap years ahead of his peers. I tried to lure him here. Work with us. But he's a bad capitalist; wouldn't take our generous offer."

"Steadfast. What's his claim to fame?" asked Bubba.

"His Feynman diagrams mathematically portray how subatomic particles behave. He earned a Nobel Prize for his work in quantum electrodynamics. Of particular interest to us was his work in what we now call nanotechnology. Feynman was the first to put forth the concept of controlling synthesis by direct manipulation of atoms."

I'd officially stepped in it. Quantum electrodynamics? Nanotechnology? "Uh-huh. Wow! Geez," I said.

What? "Wow! Geez."

Winston shot a glance at Betsy and grinned. "Ah, but I hired two of his protégés. They are running with it in full stride. With funding, equipment, and brain power, you can make radical leaps in short order. Nobody in the world knows how far we've gotten."

Betsy gave him a stern look. He didn't seem to notice the sophomoric cloak I wore after my "Wow! Geez," response. I tried again. "What practical applications are you thinking of?" *Better?*

"With nanotechnology, we can deliver drugs to very specific organs and cell types. If you combine that with genetic manipulation, you can achieve wonders. Nobody is going in this direction yet." He glanced at Betsy again and stopped.

She nodded and pointed to her watch. He rose. "Nice to meet you guys," he said. "I understand Betsy is going to have a beach party when you return. She's got a prime spot a few miles down the road. I insist we talk before you leave for South Africa."

Winston took one step out the door, clearly engrossed in thought. He stopped, back to us, and turned his left ear in our direction. "Bubba, when are you guys heading out?"

"Friday."

"I see." Without looking back, he set stride down the hall.

CHAPTER 6

With the phone in his left hand and a dart in his right, Gus whipped the dart across the room and buried it, barrel deep into the board. He shouted into the mouthpiece, "My God, Winston, you're a genius in the lab, but you are cack-handed as an operations director. We're on the verge of launching, and you can't even get the bloody manufacturing protocols delivered to the pharmaceutical firm. We've been at this for how many years now?"

Winston's face blanched to the shade of a bowl of curd. He could picture Gus's jowls wilting from the heat of his own ire. Gus's organization funded his research—a technology that would change the way man fought disease and simultaneously bring permanent prosperity to their homeland.

"Three times you've failed. We're quids in on this, mate. Over a billion pounds," said Gus.

Winston stirred the honey dipper, rolled it over his tongue, and took a breath. "Gus. You're more than kind. The Column has given everything I've asked for. This is my fault. I apologize and I will fix it. I don't need to remind you, I have a personal stake in this too."

Gus was more than a leader. Winston's parents were his friends. He had advocated for Winston, shared in his suffering, and believed in his approach. He softened. "Humph. Who thought a simple delivery of procedures would be a roadblock?"

"I'm humbled Gus; should have been more diligent. We all want the same thing."

"How are you going to stop these hijackings, Winston?"

"I'm making it my mission to find who's responsible. It's someone inside, I'm sure."

"Mm. Just make sure nobody knows about the next attempt," Gus said. "Nobody. If you have a birdwatcher inside, they'll figure it out, bugger it up again. Understand? After all this effort and money, I want to make sure we get the glory."

Winston smiled. A Nobel Prize for the technology would be a certainty.

"Gus, I just met with two guys. Upstanding pals of my dear friend Bubba. Someone I know and trust. They've never been to Africa before. Nobody knows them. If I hit them with a compelling story, I'm sure they'll help. But I may need help from your contacts in the Scouts."

"Ha, you and your charm Winston . . . yes, of course the Scouts will help."

"One more thing. I've discovered a way to accelerate production. It will take a couple of weeks to validate, but it will save a lot of time in the long run." Winston pulled the phone from his head, stared at the earpiece, and waited for a harsh rebuke. But Gus and Winston needed each other. His technology was the answer and Gus knew it.

CHAPTER 7

Betsy's administrator drove us to a taxi stand. Honk, honk. Loud negotiations, babies crying, rudderless cars jockeying for position. Charred spices from sizzling street meat bathed one nostril while diesel fumes bathed the other. We jammed into the back of a boxy Renault. The cabby accelerated and pinned the speedometer at ninety miles per hour, bald tires liquifying in the heat. I shouted over the swoosh of air blasting past the windows. "You've made some unusual friends here, Bubba." Mad Dog emitted a grunt that landed somewhere between astonishment and discontent.

Mike's bungalow was on the beach. Platoons of fiddler crabs sidestepped clumps of oil tar that smattered the shoreline, a gift from the tankers that motored in and out of port. "Oil companies flock to Liberia to register their tankers," Mike said. "No US labor laws. No minimum wage or union pay."

It took a day to shake the jet lag. I still felt strange being the odd White person. I knew it was mostly in my head. "Hey White man, are you going to buy this fruit?" *Not entirely.*

"Don't forget to go to the immigration office," Bubba said.

He was right. Our Liberian visa stamp read:

```
REPORT TO IMMIGRATION GENERAL OFFICE
MONROVIA WITHIN 48 HRS.
```

A taxi took us within three blocks of the immigration office. Broad Street was impassable due to wreckage wrought by the rice riots of the previous week. More than a hundred killed. "I spent the night belly down on the floor of my apartment listening to gunfire," Bubba told us.

In the right lane was a flipped Ford Mustang. Four kiosk carts were splayed across the road. We picked our way around the rubble—a burned Liberian flag; a banner with a picture of President Tolbert with red lettering casting him as a "Generational Traitor"; a buckled bus stop sign promoting the OAU conference; a tear-gas mask; three feet of a severed fire hose hung from a hydrant. Graffiti on the Palm Hotel read, "President Tolbert Mr. Badman."

"It's not just about the price of rice," Bubba said. "Tolbert insists on holding the OAU conference in Liberia next summer. It's like hosting the Olympics. The conference site will cost over a hundred million dollars."

"OAU?" Mad Dog asked.

"Organization for African Unity. People are hurting, and he raises the price of rice."

"Is he one of these president-for-life guys?"

"He's in the True Whig Party—the Americo-Liberians—initially freed American slaves; been in control since the late 1800s. But Liberians want a true two-party system. Tolbert calls his opposition evil. Satanic. It's divided the country. Family members don't speak to each other. Police have been seen fighting with soldiers."

I stepped over a dead cat and a tuft of hair held down by a ski mask and climbed the steps to the Bureau of Immigration. This wasn't what I'd imagined. Rice riots, oil tar beaches, loud taxi stands, political unrest. Africa was so distant from home. Exotic. *Why did we even come here?* To visit Bubba, yeah. Travel West Africa—immerse ourselves. Explore. Hook up with an overland trip and rough it through savannahs filled with elephants and giraffes. Our dream was to climb Kilimanjaro; maybe hop a dhow and sail up the Nile through the Sudan and Egypt.

An immigration officer saw us right away. His brass name badge said he was Gartee Padmore—khaki safari shirt, flapped pockets, chrome pins on his collar, Liberian flags patched on each shoulder. His Ray-Ban aviators were intimidating. But then he smiled.

"How can I help you fine young men?"

Bubba offered Gartee a Liberian handshake—one or two traditional shakes followed by sliding the hands apart and pinching the tip of the other person's middle finger between the tip of your thumb and middle finger. If you applied pressure and got off a good snap, the shake was a success, a measure of your credibility.

"I work at the Ministry of Forestry," Bubba said. "We will be traveling to the Ivory Coast, Upper Volta. Possibly other places."

Gartee examined Bubba's passport. His visas were in order.

Mad Dog and I handed him our passports. I tried to enrich his understanding. "We got our visas at the Liberian embassy in Washington." *Sure—that will help.*

His eyes shifted from my passport to Mad Dog's and back. "Your Peace Corps friend can come back to Liberia. But once you leave, you cannot come back."

Huh?

"The visa says we can visit for three months," argued Mad Dog.

He pointed. "Yes, but you can only enter one time. This is a *single*-entry visa. You can stay for up to three months. But once you leave Liberia, you must obtain another visa."

"Can't we get an extension?"

"No. If you leave Liberia, you must go to a Liberian embassy in another country and get another visa. However, due to the riots, Liberia will not issue new travel visas until things settle down. If you had gotten a *multiple* entry, you could come and go as you please."

Bubba had learned the practice of *dashing*—offering a small bribe. It was near standard practice. "Is there a special fee that allows them to get a multiple-entry visa here?"

Gartee smiled. He took no offense. "I'm sorry. Only embassies issue visas. We enforce the immigration laws. The ban on new visas may change, but you would still need to get them at a Liberian embassy in another country."

We turned, descended the stairs, and examined our passports.

```
SEEN AT THE EMBASSY OF LIBERIA
Washington D.C. (Consular Division)
No. 826 Feb 13, 1979
THIS VISA IS GOOD FOR Single JOURNEY
WITHIN THREE MONTHS FROM THE DATE
HEREOF . . .
```

Damn! We'd already bought our plane tickets to fly from Liberia to South Africa.

CHAPTER 8

Travis: Meeting Cameron

Travis climbed to the second floor of a maisonette in the Newham section of London. He knocked. The peephole darkened. A crisp voice asked, "What's your favorite room in the house?"

"The Attica."

Throw bolts scraped—one, two, three of them. Clank, a door jammer security bar. The door seam cracked, releasing a fog of apprehension into the hallway. It opened. A waxy-haired man with oversized, double-bridged eyeglasses studied Travis head to toe. Travis stepped in. On the blind side of the door stood a leather-faced man in a tight, black shirt that advertised his muscles. He held a 45 caliber Colt M1911 in the high ready position.

"I ain't armed," Travis said. He eased his rucksack to the floor and raised his arms.

"I'm Cameron." Cameron slid the rucksack to his colleague for inspection and patted Travis down. He smiled. "Welcome, Tom. You are highly respected in our circles. Sorry things got sticky for you in the States."

"It's Travis . . . my name, Travis."

"Yes. Sorry. I understand." They sat. Cameron offered tea.

"US Marines 1963. Training at Guantanamo. Special demolitions. Advanced covert certification. SERE training. Unblemished stealth missions in 'Nam. You're a gift, Travis."

"Gift?"

"That you are here . . . that you're considering joining us. I think you'll find that our ideologies are aligned."

"Mmm."

Cameron explained that he led the recruiting arm of Weathermen Africa. He'd clearly been briefed on Travis's history, yet insisted Travis tell it in his own words.

Travis understood. Cameron wanted to hear him speak, assess his tone, listen to the timber of his voice, the points of emphasis in his wording. He had to know if Travis was nervous or restrained, clearheaded or driven by ego. What was his relationship with risk and uncertainty? Others had mistakenly undervalued Travis's record, thinking he was a hothead with a cause. They'd overlooked the cleverness his record implied.

"What turned you into a revolutionary torpedo?" Cameron asked. After Vietnam, you went to prison for armed robbery. You were a two-a-penny thief."

Travis cocked his head. "In 'Nam . . . I seen the lives of the locals. Different backgrounds. Different values. Family structures. The war . . . it wasn't what they reported in the news. We weren't tryin' to help them. We tried to force our way on them; make sure they were on our team; protect our corporations. Still—I did my job." Travis's earlobes flushed pink; chest deflated. "It ate at me. Tryin' to reconcile what I was doing. I was a kid. A kid that was supporting a government that disrespects life. Later, when I was in prison, I seen how anger and despair was procreated by the segregation policies of a decomposed system."

Cameron sat back and grinned.

"I met Curtis LaDuke in prison. He got me to read Che Guevara and others who made a difference. The more we talked, the more we realized we could do it too—influence change. The elite reap the benefits of society—always. Attempts to correct injustices are crushed by the law. We started an underground effort to strike at symbols of US imperialism, end global racism, and bring down predators of Apartheid. We're tryin' to send a message to the people that there is a purposeful dictum around which to rally; that it is possible to end their struggle if we unite."

Cameron laughed. "You have an odd way of speaking, Travis. Unrefined, but modulated and articulate." He paused. "And thus, you created the United Freedom Front?"

"Yes." Travis pushed the base of his spine into his chair.

CHAPTER 9

Craze: Crimes and Misdemeanors

I took a dark blue pen from Mike's kitchen counter and made a quarter-inch mark on the corner of a blank page in my passport. Bubba fetched four Club beers from the fridge. "What are you doing, Craze?"

"The word *single* on our visa is handwritten. I want to see if I can erase it."

Bubba snorted.

"Just testing it." I glared. "On a blank page." Mad Dog nodded.

"We have to get back into Liberia so we can use our tickets to South Africa. Most countries won't fly there. They've adopted the Lusaka Manifesto—sanctions on South Africa's apartheid policies."

I touched the corner of a grade-school eraser to my tongue and gingerly tried to remove the pen mark, a skill that kids with marginal report cards learn by the time they reach middle school. The ink came off, but the dampness raised flecks of paper on the page, and the watermark had rubbed off. "Not good enough," I said. "Wish we had some acetone. In the lab we use it to fix malarial slides—helps the red blood cells stick to the slide so we can look for malaria within the cells. It's a good solvent. Could probably dissolve the ink."

"How about nail polish remover?" Mike asked. He went to his bedroom, returned with a vial. "Girlfriend."

Mad Dog tried this time, dabbing lightly with a miniscule amount of nail polish remover. It worked. The ink was gone, and the watermark was intact. The Dog carefully removed *single* from our passports. After some practice, I wrote in the word *multiple* in its place. Exactly what Gartee said we needed.

The next morning, we went to the waterfront, where eight guys, each with a suitcase full of money, sat on the sidewalk at the Our Lady of Grace International School on 15th Street. Bubba asked a man in his sixties who sported a six-inch, braided beard, "What is your price?"

"How much? What sized bills?" asked money changer guy.

Bubba turned to us. "Let's do $200 each—get enough francs for buses, hotels, food, in the Ivory Coast." He turned to the hawker. "$600 US. All twenties. New bills."

The changer offered 229 Francs (CFA) per dollar, twenty percent higher than the bank rate. Bubba clicked his tongue in disapproval. He took a bill and sniffed it. "Straight from the States."

Mad Dog yanked Bubba aside. "Is this legit? Doesn't feel right."

"It's the norm. Everyone going to French West Africa does it."

"But is it legal?"

"Hell, you altered your passport. You're worried about black market money?"

"Two thirty-six," shouted a different entrepreneur seated two illegal money changers from the first. "Two thirty-six; let's go now."

Bubba looked to yet another changer and asked, "Is 236 the best we can do?"

A large man with beefy biceps and an eleven-inch full tang military knife sheathed in his belt approached. "You pick one man. You talk with that man." Nod.

We settled at 240. "Why would they give us more than the bank?" Mad Dog asked.

"Expatriates own hotels, grocery stores, laundromats in these former French colonies. They get CFA in their daily business but will pay a premium for hard currency that holds its value."

"So, it's illegal."

"If you want to get technical."

CHAPTER 10

Craze: ATCG

We returned to Mike's house after completing business with the guys bearing suitcases full of money in the shadows of Our Lady of Grace. Winston had dropped by and left us a sealed envelope. It contained an invitation to return to ACORN for a deeper discussion. He said he had a proposal for us, "a simple and powerful task that will help the people of Africa." He insisted we come the next morning and stressed that we not mention it to anyone.

We laughed. "What a hugger-mugger," Bubba popped.

Mad Dog scowled. "Huh?"

"Hugger-mugger. Sometimes Winston puts on a shade of hauteur . . ."

I laughed, knowing that the word *hauteur* irritated Mad Dog. "Let's go," I said. The center had mystique, with its rainforest setting, squealing chimps, high security, and its idiosyncratic chief research officer. And what of Winston's titillating proposal?

I knew a fair amount about hepatitis, and my mind continued to toy with the notion of working at ACORN after we finished our trip. Raw science. Betsy told us they were working on a vaccine for Hepatitis B and researching a new strain called Hepatitis C. Maybe Winston could find a place for me. If ACORN was what he claimed, leap years ahead of its peers, it would be a great career move. *You self-indulgent prick. When you left Alex, she was as fragile as a green crab's shell in May.* I had to put our relationship first. *Hm—maybe she'd come with me.*

No, you idiot! Maybe?

We arrived at 10:00 a.m. The musk of cadmium orange blossoms from two African tulip trees near the entrance bathed our sinuses. Winston's ponytail was brushed out; his broad Tony Bennett smile warmed the atrium. He put his hand on my back as we walked down the hall.

"I owe you fellows an apology . . . for running off so abruptly the other day. Rude of me." He rubbed his temple with his index and middle fingers. "I'm working on that."

Bubba flicked his hand. "Stop your guttering—there's no hope. Where's Betsy?"

"At the Foreign Ministry making a pitch to import pygmy chimps from the Congo."

Winston's office smelled of coffee and a platter of sliced grapefruit, pomelos, coconut, and bananas. "I have something for you," he said. He pulled three leather pouches the size of a McDonald's fish filet from his desk drawer. Inside each was rawhide string with six aggry beads, a metal ring, and an animal tooth wrapped in leather thread. "It's a West African talisman." He hung them around our necks, saying to each of us separately, "May this grant you safe passage on any journey, physical or spiritual." His eyes were moist. I wondered if he had many friends.

"We love you, bro," Bubba said. Winston laughed.

"What's with all this security, Winston?" I asked. "Feels like overkill, like we're on the Jetsons. And what's up with these labs. What are you sequencing?"

He grinned. "You are perceptive and direct, Craze. Yes. Well, we do more than hepatitis research. I want to tell you about something that is . . . sensitive. You'll understand. His cheerful wag evaporated. "I trust you can be discreet," he said. He made us individually pledge our word while in the gaze of his stoic fisheye.

Bubba tipped his head. "The hell, Winston? You been holding out on me?"

"It's not as cloak and dagger as it sounds. But we've taken some lumps. Learned we must be more careful." He sat. "We're working on a malaria project. Horrible affliction—you will surely see it in your travels. People shaking. Abdominal pain. Fever. Death for some."

We nodded. "A hundred fifty million people infected each year. Craze, to answer your question, we've developed genetic techniques that attack certain diseases at their constitution. I'm not talking about treatment. We can wipe these diseases from the Earth."

It was a self-aggrandizing claim, but Winston was odd enough to be credible. "Sounds awesome. If it's so good, why so secretive?"

His eye twinkled and he slipped into professor mode. "Do you remember any genetics from high school or college biology? How the sequence of nucleotides in our genes tell the body which amino acids to make and how they should be strung together? How proteins are simply strings of amino acids joined together, some long and some short?"

I glanced at Mad Dog's and Bubba's wooden faces. It had been a while for them. "I remember there are only twenty different amino acids," Bubba said. "Right?"

"Good. Now each chromosome is made of thousands of genes—DNA. And DNA is just a series of nucleotides strung together."

Bubba lit up. "I'm there. ATCG baby. There are only four different nucleotides."

Winston winked. "Yes. Adenine, thymine, cytosine, and guanine—ATCG." He drew on the blackboard. T-T-G-C-A-G-A-C-C-A-G. "Genes are simply long strings of those four nucleotides. Pair two strings together and you have DNA, the double helix we know and love."

Where is he going with this, I wondered. And what does it have to do with malaria? I didn't ask questions, but my sternum tightened. *Just talk, Winston.*

"Craze, I'm sure you know that each group of three nucleotides on that string code for an amino acid." He went to the board again. "Gentlemen. When DNA is processed by the cells, the mechanisms look at the nucleotides, the ATCs and G's, in groups of three. If three consecutive nucleotides on the strand are ATG, then the amino acid methionine is made. If the next three in the string are TGG, then tryptophan is made. CAA makes glutamine, etc. You end up with a unique string of amino acids—a protein."

Ten seconds of silence. My pinky twitched. Another ten seconds. "Malaria?" I asked.

"Yes. Malaria. Some of the best genetic engineers in the world work in that building over there. Stanford. Cambridge." He picked up a mangosteen and tossed it to Mad Dog. "Cornell."

"One team is studying the DNA of the mosquito that carries malaria—the Anopheles mosquito. They isolated the gene that codes for the sex of the mosquito, important because only female mosquitoes carry the malarial parasite. Another team identified a gene that can be manipulated to make the mosquito resistant to malaria. If a mosquito can't get malaria, it can't transmit it to humans."

Okay, that's pretty cool. I was feeling better. He can be pretentious and a bit of a dink, but this was heady stuff. But the word "manipulated" bothered me. I asked what he meant by it.

"Ah, that's the best part. We've developed a technique that not only can find a specific nucleotide on a gene, we can replace one nucleotide with another. For instance, we can replace a C with an A or replace a T with a G. We've come up with two possible ways to eliminate malaria. We can either wipe out the Anopheles mosquito altogether, or we can make the mosquito itself resistant to malaria."

Impossible, I thought. "How do you know which gene to manipulate? And how do you cut and replace the nucleotide on that one gene without doing the same to other genes?"

"The sequence of nucleotides that code for a protein is unique. A fingerprint. If you know the sequence of ATCGs on either side of the one you are interested in, you can find the specific one that you want to edit. Suppose you are in a traffic jam on a road with only one lane. And there are only four different cars on the road: Accords, Thunderbirds, Camaros, and Gremlins. If you know the sequence of the hundred cars ahead of you and the hundred cars behind you, it would be a unique string. Knowing that long sequence would allow us to identify where your specific car is."

"Didn't the National Academy of Sciences halt this type of research in the early '70s?" I asked.

"That's one of the reasons we are in Liberia. Similar to their shipping registry, there are few regulatory barriers on medical research. We can move quickly; keep a low profile."

"But why the hush-hush?"

"People are afraid of anything to do with modifying genes. A general phobia. Last year, Ethiopia refused to accept forty-four thousand tons of food because it was genetically modified to make it less susceptible to rotting or bruising."

Bubba sniveled. "Next time don't tell 'em."

Winston sneered. "The other problem is that gene editing could be used for . . ." His lips fluttered, pen went clack-clack, ". . . unscrupulous purposes."

My chest tickled like that first drop on a hyper coaster. "This could be used for all kinds of genetic diseases," I said. "Cystic fibrosis, hemophilia, Huntington's, Tay-Sachs." As the words exited my mouth, I felt a little stupid. For a half second, I thought I was enlightening him. A smile crossed his face.

Mad Dog, who'd been following along quietly, asked, "What's this got to do with us?"

CHAPTER 11

Travis sat erect and listened to Cameron recount his resume. "Wanted for over twenty bombings in protest of South African apartheid, U.S. imperialism in Latin America, and racial injustice in the United States?"

"Sounds right. We want to put pressure on these companies. Let them know what it's like to live in fear. That we ain't going away. Nothing ever gets changed with peaceful protests. Sometimes people are gonna get hurt."

"Like the Suffolk Courthouse explosion in Boston?"

"Mm . . . yeah, like that."

"What triggered your letter to the FBI demanding they release the man who tried to kill President Truman?"

"The government needed change. Maybe needed to be brought down. Collazo tried to do that."

Cameron laughed. "Well, you aim high."

Travis shifted, surprised at how much Cameron knew. "What's Weathermen Africa working on now? South Africa? Apartheid?"

"Not exactly. Our focus is on the Bush War in Rhodesia—to the northeast of South Africa. We want to put an end to White minority rule there."

Travis leaned forward, ears perked as if he'd swallowed two shots of espresso. "Okay?"

"What you need to know is that in 1965 Southern Rhodesia defied the United Kingdom. Africa was being decolonized and the UK had a policy of No Independence Before Majority African Rule—NIBMAR. But Southern Rhodesia issued a Unilateral

Declaration of Independence and changed their name to Rhodesia. Led by Ian Smith, they founded a government that guaranteed White minority rule—a government that isn't recognized by any nation on earth."

Travis's nostril twitched. He reached his hands behind his neck and locked his fingers. "What do you got in mind for me?"

"The Bush War has been going on for fifteen years—since '64. If we can end minority rule in Rhodesia, it'll put pressure on South Africa. There are two factions fighting the Rhodesian forces: ZAPU led by Joshua Nkomo and ZANU led by Robert Mugabe. Each has their own military arm. Together they are called the Patriotic Front. But sometimes they fight each other."

"Hm—a bucketuh crap. What are they fightin' about?" Travis asked.

"Tribal lines . . . ideology . . . power. Nkomo is from the Ndebele people from the western part of Rhodesia. Mugabe is a Shona, from the north and central parts. Both socialists, but Nkomo is backed by the Soviets, and Mugabe is backed by the Chinese. They both want to put an end to White rule, but each wants to take the reins when it's over."

"And you want to get rid of Ian Smith and his self-appointed arbitrators of societal structure." Travis thought, Shit, I've been blowing things up from a distance in the States. I could be on the front lines of the real battle.

"What do ZAPU and ZANU stand for?"

"Nkomo's organization is called ZAPU, the Zimbabwe African People's Union. They use conventional warfare but are best known for their guerilla tactics."

Travis recited under his breath a couple of times, "Nkomo, ZAPU, Russians."

"Mugabe is the head of ZANU, the Zimbabwe African Nationalist Union."

Travis uttered to himself, "Nkomo—ZAPU, Russians. Mugabe— ZANU, Chinese. Nkomo—ZAPU, Russians . . ."

Cameron chuckled. "Not bad."

It was a war Travis could believe in. He had genuine anti-apartheid convictions and was intimate with guerilla warfare. In

Vietnam, he blew up caves, tunnels, and hiding places of the Vietcong. Close-up work. Dangerous. Required stealth. He'd learned cat walking, mud and leaf walking, and how to break the shape of silhouettes. The art of camouflage and blunting reflectivity were indwelling obsessions. Leave no residues. Blend body odor. No unusual smells. Move undetected using shadows.

Cameron straddled the bridge of his nose with his thumb and forefinger and touched the corners of his eyes. "What we have in mind for you is risky. I'm reluctant to tell you details if you aren't on board."

"Jesus, I have to hear what it is first. In general, I'm on board, but . . . Norah and Jaxon. What about them?"

"We'll set them up with a flat in London. We can provide contacts and money. Norah will have a good midwife. We'll get Jaxon into school." Cameron's voice dropped to a whisper, as if talking to himself. "You could change the bloody war, Travis."

Travis didn't think it over. "Let's hear it."

Cameron was direct. Travis was to join the Rhodesian Army as a mercenary and become a counterintelligence agent for ZAPU. He was to funnel information on the Rhodesian Army's tactics and battle plans back to ZAPU via a handler in Rhodesia. He was to be a spy.

CHAPTER 12

Craze: The Proposal

"I need your help, Mad Dog." Winston seemed like he wanted to cultivate a sense of duty within us before explaining. "We rejected the idea of forcing all new mosquito offspring to be male and thus eradicating the mosquito completely. Don't know how it will impact the food chain. We opted to make mosquitoes resistant to the malarial parasite, thereby preventing the spread to humans."

He told us that they planned to use something called a gene drive. It's a way to force the resistant gene to be passed onto the offspring. He talked about manufacturing a gene editing protein that would be incorporated into bacteria as a plasmid—a DNA structure that can replicate within the bacteria separately from the bacteria's own DNA. They would stick the bacteria onto nanoparticles in order to deliver the component to specific cells in the mosquito. Once inside the cell, the plasmid would edit the mosquito's genes. He was getting over our heads.

Mad Dog fidgeted, shifted his torso toward the door.

"Uh, sorry. Carried away, yes?" Winston bowed. Bubba grinned—he'd seen this before.

"Here's the thing. At ACORN, we strictly do research. We're not set up for large-scale production. So, we've partnered with Kalumba Pharma Ltd., a firm on the outskirts of Lusaka, the capital of Zambia. Kalumba has the transfection, electroprorata, and other equipment needed to produce the large amounts we need to make this work. Their personnel are familiar with the bacteria and cell types, and they know how to follow stringent manufacturing protocols."

"You still haven't said how we can help."

"That? Yes. We've tried to deliver the protocols to Kalumba three times. First, we tried certified mail. The package never reached them. Then we put our director of clinical pathology on a plane to Lusaka. Someone ransacked her hotel room while she was at dinner. Took her briefcase. She was to deliver the protocols the next morning."

"She was targeted?" I asked.

He paused. "They didn't steal her camera. It was in plain sight on the nightstand. Initially, I suspected a bioethics group. Then I thought, How would they even know she was there?"

"Mm."

He told us of a third attempt and another interception. He'd employed a private currier who was robbed at gunpoint.

"There are groups that oppose any genetic manipulation—claim we're playing God. But after the third time, we are sure someone on our staff is tipping them off, possibly even coordinating this. Someone who opposes using the technology."

"You mean like a mole?" I asked. "Why, if they've worked so hard on it?"

"It can happen with scientists. They pursue raw science but later have misgivings on how their work is applied. Einstein was aghast after Leo Szilard explained to him how his nuclear fission formulas could be used to generate the chain reaction needed for an atomic bomb. Arthur Galston created a hormone to help soybeans grow, and someone else used his technology to create Agent Orange."

Winston paced behind his desk. "You guys will be flying to South Africa. Your trip will take you quickly into Zambia. I can have someone meet you as soon as you cross the border into Zambia. Would you be willing to deliver the protocols to him? The person you meet will securely take them to Kalumba."

"Why us?" Mad Dog asked.

"Nobody knows you. You're not on anyone's radar. And you're going there anyway. I will start a rumor that I am going to deliver them myself. To throw them off."

"What do we get out of it?" Mad Dog fingered at the talisman that hung around his neck.

Winston laughed. He looked directly at Mad Dog, offered an apologetic bow of the head. "Ah, good. Pardon me. If you deliver the protocols by end of April, I can arrange to have a friend in Tanzania, Mr. Motondo, take you on a private trek up Kilimanjaro. He'll take you to the Kibo lava formations, show you a rare fossil pit, will stomp on your souls with stories. He knows where all the mountain's ghosts are and what they want."

My heart raced. *Kilimanjaro! Good score, Mad Dog.*

Winston's eyes wandered to mine. "And . . . if it fits your aspirations . . . you could help us in our efforts to refine lipoprotein adherence to nanos when you finish your trip. Might get your name on a couple of papers."

With my palm, I covered my lips, hiding an ear-to-ear grin.

"Good," Winston said.

Alex would kill me. "Why the end of April?" I asked.

"Nobel Prize. If you deliver by then, I'd have time to gather data and make the submission deadline. The most important thing is to get rid of this horrible disease, yes. But a Nobel prize . . . well. I'd have the money and cache to expand to other diseases."

"But we're leaving for the Ivory Coast tomorrow," I said. I wanted to help but was wary of what the heck was going on with these interceptions.

"Timing is perfect," Winston said. "I am adjusting the protocols—will be ready by the time you get back. I'll package the documents in a way that nobody will know you have them. Guys, if you agree, you can't tell anyone. Not your mother. Not your girlfriend. I'm not even going to tell Betsy. The more people that know, the higher the risk."

Mad Dog glanced at me and then turned to Winston. "Craze and I need to talk."

Winston sensed I was on board. I shot him an artful nod when Mad Dog wasn't looking. Then I turned to Mad Dog and whispered, "Kilimanjaro."

Winston winked. "Just think about it. Let me know when you get back."

He knew he had us.

35

CHAPTER 13

We hopped a ride on the bed of a pickup truck with Winston's proposal parked in a side lot of our consciousness. Hell, I'd have helped Winston out even if he hadn't offered the Kilimanjaro trip or teased me with the possibility of working at ACORN. The destination was Foequellie, a blip village four hours north of Monrovia where a Peace Corps party was slated for the weekend. Small fires burned in the woods just beyond the edges of the hardened laterite road that transected the belly of Liberia. "What do you think those fires are all about?" Bubba asked.

I sighed. "Camping?"

He put on an annoying smirk that he keeps in his pocket. "Kpelle people. The huts with the grass roofs are their homes." *Okay, let him be pleased with his worldliness.* I was happy for a glimpse of the Africa *National Geographic* had etched into my head. We arrived around 10:00 p.m.

Foequellie had no electricity. Water was fetched and boiled. Peace Corps Volunteers, PCVs, had erected eight tents in an open space outside of a mud brick house. We slept. At 7:00 a.m. I woke when the sun seeped through a slit, only to see a pair of small, brown eyes squinting through. I moved, and the eyes ran off. *Giggles.* In a safe arc around our tent sat thirty little kids gawking at us as if we were from Mars. Mad Dog rose, squeezed out of the tent, and gruffed past the children. He didn't speak, searching for a place to pee. His size and solemnity caused them to huddle and whisper. I beamed, stomped after him, swerving between the kids, screeching, "Buk-bahhhk." A boy yelled, "Chicken, chicken."

It was a glorious day in the lives of the locals, as if tectonic plates had shifted beneath Foequellie. Hundreds gathered, bewildered at games where you used your hands or clubs to strike a ball instead of your feet. Palm wine and local beer overflowed and penalized many. The kids killed and skinned a goat for the Kpelle women to cook. Pieces of guts, heart, liver, blood, and teeth went into the soup along with a mound of questionable greens. I cocked my head, looked at Mad Dog. Without a word, he understood my meaning. *This is what we wanted when we left Norwell.*

"It's called chop," said a cheery-eyed woman who offered us plates with pride, upholding a smile in defiance of an unattended curvature in her spine. We ate.

The setting of the sun behind an orange haze provoked a night of dancing thanks to a lonely Victrola, the kind embedded in a suitcase the color of a cirrhotic liver with an English terrier musing at a gramophone on the cover. It was powered by a car battery—ingenious.

Bubba laughed. "Boys, we're in for some polyrhythmic tribal music or Liberian highlife superstar tunes." But when the DJ turned the volume and base knobs fully to the right and the tone arm hit the vinyl, "Stayin' Alive" pounded out with full distortion. A boy grabbed my wrist and schooled me in the meaning of uninhibited merriment. After three hours and another jug of palm wine, we crashed to the sound of "More Than a Feeling."

The Lord ushered us into Hotel Penance that night and administered pangs of regret in the morning. He demanded contrition. It was an establishment we'd visited many times together. Bubba would rise first, dive into caffeine, and grouse. I would drink juice and grope my way to equanimity. Mad Dog would rise last, sigh, and drive himself to physical exertion in an activity that would "sweat out the toxins." At 10:30 we dragged ourselves to the dust bowl road that led deeper up-country and waited for any form of transport to come by. It was a lifeless afternoon; furious heat pressed soggy air into our pores. Two hours passed. We stewed in the shade of a tree with some town folk. Nobody hurried.

I asked Mad Dog what he thought of Winston's proposal. I didn't offer my thoughts, knowing he doesn't respond well to persuasion.

He puckered on a White Owl blunt he'd brought from home. "Did you see the clicking?"

I half-closed one eye.

"Pen clicking for no reason. Stress. He's holding something back. A secret."

My eyelids dropped. I held silent. Mad Dog was prone to conspiracy theories. His aunt swore she'd ridden in a UFO, and he credits aliens with helping the US Navy teleport a war ship from Philadelphia to Norfolk, Virginia, during the Second World War.

Bubba defended. "He's a good guy, Dog. Eccentric, like all geniuses."

"Darwin had to have every hair in place," I said. "Tesla was obsessed with toe exercises, talked to pigeons."

"Isaac Newton died a virgin . . . and he did it on purpose," Bubba added.

"It's a feeling," Mad Dog said. "We've got a time to stew on it."

Bubba's endorsement was a good step. I let it drop. We'd just had our first true African experience, and I didn't want to taint it. I daydreamed, imagined we were agents like Napoleon Solo on *The Man from U.N.C.L.E.*; three guys on a secret mission in the jungles of Liberia. I thought of Alex, of the time we climbed Mount Katahdin together, the time we camped on the beach on Prince Edward Island for ten days. In the wild. Unencumbered.

"Here we go, boys. Buckle up," Bubba shouted. A dust cloud rumbled in from the south.

CHAPTER 14

Ron Reid and Gus were boyhood friends—went to Chaplin High School together, played soccer, hunted birds in the bush. In their twenties, they took separate paths but retained a common trait. They were patriots. Ron became a master of covert operations, while Gus dominated the business world.

"That's right, Ron. Winston thinks there is a leak inside the research center. He's going to use all new players this time. Unknowns. And he's asking for your help."

Ron's voice vibrated as if being pulled through flakes of shale. "Sounds like you need a common delivery boy. We do elite ops, Gus. You don't need our help for this."

"Listen to me, old chap. It's too important. Nothing is too extreme. This prick is either sabotaging the deliveries himself or is tipping somebody off. Winston is trying to figure out who it is. In the meantime, please assign this to someone who is rock solid. All your guy has to do is meet these two guys, get the documents from them, and deliver them to the pharmaceutical. That's it. I understand Winston's thinking. The mole, or whatever we want to call this guy, won't suspect these guys."

"What's so important that you need one of my guys?"

Gus explained the implications of the new genetic technology and what it would mean. Ron gasped. Through the phone, Gus could sense a broad grin swim across his face.

"Ron, one final request. Winston developed a device that emits a tracking signal every half hour. It's about the size of a poker chip. One of your guys will have to plant it."

"Absolutely." Ron paused. "You sure you can trust these guys? Would they help if they knew what we were doing?"

"They won't know. They've been told they'll be carrying instructions on how to eliminate malaria."

CHAPTER 15

Craze: Money Bus Blues

Bubba laughed as Mad Dog and I disentangled ourselves from the stockpile of humanity and small animals wedged into the rear of the Isuzu pickup truck. The metallic taste of blood coated my tongue, a consequence of speaking words with the letters "th" during an untimely bump. Mad Dog couldn't stand erect, likely due to a compressed disk in his back. Chicken feathers stuck to the sweat in the creases of our necks, souvenirs of our first money bus ride.

At a village on the outskirts of Sanniquellie, the driver yelled, "Last stop. My home." It was late. A passenger guided us to a couple, Jerome and Fatu, who offered us a spot on the floor of their ten-by-ten mud-square home, covered with a sheet of corrugated tin. Jerome—late thirties, wire brush goatee, discarded western shirt with wagon wheels print on the collar—introduced us to the bucket bath, where you wash your hair, sweat, and grime with a single bucket of water and a tin cup. I was bizarrely delighted at this minor intimacy of daily life. I thought of how Alex would laugh at me if she could see. But she'd understand.

Fatu made rice with a fiery chop that stopped my heart. She giggled when she saw beads of sweat puddle on our foreheads. After supper, Jerome pointed to the moon, twisting the cavernous lines of his face. "Did the USA really go there?" he asked.

"It may have been staged," Mad Dog said. We slept.

Our morning money bus rattled through dense bush to the Liberian border, where an officer sat on a fatigued Baule chair that wobbled atop ten-inch wooden legs. A Česká zbrojovka bolt action rifle rested on his lap. The gravity of having tampered with our visas pressed a rueful slab of distress onto my chest. The officer was in his mid-twenties, wore a khaki vest over an olive T-shirt with a hole near the belly button. "Mulbah" was etched into his name tag. Three vertical scars embellished Mulbah's cheeks, each an inch long and crafted with care. I wanted to ask about them, but his rifle weakened my curiosity.

His sidekick, Samuel, a boy in his teens, thrust his shoulders back to project importance. His scars, dark purple and irregular, looked like they were codified with broken glass. A Browning single-action pistol was stuffed into his belt, inexplicably pointing at his right testicle. *A pistol in the hands of a boy-man with an unstubbled face in isolated brown-water territory!*

"We are going to the town of Man in Côte d'Ivoire," Bubba offered.

"Passports," grunted Mulbah, still seated, elbows on knees. He inspected Bubba's photo, grinned, and rubbed his face, acknowledging Bubba's six-day scruff. He handed the passport to Samuel, who held it upside down and stared. *He can't read.* I felt bad. Mulbah motioned to Mad Dog for his passport, my chest now a breathless vacuum.

"What is this?" Mulbah pointed at the word "multiple" on Mad Dog's visa.

"We can enter Liberia multiple times." Mad Dog's temples pulsed. *Geez, he's ready for a fight.*

"Mine's the same," I said. "Here. Got our visas at the embassy in Washington, DC."

"Multiple?" he repeated. But he shrugged and switched into his other role, a customs agent. The allure of searching the packs of three white men from America was too tempting.

He picked through Bubba's first, item by item. Bubba sidled up to me and whispered, "There's six joints in the bottom right pocket." My face went gray. Thoughts of the movie *Midnight Express* filled my head. *What's wrong with you? They have guns. What will Alex think if we're arrested? Dad?*

Mad Dog didn't hear Bubba's bombshell but picked up on the vibe. His eyebrow shouted, "What the hell is going on?"

I wrapped my lips around Bubba's ear. "You fucking idiot."

Mulbah reached for the zipper of the pocket that had the joints. I rifled through my pack—Swiss Army knife, journal, granola—and found a plastic compass I'd brought from home. I handed it to Mulbah. He palmed it and gazed, transfixed on the needle. His torso flinched when he realized that the needle pointed in the same direction, regardless of how he rotated the housing. His hand trembled, but fear gave way to astonishment. He smiled and handed the compass to Samuel. He held it upside down. Rotated it. Magic.

I started to recite fragments of information I'd absorbed from Hank, who worked at Robert E. White Instrument Services in Boston. "The inner core of the Earth is made of iron. It spins at a different rate than the outer crust, which creates a magnetic . . ."

"Can I have?" Mulbah uttered. I realized it wasn't a question.

I feigned graciousness. "Yes, please. It is a gift . . . for you."

Mulbah abandoned Bubba's pack and its hidden doobies, decided mine was more interesting. He found my shaving cream and pushed the button. It shot over his shoulder, landing on Samuel's pistol. He stood, face decidedly unnerved. I started to explain, but he'd had enough. Stamp, stamp, stamp. Three exit visas. "Good journey, gentlemen." I wheezed.

Mad Dog waited until we were out of hearing distance. "What was that?" I clenched the muscles in my neck and threw a thumb toward Bubba.

"I had some weed in my pack. Heard these up-country borders were easy."

Mad Dog boxed his lips like he'd eaten a bad kumquat and gave Bubba a death glare.

"Don't be so sanctimonious. You forged your visas for Chrissake."

The Dog groaned slowly from his diaphragm, "Get-rid-of-them." He raised his shoulders to his ears and flicked his head toward the jungle.

Bubba stared into the bush, unrolled a joint, licked the golden flecks off the paper, and swallowed. He tossed the rest into the jungle, pretended to wipe a tear. "Bully!"

It was a ten-minute walk through no-man's-land to the Ivory Coast border post—no building, just two guys in fatigues and berets, one lying in a hammock, one sitting on a stump. Both carried AK-47s and seemed inconvenienced by our arrival.

"Vos passeports, s'il vous plaît. Où allez-vous?"

We made out the word "passeports" and handed them over.

Bubba tripped over his three years of high school French. "Nous allons a Man en Côte d'Ivoire." After a brief conversation, we were stamped into the Ivory Coast.

"He said we have to go to the police station at Danané, an hour up the road by bush taxi." As if on cue, a taxi came and dropped off a woman, who placed a coconut on her head and walked with grace toward the border. The driver took us to the Danané police station where they slapped a half-page stamp into our passport.

The money bus from Danané to Man—a blue Isuzu pickup, left side mirror gone, right side mirror duct-taped to the bracket, windshield cracked diagonally left to right, unburdened by functioning shocks and mufflers, requisite threadbare tires—had more people jammed into the back than there are seats in purgatory. The fuel gage was typically one thimble above empty. Luggage and two goats were tossed on the roof. We sat on one of the two planks that ran along either side of the truck bed. None of the roads were paved.

A mom, dad, and daughter squeezed in. Dad sported a maroon jacket with a conga line of buttons along each arm and proper shoes with laces. Mom's dress was full length, brilliant yellow with a print of red birds. Her dhuku, head wrap, was a stunning red with yellow polka dots. The girl—demure, head down, withdrawn—looked to be around twelve and wore a diluted cabernet dress with navy blue flowers.

After driving a hundred yards, the driver stopped; tank was empty. After catching up on family matters with the gas station owner, he banged the roof three times and turned the key. *Sput, sput, spurtle . . . rrenga, renga . . . vroom.*

The girl sat on the floor of the truck bed and folded herself into a sitting fetal position. Her head and shoulders quivered, inducing her to fist her hands and place them over her eyes. She hunched further, as if trying to will the shaking to stop. I couldn't look away. Her lips trembled. Mom and Dad didn't acknowledge. A seven-year-old girl offered water.

Bubba asked the father, "Est elle bien?" *Is she okay?*

"Malaria," the dad said.

"God," I replied. I'd seen malaria on my job, even knew how to differentiate between the four species, on a blood smear. But I'd never seen the actual patient. Plasmodium falciparum, the most prevalent species in West Africa, has a mortality rate of ten percent. The girl's parents sat, unengaged, as if the girl had a common cold.

Mad Dog sat on the plank, next to the mother. He offered the girl his seat, which she accepted after exchanging glances with Mom. I reached over to help her move. Her arms were on fire; skin felt like a fishnet had integrated into the dermis. Once seated, her mother's arms provided comfort, but watching the girl gasp for air between shakes was hard to watch.

Miles passed. Heat and humidity intensified the body odor and vapors of chicken shit. No one complained—not the eighty-year-old grandmother, not the two-month-old feeding on Mom's breast. Bubba hatched his juvenile voice, "Eeeooo, that's called tay-tay water . . . titty water." I wanted to tap him in the nuts.

By the time we got to Man, the ride had wedged our underwear deep into our butt cracks, compressed our balls, and reshaped our disposition. Sinuses burned from exhaust that seeped through the rust holes. But nothing bruised us more than witnessing the girl with malaria. I said to Mad Dog, "Man, we gotta talk about Winston's proposal." Single nod.

A passenger named Luc was amused at the sight of three out-of-place toubabous—White-guy travelers. He spoke English and called on his fatherly instincts to help, brought us to the Virginia Hotel, a place that was "reasonable for White people." He helped us buy bus tickets for the next day's ride to Bouaké, our next destination, and made sure the clerk didn't rip us off. We offered him money, but he outright refused and disappeared down the road.

I was dying to call Alex. I needed to hear her voice; our awkward goodbye still left me hollow. In the morning I sought out the telecommunications office. A sign on the door read: "On Strike— Three Days."

CHAPTER 16

"I don't have to tell you, Bobby, nobody can know about this. Not your bar friends. Not even the chimpanzees."

Bobby scoffed, face frozen, eyes aggrieved and libeled. Winston may as well be telling his dentist to floss daily. Bobby abhorred after-work meetings; they interrupted his regular visits to the Hard Thymes Saloon.

Bobby Diggs was a former flaps and seals craftsman for the UK's MI6 service. At his final gig in Nigeria, he founded a magazine called the *Grey Parrot*, a publication that allowed MI6 to slip anti-communist persuasions into articles on glamour, culture, and fashion. His office was windowless, walls empty, desktop inhabited by a phone, a DEC VT100 computer terminal, and BIC pen—blue. Winston used money and six weeks a year at a villa on the isle of São Tomé to lure him out of retirement and serve as director of security at ACORN.

Bobby pulled a bottle from his drawer and wet his lips with a rocker of Old Tom gin. "You want me to put together a paste-and-baste set of documents? How fun."

"What will it take?"

"I need three or four days to package your documents. Cement has to dry. Outer layer needs a few coats to make it watertight. It'll be seamless."

"How seamless? If they are stolen or lost, nobody should be able to read them."

"Prance and a dance my friend. They could be holding the documents in their hands and never know it." Bobby tinkered on his keyboard.

Winston grinned, aware of Bobby's early successes. He'd developed the transport capsules for MI6's pneumatic tube system. According to Bobby, "Few people were aware that sometimes the capsule itself was the information."

"Everyone at ACORN knows about the previous failures to deliver these protocols, Bobby." Winston stroked his hair, clenched his ponytail. "I know this mole is watching me. I'm going to leak a rumor that I will personally deliver the documents this time. You and I can figure out a way to trap them. While they're busy watching me, my couriers will deliver."

Winston Walsh Office flashed in white letters on Bobby's terminal. Winston stretched his neck. "What the . . ."

Bobby's head recoiled from the screen as if he'd taken a jab from Joe Frazier. He scrambled to the hallway with a spring that belied his Pillsbury Doughboy chassis. Down the hall, left, and down two flights to the first floor. Winston followed. "Check your office," Bobby yelled. He continued to run down the hall. Winston's office door was ajar. He rushed in. The chimpanzee skull ashtray was on the floor. His chair had been pushed against the rattan wall and his cellular engineering diploma from MIT was crooked.

A piercing buzz like a massive cicada awakening filled the hallway. After a minute or two, Bobby returned. "Nothing. Can't move like I used to."

Winston stared back at the skewed diploma. "Shit."

CHAPTER 17

After a day of merciless money bus rides, deferring to adolescents with guns, and avoiding arrest for altering our passports, the girl with malaria was all we talked about. Her capacity to suffer with quiet tolerance, her dignity, the acceptance in her parents' eyes, as if it were a contract with fate, an irreconcilable pique of nature. We wondered if she would live or die.

I had to find a way to convince Mad Dog that we should deliver the documents for Winston while making him think he reached the decision on his own. It was a frustrating trait I'd had to navigate since we were ten. My mind was settled. Initially, I'd thought, what fun it would be—to play a bit role in a great achievement, à la Johnny Fry, who rode the first leg of the first Pony Express ride. But the encounter with the girl solidified my resolve. I'd seen and touched the scourge that Winston was trying to kill. I'd seen Winston's quirky brilliance. As a person of science, I felt an obligation.

When we arrived at the bus stop for an 8:00 a.m. departure to Bouaké, the driver of the 1961 Scania bus was changing the oil, after which he inspected the rubber membranes that masqueraded as tires. The crew removed them one by one, looked them over, chatted, and put them back on. A second bus appeared. They transferred all luggage to its roof. Task completed, it was time for coffee. An important-looking person came. Discussions ensued. Luggage was moved—back to the original bus. At 11:15, the fully caffeinated driver pulled out of the lot and drove two blocks. Tank empty. Needed gas.

Bubba whined, "What a shit show."

Mad Dog fired back. "Shut up."

Facial markings of the passengers varied, and their personal carriage was more solemn. Most men wore full-length, embroidered robes—white, red, beige—accompanied by close-fitting, brimless cotton hats, some ornate, mostly plain white; Muslims, most of them Mandinkas, descendants from the ancient Mali Empire. Sejadahs, prayer rugs with a pointer that is pointed toward the Great Mosque of Mecca, were pulled out twice during the ride.

"Every people must five times in one day pray," we were reminded by a non-Muslim man who remained on the bus with us.

We watched them purposefully face Mecca and alternate positions—stand, bow, raise hands, sit with hands on thighs, and prostrate themselves. It was a moment to confront our level of naiveté, how malnourished our world view could be. *This* was the source of my travel addiction, my way to fight what I call the *passing glance syndrome*—reading a story in a newspaper and flipping the page, glancing away, reducing Hanoi or Paris to a five-letter word. I'd watched Vietnam on TV. Read accounts of the Arab-Israeli Six-Day War and the ouster of President Allende in Chile. A force made me want to see and touch. I didn't want to flash people and places away with the turn of a page and stuff them into the "you don't need to dwell on this" corner of my brain—next to the room with Santa Claus.

Bubba and I were raised Catholic. Mad Dog, an atheist despite attending the First Parish Church of Unitarian Universalists as a kid, was less burdened. I'd always accepted the rituals in Catholicism with minimal scrutiny. Eventually, I thought about reversing the lens. How would a Martian assimilate, watching us drink the blood of Christ, eat his body, bless ourselves when holy water was cast upon us during mass? Our most public individual display of our faith is when our foreheads are crossed with ashes. These people prayed openly, on the side of the road.

After eight hours, we pulled into Bouaké, heads, necks, and vertebrae intact. I missed Alex and wanted to share everything with her: The chaos; the heedless sense of time; Victrola record players in the jungle; the sanctity of the local people. She would delight in it. She'd have found a way to enhearten the girl with malaria—she does that. I wanted to know what she'd think of the long-haired scientist in Liberia. She's good at reading people.

I still hadn't written to Alex or Dad and vowed to do so when we got to Bobo-Dioulasso in Upper Volta. As we fell asleep that night, Mad Dog uttered, "The girl with malaria—that was bad." I understood his meaning. *Maybe it would be negligent if we didn't help Winston.*

The 8:15 a.m. train to Bobo-Dioulasso, a coal-fired steam engine that looked like my old Lionel set, chugged to the platform at 9:05. A mass of humanity rushed the moving train, running alongside, fighting to board and seize a few inches of space in second class. Once a spot was established, they leaned out the windows and pulled their loved ones in from the platform. The train stopped and station workers yanked at the feet of those hanging from the windows, lashed at them and tied ropes around their ankles to pull them off.

We had first-class tickets per Winston's advice. Conductors guided us onto the coach amid the chaos, granting us a deference that was undeserved yet uncomfortably accepted. At random, the train moved twenty feet and stopped. "It's called bluffing business," Bubba said. "Start, stop, start." It went on for three hours before we left the station.

At each stop, locals ran to the train to sell food, clothing, and something we'd never seen before—bottled water. Each station brought us deeper into the sub-Sahara; each kilometer brought denser infiltration into our first-class car. People trickled into the aisles and marked their territory. Some sat on the floor. Stale breath filled the cabin. Heavy atmospheric pressure pushed the stench firmly into nasal membranes. The woman sitting behind me reached out the window, bought a ten-pound hunk of rancid meat, and stuck it under my seat. It reminded me of the most infamous prank my Caper Crew friends pulled in high school.

It was my senior year. Our psychiatry teacher was loquaciously educating us on layers that differentiate psychoanalysis from psychotherapy. A tiny, pixie-nosed, teacher stood outside the room on tiptoe and peered through the rectangular glass pane on the door. Mr. Napoli, "Nap," the vice principal and football coach, aligned his woodchuck face next to hers—creepy. Moments later I was called to the office over the intercom. All Caper Crew members glared at me with eyes that would roast a bug.

That morning, six of us had spread ten pounds of sun-warmed limburger cheese throughout the school, hitting every locker handle, stair railing, and doorknob—and the heating grills in the lobby, which blew hard on a cold January morning. The smell assaulted each victim as they entered the school; most made faces, a few checked the bottom of their shoes. We took pleasure in being the only ones who knew what the odor was. The entire student body was bussed to the gymnasium of the junior high school.

The principal, Mr. Barrows—Vandyke mustache and jet-black hair flanking his bald crown—called me a miscreant. Nap, in his short-sleeved, too tight, white shirt, was pleased as an osprey circling an Atlantic herring. Bubba, Hank, and I were suspended. The others escaped, unseen. It's the only time anyone in the Caper Crew was ever caught pulling a prank.

One guy moaned a song while playing a one-string shelled instrument. A small donkey magically appeared at the end of the aisle. A woman held two live chickens upside down under her skirt. First class had become a menagerie. The moaning man sat on my lap and started singing. A bold move. The congregation stared, unsure of the outcome—would I take offense? He finished his song and surveyed the crowd to make sure they were watching, and then kissed me on the cheek. He offered a brief discourse in a local dialect. The flock roared with laughter. I checked my wallet in case it was a pickpocket distraction. All was secure. I had to laugh . . . it *was* funny. At the next stop, he shook hands with us, said au revoir, and left the train with his six wives—still singing.

CHAPTER 18

Winston bent forward and pulled on the ribbon that secured his ponytail. Hair fell to his lap. He stared at his waste and the extra belt hole he had to punch. After brushing out his hair, he retied the ribbon, let it out, and repeated the process—three times. Gus hadn't called yet.

Winston had finished tweaking his genetic editing process and was amending the written protocols for wide-scale production. He hadn't identified the malcontent who had sabotaged previous attempts to deliver the protocols, but it was surely the same person who'd broken into his office. Finally, the phone rang.

Gus never shared his phone number, an identity protection foible that agitated Winston, but he put up with it because Gus was the money man. Winston pulled at scruff on his chin, anxious that the Column, Gus's organization, wasn't losing faith in him.

"Good to hear from you, Gus."

"How are the procedures coming along? Ready to go?"

Winston dared hope that Gus had come through. It seemed like he wouldn't ask such a question if he hadn't arranged for the help Winston wanted. "Yes, ready. Bobby Diggs has already packaged the information in a secure manner; did it in a way that nobody will suspect."

"What about the mole? Tell me you found him."

Silence. Nausea crept into Winston's gut, triggered by anger and shame. Anger at the colleague who'd betrayed him. Shame that his esteemed confidante would be disappointed with him.

"So, you didn't find him."

"Almost." Winston didn't tell Gus about the office break-in.

Gus grunted. "Keep looking. I spoke to my contacts. We can give you the help you asked for. We've identified a handoff point. Your guys just need to get it there. I've also got someone who can test out your new tracking technology. Just send me the units ASAP."

Winston was gladdened on both points, but he wanted to do the tracking himself. Gus wouldn't hear of it. "I represent the Column. Ron insists that a single point of contact coordinates all of his communications with the Column. And he'll need two tracking receivers. One for the guy he sends and one for himself—so they can both track the transmitter."

"Okay. Will do. Thank you, Gus. You always come through. And Gus. I'm not telling the Americans about the tracking device. Just a safety precaution, but the idea might spook them."

"No worries. We can plant it. It'll be a true test."

CHAPTER 19

Craze: The Hee-Fee

By the time the train pulled into Bobo-Dioulasso, our spirits were defeated. Africa didn't feel like an adventure anymore. Bubba's face hung low, his nose stuffed into his fetid armpit. Mad Dog was slumped, glassy-eyed, muttering something about Area 51. We were soggy shingles on a fish shack—crammed by the masses, exhausted from the anxiety of knowing that if you give an inch, someone will take it. Bladders, strained and taught, were unsung martyrs in the battle for our turf. Vapors from the rancid meat were so ghastly I could taste the putrescine from the breakdown of amino acids. I'd had it, broken after three days straight of hard travel.

Someone accidentally elbowed Mad Dog in the face. He blinked twice—it was inconsequential compared to head blows he'd taken on the football field. We got off, strolled through the train station, and exited into the city square. A plaque told the story of Chief Tiéfo Amoro, who killed himself to avoid surrendering to Samori Touré, swearing he'd never become a slave. Bubba cracked, "Looks like someone had a worse day than us."

We looked back at the Bobo train station. The clay ground looked like the Fenway Park infield after they water it down before a game. Sprouting from the clay stood a magnificent, arabesque station, the lower half a brushed milk-chocolate color to mask the sullying influence of the surrounding dirt; the upper half white as teeth that saw too much peroxide gel. Four entrances were flanked by square turrets, and the roofline boasted an exaggerated saw-tooth pattern. It was the transportation hub of Bobo and the bravado of the design shouted, "Damn right I am." We walked. Right on Avenue de l'Unite. Left onto Ave de la Nation.

A boy, around eleven years old, whose primary language was neither French nor English joined us. "Bonsoir messieurs. Mon nom est Felix. Vous avoir bessoin hotel?" Mad Dog jerked his head toward Bubba. Felix started walking and said, "Come."

We passed a square where crowds carried signs that said "Trade Unions Against Lamizana" and "Oust President Lamizana." Felix ignored them. He turned down an alley that was wide enough for a thinly painted Volkswagen Beetle and popped his head into the door of an unremarkable two-story building with a hand-painted sign that said "Hee-Fee Hotel." After a ten-second conversation with someone we assumed was an adult, he led us to the top of a sunken stairwell and gave a snap-nod. The door was eight stairs down. Number 2. Felix made his bid. "3,000 CFA."

Bubba faced me as if handing me the decision. "Dude, we know your standards. Let's see how low they are." He turned his palm up, twisted his freckled cheek.

Felix sensed hesitation and went into sales mode. "Fine, fine, fine." He pointed down the stairs at the door. "Hee-Fee fine fine." He took two steps down, paused, and looked back. Then adjusted his price. "2,000 CFA."

The little shit had overbid his father—or whomever he talked to—so he could pocket 1,000 CFA for himself. Head still, my eyes rolled to meet Bubba's. Indistinct shrug. "Let's take a look."

A single light bulb hung from the ceiling. An 8 x 10-inch picture of Gérard Kango Ouédraogo, a former prime minister, was the only adornment. Mosquito netting hung from the ceiling and encircled a double bed that was low to the floor and backed by an iron-railed headboard. The waste pipe of a sink punched through a hole in the wall and emptied into the alleyway. A single straight-back chair stood in the corner.

Felix squatted and waved his hand over an empty spot on the floor. "I bring roll mat for third man," he said in English.

Bubba asked, "Where is the bathroom? La toilet?"

"A la extirieur. Porchaine porte. Nexta door."

Bubba turned to us. "It's outside. Next door down."

Mad Dog dropped his pack and said, "It's fine. We'll take it. I'll take the floor."

Bubba nodded to Felix and said, "Bien." Felix stuck out his palm. I laughed and forked over four 500 CFA notes.

Felix left to find the roll mat. Bubba searched for the toilet; his face bore a look of urgency. Dog and I sat on the bed. Mad Dog asked, "What are we doing here?"

I wasn't sure what he was asking. Mad Dog doesn't rattle easily.

"What are we doing at the Hee-Fee? What are we doing in Bobo? What do you mean?"

"Not sure. Thinking out loud." He dropped his head. "Are you enjoying this?"

"Enjoying? Mm, wrong word. I like seeing how people live. How they eat. How they maintain a purpose, despite having so little. I like trying to understand their motivations." I laughed. "People think travel is glamorous.

"Huh!"

"Tell you what I love. Not getting up at five in the morning, not fighting rush-hour traffic, not watching *Happy Days* at night."

Water dripped from the faucet. A muffled prayer from a nearby minaret squeezed through the door crack.

"Tomorrow . . . no travel. The outdoor market in Bobo is supposed to be splendid, governor," My British accent was abysmal.

"Different than I thought. I expected poor people. Y'know? 'Africa poor.' Mud huts. No electricity. Fetching water. I didn't think about the fight. The daily struggle to provide. To survive. Boys have one filthy shirt with no buttons. If they have shoes, they're two sizes too big and the soles have a hole in them. Kids are shaking with malaria. The woman with the lump in her neck. The guy with the spinal deformity. Shit."

I paused, spoke quietly. "Seeing these things. Knowing it. Letting it seep into your pores. That's worth something, yeah?"

"Okay."

I thought, This is coming from a guy whose mother is a diabetic, father is blind, and sister was born with a mitochondrial disease that gave her learning disabilities, kidney problems, and weak muscles.

"It's shit luck what we're born into, Dog. One gets a thirteen-room Georgian colonial; one gets a job in the body shop; one gets a mud hut with twelve siblings fighting for fufu."

He pulled on the talisman that hung around his neck.

"You're glad we came . . . aren't you?" I asked.

"Sure. I love seeing kids with distended bellies next to pretty girls in pretty dresses. Mothers in rags projecting dignity while trying to sell one more piece of fried dough." He laughed. "I like that fried dough."

"Ha. I wish we'd learned more before we left. Sounds like Liberia is about to blow. A guy on the train was worried about Marxists in Upper Volta. Idi Amin's butchering people in Uganda."

Bubba broke through the door, squeezing his butt cheeks with all his capacity. His face and posture told a story of despair. "Guys. Got runny belly. There's no toilet paper. Quick. Roll in the top pocket of my pack . . . *now.*" He squeezed harder. "The shitter is a rectangular slot in the concrete floor, three inches wide."

Felix opened the door and tossed in a pad that was one-inch-thick and three feet long. He laughed, closed the door, and recited, "Fine, fine, fine," as he walked up the stairs.

Bubba's face oscillated between pain and panic. Mad Dog tossed him the roll.

When the emergencies were over, Bubba's mouth ran worse than his belly. Mad Dog and I ignored. Bubba and I anchored the mosquito netting around the bed with our shoes. Mad Dog rolled out the mat, hopped into his sleeping bag, and edged up to the wall. It was 1:00 a.m.

I crashed, asleep within seconds. After twenty minutes, Bubba jabbed my back, whispered, "Craze, you hear that?"

I did hear. Those pleural sounds from Mad Dog's direction—rapid, electronic squeaks, like the scratch pin on your brake pads when they wear thin. More sounds, from the wall near the sink. Asthmatic, 78 RPM grunts—agitated. My skin rippled. I jumped to the light switch.

Mad Dog screamed, "Holy shit," and invoked the name of his non-existent savior.

Mad Dog never screams.

I hit the switch. A rat was at Mad Dog's head. It scurried across his sleeping bag. But there, stuck in a space between the drainpipe and the hole in the wall that had been cut for the drainpipe, was another rat. Snorting. Hissing. Stressed. Feet flailing—too fat to get through.

Mad Dog jumped up. He shrieked and said, "That thing was on my wrist." He snapped up the chair. Raised it. Swung down at the rat. "Fuck you!"

Missed.

The rat ran in circles beneath the sink, waiting for the fat rat to get through the hole. The light had increased the urgency level for the fat rat. Finally, with a gritty effort, it squeezed through the hole into the sanctuary of the alley. The second rat, less rotund, wiggled through the escape portal like a bail bondsman was on his tail.

"That thing nibbled at my wrist." We checked. No blood. We scoured the room for rodents. Mad Dog wrapped the end of one of his flip-flops with a sock and stuffed it into the space between the drainpipe and the wall. Hearts beat. We were wide awake.

Mad Dog declined an invitation to squeeze into our bed. It would have been cozy; he'd have no part of it. "My fucking word, what a night. I'll be fine," he said.

Bubba cackled, "Don't you mean you'll be fine, fine, fine?"

We tried to nod off but were still panting and full of epinephrine. Any sleep gained that night was shallow. When I awoke at 6:15 a.m., Mad Dog was on the bed, curled up at our feet.

CHAPTER 20

Alex flipped through the mail and tossed it onto the kitchen table.

Josie sighed. "Nothing? Not even a postcard yet? What are you doing, girl? You haven't heard a word since he left you standing on that curb."

Alex squooshed into the beanbag chair and dropped her hands to her lap. A tear welled. "Stop," she finally said. "I love you, Josie, but I don't need your bitching. I need your support."

Josie slackened and spoke softly. "I like him, Alex. You know I do. I just hate to see you brooding like this. Okay, let's try this. Tell me what you love about Craze."

Alex turned up her lips as if a puppy had licked her face. "Well . . . at first, I liked how he was unaligned. Athletic, but took a role in *West Side Story*. Creative. Spends time on people—puts together slides and music for their birthdays. Can hang with the nerds. Sarcastic, but not mean. Funny. And he listens. Asks questions. He's the first guy who didn't like me just for my tits."

"I'll give him an Amen for that Alex."

"Before we started dating, he changed my mother's tire in the parking lot at Star Market. Didn't even know her, but Mom remembered him when I brought him to the house. When my grandma got sick, he had Springsteen tickets at the Music Hall and gave them up so he could be with me when I visited. He volunteers for Oxfam, I don't know. And damn it, I still feel it when we're alone . . . you know."

"You made a man out of him, girl. He was unspoiled goods when you got hold of him."

They laughed. "Well, he still has a gentle kiss . . . but I have corrupted him."

"Thoroughly."

Alex paused. Her burned heart thumped, and the sides of the beanbag chair slumped around her shoulders. "And I miss him when he's gone."

Josie slipped behind the chair and hugged Alex from behind. She melted into the crook of Josie's elbow.

Alex's words dropped to a whisper. "I like Craze for his independence, I do. He's not afraid. He makes me feel . . . cherished. When I realized that I loved him, I said to myself, It's him."

"When he's here."

Alex's cheeks turned dry. She scooched up in the chair. "Yeah."

CHAPTER 21

We didn't leave Felix a tip. Early morning storefronts were rolled up; most offered baked goods that houseflies used as landing strips. We bought a loaf of bread and fried dough at Les Miettes and crossed the street to a sidewalk café au lait stand—a makeshift table with plank benches supported by plastic milk crates.

"Anybody seen a telecom office? Or post office?" I asked. No response.

Mad Dog stared at an elderly man who was in respiratory distress and convulsing on the sidewalk, eyes empty and pleading to die. The coffee-meister said, "Malaria," and smiled, as if Mad Dog had asked him what time it was.

We each plunked 60 CFA on the table. The meister poured coffee into a glass bowl, the kind you eat your cornflakes out of, and topped it off with a godless amount of white goo from a tin can. At the end of the bench was an elderly man with a white beard and kufi cap who tapped on a goblet-sized drum. A scar-faced man in western clothes played mancala with a thirty-something clad in a Rolling Stones *Sticky Fingers* T-shirt. In the shadow of the large coffee urn sat a man, back against the wall, begging, his left leg broken and never attended to.

The guy shaking with malaria was my cue to see if Mad Dog might drop his skepticism. "Hey. Are we going to deliver those gene-editing documents for Winston?" I asked. Admittedly, I was seduced by the idea of being part of the story. It didn't bother me that Winston was peculiar—I'd met my share. And each time I thought about working at ACORN, I felt like a kid who woke up and found a new bicycle in his bedroom. But Dog and I would be traveling for months. I wasn't going to stress our friendship if he wasn't on board.

"Sounds like hocus pocus. How do we know he won't screw up the whole ecosystem? This isn't medicine. He's not Mother Nature. Why can't he hop on a plane to Zambia himself?"

Bubba spoke. "I get the feeling he doesn't like to fly. And it sounds like he's being watched. If Winston goes to the airport, he'll be followed."

"That's supposed to make me feel better?"

"And he has to figure out who the internal dissident is—and hang him from a banana tree."

A European guy—coarse, woven shirt, fifties, gray mustache—who'd been futzing around at the fruit stand across the street, walked over to the table and joined us. His front tooth was chipped, and his pupil peeked under his left eyelid, which was nearly closed. He wore a camouflaged bush hat and carried a rusty shoulder bag that had a bird insignia patch on the end. With a nod, the coffee-meister served him a bowl.

"Bonjour gentlemen. What brings you to Bobo?" *What kind of accent was that? Not French. Sort of British, but not.*

"I'm in the Peace Corp," Bubba said. "Work for the forestry service in Liberia. These are my high school buds. Took some time off so we can see a few things in West Africa."

"High school chums. Brilliant, I smaak that. Didn't see you at the hotel last night. I was up pretty late at the bar." He made it sound as if there was only one hotel in Bobo.

Bubba groaned, "I don't think you stayed at our hotel—the Hee-Fee. It's a rat hole."

"Hee-Fee? Never heard of it. Ag, shame man. Everybody stays at the l'Auberge. You have to get out of that place." *Hm. Definitely not Australian.* I asked where he was from but got a hazy, "I'm from all over." Told us he was in Upper Volta on tobacco business.

We told him we planned to go to the Grande Market. He insisted, "Aw, you've got to go to the Grande Mosque. If you haven't seen it, you haven't been to Bobo. Go today. Get there before noontime prayer if you want the full experience."

We thanked him for the hotel tip and the advice and withdrew our asses from the wooden planks. Just a minute up the road, Mad Dog stopped and pointed out a pile of shit on the sidewalk—possibly human. He pondered. Offered his thoughts.

"Those are the same flies that took a walk on our pastries at the bakery." I grimaced. It took Bubba a few seconds to calculate the meaning. He covered his eyes.

We walked.

The l'Auberge was on Avenue Guillaume Ouédraogo. It had a pool with colored lights on the perimeter, a bar, and a receptionist. A "white man's hotel" as our friend Luc from the Ivory Coast would say. Expatriates walked in and out, most speaking French, with some German or English mixed in. 4,000 CFA—around $17/night. Easy decision. "Check us in."

Bubba whispered to Mad Dog, "I hear the rats here say please and thank you."

Settled and showered, we drank orange juice by the pool.

"That guy was a character—with the eye, the tooth, the hat. The accent. And the bird emblem on his bag—looked like a military thing," I said.

"Yeah. Not the French Foreign Legion grenade emblem. I've seen those," Bubba said.

"Let's do the mosque," Mad Dog said. "That guy knows the ropes. Grizzled. I liked him."

The Grande Mosque of Bobo-Dioulasso was proud. It looked like God took a mighty handful of wet mud and dribbled a dozen towers connected by walls in a rectangle pattern. Wooden beams projected out from the walls like an oddly shaped pincushion.

Bubba shared his observations. "It's red mud."

A historical marker explained that the mosque had been built on a deal. When Bobo was called the Kingdom of Sya, it was threatened by a nearby kingdom called Kénédougou. Sya needed an ally and found one in the Islamic religious leader Almamy Sidiki Sanou. In exchange for his help, Islam was to be allowed in Sya, and the mosque was built.

My Catholic wariness visited. I'd been to the Middle East before but had never gone inside a mosque. "Can we go inside?"

Bubba was circumspect. "Can Catholics go in there? I've never even been inside a protestant church."

"Should be okay. That guy said to come for the noontime prayer. He wasn't a Muslim."

"We're here. We're going in," Mad Dog said. "If lightning strikes, I'll send you home in a nice pine box."

"You're an atheist. You've got nothing to lose," Bubba countered.

We stepped through the door. Bubba looked back, surely thinking it was the last time he'd see daylight. Mad Dog acted like he belonged there. I was struck by what happened to the change in your psyche by just walking three feet through a door—how you are enveloped by a sense of insecurity and audacity, simultaneously timid and bold.

Shoes, twenty to thirty pairs on a large rug, told us that our shoes had to come off. We complied. The mosque was dark and solemn. Structural mahogany trunks spanned above us. Dark hallways and open side chambers. Floral incense seeping in from the far end of the mosque.

It was nearly time for the dhuhr, the prayer that begins at the solar noon. People prepared; some had already placed their rugs on large platforms that were built to provide a clean setting.

Do we belong here? I don't think I should fake like I'm here to pray.

We made ourselves invisible in the corner. Ardent followers of Allah granted us their version of respect. They ignored us. We watched as dignity cast itself into their bodies and brought them to a place apart from the outside world, the complexity of their faith weighing heavier within the intimate margins of the mosque. After dhuhr, we made for the exit. Mad Dog whispered, "I'm glad we did that."

We culled our shoes from the pile at the entryway. Bubba deliberated. "Whoever invented round shoelaces?"

"I need to read up," I said. "When I think of Islam, I think of Arabs and Iranians. Not African tribes with scarred faces."

"Flat shoelaces stay put," Bubba said. "The knots on round laces slip apart . . . because they're *rowwwwwnd.*"

We stepped out of the door into the light. Bubba mumbled something about plastic vs. metal grommets. Worshipers passed us, returning to their daily lives. Mad Dog's face soured. He walked a few steps and bobbed up and down like he was skiing the moguls at Killington. He stared at his feet and lifted one leg to look at the instep; did the same with the other leg and declared, "These aren't my shoes."

CHAPTER 22

A thirteen-hour flight and a nine-hour bus ride to the border of South Africa and Rhodesia left Travis hollow-eyed and weary. He'd used his travel time to study the landscape, plants, history, and politics of southern Africa. The discussions with Cameron, the London recruiter for Weathermen Africa, left him intoxicated with the idea of ousting White minority rule in Rhodesia. He'd formed the United Freedom Front to bring justice to the oppressed, and the minority government in Rhodesia was a bully. Returning government to the exploited peoples of the land was a concept that hot-wired his credo. But it made him nervous—what if he failed?

He got off the bus. Tin-roofed stands displayed oranges, sorghum, peanuts, cassava, and hard-boiled eggs. Multicolored umbrellas protected patrons from the sun. Phone poles supported two wires that ran from South Africa into Rhodesia, crossing the Limpopo River where two wispy-maned warthogs foraged. Whiffs of wood-roasted maize filled his nose. Travis entered the market and found the table he was looking for—yellow tarp, teak carvings of elder tribesmen, rhinos, and secret keepers. A man wearing a green leisure suit with a pack of Rothmans cigarettes sticking out of his shirt pocket smiled.

"Hello, Travis. I'm Sipho. Come. I know a place we can talk."

They walked.

Sipho stopped at a country grill. A four-foot coil of sausage seared over an open pit at the entrance. The proprietor greeted Sipho and led them to the back. They sat. Sipho handed Travis a canvas satchel. "A few items for you. Use the mefloquine or fansidar if you get malaria. You can get malaria even if you've taken your weekly chloroquine pills."

"Good to meet you."

"The hypochlorous water tabs need thirty minutes to work. A 32x monocular is built into the pen. Backwoods repellent is from the States—you won't get these from the Selous Scouts. Too scarce. And some Rhodesian dollars. Officially Rhodesia doesn't hire mercenaries. They claim they get 'volunteers.' You'll get $2,100 a month for your volunteer service."

"The Selous Scouts?"

The waiter delivered tea, macadamia nuts, and shortbread. Travis folded his arms, eyes drifted down as he recalled some background Cameron had given him on Sipho.

Sipho lit one of his Rothmans. "Yes. The Selous Scouts. I reviewed your experience with Colonel Ron Reid. He liked your covert training. Your assignments in 'Nam. He's considering bringing you into Rhodesia's special ops force: the Selous Scouts. I only briefed him on your military qualifications, not . . ." Sipho took a long drag and blew a cloud of smoke into his palm as if he were a magician making something disappear. ". . . not your activities with the United Freedom Front."

"Special ops?"

"Yes. They're involved in anything that's critical. It's a big win for us." Sipho smiled. "If you can survive training camp."

Sipho took stock of Travis. Wiry. Elongated muscles. Erect posture.

Travis shrugged, blue eyes peeking through their natural squint. They locked onto Sipho's. "What happened to you, Sipho? Cameron said you were a big shot on the other side—a fully encamped benefactor of White Rhodesia. Supporter of the Rhodesian Federalist Party. How do I know you ain't gonna turn on me? Why'd you switch sides?"

Sipho's smile tightened. "Alas, I'm a businessman, Travis. Yes, I facilitated arms shipments for the Rhodesian Army, had a few parties for their upper crust, high-end influentials—liquor, gambling, women. I'm respected. I'm rich. For a long time, the country has been ruled by a 5 percent minority. It's not sustainable. The government isn't recognized by any country in the world, and I want to be on the right side of it when ends."

Travis waited, peering harder into Sipho's eyes. "That ain't all of it. An apolitical businessman? You could just pack up and leave at any time."

Sipho leaned back, flipped an ember into the soapstone ashtray. "Year and a half ago, my fifteen-year-old son . . ." Travis sensed Sipho's throat binding. ". . . was killed in a movie theater. Rhodesian forces. They thought it was a front for ZAPU infiltrates. Blindly raided the place. Shot first. No resistance. No ZAPU sympathizers. Just a macho raid. A fuckup. Something they forgot about by afternoon tea."

"Sorry Sipho. That's vile."

"Mm. It was enough. I'd witnessed the disdain and subjugation they foisted on the Ndebele and Shona for years. Didn't affect me— I shamefully ignored it. Don't get me wrong. I may be helping ZAPU and ZANU now, but I'm not a socialist. Still . . . I know how this war is going to end, and I don't want them attacking my businesses or my family like they've done with some of the farmers and gold mines. I love this place. The air. The wildlife. The power of nature. I love the butcher in the corner shop, my mechanic, the woman that cuts my hair.

"And you like bein' a big shot."

Sipho scoffed. "Indeed. When this is over, the winner must look favorably upon me."

"You sure they don't know you switched?"

"I was a loyal supporter for years. Schmoozed into relationships with all the right dignitaries. Since killing my son, they've bent over backwards to please me. Yes—I'm as free from suspicion as one could possibly be."

Travis was taken by Sipho's poise and credible tenor. He uncrossed his arms.

"And you, Travis?" Sipho leaned forward, looked under the hood of Travis's eyelids. "Who hurt you?"

Travis winced. The question was intimate. "I was a punk. Deserved the time I did at MCI-Walpole." Silence. Sipho waited. "My younger brother—he has cerebral palsy. Delayed speech.

Uncontrolled fidgeting. Socially awkward. Goons tormented him to the point where he crawled within himself. Couldn't come out. Tough guys, reveling in the power of makin' someone feel small. I started to look at people differently. I seen how the elite will do anything to hold onto power. Nah, nobody hurt me. Ugliness just opened my eyes."

Sipho nodded. "But that's not what set you on the road to revolution."

"Look, I've been over that with Cameron. You want me here or not?"

Sipho steered the conversation to seminal events in Rhodesia's past. He talked about Cecil Rhodes, who had moved from England to South Africa when he was seventeen and eventually monopolized the diamond mining industry with his De Beers Consolidated Mines company. How Rhodes was a leader of the British South Africa Company, an organization formed to exploit the rich mineral deposits in southern Africa; and how Rhodes created the Pioneer Column, an unrelenting unit that coerced the king of the Ndebele people to grant the British South Africa Company mining rights on land that would eventually become Rhodesia.

"Why would he agree to that?" Travis asked.

"Coercion. The Pioneer Column murdered the opposition, abducted young women and men, conducted persistent hell-born acts of terror. It was like protection money in your country. 'We'll stop if you give us what we want.'"

"Christ. Johnny Torrio Black Hand Chicago extortion." Travis flicked his chin upward.

"The Pioneer Column marched in, planted a British flag, established three towns. Before you could blink, they'd annexed all of Mashonaland and founded a colony whose constitution assured a predominantly European electorate. In 1923, the British government took over and named it Southern Rhodesia."

Travis muttered, "Jesus, Mary . . ."

Sipho popped a macadamia nut into his mouth. "Rest up, Travis. We cross the border into Rhodesia tomorrow. I've arranged for you to meet Colonel Reid."

CHAPTER 23

Bubba looked at Mad Dog's feet. "What do you mean? They look like your shoes."

Mad Dog's penny loafers were tired and worn, not hard to mistake. He bounced up and down, walked, took one shoe off, reached inside, felt around. "I know what my shoes feel like."

I stepped back. "You sure? What are the odds there was another pair on the shoe rug? Same shoes? Same size?"

The Dog bit his lip. "Bobo's killing me. The rats. My shoes."

"Those square leather laces are the best," Bubba said.

We walked.

Mopeds cried *ying ying*. Buses and taxis jammed and jockeyed. Pedestrians moved with purpose. Hawkers sizzled banana fritters coated with the exhaust of leaded gas. We swung up Coulibaly to the main gate of the Grand Marché—a rectangular portal that had watched centuries of emirs, sultans, desert dwellers, thieves, holy men, and a few gods breach its threshold. Masses of mortals flowed through it in straight lines and zigzags. *This is the Africa we came to see.*

Bubba spotted the telecom office. "Hey, Craze. Different country. Maybe they're open."

I begged them to wait. I had to call Alex.

Bubba said, "Craze, do you remember when I got that kidney stone and had to fly home to Oregon for a few weeks? I sent you a letter before I flew back to Liberia. D'you get it?"

"Huh? What? No." I was dashing off to the office and barely heard him. I still had the kind of love where I couldn't do anything without thinking of her. Shopping for socks, planting tomatoes, doing compatibility testing for a kidney transplant. She was always on my mind.

Alex's phone rang. *What am I going to say?* Three rings. Four. *Damn it. Forgot about the time difference. She's still at work.* Voicemail. "I love you. I miss you. I miss your voice. I miss your laugh . . . damn, I hate talking to answering machines. Forgot about time zone. I love you."

Food, medicines, pots, pans, and wares from all corners of the Sahel, the region that stretches across the Sahara from the Atlantic to the Red Sea, filled the market. Mossi and Fulani people were prominent. Women's faces were bedecked with tattoos, some with dots that ran from the side of their eye to the corner of their mouth. Men peaked through shemaghs, full desert head wraps that, through a slit, revealed a set of exacting eyes. One guy wore a ski hat.

We window-shopped. Pangolin heads: to treat infertility and ailments of the spirit. The fat of Saharan sand boas: for rheumatism and gout. A pile of three-inch-long grubs: snacks. One guy hosted a table of black fish that were flat like a flounder, had bulging heads, and were dried and curled. Mad Dog, the Buzzards Bay angler asked, "What kind of fish?"

He frowned, glared at Mad Dog like he was an idiot. "It's fish."

The number of impoverished persons within and beyond the market walls shook us. Appeals for help were sometimes meek, sometimes not. An elderly starving woman's eyes can penetrate you, wrap your heart in a cloak, and make it sick. Each crease in her face told a story of anguish and struggle, but there were no subtle parables to be inferred. Her only goal was to survive. A morose veil plagued the outskirts of the market—a festering infection enveloped a boy's lower leg; a shirtless man whimpered, his serous skin taut across his jutting ribs; untold souls with jaw deformities and empty eye sockets.

I was starting to believe in the Devil; wondered if there was a way to hide within myself; wondered how my anima allowed me to look away. If I passed by, should I surrender the assertion that I am human? I can't help everyone, I told myself. *If I give to one, the rest will come running.* I protected myself in a mantle of numbness, aware that blight was infecting my character. *I'll give something to the next person I see who is alone.*

We had tea. I'm not sure what allows you to assimilate a cup of tea at one booth while those in your passage pursue survival. But you do. Mad Dog shifted his chair back from the table, crossed his legs, and stroked his fledgling beard with the web of his right hand. "Craze, I know you want to deliver the documents for Winston. I don't want to have that hanging over us until we get rid of them. What if we want to change our plans?"

"Dog. We're already slated to join the overland trip from Johannesburg to Nairobi. That's a hard date—it leaves a couple of days after we get to Jo'burg. We'll be at Victoria Falls just a few days later. Not a big deal."

Blank face. He wasn't listening. "Explain it to me again. Exactly what he's doing."

I could hear waves splashing in Mad Dog's head. Measured. Rhythmic. Bound by their own force but accepting of influence. "He's changing DNA. Altering it to achieve an outcome."

"To get rid of mosquitoes?"

"To make mosquitoes resistant to malaria. If it works, it could lead to cures for diseases like Cystic Fibrosis. That's a disease where one single nucleotide in the person's DNA is wrong."

"You're okay with it? He's not going too far?"

Bubba squawked, "What the . . ."

From behind, a man had placed his hands on Bubba's shoulders. He said, "It's a treasure, isn't it?" It was the man with the chipped tooth and rusty shoulder bag with the bird insignia—the guy from the café au lait stand.

Bubba chided him. "Jesus, you scared me."

He lifted his hands from Bubba's shoulders. Still standing behind Bubba, he smiled and circled his lips as if to say "Oooooh."

I said, "It's been good. We're going to buy some of that country cloth."

"Don't miss the north end of the market. Dutch prints. In-your-face rolls of fabric stamped with colors made from fruit and leaves—fixed with copper and zinc. Fabulous."

"Sure," I said. Bubba was pale and annoyed.

"I'm off. Don't eat any fish pies," he said, strolling away, whistling "Dock of the Bay."

Over the next four days we visited the Cathedral de Notre Dame de Lourdes, a mausoleum that honored a woman who helped the Samori Touré defeat his enemy, and Dafra Pond, where people seek favors by offering sacrifices to the great catfish in the pond.

From Bobo we hitchhiked to Banfora, caught a ride with a guy named Gabriel. He invited us to dinner. His wife cooked for us and stood outside while we ate. I asked why he had so many children—eleven. "Half die before age five. You hope one will be successful and take care of you when you are old."

Gabriel took us to a nearby bar where we met a Peace Corps guy. He joked: "During your first week in Africa, if a fly lands in your beer, you ask the bartender for a new one. During the second week, you simply shoo the fly or drink around it. During the third week, you complain if there isn't a fly in your beer."

We'd just finished our second week and were still skirting around Winston's proposal.

CHAPTER 24

Travis: Colonel Ron Reid

Ron Reid, founder and commander of the Selous Scouts, had no socks on. He had a peculiar tic where he repeatedly tapped his belly with the inside of his left wrist. "Sipho tells me you went through the Survival, Evasion, Resistance, Escape course in the US. What level did you reach?"

Travis was distracted. Reid was now tracing the contour of the windows and doors on the back wall with the brim of his camo hat. "Er. All of 'em . . . sir. BMT. SST-OC and SST-AC."

Reid's eyes quieted. "Basic—ding. OC—orientation, right? What's AC stand for?"

"Specialist Apprentice Course, sir. Forest, tropic, desert, arctic . . . open ocean and coastal. Survival. Hand to hand. Also did Deep Scarlet resistance."

A sticky, salt-like aroma from Reid's breath dominated the room. Ian Smith stared at Travis from a portrait on the wall.

"I admire you, sir. What you done with the Selous Scouts. How you're tacklin' the head of the dragon here in Rhodesia. Protecting your way of life. It's inspiring."

"Impressive pedigree, Travis. We like Vietnam vets. I have a question. I expect an honest answer. Why are you here—in Africa—willing to fight with us?"

Travis bowed his head and spoke as if he were in a confessional. "I intend to settle here, sir. I seen an article in the *Soldier of Fortune* magazine. It talked about your free and easy life here. A place where you can be a man among men. Beautiful nature. Prosperity. When I finished in 'Nam, I found out the US wasn't my home no more. No jobs for combat vets. Crazy inflation." Travis raised his head; his eyes now glistened, and he allowed them to meet Reid's. "You're fighting to preserve western values here. We can't lose any more countries to Communism. Christ, you raised the standard of living here, and this is the thanks you get?"

Reid tapped his belly with the inside of his wrist. He leaned forward, eyes firmly on Travis, right hand over his mouth. He looked to the ceiling and sighed. A full minute passed. "Initially we thought we'd place you in the Crippled Eagles, Travis—a group of soldiers from America. But Sipho was right . . . something about you. How would you like a chance to join the most formidable bush unit in the world?

Travis smiled.

"Training starts in three days."

CHAPTER 25

Craze: The Katiola Burn Out

Geoff Smith, an English teacher in Katiola, a town in the north central Ivory Coast, was a celebrity among Peace Corps Volunteers from Timbuktu to Cameroon. We wanted to find out if the legend lived up to the lore. Bubba found him.

Our stomachs twitched, in the same they did way before our annual Caper Crew Burn Out, a tradition that started in the eighth grade when Mad Dog, Bubba, Hank, Clark, and other friends slept in the woods on the last day of school. In the dark drizzle we threw notes from the school year into the campfire and dubbed it the Burn Out. By junior year we'd discovered alcohol. Each year, Caper Crew members from Massachusetts, Alaska, Delaware, Maine, Georgia, New Jersey, and Oregon hypnotically migrate to a tiny cottage on the west end of the Cape Cod Canal for a drinking contest. There were rules. Nobody can "chalk" their own beer. If you pass out, but wake up before the sun goes down, you can continue. Otherwise, you're out.

Geoff led us through the village with a gait that was crafted to assure people would see him and extend their salutations. He'd raise his hands over his head, thumb to thumb, and chant "Cómo sava . . ." We stopped at a cook shop where fire flickered beneath an iron cauldron that rested in the crook of three rocks. He ordered in French. The woman brought four Flag beers.

Bubba sneered. "What did you order, Geoff? Goat head? Pig tongue?"

"Good stuff. A bowl of stew for each and a plate of fufu with guinea fowl."

The stew was parched orange, charged with West African bonnet chili peppers. It induced tears and nasal discharge within seconds.

"Snot pockets," Bubba said. "Plastic liners in your pants pocket to keep boogers from your handkerchief from contaminating your pockets,"

Mad Dog inspected his stew. "Are those ribs?"

We gazed and then dissected what was in our bowls. "What are we eating?" I asked.

"Good, in't it?" Geoff said. "She's masterful. Her guinea fowl chop. The best."

He is intentionally being evasive, your honor. I glared.

Satisfied, he said, "It's rat de brousse." He paused for dramatic effect. "Bush rat."

I dropped my knife. Mad Dog took another bite, still harboring a grudge from the Hee-Fee. He declared, "I'm eating the whole fucking rat." We chased it down with another beer.

Geoff led us on a pub crawl. In the course of the day, we downed two tchapalas, a local brew plucked from a sizzling clay pot atop a fire, shots of ogogoro, fermented from the Raffia palm tree, hoppy beers from Mali, boukha, a spirit of distilled figs from Tunisia, and akpeteshie, god knows what from Ghana. At one point Geoff offered us smoked termites, which we ate, following his lead as if he were Jimmy Jones of the 1978 Jonestown massacre.

At the final bar, a Welch guy named Lewis roosted at the end. He'd been in Africa eleven years and was mining diamonds in Kokoumbo, a few hours south. Mad Dog told him of our plans to go to South Africa and work our way up through the game parks to Kenya. Lewis scowled, mouthed the lip of his bottle, and launched into a fatherly mode, warning us of war in Rhodesia, covert operations in Zambia.

"I'm not breaking shit, man. You never know who's who in that part of Africa. When you're in South Africa, stay in the areas marked 'Whites Only' or 'Europeans.' Take the right buses. Go to designated stores. Take care as you move north. The Rhodesian Bush War has been going on since the '60s and has ramped up in the past year. Trust no one."

"You guys aren't going to Rhodesia, are you?" Bubba asked.

Lewis interrupted. "All of the overlanders go to Vic Falls on the Rhodesia–Zambia border, yeah."

I nodded. It was where Winston wanted us to deliver the documents to—where we would meet a guy that would deliver them to Kalumba Pharmaceutical in Zambia.

"You'll have to go through Botswana to get to Zambia. You could go through Rhodesia, but I wouldn't recommend it. From Zambia, you'll go on to Tanzania. Forget about South West Africa or Mozambique. One is fighting for independence and the other is in a civil war."

"You never said that Zambia is at war," Mad Dog said. "What's the problem there?"

"Joshua Nkomo . . . ZAPU . . . The Zimbabwe African People's Union. They work out of Zambia. Backed by the Russians. Their military arm is called the Zimbabwe People's Army, or Revolutionary Army, something like that. They funnel fighters, weapons, supplies through Zambia into Rhodesia. They can be vicious, and Rhodesia is known to retaliate. Zambia's not at war, but they let ZAPU run unchecked through their country, and Rhodesia doesn't like it."

Bubba babbled . . . "Shit, guys."

"Which overlander are you gents signed up with?" Lewis asked.

"Trindell Travel. They're headquartered in London."

Lewis ordered shots of banji. "Never heard of 'em. I know people from Encounter Overland. When you get to Jo'burg, look them up. They are on top of things." Fumes from the banji burned my nostrils. Sewing needles penetrated my esophageal wall.

When we rose to leave, Lewis waxed. "Good luck, mates. The blokes on these overland trips know what they're doing. Aw, it'll be the time of your life. Over the top of the dishes."

CHAPTER 26

Betsy stopped at the door and sniffed the thyme that lined the entrance to Hard Thymes Tavern, a popular establishment with the cocoa laborers from Chocolate City, a suburb of Monrovia. The bar top, shaped in the likeness of a yellowfin tuna, was cut from the rusted hull of a grounded tanker. Seats were made of leftover fragments from the Firestone rubber plant. Bobby Diggs sat in the center stool and stirred cocktail onions into his gin.

Betsy put her hand on his arm. "Would love to join you if you don't mind, Bobby."

He peeked over his shoulder. "Flippin' hell. By gum yeah. Sit. What are you doing in this toad hole, Chief?" The barstools were high. Betsy could have negotiated them, but she insisted Bobby assist her. She ordered watermelon punch.

"I'm meeting the new veterinarian here. She's starting at ACORN next week—flying in from Nigeria tonight."

"Ah, my old haunt. Nigeria. My swan song from MI6," Bobby said.

"I'm aware. You do good work for us, Bobby, keeping a place like ours secure. All the intellectual property. Equipment. We're lucky to have you." Betsy stabbed a cube of watermelon and leisurely sucked the punch out of it. Juice dripped to her chin.

"You'd think the CEO could find a better joint than this to meet someone."

Betsy stood on the bottom rail of the stool and reached across the bar for a napkin. Before reseating herself, she paused and allowed her face to pass close to Bobby's, close enough for him to inhale her breath as she spoke. "She's been to Monrovia before. Knows this place." A career woman in her midforties, she understood the influence of a delicate tease.

She nestled into her seat. Sipped her punch. "I appreciate the work you're doing to find the bad seed at ACORN. Must bring you back to your roots—a true investigation."

"Don't worry, Chief. I'll find them. I'm sure you know, Winston and I have a good plan to get the documents delivered, and to nab the Judas who sabotaged the previous attempts."

Betsy crossed her legs; her skirt skated up her thigh another inch. She and Bobby chatted for over an hour. The new vet never showed up. "It's not unusual for flights to be canceled in Africa," she said.

CHAPTER 27

"Hey, Craze, let's go." Mad Dog stood next to a green Peugeot taxi. "This guy's going to take us to Yarmasuck . . ." He turned to Bubba. "Where?"

Bubba laughed. "Yamoussoukro."

Mad Dog yelled, "Yamsooko."

Alcohol dehydrogenase enzymes were in mid-assignment, ridding acetaldehyde and other malicious toxins from our systems. Our kidneys blocked antidiuretic hormone, causing dehydration, vasodilation, headaches. Bubba's attempts to bargain with God went unheeded.

We said goodbye to Geoff. I folded a piece of malachite Dutch cloth that I'd bought in the market—silver leaf vine with fire brick banding—and settled in for the ride. I planned to have it sewn into a West African dashiki shirt for Alex when we returned to Monrovia.

Alex's question galloped from one corner of my mind to the other. "Will you marry me when you get back?" How could I have been so aimless and unprepared for *that* question? Did I love her? Absolutely. Did I want to marry her? Yes, absolutely . . . sometime.

Why was I hesitant? I'd known her for twelve years. We'd been dating for eight. Was my life so grand that I couldn't bear to change it? I'd been listening to a voice that made me think I should never get married. I don't know what led me to that ism. I'd always thought, If I ever want to get married, I want it to be Alex. If.

I'm not sure how or why she chose to be with me. She was openhearted and fun. When she entered a room, it became coated with a mist of joy. Initially, I tried, unartfully, to gain her interest, but never expected to get anywhere. She was out of my league. Buoyant, warm, optimistic, nonjudgmental; cared about the world and the people in it. She had the best laugh in town, a caramel-coated echo, which, escorted by pure eyes and corn-fed cheeks, gladdened those around her. She was sexy and pretty in an approachable, anti-diva way.

I was a chair. A comfortable kitchen chair. Somewhat invisible, but not. I fit into the orbit of most groups—good student, good athlete, decent guy. There, but nearly imperceptible to women, save for an unrequited crush that left me despondent and full of self-doubt.

We worked on the yearbook staff together. Eventually, I built up the courage to ask Alex to the senior prom. I was petrified, had no doubt what her answer would be. I wondered how gracious she'd be in letting me down. I wanted to enlist the East German Army to standby and throw a wall around me as soon as the rejection came in.

She said, "Yes." *Are you kidding me?* And she seemed happy about it. Panic. *What does this mean? Maybe she actually likes me. C'mon, think. Could it be that her smiles were real? She smiles at everyone. Maybe she gets me. Or maybe she's happy to go to the prom with someone who is safe. Maybe she can see deep into my soul. Ha, is there anything to see?*

We spent days going from the opulent capital to the tiny villages. Rattling red roads that looked like a bulldozer made a single swipe through the slick mud had become the norm. Termite mounds pushed ten feet into the air. "That's where the bugabugs come from," noted Bubba. Mud homes with thatches of grass, reeds, and millet stock. It was the heart of Africa, and we'd forgotten that we were toubabous. We'd become charter members of the Afro-endurance club, where grime was a state of mind and time was not an enemy. We accepted the place and the pace of the land and relished the graciousness of its people.

"When Muslims pray, are they praying to the same god as Catholics?" Mad Dog asked.

"I don't know. Does it matter?" Bubba asked.

Mad Dog was a declared nonbeliever but his mind housed shadows of curiosity. "It matters if you want to know the truth."

"I know Jacob asked his sons who they'd worship after he died. They said they'd worship the God of Jacob's fathers—the same God that Isaac, Ishmael, and Abraham worshiped."

"Uh. That doesn't connect the dots for me."

"Some people say it's the same God. Others say it's not. For Catholics, Jesus was . . . is God. For Muslims, Muhammad is a man who received his instructions from an angel."

Mad Dog pushed. "For Christians, it's not just Jesus being God, right? He's part of this holy trinity thing. The Father, the Son, and the Holy Ghost. Which one of them is really God?"

"All three of them. Together."

Mad Dog was displeased. Bubba tiptoed to the edge of blasphemy.

"Think of the Beatles, right? Let's say John is the father—the force that brought them together. Paul had all the natural talent, was the best communicator, and articulated the Word. He's the Son. George? He's the Holy Spirit. Brings the spirit of goodness and virtue into people's hearts. Only together are they one. Only together are they the Beatles."

Mad Dog shook his head. "You're whacked. I'm reporting you to the Pope."

Bubba whined, "For comparing them to God? It was just a metaphor. Don't report me."

"You left out Ringo. Where's Ringo? Ignored him like he was a piece of burnt toast."

I noted, "Ringo had some innovative licks on 'The End' and 'Come Together.'"

Three days later we were in the town of Man again, on our way back to Liberia. I jumped ankle deep into a puddle from the back of the money bus. *Perfect.* We found the same Virginia Hotel that Luc took us to when we came into the Ivory Coast. It was midafternoon and Mad Dog's colon was punishing him for reckless malfeasance. Bubba and I decided to stroll the outdoor market while he convalesced. I put my sneakers on the windowsill to dry and borrowed Mad Dog's shoes.

We walked past a man pushing a square wooden wheelbarrow full of maize and into the market. Bubba rattled, "Ringo was John the Baptist."

I sighed and gave him a look. "How do you figure?"

"He's essential to the story. Can't leave him out. But he's not critical to the unit. Ringo wasn't fit to untie the sandals of the other three."

We visited a stall that was tended by a woman with a goiter the size of a croquet ball. She was older but had the loving eyes of a young mother. A Mise en Rose coopered barrel that embraced fifty gallons of peanut butter flanked her hip. She dug beneath two inches of oil with her wooden spoon and excavated enough gobs to fill Bubba's aluminum coffee cup.

"Jesus was the only one who wore sandals."

"Huh?"

"The Father and the Holy Ghost don't wear sandals. Only Jesus wore them. In your example, Ringo would be unworthy of untying Paul McCartney's sandals. Not all three."

He glared. I answered. "All I'm sayin'."

Bubba abruptly shoved my shoulder aside and darted into the aisle between the stands. He waved me over. "I swear I just saw the guy from the café au lait stand in Bobo."

"Really? Where?"

"Right there. He was five stalls down, next to the guy in the blue kufi selling pottery. He skipped off to the right as soon as I looked at him."

We ran straight at the pottery stand, ducking under some makeshift umbrellas made of oversized garbage bags. "Let's split up. Meet you back at the peanut butter lady."

I ran into a woman carrying a giant orange sack on her head the size of an easy chair. She staggered. The sack fell. I looked back, pretending I wanted to help, but others were already doing so. I ran. A few yelled at me. "Sorry. Sorry," I said.

I zigzagged between people and stalls, but no bush hat, no rusty shoulder bag with the bird insignia, no café au lait guy. I gave up and went back to the peanut butter stand.

Bubba arrived a minute later. "I saw him. He jumped into a taxi."

"You sure it was him? These expatriates wear similar clothes."

"Same hat. Same reddish-brown shoulder bag. Chipped tooth. It was him."

"The guy gets around. Maybe he just happens to be here."

"Sure, but why'd he take off? Soon as I made eye contact? Why didn't he just say hi?"

It was probably a coincidence. Maybe the guy was afraid we'd think he was stalking us. But it felt icky—would have been better if he came over and talked. We had no recourse; picked up some bread and a proper bottle of jam and returned to the hotel. Mad Dog looked human again. We told him about the café au lait stand guy in the market, but his mind was elsewhere.

"Craze," he said.

"Yeah?"

"You know this gene editing thing. The thing Winston is doing?"

"Mm"

"Could it be used to help my sister?"

CHAPTER 28

Travis: The Selous Scout

It was late afternoon. Travis had been blindfolded, shoved into a helicopter, and dropped into the bush with a knife, a single match, and an egg. "Enjoy your breakfast, mate. If you can find your way back to the camp by midnight of the third night, you can finish your training." The helicopter pulled away, flying low and surely in the wrong direction as it wove back to the Selous Scouts training camp located on the eastern shore of Lake Kariba.

Sipho had briefed Travis on Wafa Wafa Wasara Wasara, the feral proving ground where recruits who sought the chocolate brown beret, green belt, and osprey emblem of the Selous Scouts were dehumanized, stripped of integrity, and rebuilt from their claws inward. The name is Shona for "Who dies—dies; Who survives—remains." Only one in eight survives the rigors of training. They become part of the most feared bush unit in the world, known for infiltrating tribal groups, gathering intelligence, and inflicting pernicious harm on their opposition.

Travis dropped to one knee and slid his knife into the soil. Dry. Coarse with a powdery topcoat. *Patience. Don't just start walking randomly.* He measured the surroundings. Sparse camel thorn trees, bitter scrub, and sporadic indigo, all vegetation with roots that plunge fifteen feet into the soil. Travis popped a couple of stitches inside his khaki shorts—he'd sewn the pen-monocular that Sipho gave him into the cloth backing of the zipper. Even with the monocular, he could barely detect the shadow of a tree line to the east. To the distant north was a rise of table land. *Trees mean water, food—survival. Elevation provides perspective—direction.* The choice was clear. Find the lake. Find the camp.

Travis walked north, toward the tableland. He pulled up his shirt to shield his face from a sun that bore in sharply from the northwest. A moderate wind agitated the chalky topsoil, which caked his nose hair and beard like metal shavings on a magnet. Unpleasant annoyances. Water was his priority; eyes in constant motion as he walked, searching for animal tracks, dry streambeds, clusterleaf trees and other shallow rooted vegetation. A baobab tree would have water between the corky bark and the meat of the tree. Unbroken concentration was needed, but concentration induces fatigue. An hour passed. Three. Chalk in his teeth now.

The sun dropped. Travis spotted the fingers of a bi! bulb plant writhing from the soil. Then another. He dug beneath the growth, pulled up a volleyball-sized bulb, cut it open and shaved the white, fleshy scales with his knife, creating a mound of spongy tissue. He rolled the flesh into a ball, held it over his mouth and squeezed. Water. He drained several balls into his mouth and then used the damp sponges to wipe his face, neck, and arms.

The land rise was hours away and the sun was setting. There was no moon in sight. Travis cut a bundle of dried grass and settled on top of it between giant clumps of savanna grass. The match remained dry in his pocket as he slept. In the morning, he tapped a hole the size of a dime into the top of the egg and drank the uncooked yolk and albumin. Ripping a strip of cloth from the bottom of his shirt, he made a sling to carry a bi! bulb.

After seven hours he reached the base of the tableland. He climbed. A blister had formed on the tip of his nose. Exertion and lack of glucose brought hunger, not as pain but as a clammy syncope of fever, perspiration, mild hallucinations, and disquietude. He thought of his father, a longshoreman who made him unload cod with bare, frozen hands in the dead of winter at the age of twelve. He had to learn toughness, his father told him. A father who died at the age of fifty-one, forcing Travis to dissect shards of love from a mountain of gruff authoritarianism.

Shit, it's barely been twenty-four hours, he thought. Unapologetic pangs of hunger. Attention shifted to edibility testing: smell test, skin test, mouth test, swallow test, eat. By the time Travis reached the top of the ridge, the sun had set. Night number two, heart fluttering cold. He looked for a place to make fire and found a lone baobab tree nestled in a sheltered col. He gathered branches and scrub and used his match. Once the fire matured, Travis used the husk of the bi! bulb to cook spinach made from leaves of the baobab. Then he extracted nuts from the cream-colored pulp of the hardened reproductive pods. Travis slept, warm, hydrated, and fed.

Dawn was critical. He couldn't see the lake, but the cool morning air had created a bank of steam fog in the distance. Three birds flew in the direction of the haze—a haze he knew would disappear as soon as the sun warmed the air. Fog, fed by water. Birds flying toward it. He'd established his direction and walked. Around noon he found an African mangosteen tree and ate. The density of vegetation increased. He reached the lake in the late afternoon.

Travis searched the shore and found a washed-up dinghy. He paddled hundreds of yards offshore and waited for dusk. As the sun set, a swirl of smoke rose from behind an extended peninsular to the northeast. Scouts cooking high tea . . . dinner. Two hours of paddling brought him to the camp. A scout saw him and grunted whoop-whoop. Travis raised an oar and waved it over his head. The other scouts broke into a haunting chant, "Selousi shumbi. Selousi shumbi."

A night of rest was followed by two-and-a-half weeks of abusive strength and fitness tests designed to probe for weaknesses. Next came combative sessions and exercises meant to catechize a warrior mindset. The commander conducted drills in fast roping, high and low freefall techniques, and helocasting—jumping from a helicopter into water. Given his expertise, Travis was asked to assist in a session on explosive breaching techniques. After completing a hundred-kilometer endurance march with heavy cargo, he was officially a Selous Scout.

He went on patrol with a small band of scouts, shadowed their moves, learned their swagger and code of conduct. The scouts had informants in the villages: Black Ndebele or Shona who accepted payments that would help their families. They interrogated villagers. At one point they shot two men in front of their families.

Mothers screamed. Neighbors ran. While on patrol near Chirundu, a group of four women displayed their identity tags to the scouts. One woman carried an infant on her back. The scouts shot the women, claiming they were transporting contraband—illegal newspapers, flyers, magazines—but their bravado and hoots convinced Travis it was done for sport. *I swear they are doing it just to impress me. Is that possible?*

"Was that necessary?" he asked the lead scout.

"When White people were under siege in Bulawayo, Cecil Rhodes told his men to do the most harm to the natives around them. He called them the White man's burden, told them to kill everyone they can, even those who drop their guns and beg for mercy. News travels. Their resolve in this war will diminish, yah?"

Two women died immediately. The other two shimmied on the ground, ashen cheeks of panic, staring into the eyes of their assailant; eyes infected with the joyous tears of Satan. The lead scout walked to one of the women, placed his rifle to her head and fired through it, into the ground. Travis didn't flinch. The second woman screamed. She bellied toward the stream, perhaps thinking it could carry her away. The commander held her neck down with his foot, drew a pistol, and held it her temple, horizontal to the ground. He fired. Travis saw a man who was having fun watching bone and brain fragments spurt from the exit wound.

They turned to leave. Travis saw the baby. "It's still alive."

A scout removed the baby from its mother's pouch and held it upside down by the legs, like a chicken. "We don't want this Jim Fish to come back to haunt us. Let's let the tiger fish have a go at him." He tossed the baby into the river but was compassionate enough to whack its head against a boulder before doing so.

Travis struggled to remember his role. Get information. Report it to Sipho. He willed himself to contain his emotional suffocation. This was not war. It was imperious butchery intended to intimidate. To impose fear. Travis supervised his words, forcing them to express things that were in conflict with his instincts. "They'll have a good feed today, mate."

Vomit filled his brain.

CHAPTER 29

I sat on the edge of Mad Dog's bed. *This is it. If I say yes, gene editing could help your sister, he will certainly be on board to help Winston.* But I was embarrassed that the thought even entered my head. I wasn't going to risk our friendship by bending the truth.

"I don't know, Dog. She has a mitochondrial disease. Your mom told me it was congenital muscular dystrophy. Genetic, yes. One or more of the ATCGs have mutated. In principle, Winston's technology could lead to a cure."

Mad Dog sat, plank-faced, gaze fixed on the ceiling. I flicked the button on my shirt with my thumb. "But . . . it's complicated. There might be more than one mutation. I don't know. It takes a long time to sequence DNA. And . . . I'm not sure it would reverse damage that's already been done to her."

He lowered his eyes to meet mine. "I get it. But it could help others? Down the road?"

"Yes. Maybe prevention."

We slept.

In the morning, we caught a VW bus headed for the Liberian border, the same border that Bubba tried to sneak pot through. The driver stopped at the police station in Danané so we could get our exit stamps. The officers looked at our passports, chatted privately, and told us, "No stamp necessary." We asked if they were sure, pointing out we'd gotten our entry in this same police station. They feigned being insulted and did so with authority. "No stamp necessary."

It took two-and-a-half hours to slog the final seventy-five kilometers to the border. The driver dropped us off, turned, and headed back toward Man. The Ivory Coast soldiers lazed in their border hammock—different guys but the same shtick. AK-47s. Fatigues. Berets. Bored. They lay in opposite directions, feet to head, and reluctantly stirred as we approached.

"Passeportes, s'il vous plaît," said the older and more rotund soldier. He switched to English. "Please." He flipped through the pages and stopped. "Where is exit stamp? You need a stamp from police in Danané."

"We went there. They said we didn't need one," I said. I saw him cast a mental wink at his partner. He pointed his finger down the road, grinning. "You have to go back to Danané."

Three Americans at a jungle border. No taxis or buses. Over two hours to get to Danané. Two hours to get back. He didn't mask his intent. "This will cost you plenty money."

We exchanged glances. The soldier knew his price. He said, "1000 CFA each."

Four dollars! Don't let him see you smile. Look dismayed and hand him the money.

Mad Dog poked his tongue into his cheek. He didn't like being made a fool. The police in Danané had set us up for their friends.

You're not on the football field, Mad Dog. Let it go. Let them have their win.

I pulled a 1000 CFA note from my wallet and held it out to the fat guy. Mad Dog raised his voice and spoke with purpose. "Don't pay 'em, Craze. This is bull."

I turned, leaned into him, found my quiet voice. "Four bucks each, Dog . . . it's okay."

The younger soldier smiled, raised his arm, and pointed up the road . . . toward Danané. The fat soldier dropped the rifle from his shoulder, slapped the butt on the ground, and wrapped his right hand around the barrel like it was a walking stick. He positioned himself between Mad Dog and the road to Liberia.

Dog's competitive compass outpaced his common sense. "You guys know this is bullshit?" He took a half step toward Liberia. "Is this how you . . ."

91

Dut—splack. The fat soldier had pulled the rifle barrel up, gripped the stock with his left hand, and butt-stroked Mad Dog. He'd aimed for the chin, but Dog flinched, and the blow caught his upper chest. He dropped to the ground.

"Shit," Bubba yelled.

I wasn't sure what to do. *Will I get hit if I try to help him?* Mad Dog was stunned but conscious, shirt torn, short breaths. I thought his collarbone might be broken. Bubba yanked 2,000 CFA from his wallet and handed it to the younger guy, saying, "Here. Here."

Mad Dog stood. The fat guy flounced and waved the barrel of his gun in the direction of Liberia. He called out, "Merci messieurs. Bon voyage," and spat on the ground. We walked.

The Liberia post was ten minutes away. Bubba asked Dog if he was okay. No answer. Bubba's voice took the tone of a Sunday sermon. "You gotta get through the border with the multiple entry visas you've concocted. Get composed. Dashing is a way of life here. If they need a bribe, we'll pay it and move on. Be smart."

"Got it. Sorry," said Mad Dog. He ran his thumb and forefinger along his collarbone to see if it was broken. "I'm all right. Going to hurt. Why's everything so hard?"

Bubba lashed. "It just is."

We arrived at the border, fearful that our altered visas might send us to jail. I still hadn't assembled a complete breath since Mad Dog got whacked. My left hand slipped deep into my pocket and cupped my balls, an inexplicable reflex of self-protection. Mad Dog pulled on his shirt to hide the red mark on his chest.

Mulbah, the guard we met on the way out of Liberia wasn't on duty. But Samuel, the fourteen-year-old trainee with the single action Browning was. He greeted us with the Liberian finger-snap handshake, a happy hello, and went into the small guard house to get his boss.

Bubba stepped forward, whispered to us in a cocky undertone, "Showtime." Samuel introduced us to Momolu. Bubba snapped a handshake, discussed his job at the Ministry of Forest Services, discovered that Momolu had seven kids, belonged to the Krahn people, and lived in Kahnple. His wife crafted buttons from the nuts of the toddy palm tree. Bubba bought a dozen.

It was clear sailing. Momolu mouthed the word "multiple" when he looked at my visa but didn't ask questions. Stamp. He took Mad Dog's passport, found the Liberian visa, stamp.

BUREAU OF IMMIGRAION & NAT. MINISTRY OF
JUSTICE GRANTED TEMPORARY VISA OF 17
DAYS *Momolu Seckey*.

Momolu told us a money bus usually came at three o'clock from Ganta. A cloth rug lay on the ground across the road from the guard house. A middle-aged man sat on the corner of it, arms wrapped around his knees. I asked Momolu if we could wait there. He nodded.

"Nice job, Bubba," I said. "For a minute there I thought you and Momolu were going to hold hands and skip into the jungle." We slipped off our packs and sat on the rug. Mad Dog remained standing, stretched his back, legs, twisted side to side, rubbed his collarbone.

Bubba opened up. "Okay, Craze. You remember when I went back to Oregon for a few weeks before you guys came over?" I did remember. While in Liberia, Bubba had developed a low-grade fever and felt a cutting pain in his left back. The Peace Corps sent him home to Oregon for evaluation. He had a kidney stone and an infected urinary tract. Both were treated and he flew back to Liberia a few weeks before Mad Dog and I flew from Boston to Liberia.

I said, "Yeah. I'm glad they figured it out. We thought we'd be traveling without you."

Bubba seemed to be calculating his next words. How to say them. "Well, you know how Alex went on a vacation out west with her roommate?" I nodded. Alex and her roommate had gone on a road trip—they'd talked about doing that for a while.

"Well, before heading back to Massachusetts, they came to visit me while I was in Oregon for my kidney stone."

Okay. She stopped in to visit him. No big deal.

I said, "That's cool. What's with this blood-thickening tone?"

Bubba's voice was subdued, but clear. He looked down. "I don't know, Craze. We had an earnest conversation about where you and she are in your relationship. I didn't get good vibes. Got the feeling she's tired of waiting. You've been together a long time. I sent you a letter, before I flew back to Liberia."

"Didn't get it. Must have left before it arrived. I was at her place the last two days."

Her parting question migrated to my forebrain. "When Dog and I were getting into the car, she asked, 'Will you marry me when you get back?' It took me by surprise. Life has been good. We hardly ever fight. I didn't know marriage was important to her." Bubba lifted his head. I stared forward. "She goes to all my ball games . . . loves the Caper Crew. She came to see me when I lived in Sweden. Met me in Munich to go to the Oktoberfest. Supported me when I went to work in Israel."

I tried to look at Bubba but found myself focused on a coconut on the ground, trying to make sense of the marbles that were bonking around my head. "She told me, if you don't propose soon, she'll probably start looking elsewhere," Bubba said.

"You're telling me this now?"

"It's all in my letter. Wanted to get it down word for word so I didn't screw up. I figured you got it."

A hoary bat swirled at my throat.

"Craze, think about what you just said. *She* went to your games. *She* visited you in Sweden. *She* went to Munich. Sounds a little lopsided."

"Thanks." There aren't many people who could say something like that to me, but Bubba was one of them. Still, I was defensive. "I do things for her all the time. I'm the romantic. I never forget her birthday. Love bringing her flowers. Love her parents. I'm pretty sure they love me."

Bubba was blunt. "At some point, romance isn't enough." He lingered. "And there's more."

"Huh?"

"What did you say? When she asked if you'd marry her, what did you say?"

"I don't know. I was confused. It was unexpected. What do you mean there's more?"

"Listen to me." Bubba looked through my pupils, like he wanted to stick a switchblade into my soul. "'Will you marry me when you get back?' Craze. That's a proposal. She proposed to you. What was your answer . . . to her marriage proposal?"

Mad Dog was still standing with his back to us. Doing trunk twists. He said, "You need to marry her, Craaaaaaaaaze," adding a dose of gravel to my name.

The middle-aged man sitting on the rug said, "Yes, you need to marry her, Craze."

I chucked a glare his way and returned to Bubba. "I just said . . . I said, uh, we don't have to talk about this now. We'll talk when I get back."

Bubba's voice was chafed. "And? That's it? That was your answer to her proposal?"

Mad Dog certified. "Yup. That's what he said."

I'd been indicted, tried, and convicted. "What'd you mean when you said there's more?"

The time for the final quiver had come. Bubba told me she'd met a guy from British Columbia while she was on her trip. He was adventurous like me, gave her feelings that stirred her. He made her laugh. Made her see promise in a life that didn't include me. He wanted to settle down. Have kids. Bubba said he was "sure they slept together." She told him that the experience confused her; she still loved me and felt my love for her. It had nothing to do with a biological clock thing. It was a relationship clock. If I didn't know the answer by now, she might move on. Bubba said she was still interested in the guy, knew he'd visited her once, maybe twice. Holy shit.

Bubba's words surrounded me like a cloud of despair. I felt exposed. Worse, I was embarrassed by my unconscious disregard for her aspirations, a scab on my self-awareness. What the hell! *She's the catch, not me. She's the one everybody loves. She wants to marry me. How did I screw this up!*

The money bus came. We piled into the back with three others. My heart pounded. For a full minute I couldn't figure out where I was. In Africa. In the jungle. Just slipped past immigration with an altered visa. I wasn't able to sit comfortably and couldn't figure out why.

CHAPTER 30

Craze: The Invitation

A local couple in Ganta, Nathaniel and Way'etu, offered us food and a place on their floor for a small fee. While we were eating, their eight-year-old son, Lester, giggled and whispered in his mother's ear each time he looked at Mad Dog. After dinner, Mad Dog asked Nathaniel what the giggling was all about.

"Lester thought you were the spirit of his pet bullfrog that died last week."

Mad Dog flinched, like he'd stuck his face in a bucket of ice water.

"We are Vai people—from the Lofa River. We allow Islam to coexist with our own beliefs—good and evil spirits turning themselves into animals. Objects. Other people."

At bedtime, Bubba, bead of Colgate hanging from his mouth, whispered, "Maybe we'll start calling you Mad Frog." He was pleased with himself.

We hitched a ride with a neighbor who had a 1963 Studebaker pickup truck that wore the pummeled scars of bush driving. He and his partner were delivering two hundred liters of palm oil to Monrovia. As we started to hop into the bed of the truck, Lester shied his way up to Mad Dog and held out a four-inch-tall plastic figurine of Chewbacca. The figurine had been in the box that Lester kept his pet bullfrog in, his bullfrog's friend.

Mad Dog's face flushed. If a Vai spirit was in him, it surely consumed the moment. He dropped to one knee, leaned on his elbow, and placed his fingertips on his forehead, covering the right side of his face with his hand. He gazed at Lester, and said, "For me?"

Lester nodded. He hugged Mad Dog and ran into the house. Mad Dog hid his face and wiped his brow with his sleeve, brushing his forearm across his eyes. If moisture had formed, it wasn't going to reach his cheek. He slid the figurine into his shirt pocket.

Once underway, I took a poke at Mad Dog's atheism. "That was quite a gesture Lester made. Almost reverent."

"Yeah . . . the kid got to me."

"What do you mean he got to you? He got to your leg? Your hair? Your heart?" I waited. "Did he get to your soul? A soul that defines your being? Or is what you're feeling just a bunch of molecules reacting to other molecules?"

"Fuck off."

The rest of the ride was silent except for an intermittent, "Ribbit, Ribbit," from Bubba.

It was a relief to see Mike's beach house. We took a moment to sit on the porch. Without warning, Mad Dog's usually restrained Barry Goldwater demons surfaced. "Is this how the Jimmy Carter liberals spend taxpayers' money? Renting beach houses for the Peace Corps?"

Bubba's eyes popped. Mad Dog's tendencies seldom actualized in speech. "PCVs don't get paid shit. If they can find a good place for a cheap price, they take it."

"Vietnam vets are homeless, and my tax dollars are paying for someone's beach house? What does the USA get out of this, paying Peace Corps people to run around the globe?"

I said, "Dog. The Peace Corps spreads a lot of goodwill for what amounts to chump change. If these countries prosper, we prosper. If they buy more things from us, it adds to *our* economy. Firestone and Goodrich grow rubber for our tires here. Besides . . ." I aimed for his soft spot. ". . . some countries in Africa have turned to communism. You want the commies to have free reign on influencing these countries?"

Mad Dog was inspecting his shoes again, still swearing they weren't his.

I said, "Liberia, was founded to give freed slaves a place to live, right Bubba?"

He smirked. A year in Liberia had taught him some unseemly details. "That's the party line. But it's not as sanctimonious as it sounds. The concept was motivated by racism."

"Huh?"

"After the Revolutionary War, the number of free Black people was increasing, particularly in the north. The American Colonization Society was afraid that those still enslaved might form a rebellion. They set up 'voluntary' relocation to Liberia: slaves were freed, but only if they would emigrate to Liberia where they were promised a life free of White bigotry. But the real fear of the ACS was that the free Black people would blend into the mainstream culture in America. Eventually, the Society's intentions were exposed by White abolitionists, and the program ended."

Mad Dog shook his head, listening. "How'd you get onto that topic? Just don't like seeing money wasted on liberal programs."

My heart skipped. I realized a letter from Alex might be waiting for me inside. Then I remembered I hadn't sent her anything, just left one stinking voice message from Bobo. It was there, on the kitchen counter. I fumbled with the flap like it was laced with anthrax. She wrote:

```
Dear Craze,

    My butt is sore. I played Hearts with
Mom last night, and she whipped me. She
says hi. Dad too. Mom's still mad at you
for breaking her vacuum cleaner. Ha!
    Devon, the 16 year old guy at Fernald
with Fragile X syndrome made me a Miss
Piggy doll out of play dough, M&M's, and
a pair of his socks. So sweet! Carl, the
man with Lou Gehrig's, you met him at our
field day. He flipped the bird to a board
member while he was giving a tour. That
guy's uncle was on the team at Fernald
that exposed children to radiation in the
'50s. Carl has good instincts.
    Jake bought his first car, but Dad
won't let him drive it until he gets a
new muffler. Someone trampled on an
```

```
azalea in front of our apartment. Our
landlord tried to blame us. BITCH. I
can't imagine the incredible things you
are seeing. Be safe always. Got your
voicemail. Maybe you can write or call
soon?

Love,
Alex

P.S. Your dad said you can call him
collect any time.
```

I was petrified as I read, dissecting each word, searching for microscopic nuances. She loved her job as a physical therapist at the Fernald State School in Waltham, a place that once was called The Experimental School for Teaching and Training Idiotic Children. She always talked about work. But the letter was mostly just stuff. She signed it, "Love, Alex." *But what are you thinking, Alex? Okay, she's living her daily routine while I'm on a ramble. What do I expect?*

She never mentioned the question, marriage. I felt increasingly unsettled.

It was Friday evening. The telecom office in Monrovia was closed on weekends. We went to the US Embassy the next day. They wouldn't let me call the US unless it was on official business or an emergency. But we could use their pool. I wrote to friends and family. To Alex. Told her about our forged visas, the border crossings, people getting whipped off the train, the Hee-Fee rat night, the wares and people of the outdoor markets, the café au lait guy, Mad Dog's shoes, and the kindness of so many people. I told her how I missed her each time I saw a yellow oleander, the color she wore when I last saw her. How I wished she were with me. Words about why I loved her and how I fell in love with her flowed with an elegance that surprised me. I even told her of Winston's intriguing proposal.

I didn't address *the* question—couldn't do that in a letter. But I asked her if she could join us in Kenya for a few weeks before Mad Dog and I headed into the Sudan and up the Nile into Egypt. I'd checked with Mad Dog. He understood the position I was in and was fond of Alex. "It'll be fun," he said. Eleven pages, the embassy post office charged me over a dollar.

We moved into Bubba's apartment because Mike's roommate had returned. It was small and had no furniture. We slept on the floor, a rat-free floor, which meant it was fine, fine, fine.

An envelope with a note had been slipped under his door.

```
Hello Bubba,

Welcome back. A reminder, you are invited
to come to Betsy's lagoon for a beach
party. We want to give Craze and Mad Dog
a nice send off before they leave for
South Africa. You will stay the night.
We've arranged transport to get Craze and
Mad Dog to the airport. It will be fun.
I trust they've discussed my proposal.

Winston
```

CHAPTER 31

Travis: Wimpy's

It was 1:10 a.m. After spending a few weeks in the bush, the Selous Scouts in Travis's unit slept comfortably on their cots in Bulawayo, the second largest city in Rhodesia. It was in the center of Matabeleland, home of the Ndebele people in the western third of the country.

Travis slipped out. Barely a shadow wavered as he navigated his way to the Weathermen Africa office, located in the rear of a Wimpy's hamburger store off of Fife Street. Sipho sat on a sofa, drinking tea, and studying the sports page.

"All right, mate. Good to see you. You look a bit knackered, scruffier than our first go. You survived. You're a Selous Scout man. Well done."

Hearing Sipho's voice alleviated some of the tension that had been pressing on Travis. He was free of the masquerade that defined his assignment, perpetually living a lie while pretending to be collegial with a band of unripe thugs. Sipho asked to hear details of his training, numbers of scouts, who the leaders were. Eventually they discussed operations.

"We're gonna start training for a mission. They're calling it Operation Excision but haven't said where it is or when. From what I hear, it's deep into Zambia, maybe Lusaka."

Sipho stiffened. "Lusaka? Hm, that's it? Nothing more?"

"I get the impression they only give us bits of info when we need it."

"Of course. Still, try to get more. Where? When? Number of men? Whether the infantry, C Squadron, or Special Air Service are involved, or is it strictly a Selous Scout operation."

"It's more than the Scouts. The army built a training ground, including a mock house. I know I'm supposed to blow up some buildings. Heard something about crossing Lake Kariba."

"Lake Kariba is 250 kilometers long, Travis—makes up half our border with Zambia. They're probably planning to cross the lake into Zambia, instead of going overland. That's good info. Tricky. Try to find out where they plan to land their boats."

"I'll learn more tomorrow." Travis fidgeted. His lips stumbled. "Sipho, I wa . . . I was. Well. Surprised to see how many Black soldiers are in the Rhodesian Army. Hell, there's a lot of them in the Selous Scouts too. I don't get it. If the Whites are so oppressive, why do the Africans support them by joining the army?"

"Ah. You are new to the confutations of African life, my friend. First, it is a paying job. Hard to come by, especially with the international sanctions levied on Rhodesia. African soldiers make around $2,500 a year."

"A year?"

"Not what the White soldiers get, but a lot of money for them. Puts food on the table. Maybe a motorbike. They don't fight to maintain White rule. But they don't all support the socialist agenda of the Patriotic Front either. Don't equate joining the army to mean they don't want to be free from White rule."

It was a conflict Travis understood thoroughly, being forced to choose between your family and your cause. He digested Sipho's words and tucked them away.

Sipho said he'd wait for Travis until 1:00 a.m. each night for the coming week. But the following morning, Travis was whisked off to a training facility in a far corner of Rhodesia, where he learned of a surgical assault that would flip the war on its head. He had no means of getting the information back to Sipho. Travis was on his own.

CHAPTER 32

Craze: Betsy's Lagoon

Thousands of fiddler crabs skittered as Betsy beached her boat on the sand. Her place was a few miles from ACORN on an island across the mouth of the river. A couple of Peace Corps friends and others from ACORN landed next to us in a second boat. The smell of wood fires and the oil scent from nearby lemongrass mingled with the beach spray. Curls of freshly cooked cornbread filtered in from a nearby bakeshop.

An army of children emerged from the undergrowth, where the beach met the forest. Betsy nodded. They hopped aboard and carried the coolers, food, fresh water, and cooking gear on their heads to her camp: two grass huts, which offered relief from a tireless sun during the day and transformed into sleeping quarters at night.

Winston was already there, up shore talking to a fisherman. We waved. We still hadn't rubber-stamped a decision on whether we'd deliver his manufacturing protocols to the liaison in Zambia. As much as I wanted to say yes, I wasn't willing to screw up the karma of our trip if Mad Dog wasn't on board. I'd done my best to allow him to come to a decision on his own. When he asked if gene editing could help his sister, I was sure he'd come around. But I knew that nothing was ever sure with Mad Dog until he came to his own conclusion.

The three of us dug our toes into the bright, pulverized silica, and ankled along the water's edge to the lagoon, a tropical atoll with a narrow outlet to the sea. Isolation was total, but others would arrive soon.

"Craze, do you understand what Winston is doing at the center?" Bubba asked.

"Yeah. Most of it." I was looking at Bubba but was really trying to convince Mad Dog. "The function of DNA is to make proteins—enzymes, collagen, hair, hemoglobin, etc. It defines the order that amino acids string together when a protein is manufactured by the cells. Winston is accelerating, or better said, guiding nature in a positive direction. It's mind bending."

"I knew there was serious shit going on but had no idea," Bubba said. "Gene editing. Nanoparticles."

"Guys, this is up there with penicillin or the smallpox vaccine. I had my doubts about Winston, but I give him props. Screw the bioethicists. Who wants to have malaria on this earth? If Winston doesn't do it, someone else will."

"What about his story about a mole or moral crackpot at the center? Sounds iffy."

"Mm, yeah. That's why he asked for our help. To throw them off. All he's asking us to do is carry the info for a few days and then hand it off. We'd be part of something historical," I eyeballed Mad Dog, "and get that trip up Kilimanjaro."

Bubba faced Dog. "What's going on in your head, Mad Dog? You in or out?"

I was ten years old and rode my bike to visit Mad Dog, who went by his given name then, Dave. Dave opened the door. The hi-fi played Glenn Miller's "Moonlight Serenade," but the music was interrupted by the steely voice that his father had adopted over the past few years. Dave knew he had to own up to whatever he'd done wrong. He may have failed to push in the kitchen chair completely, possibly left his bike by the back door instead of putting it in the shed.

"David, you left your slippers in the wrong place. I tripped over them, could have killed myself. And the sugar bowl wasn't where it belongs."

"Sorry, sir. I'll put it back on the counter next to the coffee machine."

Mr. Hill scoffed. "Now put the needle back on the album, second cut please."

Dave handled the tone arm gently, afraid of scratching the record. His house was always filled with the sounds of classical music and the big band era. Mr. Hill once told me he felt the beat of the tympani on his chest, that he could ride saddle atop the notes of Mozart's "Sonata for Two Pianos." He cherished Pavarotti's voice when it pled the crescendo of Puccini's "Nessun Dorma."

Mrs. Hill came in from the garden. The needle reconnected with the vinyl. She smiled at me. Dave nodded. Mr. Hill shouted, "Remember to mow the lawn today." Dave didn't reply.

Mr. Hill had lost his sight two years prior when he fell off a ladder while painting. Retinas detached in both eyes; in an instant he was blind. It left him bitter. Once, he blindfolded Dave and made him eat and do chores without sight for an entire day. He turned to Christian Science to help battle the goblins that haunted his spirit. Before losing his sight, he'd immersed himself in photography, employing a folding focal plane camera on a tripod, the kind with the accordion-like body, rubber ball trigger, and slot in the back for wood-framed dry plates. Dave would sit with him in the dark cellar and watch photos magically appear: milk splashing in a bowl, the geometry of its droplets captured in midflight; a portrait of a breathtaking woman with shadows cast perfectly to amplify her complexity; a series boasting the prowess of the B29s he flew during the Second World War. He could personify a vase or a simple metal cylinder. Mr. Hill not only lost his sight, he was robbed of an avocation that celebrated beauty and artistry.

In time, Dave grew to admire his father. He walked the streets with the aid of his cane. He could still fix things. "But what good is a tool if you can't put your hands on it?" he would say.

The obligations thrust on Dave were unjust, but at the age of ten, he accepted his position. His sister was born with a mitochondrial disease. Mentally impaired. Needed special education and care. Mrs. Hill relied on Dave to be the little man of the house, her partner in keeping the house whole.

Newspapers named Dave all-scholastic defensive end, best in Massachusetts. With offers from thirty colleges, including the football beasts, he opted for education at Cornell, where he earned the name Mad Dog. That his father couldn't watch him play football or look at photos of the places he'd been left Dave heavyhearted. His youth taught him to be cautious, thoughtful; everything must align. Ask questions. Don't be impulsive or pretentious. Make sure you understand.

Mad Dog said, "Uh-boy." He looked at me. "It's hard to say no. We wouldn't be doing anything wrong." He fixed his stare on the water and recalled out loud our experience with the young girl who had Malaria on the money bus, and the man on the sidewalk in Bobo. He was moved, but wariness lingered. "I don't know Winston. How do I know I can trust him? And how are we supposed to meet up with this third party?"

"Good questions. I see a guy who is brilliant, but insecure and awkwardly charming. The guy's talking about a Nobel Prize for God's sake. He's been burnt three times. In principle I'm in, but only if you are."

"Hmph."

"Winston entrusted us with a lot of information. Getting rid of malaria? To even play a small part, it's a caper. We are the Caper Crew after all. You have any other questions?"

"Yes. Where are we going to find this guy we're supposed to meet? How will we know it's him? What does Winston mean when he says he'll package the information so that nobody will know we have it?"

Bubba tightened his neck, crossed his eyes, and contorted his lip, something he did before using a creeped-out idiot voice he was fond of. "Ooh, maybe he's going to use invisible ink. Or maybe the guy will have a gold front tooth."

I was a little pissed off. "This is serious shit, Bubba."

Betsy effortlessly directed cooking activities, organized games, and met with the elders amid the backdrop of atomized brine from the tidal flat and the crimson shadows of mahogany trees. Meat sizzled over a hickory fire. Women chatted and laughed as they carved. The feast was outrageous. Chicken peanut soup, corn, cornbread, rice, rubbed goat ribs, fufu, habanero-spiced shrimp skewers, sweet potato ginger pone, and a boiling pot of beef palava. A hand-carved bowl with pineapple, mango, sour soup, palm cherries, and breadnuts centered the table.

It's rare to find high levels of intellect and grace residing in the same mind. Betsy could break bread with the elders, win over undiscerning politicians, and discuss the relative strengths of carbon-nitrogen bonds with chemists. Winston could learn from her. When she asked us countless questions about our trip, we felt like it was the only thing on her mind. Minds like hers are fueled by intense curiosity. It separates them from the book-smarts. The topic has no relevance; it could be mushrooms, the rings of Saturn, the effect of volcanic soil on grapes, or the left-handed hatch strokes of Leonardo.

Winston was rudimentary. He loved the story about Mad Dog's confrontation with the rats in Bobo but was starkly disappointed that we hadn't sampled any women at the local knock shops. Bubba tried to soften our underachievement. "One night at an outdoor bar, some scorching women in tight shorts sat on our laps and masterfully convulsed their butt cheeks on our cocks. They asked, 'Do you want me to shake your point?'"

"And . . .?" Winston forced us to answer. Wanted us to say it, probably for his amusement, but it felt like he was trying to instill a layer of superiority. *Like he needs it.*

Bubba laughed. "Hey, I'm fond of my wiener and happy to pass up the opportunity to acquaint it with a venereal disease. We don't have a war chest of pharmaceuticals like you."

"Accepted." Winston bowed.

After our gorge, we strolled to the shore with Winston and sat on a raised beach ridge under a single tamarind tree bursting with fig buds. Bubba yammered. "I can barely move. Gluttony, I have met thee and hold ye no remorse, yet I do not wish to congregate with thee oft."

Winston laughed. Mad Dog and I looked at each other and shared a familiar glance of stupefaction. I said, "You're a friggin' cretin . . . you know that, right?"

Bubba's face twisted into a sponge. His idiot voice resurfaced. "Oooooooooh."

I begged myself not to laugh and put my nose up to his. "You are a seriously flawed individual." He shriveled, feigning indignation.

Winston got to the point. "Have you talked over my proposal? It would be very generous of you and would be a colossal help to our cause. It may not seem like much, but we don't know where the leak is. No one will suspect you. I've arranged for a trusted contact to meet you as soon as you cross the border into Zambia. Give him the documents, and your work is done. In the meantime, we must find the altruistic misanthrope that has sabotaged the previous deliveries."

Mad Dog asked, "What do you mean we're going to meet some guy in Livingstone? Who is he? Where do we meet him? How will we know who he is?"

"Good. There's a place on the Zambian side of Victoria Falls called Leopard Spot Campground. All the overland tours go there. We've checked. The company you're with, Trindell Travel, uses that site. You won't have to find him. He'll find you."

Mad Dog formulated the scenario in his head. "He doesn't know who we are. Won't it look strange if he comes wandering into our camp?"

"It's Vic Falls. Big tourist attraction. That campsite is a sociable place. There can be three or four overland trucks there at any time. People wander around, talk about where they've been, where they are going. It won't be unusual at all. And guys . . . the trip you are on typically has Europeans. Two Americans won't be hard to spot."

A hairline movement in Mad Dog's jaw told me his bulwark had shifted.

"One more question. You said something about providing the documents to us in a way that nobody would notice. What do you mean by that?"

Winston grinned. "Oh? That's the fun part. We learned this technique from a former MI6 guy who is now the director of security at the center. Have you ever seen those Russian nesting dolls? The Matryoshka dolls? The ones where you open the doll and there's another one inside. Then you open that one and find another, smaller doll, etc.?"

This hit a spot with Mad Dog. "I have one of those dolls . . . bought it when I rode my Honda 750 to Alaska."

"Very good. Anyway, there are similar dolls in Africa, a tourist thing. They don't have the doll shape; they are nested cylinders. But it's the same idea, one doll nested inside the other. Each doll is a representation of African royalty: Osei Kofi Tutu, ruler of the Ashanti Kingdom; Musa Keita, the king of kings in Ancient Mali; Oba Ewuare, king of the Great Benin Empire, blah blah. Quite nice. We made one with eight nested dolls. The tallest is about ten inches. You'll only have them for a few days, maybe a week, before they're taken off your hands."

Mad Dog and I had a prolonged visual exchange, a silent conversation that only lifelong friends can have. Finally, an answer, I thought. I said to Winston, "We're in."

"Let's do it," Mad Dog said. He stood, resolute, looked Winston in the eye, offered his hand and snapped off a fine Liberian handshake. "We'll get 'em there for you."

It always thrilled me to watch this kind of transformation happen with Mad Dog. I thought, *This* will be a great story to tell his father.

Mad Dog had one final question. "So, where are the documents?"

CHAPTER 33

Craze: Old Man George

Old Man George plunged his paddle into the waters of the river. His hollowed-out mahogany tree provided our last mode of transportation in before flying to South Africa. A gentle giant in his mid-sixties, with muscles upon muscles, younger men in smaller canoes could only nip at his wake. Whether a deferential bow, a nod from a fisherman, a yielding of the right of way, or children running to catch a glimpse, his passage was a venerate occasion.

The Chewbacca figurine that Lester had given Mad Dog dangled from a gear loop on his pack, tied off with a rawhide shoelace. Acknowledging this quirk of Mad Dog's personage would be an affront to his privacy standards, expose a morsel of his inner pathos. Still, I said, "Nice touch with Chewbacca, Mad Dog."

"Yep."

Before breakfast, Winston had taken us to the Krahn sacrificial table in a cave near the village. At the entrance he removed the dolls from his shoulder satchel. They were stunning, each a dignified African king, queen, princess, or warrior adorned with gold neck rings, carmine head wraps, a vantablack akrafena sword, extreme piercings, and silvery body paint. The walls of each doll/cylinder were made of paper scrolls tightly wrapped into a tube, held together by an adhesive, like a toilet paper roll. The outermost layer of each doll was sealed with shellac.

"What do you think?" Winston asked.

"Simply beauteous," I said. *And clever.*

"I want you to feel comfortable. It looks like a harmless African tourist trinket."

I counted eight dolls, each larger than the other, the smaller doll nested within the larger one, but unlike Matryoshka dolls, they opened on the top instead of the middle. "So, we just hand the guy these dolls, and we're done, right?" I asked.

"That's it." He told us of specific solvents that were needed to dissolve the coating and separate the layers. But we needn't worry, that was the pharmaceutical company's problem.

"They're amazing," Bubba said. Mad Dog smiled. He'd inherited his father's appreciation for artistry, but I could see plumes of conspiracy theories burning in his head.

"The largest doll will roll out to eight feet. Each successive doll will be shorter. You can fit a lot on that amount of space."

After breakfast, we said goodbye to Betsy and Winston. I wanted to assure Betsy that the dolls would be safe, but honored Winston's directive to not tell anyone. We'd come to feel close to this little corner of Liberia. The prospect of leaving Bubba left us pitted. Unbalanced. During breakfast, we mourned the loss. He belonged with us, and we told him so. I said, "It's going to feel empty. One leg of the three-legged stool gone." I hugged him and kissed him on the cheek. "What will we do without our beloved goofball?"

Our flimsily conceived rollick had deepened a friendship that was already strong. This goodbye was not detached or vacant. It was cluttered, intimate, bonded by the experience, sights, sounds, and smells of West Africa. A fraternity forged within the events of life.

Our canoe approached the airport. I coaxed Mad Dog to speak. "Well, Dog, I'm ready for new scenery. Goodbye forged visas, retinal scans, sneaking pot through the border, rats at the Hee-Fee Hotel, the wonderful people of Upper Volta, the African Burn Out, and the kindness of Luc in Man. Ah, and getting butt-whipped at the border and the rancid meat affair."

"Thanks for sticking with me, Craze. I know I've been down a few times." His voice perked. He raised both arms to the sky. "Ready to see my first giraffe."

I laughed. "And how about this super-secret mission we're on. Got to admit, it adds a touch of drama, and a story. Meet a mysterious man at Victoria Falls. Pass him the secret Matryoshka dolls. I hope history books are kind to us."

"Yeah, maybe this Winston guy is OK. He's clever. Can't completely warm up to him. It doesn't bother you, all this secrecy? Shit, he's trusting us with Nobel Prize information."

"He's not just analytical, Dog. He's intuitive. They aren't exclusive traits."

Old Man George dropped us at the riverbank near the airport. With a humble nod, he was gone. Our Air Afrique flight originated in Paris and stopped in Monrovia, and Kinshasa, the capital of Zaire, on its way to Johannesburg. It was scheduled to depart at 2:00 p.m., but we were told it wouldn't leave until 9:00 p.m. Africa.

While sitting on the plane during our stopover in Zaire, the flight crew walked through the cabin wearing surgical masks. They sprayed a powdery disinfectant on everything and everyone. We shielded our eyes. Our flight was going from a Black African country into a White-ruled apartheid country. They had to get rid of the cooties.

The plane took off. Winston's dolls were nested in the overhead in the rear pocket of my pack. Our eyelids were in want of sleep. Heads sagged. Mad Dog spoke.

"Craze."

"Yeah?"

"What about Alex?"

"I know."

Part II
Botswana

Bernie, Emilie, Doug, and Jerry cutting wood for cookfire

CHAPTER 34

Craze: Michael's Tavern

The flat-faced immigration officer in Johannesburg looked like his best friend had stolen his wife. I asked, "Could we please get a loose-leaf visa?"

It was something I'd learned in Israel, getting a visa on a piece of paper in lieu of a stamp in your passport. Arab nations won't let you into their country if you have an Israeli stamp in your passport. Similarly, if you have a South African stamp, you're denied entry into many African countries, some that we planned to visit later.

The officer, framed by the backdrop of the orange, white, and blue flag of South Africa, perched his voice atop a snide stallion. "Why do you want a loose-leaf visa?" I was sure he knew the answer. But it was more satisfying to be a prick.

I wanted to say, "Because I can't get into other African countries if they know I've been to your racist country. They have sanctions against people who travel to a country that embraces apartheid." But I didn't. "I'd like to be able to put it in a scrapbook when I get home."

Mr. Snide Face smiled, dipped his stamp into a saturated ink pad, and branded a full-page stamp in my passport. It shouted, "This guy has been to South Africa."

First impressions came without effort. Busses and bus stops labeled with signs that said, "Whites" or "Asian, Colored, and African." The same was true of liquor stores and retail shops. Sometimes they were labeled "Non-Whites." More succinct. Benches on the sidewalks were designated "European only," an attempt at political correctness.

I read Mad Dog's lips. "Holy shit."

We passed a newsstand where foreign newspapers—British, Dutch, International Herald Tribune—were heavily censored, words and sentences manually blacked out on every page. *My god, somebody makes these decisions every day and tells a team, armed with magic markers, which words stay and which words go.*

The city was clean, vibrant, and beautiful, the April autumn air dry and fresh. We found a room in the Marshalltown section of Jo'burg, not far from Rissik Street, where Trindell Travel was located—the office of the overland tour we were booked on. It was clean enough, with two twin beds, a pedestal sink, mirror, showers down the hall.

We dropped into a place called Michael's Tavern for supper—fish and chips—and forty-five-cent Carling Black Labels. Mad Dog hadn't gotten much sleep on the plane and went back to the hotel after supper. I decided to stay and play pool.

The pool table was a conduit for observation and conversation. Guys trying to look cool. Exaggerated fist pumps. Bad shots triggered obtuse logic on how it fit their strategy. They weren't joking; they expected you to buy it. Guys freely turned to politics, especially once they learned I was American. Most visitors were Brits, Aussies, and Dutch. My sozzled buddies knew what their international image was and were determined to defend it, without any prompting.

"Hey, Yank, this is the greatest fucking country in the world."

"America would be shit without South Africa." *Really?*

They tried to show me that they weren't as demonic as the world lens portrayed them, that they were more enlightened than advertised. A kid named Sebastian made his pitch. "We know it's wrong . . . apartheid. But we were born here, mate." He waved his cue stick in an arc above the bar crowd. "Our parents were born here. Our ancestry goes back to the 1600s—same time your Pilgrims went to America. We're not visitors, this is our home, mate. What can I do? I can't change the government. Just living our lives in the country we were born in."

I ventured. "Seems like it's home to others too. Not just the White folks."

Sebastian pulled out a preloaded response that I eventually learned was in every South African's pocket when they spoke with an American. "The United States was initially occupied by Indians. Same thing. Look what you did: took their land, put them on a reservation."

I was rattled. "But that doesn't mean it was right." *Ugh . . . am I guilty of going about my life with an inert conscience on this subject?* I'd just been schooled on the power of apathy.

A friend of Sebastian's, a more enlightened chap, joined in. "You know, we believe that—on the inside—Black Africans are mostly equal to White people." Oh God, I thought. "Well, maybe not as intelligent, but basically the same."

I gulped. Decided I valued my life. I treaded lightly. "Could a Black African or non-European walk into this bar right now? Have a beer? Play a game of snooker?"

"Yes, he could, mate . . . mm, not in *this* particular pub. But he could so at another one."

On the wall behind him was a framed poster, a photo of a sign on a beach that read, "Under Section 37 of the Durban Beach by laws this bathing area is reserved for the sole use of members of the White race group."

Something about the specificity and un-ambivalence of the words pulled a garrote around my view of mankind. The words "race group" amplified a hostility that unfolded cells that harbor shame. *I belong to the same species as the person who composed those words.*

Which was worse: The undisguised hatred that made it acceptable to post such a sign on the Durban beach, or the fact that a bar owner found it acceptable to hang the poster and knew it wouldn't cause a ruckus? Patrons would accept it as normal decorative fare . . . and he found no hypocrisy in hanging it next to a poster of Kaizer Motaung, a Black South African soccer player.

The message seemed to be that the key to living life unaffected by apartheid was to be apathetic, at least for youthful, White, snooker players. Ignore politics and accept that injustices are not of your doing. Be happy that censored newspapers allow you to veil your scrutiny. Do these things, and you will see a beautiful place filled with paintbrush lilies and plumbago shrubs. Still, I thought, no matter how numb you allow yourself to become, it would be a mighty effort to ignore the bigotry.

I wondered what they felt as they grew into their conscience. Was clean air, natural beauty, and a pleasing lifestyle enough to stifle awareness, to make them turn a blind eye to hateful policies? Or did they secretly buy into it, accept that a bar owner could hang a heinous poster on the wall, drive by road signs that said, "Caution Beware of Natives." Could they be brought up to have such consequential disregard for other humans that they were willing to look away and not speak? Were they afraid to speak?

I walked. The night air was still, the moon nearly full. "Werewolves of London" leaked onto the sidewalk from a window at the Ace of Spaces Disco. I thought of my own providence, bouts with selfishness, bouts with pride. I wondered what Alex was doing. Wondered how often she thought of me. From nowhere, a vision of the impoverished old woman I saw in the Bobo-Dioulasso market popped into my head. I hadn't given her money because I was afraid that others who shared her plight would come running. I promised myself that I'd give to the next needy person I came across.

I never did.

CHAPTER 35

Winston: New Pioneer Column

Winston Walsh sat in his office, studying bands of green, fluorescent dye on an electrophoresis plate he was using to test his next-generation method of DNA sequencing. But his mind was fixed on the dolls and the fact that Gus Cooper hadn't called. He trusted Bubba's endorsement of Mad Dog and Craze. Craze appreciated the science, and Mad Dog's handshake held more integrity than any written contract. He questioned his decision to let them deliver the protocols, but someone inside ACORN was watching him and had foiled him multiple times. He had to catch the turncoat.

The phone rang. Gus spoke in Afrikaans. "Hoe gaan dit Winston?"

"Dit gaan goed met my. What have you heard, Gus? How is the tracking working? Have they landed in Jo'burg?"

"Working perfectly. Yes. Mad Dog is in Jo'burg. Signal is strong.

Winston took his first full breath in days. "Thank God.

"By the way, what kind of names are those?" Sarcasm hung from Gus's lip like drool on a Neapolitan mastiff. "I'm putting my faith in you, Winston. Mugabe and Nkomo are giving us the squeeze on the battlefield and on the political front. If there *is* an election, we may see a name change from Rhodesia to Zimbabwe–Rhodesia. This operation has to be in motion before that happens. We'll scare the bejesus out of them."

"These guys are solid, Gus. They bought the malaria story and are proud to help advance a monumental achievement in history. The important thing is that nobody knows them. The Matryoshka dolls are in good hands."

Gus was a founding member of the New Pioneer Column, an organization with roots in London. Its members were wealthy to a degree that ordinary men can't comprehend. They were current owners or heirs to mining companies in southern Africa. They extracted gold, diamonds, platinum, chrome, titanium, palladium, nickel, copper, and asbestos from the land, and now they watched the Rhodesian Bush War threaten their domains.

If Ian Smith's government is ousted, the mines and other assets would be nationalized. Ownership would be transferred from private individuals to the state. This had already happened in Patriotic Front strongholds; mines were taken without any compensation to the owners. If Rhodesia fell, South Africa would be next. Most of the New Pioneer Column members owned mines in both countries. Their ancestors had provided the intellect and technology that brought jobs and prosperity to the people of Southern Rhodesia and South Africa. They built infrastructure, cities, and government. The New Pioneer Column members were indignant at how contemptuous the native Africans were. How could they rebel after they'd done so much for them?

The original Pioneer Column, led by Cecil Rhodes, terrorized with physical brutality, fear, and force. The New Pioneer Column paraded an equally powerful form of terrorism: money. They were in it for the long game, a permanent solution that would quell the opposition and impose a level of superiority that frightened their enemy such that they'd never rebel again.

"Is everything in place on your end?" Winston asked.

Gus grunted. "Of course. Got the perfect guy to meet them. Experienced. Impeccable."

"And this guy knows that Craze and Mad Dog think he will be bringing the dolls to Lusaka, right? He knows the malaria story?"

Gus snarled. Winston could hear the unsaid, "Tut tut." He

envisioned Gus's percoid face and sea urchin eyebrows as he said, "Calm down, son. We know the plan, and we've identified the right guy. He'll be fully briefed. He's a pro. Will know the whole malaria story and will tell Craze and Mad Dog he's taking the dolls to a pharmaceutical in Lusaka. It's an easy plan, Winston. Just make sure you find out who the mole is at your facility. And get rid of them."

"Plan in progress. Just being cautious, Gus. As long as he doesn't slip and tell them the dolls are going to Rhodesia."

"Don't worry. Once Craze and Mad Dog make the handoff, they'll be out of the picture, can continue with their happy safari."

Winston decompressed. "No disrespect intended, Gus. You know me, same as you."

"Of course. We're both trying to cover all angles. With your genius and our backing, we are going to shake the world all right."

CHAPTER 36

Travis: The Stink Bomb

Quiet ripples pressed around the bow of the skiff. The Duffy Electric Company engine was inaudible in the predawn breeze. Max, a Selous Scout familiar with the contours of Lake Kariba, wrapped his fingers around the tiller. Travis sat in the front, trying to piece together his plan. It was his first mission, and it was sanctioned by Rhodesian President Ian Smith. He was to drive to Lusaka, deploy unexploded ordinances in advance of the operation, participate in a raid of Joshua Nkomo's house, and kill him.

Killing the leader of ZAPU would devastate the soldiers fighting against Rhodesia. A full-sized model of Nkomo's house had been built at the Ikomo barracks near Salisbury just to train for the raid. A secondary objective was to destroy a building that served as both a safe house for Nkomo and a strategic planning office for leaders of ZAPU's revolutionary army.

Travis had been whisked away so fast he never found a way to tell Sipho about the raid. His mind ran in circles. He couldn't let them kill Nkomo but had to maintain his cover with the scouts. He questioned why he was about to risk his freedom, his life, to prevent the assassination of a man he'd never met. *Jesus Christ!* But the courage of his wife, Norah, and the spirit of his United Freedom Front members spoke to him. "This cause *is* your cause. You've spent your adult life fighting for the oppressed, striving to rid the world of inequity." This was not a symbolic bombing of a corporate target. This was *it*.

Max eased the boat onto Zambian soil, where a Toyota Corolla awaited. They moved ammunition from the boat to a compartment hidden behind a removable front fender and changed from their Selous Scout togs—camo T-shirts, abbreviated shorts, ammunition harnesses—into casual business attire. Using maps generated by fellow scout Chris Coch, and Danish passports, they easily navigated sixty-five miles and two checkpoints on their way to Lusaka, where they would blend in with those attending the international conference of the People's Solidarity Organization. Max pulled the Corolla to the curb.

"There's Nkomo's house at two o'clock. The one with the gate out front, high wall all around," he said, lauding the detail of Coch's maps.

"Mm. And the headquarters? Over there, right?" Travis flicked his chin at a building lying across an open green.

Max cracked the car door open. "Let's go for a walk. Take a look about."

That evening, dressed in coffee-bean double-knit pants and polo shirts, they approached the ZAPU office building. Travis pried open the corrugated service garage door. Max admired Travis's workmanship, watching him plant an array of C4 blocks with remote detonators that could be fired with King radios retrofitted with a DTFM chip along the sill plate of the foundation. I don't care about this building, Travis thought. Nobody will be in it at that hour, and I'll gain some cred with the Scouts.

They moved on to Nkomo's house and waited. Midnight passed. The three guards at Nkomo's gate had stopped chatting. One slept, slumped against the wall. Travis and Max circled to the rear of the compound and worked their way to the wall. Max inspected the area for electronics: none. Travis kicked the ground, unable to solve the final piece of the puzzle: how to plant claymore mines at Nkomo's house but avoid killing him. Claymores were blocks of C4 with anti-personnel steel balls that exploded into a kill zone. If Nkomo was in the area, he'd die. If he lived, he'd be forced to the front of the house, directly into the oncoming Selous Scouts.

Coch's drawings showed little room for breaching the grounds. Travis looked to the sky. He knew the moon would set at 6:00 a.m.

If he waited until 4:30 a.m., it would be low in the western sky, and a three-foot-wide section of the wall and grounds would be shaded by a large Kigelia tree for thirty-five minutes. He said to Max, "I have to do this alone. Two of us means two wall breaches. Two people to see. Two people to get out of there."

"I'll give you cover."

At 4:35 a.m., Travis scaled the wall using fat-tanned leather gloves and kneepads to safeguard against broken glass bottles that were embedded in cement on top of the wall. He cut the protective barb, dropped to the ground, draped a tussock African mudcloth over his back, and blended perfectly into the ground. He bellied across the yard to the foundation and planted mines below ground level on either side of the rear exit. Claymores are curved units. Projectiles fire out and create a kill zone. He positioned the curve such that the steel balls would fire into the ground but the C4 would create enough upward thrust to make the walls collapse.

Then Travis used a trick from his days with the United Freedom Front. On the back steps he placed a stink bomb concocted from a glass jar, household ammonia, and match heads. He attached a timer and set it to detonate the stink bomb at 7:00 p.m., eight hours before the raid. If nobody saw the note during the day, the stink bomb would attract attention. The note under a stone read:

```
Raid tonight on Nkomo house. Get out.
```

Travis and Max returned to the motel and slept. The raid would start on April 14 at 3:00 a.m., the hour that the natural circadian rhythm of humans renders them most sleepy.

The 2:40 a.m. air on April 14 was quiet and crisp. Travis and Max, cloaked in darkness, stood between a baobab tree and a cinder block wall that obscured them from the dim light cast by a gibbous moon. Eyes zeroed in on the road that approached from the south, a bit to the right of the Southern Cross. The rest of the Rhodesian troops would arrive soon.

On schedule, seven land rovers painted in Zambian colors and filled with Rhodesian troops skulked in from the southeast on the T2/Kafue Road. They stopped where the wall met the road. Captain Myles Price was in command. He whispered to Travis and Max, "Jump in."

Four of the Rovers advanced on Nkomo's house. Three others trailed behind. Travis's eyes flicked about, fearful that Nkomo didn't get the message. The timer had to detonate the stink bomb; the odor had to draw attention; they'd have to see the note. Still, Nkomo's pride might get in the way. He may stay and fight. Possibly stage an ambush.

Travis and Max were dropped one block from Nkomo's house, where they hid inside a vacant parking attendant hut of the Lusaka Golf Club. Travis pulled out the first King radio. When he got the word from Price, he detonated the claymore mines buried just below the surface on either side of the rear of the house, where Nkomo's bedroom was. The walls caved in. I may have just killed Nkomo, he thought.

Nobody was manning the gates. Crossfire came from adjacent buildings and trees. Travis took a deep breath—*They got the message.* He took the other King radio and detonated the explosives at the building used by ZAPU's army. It crumbled. On Max's radio, Travis heard Captain Price give the three trailing Land Rovers their orders. They branched into separate paths across an open park that fronted the compound and attacked the areas where the fire came from. Travis saw Max collapse. He'd taken a round in his left femur.

"Shit, Travis. It's shattered."

Travis returned fire. He took out a sniper perched in a giant acacia tree . . . then realized what he'd done. He'd forgotten whose side he was on.

"Crack shot, Travis," Max grunted.

He fired several rounds at no one and tended to Max within the confines of the parking hut. He wrapped his belt around Max's thigh. Made sure he drank. The guerillas resisted, but in the end, they were outnumbered. A Rover swept by. They loaded Max into the rear. He babbled, "This guy took out a sniper from across the green." The medic ripped open Max's pants.

"Nkomo got off—bloody snake," said one of the scouts. "Your mines collapsed the rear of the house, but no sign of him."

Travis gasped. He tried to will his body to relax, but adrenaline wouldn't allow it. Three Rhodesian soldiers had been killed. They saw ten members of ZAPU's army go down, eight in battle, two gunned down on the perimeter as they fled. *Nkomo must have thought that a small, specialized unit would be used for an assassination attempt.*

When they got to Lake Kariba, Captain Price asked Travis to join him as they boarded boats that would take them across the lake to Rhodesia. "Good job, mate. Your explosives went off. I saw you throwing some rifle action. Good on you. Can't believe bloody Nkomo got off."

"Thank you, sir. Yes, too bad we couldn't nail him."

It was a good day. Travis's bombs went off, which would earn him regard with his peers and superiors. Nkomo was alive. The word of him bagging a sniper was circulating. He reminded himself, Sometimes people are gonna get hurt.

CHAPTER 37

Craze: The Call

I woke up the next morning with a meshwork of mind states vying for my attention. The distasteful evening at Michael's Tavern, the odious décor, and the casual racist demeanor of the clientele were alarming. I accepted it as a lesson in life literacy, but the difference in reading about apartheid in *Time* or *Newsweek* versus seeing, feeling, touching it was unsettling. I was Thomas feeling the wet pus in Jesus's wounds.

Another petition fed my disquietude. I had to call Alex before we left Jo'burg. Besides, Mad Dog made me promise. The kickoff meeting for our trip was that night, and we'd be off to Botswana in the morning. Any excitement I had for speaking to Alex was offset by a fear that she had real feelings for the guy she'd told Bubba about. I considered asking her to marry me, over the phone, from eight thousand miles away. I wondered what her thoughts were on the letter I wrote, asking her if she could meet us in Nairobi.

Mad Dog was awake, wrapping something about the size of a shoebox in brown paper.

"Been shopping, Dog?"

"I saw these in a store window." It was a set of eight Star Wars characters. Winston's Matryoshka dolls were on the bed. He tossed them to me.

"Since when do you like Star Wars?"

"Sending them to Lester. The kid in Liberia? The kid that gave me the Chewbacca?"

I grinned. "Cool, he'll love it."

We went to the post office at 1:30 p.m., 6:30 a.m. in Massachusetts. Alex should be home. I dialed, still reviewing the plan in my head. I'd decided that, if she was going to join us in Nairobi, I'd wait and ask her to marry me then. It would be mythically romantic, sun setting over the Maasai Mara, elephants or lions in the background.

She answered on the third ring. *Just be yourself.* She giggled. "Who's calling me at 6:30 in the morning? I hope I won a prize."

"Hey, Alex. It's Craze."

"Craze? Danny! What a surprise. Are you okay?" I tried to interpret her inflection, as if the lilt of each word would tell me something. I decided it was a happy eight words.

"God, I miss you, babe. Needed to hear your voice. I'm great. We're in Johannesburg."

She giggled. "Say hi to Mad Dog for me."

"I've lost a few pounds, got a decent beard going. You may not recognize me."

She rewarded me with her wonderful laugh, unabashed but so genuine it illuminated my spirit. We launched into conversation so effortlessly I almost forgot my angst. She'd seen my father a couple of times, would tell him I called. Her mother won a spot in the Plymouth Symphony Orchestra. My younger brother blew out a tweeter on my Genesis speakers.

"I saw *SNL* in New York last weekend. Rodney Dangerfield, Bill Murray. Richard Benjamin was the host. I . . . a friend . . . from work got tickets."

"I guess I'm not the only one having fun. Hey, what do you think of my idea—to meet us in Nairobi? Should be there in a couple of months. It would be beyond awesome if you could come." *Beyond awesome? Do better.* "You will love Africa."

"Oh . . . I've been thinking about it. What a crazy idea."

Crazy good or crazy bad?

"Wait. When do you leave South Africa? Remind me what the name of the company is."

"It's Trindell Travel. We leave tomorrow morning." The background noise from her parakeet disappeared. I thought the connection had dropped, but it came back.

"I'm seriously thinking it over. You really want me to come? What about Mad Dog?"

"He's tired of my sorry face. He's okay with it. In fact, he seemed to like the idea."

"Hm. I talked to my boss. He's checking the schedule to see if I can take that much time off. There's a lot to do and think about. I can't tell you for sure right now."

"Okay. Alex, I truly want you to come. It will be special. For the next few weeks, it will be hard for me to call. You can write to me, care of Post Restante, General Delivery, at any post office. I'll check at the post offices in Lusaka, Blantyre, and Dar es Salaam."

She said "I love you" when we ended the call.

I replayed the call in my head for the rest of the afternoon, like when I was a kid and bought the latest 45 record by Ben E. King. She was happy I called—yes. Wasn't guarded or cryptic. Why was I so nervous? She'd talked to her boss about taking time off. Bubba may have misinterpreted the whole thing. Maybe she realized this guy was just a capricious distraction. Would I have asked her to marry during the call if she'd sounded more detached? If it sounded like I was losing her? No, that would be desperate . . . and it would come off that way.

Finally, I surrendered to the fact that I hadn't learned a thing.

CHAPTER 38

We stood on the sidewalk at the entrance to the Corporation Building on Rissik Street. It was six o'clock and the April sun had already set in the early winter sky. The lobby was dark, an attempt to conserve energy after oil prices had surged when the shah was overthrown two months earlier in February of '79. A strike by Iranian field workers sent crude oil buyers into a panic that was disproportionate to the 7 percent reduction in global supplies. South Africa politicians whined. They got 90 percent of their crude from Iran.

A weak magnetic pole drew us through the lobby and led us to an elevator, which rattled to the sixth floor. The door to the office of Trindell Travel was opened, but the sliding accordion security gate barely allowed us to squeeze through.

The mood inside sparkled with the confabulated chat of adventurists. A professorial Australian was educating a husband and wife from New Zealand on the civil war in Timor. Two twenty-something guys homed up to a confident, tight-jeaned, Dutch donna who pretended to be impressed with their stories about Papua New Guinea. There were fifteen travelers, two drivers, and Marvin Kaestleman, the director of Trindell in South Africa. We were the only Americans.

I started a conversation with Emilie, a woman our age from Quebec City, whose nerdish wide-rimmed glasses couldn't distract from her high cheekbones, flowing brunette hair, and a smile that seemed to apologize for being pretty. She wore denim from head to toe and told us of her research: the impact of the Vietnam War on veterans of the Australian Army.

"This looks like a rather eclectic group," I said.

Mad Dog leaned into me and whispered, "Rather?" Then he chastened, "Eclectic?"

I gave him my shut-the-fuck-up stare and scratched my nose with my middle finger.

"You've never used those words in your life."

"Bite me."

Marvin called for our attention. His cadence was measured. British. "Hello everyone. Welcome to Trindell Travel."

The office was an oversized living room: two desks on the far wall, a dozen chairs, and a small sofa along the perimeter. Marvin told us how wonderful the trip would be; how Trindell had been doing this for twenty years; how Fergus, our driver, was an extraordinary mechanic and had done this trip four times before. The co-driver, Don, who we later renamed Co-Don to differentiate him from another Don on the trip, was a British guy who'd been living in Cape Town for eleven years and claimed to know Africa like "the back of a rhino's bottom."

We did introductions. Doug and Jerry, the two hosers that were spellbound by the hot Dutch woman, were from Windsor, Ontario. Tight-jeaned Hanna, from Amsterdam, worked in a nail spa and had recently inherited money from her grandma. Don, from Tasmania—who would henceforth be called Big-Don—was older and had thinning brown hair that marched toward a comb-over. His lips formed a permanent circle with each word he spoke, which he did with perfect diction, making no effort to mask his worldliness. Bernie and Veronica were New Zealanders, he an engineer and she a kindergarten teacher. Jalina and Chris were friends from Sydney. Jalina was reflective and oozed integrity, delivering her words with thoughtful, yet throaty, sensuality. She did something with publishing; her fun fact was that she was a lifelong dancer. Chris spoke with endless quippage and surely beguiled her math students at South Sydney High School. Quinn, a long-haired Scotsman in his midthirties with smoke-stained, disorganized teeth, wore blue tennis shoes and pulled regular tugs of Glenfiddich single malt from a bottle that was nested in the pocket of a fatigued tweed jacket. Graham and Cathy were a lovely young couple from Melbourne, and Dale, a firmly built guy from Brisbane, Australia, had allowed his belly to slide over his belt buckle. Missing were a couple from Belgium and a guy from Vancouver, British Columbia.

We troweled into more backchat with Emilie. With prodding, we learned that she was an unassuming scholar with a BS in cell biology from McGill, a master's in genetics from the University of Edinburgh, and a PhD in epidemiology from University of Melbourne. I guess there are brilliant people everywhere.

Fergus, the driver, spoke with a voice that celebrated monotony, as if his vocal cords were coated with heavy cream. He was all business: reviewed the rules of the road, tent etiquette, cooking, cleaning, and fire duties. If we planned to leave at 8:00 a.m., it meant tents down and asses in our seats by 8:00 a.m.

Co-Don, the co-driver, was to do whatever Fergus told him to do: organize the camp, drive, tell stories, help repair the vehicle. Co-Don was a fitting name because he was manifestly a low second in command. He was a freewheeling beach hound with slapdash hair that waved to his midback and was affable, but hovered close to the line where it was too much. A bullshitter can be fun if they are able to regulate their drivel. Co-Don explained the rule of three to us in his adopted, clipped, SuthEfrikan tongue. Three people, three days, three chores: cook, wash, clean.

Dale, a licensed heavy diesel mechanic, was mature and direct. "I'm sure you read about the Rhodesian raid on Lusaka last night. Nkomo's house was destroyed. What does that mean for us? Is Zambia safe?"

I glanced at Mad Dog, "What?" We hadn't bothered to buy a newspaper.

Marvin answered. "We've been talking about it all day. There are options. Understand that our trucks are painted pink for a reason. We won't be mistaken for a military vehicle. It's just a precaution, but effective. Mind you, Zambia is *not* at war with Rhodesia. Botswana is *not* at war with Rhodesia. These countries like tourists, and to date we haven't had any problems. We can't avoid Zambia completely. The Caprivi Strip in South West Africa is off-limits—too active with insurgents. There's a civil war in Mozambique. One option is to go through Rhodesia and then skirt around Lusaka when we get to Zambia.

Jalina spoke with typical Aussie inflections, where all words are boiled down or up to two syllables. "But Rhodesia is at war. How could we possibly go through Rhodesia?"

Graham rephrased. "Are you trying to get us bloody killed?"

Marvin's next words seemed far-fetched. "We could take a convoy through Rhodesia up to Victoria Falls so you can have a look. You don't want to miss the falls. Then we'd work our way along the border, where a private concern we know can help us cross into Zambia. From there we'd head toward the border of Malawi. We know that's possible."

Jalina wasn't satisfied. "But how do you travel in Rhodesia? Is it safe?"

"You travel in convoys. Convoys are protected by a mine sweeper in the front with machine gun mobiles interspersed every few cars. Military checkpoints along the routes monitor the road. The sides of the roads have been cleared to prevent surprise attacks. With their battered reputation, Rhodesia would be happy to see us."

"Crivens," Quinn, the Scottish soaker, uttered to himself.

People groaned. Marvin was quick to start talking before panic could accelerate.

"Let me be clear." The room was loud. Marvin raised his voice. "People, please. We are going to stick with the original plan. While in Botswana, you'll take bush roads to Francistown, the Okavango Swamps, and Chobe National Park. Lots of elephants, giraffes, and lions in Chobe. Then you'll go to the Kazungula ferry, which is a few kilometers upstream from Vic Falls. You'll cross the Zambezi on the ferry and drive to Livingstone, where you'll stay at the Leopard Spot Campground. You can walk to the falls from there and see them from the Zambian side.

That sounded better. It's what we signed up for. Dale drew on the brim of his blue scally cap. "Will we see any Bushmen?"

Co-Don clipped, "Yeah, there's a good chance. You must be respectful. They are called San or Saa is the plural. It means bush dwellers. They live in family bands or sometimes in language bands. We might see some Ana or Oro groups in the Kalahari or near Maun. Near the Kazungula ferry we may run into some Sua."

"Is it all right to talk to them?"

"Ask Fergus or me when the time comes. They are sweet people but haven't been treated well. They're cautious of Europeans. Over the years, they've been referred to as a zoological curiosity that should be preserved as if they were an animal facing extinction. Sorry to say, but it's the way. At one point the minister of native affairs said they look more like baboons than baboons. You can understand why they might avoid you."

Emilie gasped; she was so offended. She softly said, "Holy shit," which was intended for Mad Dog and me, but the whole group heard it.

Marvin said, "Listen, everyone. You're here to experience Africa. You may not like things you see. You may not like things you hear. But you are better off having seen and heard them. Feel free to ask yourself, 'Why?' Feel free to discuss it among yourselves. But do not stir the pot. You aren't going to change how people think any more than you will change where a buffalo decides to piss. You may see a lion eat a wildebeest. A leopard may toss a baby gazelle like a rag doll. Absorb it. Every kilometer is different. Fergus and Don know what's safe; who to talk to; how to get information; when you can and can't take pictures. Do as they say."

Talk of the Bushmen, game parks, the Okavango, Victoria Falls, and lion safety became the focus. This is what we wanted. Timid people don't sign up for a seventeen-thousand-mile trip through Africa. Trindell knew what they were doing. Excitement swelled like an aquifer in heavy rain. As the evening progressed, speculation on the spillage of war from an adjacent country was set aside. For Mad Dog and me, the dolls were getting heavy. We'd be happy to be rid of them when we got to the Leopard Spot Campground.

CHAPTER 39

Travis: Get Them Dolls

Travis stepped onto the osprey-imprinted welcome mat in front of Colonel Reid's office, wary of why the colonel had asked to see him. He made a final inspection of his surroundings and closed his eyes. With as much force as possible, he pressed his right thumb into his left palm for a count of five. A quick shake-out of his hands, two knocks, and he entered. *People always look left or right. If necessary, I'll run straight across the street, down the alley, left after the cobbler's table, and hide in the Immaculate Conception Basilica until dark.*

In one bite, Reid's pineapple jaw reduced a slice of Marmite on toast in half. He washed it down with half a bottle of Mazoe Orange Crush. "Morning, Travis." Reid flicked his hand in the direction of a folding safari chair and crammed the rest of the toast into his mouth. He grabbed the neck of the Mazoe in his teeth, no hands, and flung his head back, pouring what remained into his buccal cavity, allowing it to emulsify before he swallowed.

Did they find out Sipho switched his allegiance? Was Reid tipped off about the United Freedom Front and my anti-apartheid sentiments? He could get access to my military records. But if he did, he wouldn't find anything—because Travis is not my real name.

"Look at this bullshit in the *Post*." Reid read the newspaper aloud, his dimpled chin taut and bitter. "The day after we raided his house, Nkomo went to the People's Solidarity Organization conference and talked about the assassination attempt. He said, 'Our boys did a good job although they were outnumbered. They knocked out the teeth from one of the commandos and blew the brains out of another.' Nkomo held up a jaw with missing teeth and a brain wrapped in a bloodied Rhodesian flag. When asked how he got away, Nkomo said he escaped through a secret door.'"

And he surely wondered who left a stink bomb with a note that warned him of the attack.

"Can you believe this guy?"

Travis nodded, not exchanging pleasantries. He finished his surveillance of the room.

"You guys gave ZAPU a hanna hanna in Lusaka. That nought Nkomo got away, but you put his balls in a vise."

Travis was monotone. "We'll get him."

"I heard what you did, Travis. Got up to his house, practically into his knickers. All your boobies fired as planned . . . and you slotted a sniper from over a hundred meters."

"No big deal." Travis's shoulders relaxed in the way they did when he finished confession and the priest absolved him for the price of three Hail Marys. Reid's rifle lazed against the wall; the safety on his CZ 75 pistol was on. If Reid suspected anything, he wouldn't be so sloppy.

"There might be other ways to take out Nkomo, sir. Figure out how to put some ricin in his food or brush some parathion on his clothes. Maybe leak out information that he's workin' behind the scenes with Ian Smith to establish a position for himself in the future government. If Mugabe heard that, he'd get his guys to kill Nkomo for you."

Reid listened. He was known as a *charge in and kill the fuckers* kind of guy. Look them in the face, tell them you are going to kill them, and insert a knife into their jugular. The more personal, the better. Still, he appeared pleased with the show of ingenuity.

"Good ideas, Travis. We need men who think on their feet; men who can find a way. But I want the world to know that *we* killed Nkomo, that nobody can escape our reach. Instill fear, that's our thing. Make their troops question their leaders. Make them want to tuck their tails and go home to mommy."

"Yes, sir."

"Last night was a tactical operation. I have another mission for you. One that will support our long-term strategy and secure our position in Rhodesia for good. It will also scare the shit out of any insurgents left under the covers."

Travis knew his job. Gather information. Report it to Sipho. He knew these alpha types. They want to show off, prove their dominance. They can't help it. *Don't look too eager. Just nudge and let him spill it.*

"Ready to help, Colonel. What's the mission?"

"You're going to laugh. In a week or so, an overland tourist truck operated by Trindell Travel will arrive at the Leopard Spot Campground in Livingstone, on the Zambian side of Victoria Falls. Pink truck, can't miss it. Two Americans are on that trip. You're American; that'll put them at ease. These guys are carrying a set of nesting dolls. It's a tourist thing—a bunch of dolls nested inside each other. Have you seen Russian Matryoshka dolls?"

"Nope."

"Bah. All you have to do is get the set of nesting dolls from them and bring them back.

"And?"

"That's it. Now, if they deviate from their itinerary and don't show up at the Leopard Spot, we have a backup. A scout put a tracking device on one of them—puts out a global location signal. We have friends in Liberia who boosted its output and miniaturized it. You'll be able to track them using a monitor that's built into a camera. I've got a monitor, too, so we both can track them. I'll have someone show you how to use it."

Interesting.

"How do I get there?"

"Take a day or two off. The Americans won't be there till next week. You'll go to the town of Victoria Falls, in northern Rhodesia. Get the lay of the land. Take a look at the falls. They're bloody inspiring. Then you'll cross the bridge on the train. It's a spanner bridge that crosses the Zambezi River, connects Rhodesia to Zambia. You'll ride in a hollow that we'll carve into the middle of a lumber car. When the train gets two hundred meters past the Zambian end of the bridge, there's a place you can jump off without being seen.

"Why don't I just walk across the bridge and use my American passport?"

"The bridge is closed to people. Only freight trains are allowed to cross. Zambia isn't at war with us, but they let ZAPU operate within their borders. Soldiers train in Tanzania. Then they're transported through Zambia and into Rhodesia to fight us. We don't want them to cross the bridge, and they don't want us to cross either. But our economies are shit. We both need the trade, so we let cargo cross. Lumber, equipment, ore. Things like that."

"Someone must be drivin' the train, right?"

Reid laughed. "The Rhodesian engine pushes the cars to the midpoint of the bridge. Then the Zambian train couples to the car and drags it across the border into Zambia."

"What's with these Americans? You want me to kill 'em?"

"No. Just get the dolls and bring them to me."

"A set of friggin' dolls? What's so important?"

"Listen carefully, Travis. The Americans think you'll be delivering the dolls to a pharmaceutical firm in Lusaka. That's your story. They think there's information in these dolls that will help rid the world of malaria. These are just two guys that came for a romp around Africa. They think they're doing a good deed for mankind."

Travis rose, squinched his cheek, stuck his pinky finger into his ear. *What the hell?*

"What does malaria have to do with a long-term strategy for Rhodesia?" he asked.

Reid paused. The mission sounded lame, yet he'd just told Travis it could secure White rule in Rhodesia for good. He teetered in his chair like he had a full can of sea worms munching in his belly. The Selous Scouts were built on trust. Once you went over the threshold, trust was everything. He hadn't been fully truthful, and Travis knew it.

After a pause, Reid said, "It doesn't."

Time to set the hook. Travis put his hand to his head and exchanged eye contact with Reid, making sure his expression wasn't accusatory but reflected hurt—the kind of hurt you feel when you think your lover is cheating.

Reid inhaled and stopped. A thin puddle of air infused his lungs. He resumed his inward respiration as if he'd hit the pause button on a tape deck. The silence cleared his thoughts. His nostrils flared like a man bull. A bead of sweat moistened his temple. When he exhaled, Travis smelled the pomposity in his breath and the swamp of hatred that drove Reid, who now looked like a conquistador ready to shed his armor. Travis saw a set of eyes that harbored true hate, the kind of hate that wants to extinguish its enemy. He'd brought Reid's hubris to a cliff, where classified information dangled on his lips. Reid knows that all Selous Scouts share his degree of malevolence, Travis thought.

Reid nodded his head at the safari chair and said, "Sit down, Travis."

CHAPTER 40

The cab was pink. The kick wall was pink. The body racks, wheels, and lug nuts: pink. The two-wheeled food trailer attached to the rear by a scammell hitch was pink. Bazooka bubblegum pink. It shouted: *I am not a military vehicle.*

"Maybe we should pull a Chinese Type 63 rocket system behind us, eh?" A gangly kid with camel-beige hair rippling over his scalp jumped from the truck and landed at our feet. He wore the varnished face of a large boy and sported a blue-and-orange-striped rugby shirt.

"Huh?" Mad Dog said.

"Name's Gary. Vancouver, BC. I dig your Chewbacca."

His handshake was firm, not trying to prove anything, and his smile could charm an angry bull moose. Gary had missed the kickoff meeting at Trindell because he had jet lag. "Not yet on boor time," he said. We learned he'd been in Jo'burg installing elevators for Kotze Elevator Solutions for three years but had gone home to British Columbia a few times recently.

"In fact, I just got back from BC yesterday—but I might set myself up in the States. When we get to London, I'll keep on going, straight across the Atlantic. Had enough of South Africa." At twenty-five, he was the youngest of the group, a bit flighty, and conspicuously naïve, but his quirky vibe had an appeal. We asked him to be our cooking partner.

Heavy guardrails wrapped the bumper of our Bedford TK truck. A rack atop the cab housed tents and gear. The bed rode chest-high off the ground, supported by a tricked-out suspension, perfect for viewing wildlife. Twenty airplane seats were bolted to the bed, a center aisle with two seats on either side. A canopy that stretched across an arched, iron framework would protect us from the weather. Emilie said, "Let's call it the Pink Panther." We claimed our seats, last row. "Don't crush those dolls," Mad Dog grumbled.

"Don't worry," I said, happy at Mad Dog's display of concern for our cargo.

The forty-degree temperature of mile-high Johannesburg succumbed to the sun as we lost elevation. The European flair of Jo'burg's finely trimmed houses, swimming pools, and picture windows gave way to the rolling hills, sparse vegetation, cacti, palms, and scrub of the Transvaal. Mud houses, thatched roofs, and outdoor kitchens punctuated the restless inequity that shrouded the South African experience.

We were tourists, under no obligation to compartmentalize in the same way it appeared was necessary if you were a White South African and wanted to avoid looking in the mirror. I asked Gary, "What do these people do for a living?"

"Most work in the mines, especially here in the northeast. There are over five hundred of them. Gold. Diamond. Platinum. Lots of coal. Iron . . . nickel, copper." He told us that eight of the ten deepest mines in the world were in South Africa, some more than three kilometers underground. More than thirty-five thousand had died in those mines while the Europeans reaped the higher wages and lifestyle.

"What made you move here from Vancouver?"

"Economy at home went to shit. Inflation. Didn't want to live with Mom and Dad. My uncle lives in Jo'burg, told me I could make a living here. The price of gold was skyrocketing. Economy was strong. As soon as I came, it crapped out. My luck. But now I've got some good things waiting for me back home."

After four hours, we lunched on the side of the road, close to the Botswana border at Kopfontein. Mad Dog, Gary, and I would be in the second cooking rotation. We watched: sterilize plates in boiling water, wash hands in a bucket of mild disinfectant.

I asked Gary, "Is the Kazungula ferry the only legit way to get across the Zambezi River to Livingstone? I mean, you've lived here for a while."

He lowered his head such that he was staring up at us and conjured a John Wayne imitation. "You could put your spurs on and ride high on a hippo to the other side, partner."

I laughed. Mad Dog glanced at me and said, "I thought we left Bubba in Liberia."

"I mean it, Gary. If this ferry thing is a problem, is there any other way? We have to get there." *Kilimanjaro!*

"I thought your schedule was open-ended. What's the hurry?"

"Oh . . . we're just trying to help someone win a Nobel Prize." *What!*

Mad Dog glared as if I'd divulged Colonel Sanders' secret herbs and spices.

"No legitimate way," Gary said, brushing off my comment.

We crossed the Botswana border and stopped in the capital of Gaborone for a bathroom break and drank Fanta served in recycled, scuffed glass bottles. From there it was three hours of high scrub interspersed with tufts of brown, cauterized grass before Fergus pulled the Pink Panther to the side. No amenities, a simple opening amid the vegetation—our camp for the night. Quinn, the Scotsman, pulled on the lining of his tweed jacket and hollered, "Fergus."

Everyone turned their heads.

"No beer? No beer in the food trailer?"

Co-Don, the co-driver, was responsible for the food. He replied, "This isn't Germany, where beer is a food group. You supply your own beer." Quinn snorted.

The morning brought another three-hour slog to the outskirts of Francistown, a town thirteen miles west—as the crow flies—of the Botswana-Rhodesia border at Plumtree. We set up camp next to a giant thorn tree while Fergus went into town to call Marvin and get the latest news on the border situation. Means of communication are treasured in areas of war. When I worked in the fields of the Moshav Idan in Israel, there were two essentials: an M16 rifle and a radio. News was akin to breathing.

Fergus returned and hoisted his five-feet, six-inch frame onto the first rung of the ladder that hung off the back of the Pink Panther. The group gathered as if Jesus was about to deliver the Sermon on the Mount. Quinn asked, "What'd that fandan Marvin have to say?"

Fergus's nostrils puffed. He reached across his chest and wrapped his fingers around the back of his neck. "No change. Rhodesia is sick of seeing ZAPU soldiers cross into Botswana on the Kazungula ferry and then stroll into Rhodesia. No agreements have been reached."

Big-Don, the academic from Tasmania, clipped, "What does that mean for us?"

"We'll go to the border and assess it ourselves. That's how it is here. News is propaganda. It's usually inaccurate or skewed. You have to go there if you want the truth."

"Can't you just call the border?"

Co-Don flicked back his locks, tugged the scruff of his chin, intending to espouse his wisdom on the ways of Africa. Fergus cut him off. "It's a frontier border. The only phones are at hunting lodges, which are mostly unoccupied right now. If there is a phone at the ferry station, they won't talk to anyone they don't know. Botswana is stuck in the middle of this. They need commerce, and the ferry is the only way for truckers to cross the border."

Co-Don tried again, emphasizing his learn-ed South African accent. "Lee-sin. Wee'll just go hrrightt up there and geet the real storee."

Emilie sensed there was more. "What else?"

"There is another option. A Trindell truck is in Nairobi and will be heading south for Jo'burg. Same route as us, but opposite direction. We talked about switching trucks."

"How would that work?"

"Both trucks carry the same gear. They would go from Nairobi, cross into Tanzania, and then into Zambia. They'd leave their truck in Lusaka, and we'd leave our truck in Francistown. Then we'd fly from Francistown to Lusaka. They would do the opposite. We'd continue with their truck, and they'd continue with ours. Mind you, that's *only* if we can't get across."

"Explain again," Jalina said. "Why wouldn't they let us cross on the ferry?"

Fergus restated. "ZAPU and ZANU troops use the ferry to cross from Zambia into Botswana, where they can cross into Rhodesia by land. They want to overthrow the president, Ian Smith, and end White rule in Rhodesia. If an agreement isn't reached soon—one that prevents guerillas from using the ferry—Rhodesia has threatened to stop the ferry from operating."

Gary had been cooking supper while we listened to Fergus. He seemed oblivious to the whole thing and summed up his thoughts in a two-word squelch: "Let's eat."

CHAPTER 41

Travis: Comparing Notes

Colonel Reid had given Travis a couple of days off. It gave him a chance to drop in on Sipho in the back office of Wimpy's in Bulawayo. Sipho was delighted.

"I wasn't sure I'd see you again, Travis. C'mon in, mate."

Travis pulled Sipho into an embrace. It surprised him. Living a lie while amongst the enemy made him weary and in need of a like-minded person. "How's it goin', Sipho?" They sat.

"My back-channel friends in Nkomo's circle told me how someone used a stink bomb to warn him of the assassination. I knew it was you." Travis raised his eyebrows once. "Brilliant. Those Rhodesian bounders did some damage, but you saved Nkomo. Well done."

Sipho's praise was pure. Travis knew he'd made the right decisions . . . and his actions had solidified his position in the Selous Scouts. He briefed Sipho on the raid. Explained why he went along with blowing up the ZAPU building and how he positioned the claymore mines at Nkomo's house in a way that would minimize casualties. How his cover remained intact.

"Aw, they're already reconstructing the ZAPU building. You foiled their plan, and you're still in with the Selous Scouts. Perfect." Sipho went on to explain the importance of the mission and how much they respected Travis's decision to join them.

Travis tapped his foot. "They've already given me another assignment."

Sipho's eyes expanded as if waiting for the last number of a lottery ticket to be read.

"I met with Colonel Reid. He asked me to retrieve a set of nesting dolls from two Americans at the Leopard Spot Campground in Livingstone. These guys are on a tour run by Trindell Travel out of Johannesburg. They've been told that the dolls contain information about a genetic way to get rid of malaria."

Sipho leaned forward.

"I'm s'posed to tell them I'm bringing the dolls to a pharmaceutical company in Lusaka. I ain't sure exactly what info is in those dolls. But Reid knows. He says it will preserve White rule in Rhodesia for years to come. I almost got the dumbass to spill the details, but he stopped himself. Only gave me half a loaf." Travis pulled at the hair on his arms.

While Travis was speaking, Sipho's face oscillated between elation and terror.

"What's with the pepper faces, Sipho? Looks like you swallowed a jelly donut full of razor blades."

Sipho asked Travis to repeat the story, a technique used to look for inconsistencies. Travis was annoyed but complied. Sipho wasn't listening; he appeared to be thinking. Travis thought, *What the fuck? Didn't I prove myself enough on the Lusaka raid?*

Sipho grinned. "Travis, I know about the dolls. I know about the two Americans. I know about the handoff in Livingston. And now I know that *you* are the person the Americans are expecting to meet. This is an absurd stroke of luck."

"You know? How? Yeah, Reid wants me to bring the dolls to him instead."

"Uh-huh. Well . . . the destination was never a pharmaceutical firm in Zambia. The dolls will be taken to a pharmaceutical outfit in Rhodesia."

Travis's stare said, *Let's have it.* "How'd you know about the Americans?"

"Weathermen Africa has intelligence networks everywhere. Nearly all of Africa wants Ian Smith ousted. We have a contact inside ACORN, a research center in Liberia. Our Liberian colleague learned that the technology contained in the dolls will not be used to fight malaria. The real intent is unspeakable. They didn't tell me details—afraid of what will happen if the world finds out that the technology even exists. Our colleague said that the information in the dolls will be more destructive than any military operation."

"Yeah. Exactly what I heard from Reid. He got a boner talking about how it would unleash a torment that would make Nkomo and Mugabe's people lose faith. That's all I could get out of him. Everyone is being cutesy with this."

Sipho's face hardened. "I don't know. Biology. Genetics. Sounds like monsters under the bed. But I'm assured this is real."

Travis stared. Was Sipho overreacting? Was everyone overreacting? What could be in the friggin' dolls that is so critical?

"Our job is to stop them on two fronts. First, keep the dolls from getting to Rhodesia. Second, permanently stop the operations in Liberia. Cameron, the Weathermen Africa recruiter in London, is working with our colleague in Liberia on that front."

They agreed that Travis should still go to the Leopard Spot Campground, check in, and establish his presence, to show Reid that he was following orders. Then he should go to the Kazungula ferry at night and plant munitions beneath the hull. When the Americans and the truck got to the middle of the river, he should blow it up.

"That will get rid of the Americans and the dolls," Sipho mused.

Travis countered, "Why don't I just kill them and take the dolls?"

"If you kill the Americans, Reid will expect you to bring the dolls back to him. But if the ferry blows up, the dolls will go down with it to the bottom of the Zambezi River. You can tell Reid that you were waiting in Livingstone as planned but that the Americans never showed up. That way we get rid of the dolls, and you get to keep your cover with the Selous Scouts."

"But Sipho, I'm the bomb guy. Reid will know it was me that blew up the ferry."

"No, he won't. The ferry is a flash point. A lot of factions want to see it destroyed. Zambia is on the lookout for Rhodesian operatives coming into their country on the ferry. Rhodesian doesn't want ZAPU soldiers crossing the ferry. Bands in the Botswanan government fear that the ferry is a pawn that could suck

Botswana into the war. When the ferry blows, they'll all start pointing fingers at each other."

"Okay. That'll keep these dolls from being delivered. I hope your Weathermen Africa friends can stop them eggheads in Liberia."

"Mm. Travis, you came here to help us win this war. Time will tell, but this might be your most important assignment. Those dolls can never get into Reid's hands."

CHAPTER 42

Craze: The Epiphany

My chest heaved in the arid air, lungs in a biological skirmish to replenish my sad ass body with oxygen. I hadn't gone for a run since leaving the States. Little kids joined, laughed at me, ran for their own amusement. They poked each other and hollered at me while I grappled with ineptitude. A couple of times I ran backwards for a few yards, stuck my thumbs in my ears and wiggled my fingers, babbling, "Bulabula." They would stop, faces showing fear, and then laugh. Eventually they returned the "Bulabula" back to me, twenty strong.

Near the edge of Francistown, I passed a gate labeled "Botswana Defence Force." When I returned to camp, I asked Quinn about it. He was more world-wise than his initial impression suggested. He'd been living in Gibraltar for ten years after serving in the British Special Air Service during the Dhofar Rebellion in Oman.

"Yes, I saw that gate I did. A few barracks and some training areas."

"Army?" Mad Dog asked.

Quinn sneered. "A wee one, yes. When Botswana broke from the UK in the sixties, they decided to go without a military, aye. An dèidh, uh, when tensions in South Africa and Rhodesia started roasting in the midseventies, they put together a small army, got a few strike masters and small planes for an air wing. Even have a few boats to patrol rivers and swamps."

Fergus returned from downtown. He'd called Marvin again. It was fascinating to see how quickly people gathered to listen to his blanched monotone.

"Are we heading to the ferry?" Chris asked.

He waited for everyone to arrive. For Fergus, speaking and interacting with humans was a displeasing obligation. He just wanted to keep the Pink Panther in good repair, find campsites, deal with administrative exercises, and get us from point A to point B. Co-Don was charged with engaging with the Homo sapiens.

"First, regarding the truck in Nairobi, it hasn't moved. It's still undergoing repairs."

I was surprised that the option of switching trucks was the first thing out of his mouth. We didn't want to do that. Mad Dog and I were only going the three-thousand-mile leg from Jo'burg to Nairobi. Everyone else was going all the way to London. I asked if there was any news about the Kazungula ferry. His vapid reply reminded me of Sergeant Schultz on *Hogan's Heroes*.

"I know nothing. Last we heard, the ferry is still running. In the morning we leave for Kasane, a village a few miles from the Kazungula ferry. It'll take two days to get there. We'll use Kasane as a base to see the other sites in Botswana, and then cross the river."

I counted the days on my fingers, said to Mad Dog, "That'll work. We can deliver the dolls with almost a week to spare. Kilimanjaro here we come."

"Did you say something about dolls?" Gary asked. He was standing behind us.

Mad Dog sneered. "That's what Craze calls our girlfriends. Thinks he's Nathan Detroit."

It made no sense, but it mollified him. I raised my eyebrows to thank Mad Dog. He walked away.

The morning road was chalky, arid, and hot, no asphalt on the horizon. Sand beneath our tires was soft, and the food trailer barely plowed through it. Co-Don let air out of the tires to help us gain traction. Modest but steady progress, eight hours of it. Powdered grit found every pore, coated the hair on our arms, and embedded itself beneath our gums. Particles penetrated our lungs and caked our sinuses. By the time our roving dust cloud pulled to the side of the road, prints that bedecked shirts were opaque, shielded from sunlight by a blanket of filth.

After we raised our tents, twenty-five Botswanan Army trucks passed us heading south. They ignored us, possibly familiar with the pink tourist truck. Emilie said, "It's good that they are going away from the border, oui? Maybe they aren't needed there."

Mad Dog, Gary, and I finished our cooking rotation that night and turned duties over to Doug, Jerry, and Emilie, the all-Canadian crew. We'd been buying eggs and milk from a local family in Francistown, but with eighteen people to feed, that cache would soon be finished.

Morning brought another dirt-laden ride, made bearable by our first animal sightings. Four ostriches ran in front of the truck, eventually veering right into clumps of wool grass and blue bush. Cameras went snap. Next came our first elephant, a weathered sow standing in the road. She was un-cowered by the color pink, threw us a rooted snort, and held her ground. In time she granted us passage out of her good graces. Two giraffes and a troop of baboons set the shutters ablaze. Fergus waited until all lenses were satisfied. It fed the esprit de corps.

We came to a road sign. An arrow pointed right to the Kazungula ferry, two kilometers. Fergus stopped. Chatter ceased under the weight of our physical presence on this fickle tract of land. Lips were stilled; heads pivoted slowly. Jalina whispered, "Hail Mary, full of grace . . ." Emilie's knee bounced. Gary slept.

Fergus continued past the sign and pulled into Kasane, a rural village where the Chobe and Zambezi Rivers met. The waters bred vegetation, green grass, and full-sized trees. Fergus pulled into the grounds of the nearly deserted Chobe Safari Lodge. Blue-scrotumed vervet monkeys romped about the trees and rooftops. There were a few campsites and two rondavels. Fergus chose a spot on the top of the riverbank under a giant baobab tree. Glorious shade.

The river was the border. The Caprivi Strip, a pencil-necked extension of South West Africa that runs along the northern border of Botswana, was on the opposite bank. The eastern tip of the Caprivi Strip ended at the Kazungula ferry, a tenuous point on Earth where the borders of four countries converge: Botswana, South West Africa, Zambia, and Rhodesia.

We were the only clients of a lodge that maintained a skeleton staff in case migrant hunters or tourists showed up, usually to visit Chobe National Park, which was a few miles to the south. Happily, there was a patio with a single stone-cut table and window that served as a tiny outdoor bar. The lodge didn't have food, but alcohol, yes. And hooray, there was an outdoor, semi-enclosed shower; cold, but it had water that ran.

When the evening came, the tiny bar drew us and several locals into its embrace. Stars pierced like lasers in a black sky free of ambient light. Graham, Cathy, Quinn, Doug, Emilie, Dale, Gary, Jalina, and Chris drank Lion lager and Castle lager. Mad Dog drank Castle stout. It was hard-earned relaxation and a chance to learn about each other.

I fixated on Graham and Cathy, both in their midtwenties and in love. She was a delightful pixie, with short black hair and bangs à la Agent 99 on *Get Smart*, high, rounded cheeks, and a soft smile. Graham was an intense music enthusiast, who—from the opposite end of the Earth in Melbourne, Australia—knew about the Rat, a seedy punk rock club in Boston known for hosting acts like the Cars and the Ramones. Their unconscious tender glances, lingering touches, and private whispers showed me how much they cherished each other.

I found myself wanting to yell, "Stop it! You are making me miss Alex." I thought about the Yamaha guitar I gave Alex, and how she toiled to learn how to play "Chelsea Morning." She loved that song and wanted to sing it for me. It was full of rainbows and honey and paying attention to the sights and sounds around you. That was her, embracing the tempo of life, confronting every downbeat, doing the work to bring hope to those who needed it.

I remembered the first time she said, "I love you." It was at Dad's wedding. My mother had died when I was younger. We'd been sort of seeing each other and Alex wanted to go to the wedding. I was praying for Dad and his new wife. Alex knelt next to me, put her head down, and prayed. The sleeve of her chiffon dress brushed my hand. A surge of intimacy overwhelmed me. She pushed her hair aside, leaned to my ear, and whispered, "I love you."

Soon, Alex and my father came to love each other. And she liked how I bantered with her parents, especially her mother, who had told her how happy they were that their daughter was in love with such a fine young man. We climbed mountains, valued decency, shared a vigor for life, and occasionally cried together. But that evening, while sitting among a group of gritty adventurers with Mad Dog at my side . . . I was lonely. Afraid. Unhappy with the stock of my character. Aware that I'd missed my chance to lean into Alex's ear while she stood on the curb and whisper, "Yes."

I was in the wilds of Africa, on a caper to deliver instructions that would help eradicate malaria. I'd been schooled on slave traffic in Liberia; had gotten roiled by a "members of the white race group" sign in South Africa; and had managed to stumble into the edges of the Rhodesian Bush War, where an obtuse level of my own ignorance had been exposed: apathetic bigotry. Was I naïve, or did I fail to have the mettle to call it out? Yet, with all this swirling in my head, I zeroed in on a single thought, one that had loitered in the dark for years. Observing Cathy and Graham's love showed me how their life had purpose—and that having purpose nurtures joy. A wood owl called from a tree near the river, as if scoffing at my tardy revelation. My bosom flushed warm, like that first sip of whiskey, and the analytics in my head succumbed to lucid thought, delivering a clarity I'd never known. I wanted to marry Alex.

CHAPTER 43

Bubba: Mr. Hong's

Bubba smiled, slapped his palm on his rusted metal desk, a poorly lit home assigned to idealistic Peace Corps workers. He'd finished designing a tracking system aimed at quashing corruption in the logging industry—an affliction as pervasive as roundworms in a flounder's belly. A single mahogany tree harvested by foreign concessionaries could yield $50,000, of which Liberia reaped a hefty export tax. Loggers dodged the tax by paying off log scalers, who would then under-measure logs or make them disappear from the ledger.

The office administrator brought him a message:

Meet me for Chinese. Mr. Hong's. 7:00.

The restaurant, a local favorite, was hidden behind the Phoenix Hotel off Tubman Boulevard. Bubba walked along a narrow alley to a door surrounded by graffiti and smeared walls. There was no sign. Mr. Hong, always in a crisp white coat, bowed and pointed to Bubba's friend, who sat at a table hewn from a cross section of an abura tree. Bubba flipped a chair around and sat with his belly touching the back rails. forearms draped across the top.

"I knew you'd come," said his friend, peering through eyes that were atypically puffed and a voice that was faded and bereft of life.

"Are you kidding? Anytime." He leaned in. "You okay?"

Mr. Hong poured tea. Bubba's friend leaned back, lips flat, chin in a disobedient tremor, and said, "I know what your friends are doing, Bubba. I know that Winston recruited them. I know about the dolls. And I know what is in them."

How odd. But no big deal. Don't worry, Craze and Mad Dog won't screw it up. "Uh. They're happy to help. If this plan to wipe out malaria works . . ." His friend's disconnected stare made him stop. Then he said, "You can count on them. I know these guys."

"I know that Winston told you about the previous attempts to deliver the information. And that all three attempts failed. He suspects there is a mole at the center."

Bubba held his gaze. He figured Winston might tell his friend about Craze and Mad Dog but was flabbergasted at his friend's next words.

"Bubba . . . I'm the mole."

His mouth pickled; freckles popped from his pale Irish skin. Fascinated and petrified, Bubba stuck his neck forward. "What?"

Betsy stared at her chopsticks. Her chin quieted. She pulled her shoulders back. "I'm not a spy or a malcontent. I'm a dissident who has uncovered some bad behavior. I love my work. I love the chimpanzees, and I love what ACORN stands for."

"But why? You're the CEO. A marvelous achievement."

Mr. Hong served dumplings. Betsy picked up her chopsticks. Her jaw tightened; left heel began to clack the floor. "I'm up all night. Every night. Like I'm on amphetamines. Winston has betrayed the spirit of our professional and personal friendship. It circles in my head, eats at my conscience, poisons my integrity. I can no longer deny what is happening."

"Betsy?"

"I arranged the interceptions. I suspected Winston was using our technology for unintended purposes; hoped I was wrong, but couldn't let it go forward until I was sure. Well, I've done some digging." She tapped her finger on the table. "Now I am certain. Found hidden documents in his office safe. Spent nights combing through genetic code. He's clever." Her chopstick snapped.

Bubba recalled Winston's comment—that they shouldn't even let Betsy know. "How'd you find out . . . about Craze and Dog?"

"Bobby Diggs, director of security. We . . . chatted. He assumed Winston told me."

Bubba was still reeling. "What the hell is Winston doing that's so bad? And how did you arrange for these so-called interceptions? This is nuts."

"In college I joined Students for a Democratic Society. We were activists against the war. Marched for civil rights. Women's rights. A force really. SDS broke up, but another group formed, called themselves the Weather Underground. Weathermen Africa sprouted from them. I maintained a marginal connection with Weathermen Africa, thinking it would be more of a social thing— an attempt to hold onto the past, I guess. They call me a brush contact. When I figured out what Winston was doing, I asked them for help. A joyless decision."

"Jesus, Betsy."

She reached across and held his hand. She was shaking. "Bubba. At some point in your life, you have to make impossible decisions—like in that new book, *Sophie's Choice*. Decisions that are vile. Decisions that sicken you. That's where I am right now."

Bubba thought of the movie *Fail Safe*. A United States bomber unit is mistakenly given orders to drop nuclear bombs on Moscow and cannot be recalled by the president. In order to avert an all-out nuclear exchange, the US president allows the premier of the USSR to drop a bomb on New York City.

"Weathermen Africa? *Sophie's Choice*? You're losing me."

"I'm going to tell you exactly what Winston is doing. He made a miniscule change from our original plans, so tiny it was nearly impossible to detect. But now I have no doubt."

Betsy detailed Winston's misdirection. She gave Bubba background information on how Winston would justify it in his own mind. Bubba was horror-struck. They agreed that he would track down Craze and Mad Dog and tell them not to meet the guy at the Leopard Spot Campground. Betsy reasoned that Craze and Mad Dog would resist if she sent someone they didn't know. She would stay and permanently stop Winston's work in Liberia.

Bubba asked, "What about Bobby Diggs? He'll tell Winston he told you."

"Winston told him not to tell anyone. He'd be too embarrassed to admit it. Besides, he trusts me."

The next morning Bubba called Trindell Travel in South Africa. Marvin Kaestleman answered. The truck had already left Johannesburg, but Bubba coaxed the itinerary out of him. Marvin made it clear that plans were always subject to change.

CHAPTER 44

While we were at the bar the previous night, Co-Don, Bernie, Jerry, and Fergus went fishing. They caught a dozen tiger fish: sleek, with silver stripes and oversized predatory teeth. Good protein, but the bony framework made it hard to eat.

"Would anyone like to hear a bit of gossip?" taunted Chris, standing next to Jalina.

"Don't hold back, girls," Quinn said. "I'm up for a story, yeah."

The earthy smell of petrichor lingered from a brief night rain. Chris paused to create a sense of import. She lowered her voice. Her cheeks glistened. "Four years ago, Elizabeth Taylor and Richard Burton got married on this very spot."

Jalina confirmed, "Right here, in 1975. It was their second go-round. They broke off the first one after ten years. But true love brought them back together."

Jerry asked, "You mean they got married in Africa?"

Chris scoffed. She pointed at the ground between her feet. "No, mate. I mean right here. In Kasane. On these very grounds. A woman selling cabbage told us, said they wanted a secluded spot. They flew to Rhodesia and then came to Botswana to get married."

Jalina nodded. Chris put her hands on her heart. "Destiny."

Quinn smirked, "And how long might that second marriage have lasted?"

Jalina bit her lower lip. "They had a long go of it. Nine months."

It was a welcome laugh. Doug spit coffee into the fire. I poured milk into my coffee and handed the bottle to Gary. He asked, "What about you? You ever going to bite the bullet?"

"Got a longtime girlfriend. Miss her. Going to ask her to marry me." My head went light like I'd taken a slug of laughing gas. The words just came out. I was surprised at how good it felt. "Hey, Gary. I haven't told anyone yet. Not even Mad Dog."

He winked.

"You?" I asked.

"Not that close. There is someone I'm crazy about. Met her in the States. Can't wait to get back and see her."

We spent the day winding down from the previous days of hard travel. Fergus and Co-Don tinkered with the Pink Panther. Mad Dog and Big-Don neatened the back bed of the truck. Quinn and Hanna played backgammon. Emilie, Jerry, Doug, and Bernie gathered wood and cut it into serviceable lengths. We cooked over a fire beneath the giant baobab tree. The scent of burning mopane coals was ever present.

Twilight transformed the bar into a disco—another car-battery-operated record player. People from the nearby village joined. Co-Don shared some cane juice. Graham stole the show by bouncing around like a pogo stick. Even Mad Dog danced. He tried to copy Graham but somersaulted hard over a bench. His foot struck the butt end of an axe that was wedged against the wall, and his shoe came off. We went back to our tent.

"What the fuck?" he said. "Look."

A metal disk had dislodged from a slot in the heel of Mad Dog's shoe—the front part of the heel. A flap that had covered the opening of the slot hung by a rubber thread. Mad Dog pinched the disk and yanked it out. It was a little bigger than a silver dollar, twice as thick.

"Is it part of the shoe?" I asked.

"Never seen anything like it. But I don't usually rip my shoes apart." He stuffed the disk in pocket. "We have to look at this in the daylight."

Sunrise brought evidence of the surrounding tension. Helicopters flew along the river, barely a hundred feet above water. Three army transport vehicles passed the camp, eyeing us cautiously. Mad Dog and I joined Big-Don at the stone table. He was writing an aerogram. Kasane didn't have telephones, but it had a closet-sized post office where mail was picked up every two weeks, or less. "These bastards haven't got a clue. Are we crossing the river? Are we going into Chobe and Okavango? Fergus is a taciturn little bogan. Doesn't tell us shit."

"A bogan?" I asked.

Big-Don's eyes rounded. "I think you blokes call it a redneck."

"What's up with these helicopters? They never stop."

"Probably Rhodesian birds keeping ZAPU soldiers from crossing the river."

Mrs. Tonomo, a woman who tended the grounds, approached. "You should not be writing here. To write here is invitation to police."

Big-Don laughed. "I don't see any police. It's just a bloody letter. They're not interested in what I've got to say to my mum."

She eyed the river, crouched, and whispered. "Two weeks ago, a man sat on this patio sketching sunset, hippos in the river. They arrest him. Take him to jail. One week later he come back, got his things, and left. This is border. White men must be careful."

The gravity of the morning and our talk with Mrs. Tonomo tarnished lunchtime discussions. The frivolity of the disco had dissipated. Everyone better appreciated the circumstance we were in. Everyone except Gary. Gary was curious. Honest. Trusting. As the youngest, he may have felt a need to prove that he wasn't just a naïf rube from Vancouver.

Mrs. Tonomo fast-walked into our camp later in the afternoon. "He was reading. A Black man sit at table with him. Your friend. He ask, um . . . bad questions. What are helicopters doing? Where in the river is border? He ask if guerillas are sneaking . . . you say sneaking?"

Jalina sighed, "Oh. Come. On. Gary."

Chris was blunt. "How could he be so stupid?"

"Three men take him away. One said, 'sediriswataolo.' It means agent."

"Where will they take him?" Big-Don asked.

"Probably to Francistown. I'm not sure. This was different than man who was arrested for sketching. These men were angry."

Mad Dog, Fergus, Co-Don, Quinn, and I set off to search for Gary. We walked east in the direction of Victoria Falls, pounded by the unsympathetic afternoon sun. We talked to people on the road and visited a couple of dwellings. Nobody had seen anything, and either there wasn't a police station in Kasane, or nobody was telling us. We came to a locked rondavel that was unoccupied. A wire ran into the roof from a phone pole. From the pole, the wire ran south. I asked, "Electricity? Phone?"

"Could be either," Quinn said. "Could have a generator inside that runs off of kerosene."

After two hours of frustration, we headed back to camp. We were worried. Gary had become a friend. "Let's find him now and call him stupid later," Dog said. On the walk back, Fergus's cheeks stretched taut like a pressure cooker. He was clearly unnerved by this unwelcome dilemma, and he knew dealing with it fell on him.

While shuffling to camp, a Botswanan Army jeep passed. We hailed it down. Fergus explained the situation in his bland, squinty-eyed—always the right eye—manner. They said there were no police stations, but fragments of the old military police force still operated in the area: a unit that preceded the establishment of the Botswana Defence Force. They said our best bet was to go to Francistown and ask around.

Fergus and Co-Don finished talking to the soldiers while Quinn, Mad Dog, and I brainstormed. The walk back to camp was silent. Each chalky step magnified one certainty. Gary was gone.

CHAPTER 45

Travis shed his bush clothes for the trip to Livingstone. He hung an unbuttoned safari shirt over a New York Rangers hockey jersey and threw on some cargo shorts and a baseball cap. He stored his guns in a locker and was given a small pack that included binoculars, sunglasses, and a camera bag. Colonel Reid emphasized that Travis was a tourist. Tourists don't carry guns. This was to be a friendly pickup of some nesting dolls from two wide-eyed Americans.

Reid asked, "You all set with the camera, Travis? Any problems learning how to use it?"

"Nope. Works great. They are in Kasane now." *This thing is impressive.*

"Good, huh? The receiver sends signals to Block I satellites that the United States launched last year. I have my own. We can both track these buggers."

"I gotta say."

"It's a present from Gus Cooper from the New Pioneer Column. They help us out a lot. He's got a genius in Liberia that made it. The guy is such a hotshot, the US military asked him to field-test it, find the bugs, make sure the Russians can't hack it."

"The US military is helping Rhodesia? I'm surprised they . . ."

Reid winked. "Jimmy Carter condemns Ian Smith, sure. He has to. But they don't want to see a socialist coalition backed by Russia or China come in here. It's a game they play. One hand plays politics while the other helps us out."

Reid drove Travis to the meeting site for the 8:00 a.m. convoy that went from Bulawayo to the village of Victoria Falls. Private citizens extended guns from the windows of cars and pickup trucks, casually talking as if they'd just gotten out of church. The pace would be as fast as the slowest vehicle in the convoy, minimizing the time of exposure on the road.

The convoy pulled into Victoria Falls without incident after five hours. Travis saw the effects of war: deserted streets and hotels, a casino with no cars and broken neon signs. A lone bull elephant lumbered down a side street. Victoria Falls was devoid of people, save a single artist painting at Devil's Pool and a writer taking inspiration from the Boiling Pot. Travis looked across the canyon that was created by the falls. The Zambian side had a few tourists.

The lazy whine of a train whistle lured him around a bluff, where he was face-to-face with the Victoria Falls bridge. A Rhodesian engine was positioned at the rear of a dozen cars. It pushed them to the middle of the bridge and stopped. A Zambian engine coupled to the lead car and dragged them across the border into Zambia. *Just like Reid said.* Travis saluted mockingly. "I'll see you tomorrow evening." *I'll be in a hollow on a log car.*

Travis knew that once he got across the Zambezi he wasn't going to wait for the Americans at the Leopard Spot Campground in Livingstone like Reid wanted him to. He was going to pick up explosives from one of Sipho's contacts in Zambia. He was going to go upstream to the point where the Kazungula ferry docked in Zambia. At night, he was going to affix a generous amount of C4 to the bottom of the ferry and attach a remote detonator. When the Americans with the dolls boarded the ferry in Botswana and it reached the middle of the Zambezi, he would sink the motherfucker and everything on it.

CHAPTER 46

Craze: Assortments of Peril

Flounder faces marked the evening. Jalina stared across the river. Doug and Jerry spoke in hushed tones by the fire. Hanna cried. Gary's disappearance was abrupt, like a non-swimmer who goes under without a sound. I felt creepy, like someone was dragging a spiderweb across my face. I questioned my self-image as an adventurer. *I'm afraid. What am I doing? What do I want from all this? Go back. That's the smart thing. Toughen up and think.*

Big-Don was pissed off at somebody—he just liked to be pissed off. Quinn was unfazed and grizzled. "Well, we've got to bloody find him." Emilie evaluated the options aloud. Dale was willing to give it two days. If Gary didn't show by then . . . fuck him.

The sun hadn't set yet. Mad Dog and I walked to the stone table. He took out his Swiss Army knife and slid the tip into a ridge on the edge of the disk that came out of the heel of his shoe. "He's grown on me," he said.

"Huh?"

"Gary. We have to find him." He pried open the top of the disk. In the center was a square, caramel-colored wafer that sat atop a gray wafer. A button battery was embedded in the middle of the wafer, and a red wire connected it to tiny whitish rectangles. A thicker wire ran around the inside perimeter of the disk. Mad Dog held it up. "Whoa."

"Jesus, Mad Dog. Check the other shoe."

He poked at the heel of the other shoe with his knife. No rubber plug. No hidden slot.

"Someone on this trip? I mean, that wasn't there before we left the States. When could someone have gotten access to your shoes? And why?"

"Wasn't here," he said with conviction. "It was Bobo-Dioulasso. Remember, my shoes?"

"When we came out of the mosque? Nah. That would be fast work."

"Yep."

"Remember the protests against the president? Maybe someone thought it was suspicious that we stayed at the Hee-Fee instead of the l'Auberge? What is that gizmo anyway?"

"The guy we had coffee with on the street. Told us to visit the mosque. Had to happen at the mosque when we took off our shoes."

Fergus hollered. We gathered around the fire under the cooking tree, our name for the giant baobab tree on the crest of the river. Fergus scanned our faces. His gaze floated across the river to South West Africa. The hinges of his jaw moved. "As you know, we couldn't find Gary. For all we know, he could be returned to us at any moment."

"The hell he will," Big-Don said. "He's a victim of his own doing. You think they're going to drop him off and say, 'Bye Gary, have a nice holiday'?" Big-Don grinned like he expected a couple of chuckles. Silence.

Fergus looked at his feet. Co-Don, always willing to talk, conveyed the latest plan. "Look, people. We can't leave without trying to find Gary. Here's what we're going to do. Fergus arranged to hook a ride to Francistown with an army jeep in the morning. A jeep can travel faster than our truck. They'll make it in one day. He'll spend a day trying to find Gary, and then come back. While he's there, he can call Marvin."

"What are we going to do in the meantime?" Mad Dog asked.

"While Fergus is in Francistown, I am going to take you to Chobe National Park. We can do a couple of things we planned to do anyway."

Emilie asked, "Is the park safe? It feels a little weird to go sightseeing."

"The soldiers said the park is safe. ZAPU and the Rhodesians have no interest in the parks. This is all new for you, but it is common in this part of *Africa*. Something happens, tensions build, then they die down. Fergus will find Gary. You will see your lions and wildebeest. We leave for Chobe at 6:00 a.m. sharp."

Anxiety staggered us, but the proposal wasn't outrageous. Co-Don's affable tone sanded off enough edges to shift the mood. He was a kook, but he was savvy in the ways of southern Africa. I was happy that the Botswana Army knew what was going on with us. Tourists brought money into the country. It was in their interest to keep tourists safe.

At 5:30 a.m., we inhaled our oatmeal, gathered our cameras, binoculars, and sunglasses, and scrambled into our airline seats in the back of the Pink Panther. Co-Don rolled the protective tarp to the front of the Pink Panther. The Sedudu Gate was barely five miles to the southwest over a compact dirt road. A sense of guilt for allowing ourselves a few hours of gratification, while uncertain of Gary's fate, colored the morning spirits gray.

The sun bled over the horizon as we entered the park. We stood on our seats and held onto the metal frame, perfect positioning for photo ops. We pulled through the gate. Set against a falling half-moon, a ponderous eagle, perched at the tip of the highest branch of a barren teak tree, peered at us through its yellow eye ring. Dials on the telephoto lenses burned.

Co-Don stuck his head out the window and yelled, "Fish eagle." The morning composition lifted the pregnant mood and brought us to a different land.

Vegetation had dried to a withered straw, making animals easier to spot among the baobab, kiaat, teak, and mopane trees. Co-Don slogged the Pink Panther over to the Linyanti Swamp area, passing a pack of wild dogs with oversized, forward-facing ears and coats that looked like Jackson Pollock went wild with a bucket of black paint. The marshes rewarded us with rhinos and dozens of hippo heads sticking out of the water, some with birds perched on their heads. Their low, reverberating grunts could bend a windowpane.

I stood amid the pipeage with Jalina while Mad Dog traded notes with Quinn and Dale. Jalina, born an Aussie, was of Greek descent. She noticed the St. Christopher medal that my sister Carol gave me before the trip. "You're Catholic?" she asked.

"Yes. Irish Italian. Every night my mother had us kneel, five abreast, at the altar of the couch, and pray: Our Father, Hail Mary, Glory Be, Angel of God, God Bless, bed. I'm not the best Catholic, but we each have a spiritual side that makes us, us. I think we have free will. We're not just a glop of DNA and biochemicals."

She laughed. "I guess that's one way to look at it."

"I'm not in the *it's part of God's plan* camp. If we didn't have free will, and everything is happening according to God's plan, then why should we be judged?"

She reached for my medal, extended it from my neck, held it for a moment between her thumb and forefinger, and volleyed, "Well, apparently you have faith in St. Christopher's spirit."

She told me about her dance classes, that she worked in publishing, and how she was going to visit Greece after the trip. Jalina was smart, self-assured, and conferred accidental charm and grace. I knew we'd become friends, but her eye contact was deep. I wondered, Is she flirting?

A mother cheetah and her cub poked above the grass on the way to the Makumbu Pan and Nyomuga Pan, which gave us A-F-R-I-C-A in full form. My God. Giraffes, Cape buffalo, hyenas, immense crocodiles, and deer—gazelles, impala, kudu, eland—and a thing called a puku antelope with curled black horns that swirled like soft serve ice cream. And elephants. Legions of them offering superb pachyderm shots. Pompous bulls, mommy cows, babies walking beneath. Jalina leaned on my left shoulder to position herself for a giraffe shot. Her breath brushed across the back of my neck while her right breast pressed into the middle of my back and communicated a message. "If you don't move, I won't."

No denying this feels good. But she could just be just jockeying for a photo. It became clear she wasn't going to move. Hanna glanced at us and twinkled her knowing Dutch smile. It said, "I know that move . . . I've done that move." Alas, after a few minutes, Co-Don pulled the Pink Panther farther down the path, dislodging contact and breaking my sweat.

166

An hour before sunset, Co-Don set a course back toward Kasane. Dispositions had mellowed, adventurous palates were gratified. Thoughts returned to Gary. Some were optimistic.

Mad Dog and I had gotten permission from Co-Don to camp overnight inside the park. They would be coming back in the morning and would pick us up. We camped in a sandy area near a stand of trees on the west end of Chobe, where the green vegetation from the flood plains ends and the arid savanna begins. Co-Don reminded us, "See you lads at 7:30 a.m."

We made fire and sat together on a rock to watch the sun set. Mad Dog asked, "Did you have a good time with Jalina today?"

"Jesus, Dog. We were just talking. She's nice. She's going to Greece after the trip."

"So, after we get to Nairobi and head up the Nile through the Sudan, you're taking a side trip to Greece? Is that it?"

"What, are you, a friggin' spy?"

Mad Dog glared at me. "Alex?"

"We were just talking Dog, drop it." I turned and faced the road. We were back-to-back.

I asked. "Any chance that disk in your shoe has something to do with the dolls?"

"Doubt it. Nobody knows about us. When we were at the mosque, we hadn't even agreed to Winston's proposal yet. Speaking of which, are the dolls safe? You're such a slob."

"The dolls are fine. And I'm not a slob." *By my standards.* When my father remarried, for a while there were eleven people living in a seven-room cape. We threw dinner rolls across the table. Bathrooms were a battleground. In Mad Dog's house, the butter dish was never on the wrong shelf.

"You want to be able to brag that you helped eliminate malaria."

I snorted. We sat. The absence of light pollution put the Milky Way on full exhibit, as if someone took a paintbrush and slathered a swath across the sky.

At sunrise, snorts and grunts of a different timber approached our tent. Mad Dog poked me, stony look, index finger to his lips. We couldn't see them, but they were lions, no mistake. Several. They stopped a few feet from the tent. Their respiration rattled the flimsy side of the tent, paralyzing our instinct to breathe. A bossy snarl forced us to lean into each other. Marrow seemed to drain from my bones. *Is this how my life will end?* The Dog was ashen. I wished his heart would stop; it pounded like the baseline of "Smoke on the Water." He looked to be praying to a God he didn't believe in. I wanted the pores on my skin to close so they wouldn't breathe. A brief scramble, a tussle outside the tent . . . probably gambolling in the misty sunrise. The gush of a meat eaters' protein-laden breath penetrated the skin of the tent. *If we can smell them, they can smell us.* I confirmed my love to people who weren't there. I tried to remember what you are supposed to do if confronted by a lion. Stand your ground. If necessary, fight. Punch at the head, go for the eyes, scream like you've never screamed. We waited.

It went on for a couple of minutes, a lifetime. They moved on. We allowed time before daring to peek. There were at least four, now fifty yards away, lumbering into the scrub. Mad Dog smacked me when I stuck my camera out and the shutter clicked.

While breaking down our tent, a black land rover pulled up. An elderly gentleman, scruffy beard, worn olive khakis, and broad-brimmed bush hat, stepped out. Deep creases ran from edges of his broad nose to his earlobes. A face that told a story of survival, more so from his fellow man than harshness of nature. He was a park ranger and mounted a smile.

"Good morning to you gentlemen. Who is it you are with?"

Mad Dog said, "Trindell. Trindell Travel. They are coming for us."

The ranger deliberated. "Yes, I know that one. The pink one."

I showed him the lion tracks. He pointed to where the lions had come from, traced his finger in an arc through the air, past our tent and toward the water. Then he educated us, still pointing in the direction the lions had gone.

"Yes, every morning, six lions."

CHAPTER 47

Craze: Fergus Speaks

We threw the tent on the roof of the cab, making sure we told the lion story before allowing the truck to pull out. Quinn leapt out to get a close look at the tracks. Emilie overplayed her French-Canadian accent. "You guys are lucky, you know."

Endorphins were still giving my heart premature ventricular beats. Co-Don was silent. We knew Fergus would be angry that he'd let us sleep in the park. I assured him we wouldn't tell.

He said, "Get in."

"No Gary," was the word. Spines sagged into seats. Chatter was sparse. Co-Don drove southwest to do more sightseeing, as if nothing had happened. Wildebeest, cheetahs, and zebras brought little joy. We stopped under a baobab on the embankment of a clay-caked brook and watched hippos. A string of saliva dropped onto the gear box cover of the truck. Jalina gasped and grabbed my arm. A leopard lazed directly above us, sprawled across a belly of branches. Co-Don disengaged the clutch and let gravity pull us to safety. We camped in the park that night, uninspired by an afternoon of blue kingfishers, black herons, and barrel-chested great egrets, and a blacksmith lapwing.

Mad Dog and I spent the evening with Quinn, listening to stories of his stint in the Special Air Service fighting Marxists in the Dhofar Rebellion. When we learned he had a technical background, we decided to show him the disk that had popped out of Mad Dog's shoe.

"Any idea what this is?" Mad Dog asked.

Quinn shined a pen light on it. "Ah, yes. Dat little wire there, around the rim? It's an internal antenna. The t'ing it's connected to is probably an amplifier. I think you've got a modulator and oscillator there too. And a battery."

"What's that mean?" I asked.

"Some sort of transmitter, I'd say. Not 100 percent, but that's how it looks to me."

"Quinn. You can't tell anyone until we sort this out."

"Na gabh dragh, chum. I'm good at secrets, I am."

Fergus returned from Francistown the next evening. He sat alone at the stone table near the bar. We gathered. He stepped onto a small ledge, dug his hands deep into his pockets, and peered across the river as he spoke. "I went to the Defence Force base, talked to the army's police chief. I checked the immigration office. Then the Francistown police. I went to the post office to see if Gary left a message. I even checked the hospital and a church. No sign of him. I called Marvin. He hadn't heard from Gary."

Voices shuffled. "Where the hell?" "Poor Gary." "I hope he's all right." "What do they want with a kid like him?"

Dale spoke up. He shouted, "We can't wait forever."

Fergus looked at us this time, instead of looking at the ground or off into space. His cheek quivered and pulled on the corner of his top lip. "I left Gary a message at Post Restante in Francistown. Will leave the same message in Kasane, telling him that he should call Marvin, find out where we are, and fly to catch up to us."

My heart sank. I thought Fergus would find him. Moving on was a hard reality, but it was at odds with compassion. Gary was stupid enough to open his mouth while on the skirts of a war zone, but the thought of leaving him behind made me sick.

Jalina pushed. "So?"

Fergus fidgeted, his pale British face red and drawn. He placed one foot on the stone bench like he was ready to let his birthmark of self-importance out of its cave. He raised his head and tucked the top of his shoulders behind his collarbones.

"We are taking the ferry in the morning. It leaves at 10:00 a.m."

"Bullshit!" Mad Dog squawked.

I agreed. We still had over a week before the end of April, Winston's deadline to deliver the dolls. There was time to find Gary *and* get across the river to deliver the dolls and earn our private excursion up Kilimanjaro. "We have to go out in force," I said. "All of us. If he's not in Francistown, he could still be around here. Let's drop into every side road, hut, school, and outhouse in the area. Somebody knows something."

Fergus replied. "Decision's made. 10:00 a.m. ferry . . . tomorrow. Be ready."

CHAPTER 48

Alex: Oh Shit!

Alex pulled the pillow over her face and let out a shrill. She knew the difference: the awkward stammering when she was kidnapped by the initial attraction; the dopamine rush; the accelerated thud-thud in her chest; the bolt of lust in her body when his hand accidentally touched hers; and the *I've still got it* satisfaction.

She pulled her *Alex and Craze* scrapbook from the night table and looked at the photos: hugging each other on a roller coaster at the Tivoli in Copenhagen; Craze running a three-legged race with one of the Fernald School kids, laughing at the camera; Craze licking envelopes at Oxfam America, trying to make it look sensual. She laughed. Things had never become flat and accommodating with Craze. They'd never turned into just friends. They were still lovers.

The things she loved most were the same things that made her bone-weary. His independence, thinking nothing was impossible, surprising her with getaway weekends. It could be exhausting. She was hurt that he never moved in with her, something she initially respected but since had become a pebble in her shoe.

She giggled and thought of how she'd become spellbound by this other young man. He had an innocent heart, a sweet smile, and the air seemed to boil when he was around. *Sound familiar?* But he was also willing to pull up stakes, to leave his old life behind just to be with her.

She cherished Craze and his undaunted nature, his dissatisfaction with complacency. He knew how to find life and not wait for it to find him. He wanted it all. So did she, and it had included him. She reflected on his phone call, wondering if she should meet him in Nairobi. *Wait!* Alex covered her mouth with the palm of her hand. She reached for the top drawer of the nightstand and opened it. Letters. She rifled through them and found the latest from her new lover. Her throat tightened. She looked right. The bottom of her face was cut off by the bottom of the dresser mirror. She stared into her own eyes.

"Oh, shit."

CHAPTER 49

Travis picked up a heavy cache of C4 putty and equipment from Sipho's contact in Zambia and loaded it into his oversized Bergen pack. He hiked to a position a quarter-mile upstream from the Kazungula ferry, which was docked on the Zambian side of the Zambezi. It was 2:00 a.m. The immigration house was a hundred yards inland. The guard was asleep.

A low-profile dugout canoe rested in a thicket of bushveld bluebush a hundred yards upstream, exactly where Sipho's contact said it would be. Travis used the silent Indian canoe stroke to maneuver to the ferry, never lifting his oar from the water, projecting power on the forward stroke and rotating his oar to slice through the water on the return stroke. He lay on his back and slipped under the double-hulled platform with only nine inches to spare between the top of the canoe and the deck. It felt like he was in a coffin, a feeling he knew well from the tunnel rat work he'd done in Cu Chi and Phong Nha. Four I-beam supports ran the length of the deck. Flashlight in mouth, he pressed C4 into the flanges and connected it with thin bridge-wires and instantaneous electrical detonators. Flecks of rust fell into his eyes and mouth. It was a massive amount of C4. Nobody would suffer.

He finished and let the current of the Zambezi carry him downstream, and then turned the canoe right to paddle across to Botswana. He grounded the canoe on the riverbank, pulled it back from shore, and tied it to an acacia tree. His rucksack contained the radio, the camera with its tracking device, food, and water. He shaped to a semi-squat and worked his way through the undergrowth and the green chalcedony rocks to the ferry landing in Botswana. A stand of num-num bushes offered cover for the night and would afford good visibility of the ferry landing. He was in perfect position to watch, to make sure, that the Americans and the dolls were on board when he destroyed the ferry. The ferry only ran once a day. He would come back each morning before daybreak and wait . . . until the job was done.

He thought of his wife, Norah, and wondered if she had had their baby yet. He wondered how Jaxon would take to having a sibling that would compete for Mom's attention. He thought of his six brothers and sisters, and his father, who'd died of his second heart attack at such a young age. He prayed for his mother, who was still alive, living in rural Maine. The life he'd chosen had endless sacrifices. It isolated him from his family, evaporated his childhood friendships, and, as a Selous Scout, forced him to watch as his colleagues murdered women. He'd tipped off Nkomo and probably saved his life. Now he would destroy the blueprint of a plan that was said to be unspeakable. It was meaningful opposition, and it gladdened him.

CHAPTER 50

Quinn sat on the log near the cookfire, peeking over the top of his coffee mug. Everyone had finished breakfast. They were packing for the six-mile trip to the Kazungula ferry. He tried to stifle a peculiar grin. Mad Dog and I knew why.

"Good morning, Quinn. Did you sleep well?" I tried to match the diffidence in his Scottish puss by elongating the word "morrrning" and emphasizing the word "sleep."

He kept the mug in front of his face. "Yes, yes, I did t'anks. Like a baby I did."

I pressed. "That's nice, Quinn. Mad Dog and I . . . we didn't get much sleep. Our neighbors were rowdy. Don't you hate that, when people make noise aimlessly without consideration for their neighbors?"

"Oh, that can be a nuisance, yes it can." He lowered his mug to the ground. Doug sat next to Mad Dog. Quinn put both palms on the log. "You heard somet'ing, did you?"

Doug snickered. "We did, eh. Jerry saw Hanna's ass and legs crawl into your tent. Only heard a few squeaks from her, but you quaked like a loonie that lost its chicks, Quinny boy."

Quinn surveyed the area, leaned in, took another look. "It was the most wondrous t'ing. I was joking around with Hanna. Told her I could beat her in a game of strip poker. She called my bluff, she did. But not strip poker mind you. She said she'd play a game if I let her be in charge."

"What's that supposed to mean?"

"She pushed me down, don't you see. Said she'd leave if I didn't do as I was told. She kept asking me about old girlfriends as she tugged on my drawers. Her voice turned dark and she kept asking me in a whisper, 'Who was in charge Quinn? You or your girlfriend?' She gave me this lecherous stare and said, 'I'm going to render you helpless.'"

At that moment, Hanna walked past the back of the Pink Panther. She fixed her eyes on us and flipped a smile that was fearless. She stopped for a minute to openly primp in the side mirror, fully aware that secrets were being told. Lipstick and hair in place, she strutted off as if holding her head above water, accenting the movement of her ass. She peeked back and cast a wink that was carnal and approving.

Quinn, now looking down, asked if she was gone. His Scottish tongue danced thicker with each sentence. "Help ma boab, she pulls a length of string from her bra, like a shoelace, but longer— I'm flat on my back you see—and she loops it around my testicle, tying it off but not too tight. Then she takes the other end and passes it through that little ringlet in the corner of the tent on the floor. You know the ring you'd hook your sleeping bag to if you were on a mountain? Anyway, she passes the string through the ringlet and brings it back to my big toe, where she tied it off. She does the same with the other testicle, by jings."

"Smash it, Quinn," Doug said. We delicately raised our eyes, trying to locate Hanna, feeling drawn to catch a glimpse of the crazy.

"You see, if I moved my legs, say I bent my knees up, the string would pull on my testicles. It was bloody evil."

"Jesus, no wonder you were squealing," I said.

"She undressed. Straddled me facing backwards. I was excited at this point, if you know. But I couldn't move my legs without ripping my balls off. She rocked on me, slowly, to keep me from exploding. She turned her head, looked me in the eye, and said, 'Did your girlfriends do this to you, Quinn?' When she finally let me, my legs twitched, and I let out a loud one."

Doug grinned.

Fergus started chirping. "Ten minutes. If you're already packed, Co-Don could use a hand hooking up the trailer."

We took our seats in the Pink Panther. Emilie's spot was in the third row next to Doug. She noticed his undisciplined smirk.

"What's so amusing?" she asked.

She could be frustratingly perceptive. Emilie was a scientist. An expert observer and data collector—discerning, but unusually empathetic. Doug craned his neck in my direction, then to Jerry, and back to Emilie. He had classified information. "A stupid joke Co-Don told. You don't want to hear it." She rolled her eyes.

It was an easy ride to the ferry with a minor delay to clear a water buffalo from the road. The immigration hut was huddled amid the ferns and grasses atop the alluvium, about a hundred meters from the shore. The sun was heavy, arcing methodically across the northeast sky. After a superficial inspection of the truck, each passport was stamped with an exit visa from Botswana. The ferry was a speck on the other side of the Zambezi, poised to push off.

Fergus pulled the Pink Panther to the top of the landing, which was no more than a washboard boat ramp cut into hard-packed soil. A businessman from Malawi and a few locals were the only other passengers waiting. Mad Dog and I walked to the shore. The ferry had just launched from Zambia. Two crocodiles basked on the riverbank twenty meters downstream. A pod of hippos was submerged and grunting upstream. "They're called river horses by the Greeks," Co-Don said. "Mother hippos have their babies in the water. They even suckle under water. He droned on, happy to share his cultivated bank of wisdom.

The ferry launched from the Zambian shore. It was small, enough for a couple of cars and some foot traffic. As it approached, a voice hollered, "He graze. He graze." I thought they might be warning us about a predator nearby. Nobody paid attention. The call came again, elongated words bouncing along ripples in the river creating vibrato. "He graze." After a pause, the same voice shouted, "He dog–graze." *Wild dogs? They're scavengers, not grazers.*

The calls got louder. "Mad Dog, do you hear that?" I asked.

"Look," Jalina shouted. She was pointing to the right side of the ferry.

I peered across the water and saw someone standing on the pedestrian platform that ran along the side of the ferry. He was waving like a wild man. When he realized I spotted him, his eyes shined bright, and he started to windmill his arm in a Pete Townshend air guitar move. Then he boom shouted the signature riff from The Who's "Won't Get Fooled Again." "Ba da bahhhhhh . . . dunt dunt. Ba da bahhhhhh . . . dunt dunt!"

CHAPTER 51

Travis: Hesitation

The screaming red-headed guy on the ferry didn't faze Travis—some idiot blurting out a Who song. It wouldn't change a thing. But when Travis looked to the ferry landing in Botswana, he saw something that stopped him cold.

His chosen life required the ability to disconnect, to understand the greater cause, knowing that, on occasion, some would suffer. Any revolution is wrought with casualties that are both dispensed and born. But what he saw on the shores of the Zambezi in Botswana made him face an unexpected test of the revolutionary's creed. Could he stick with the plan? He was shocked by a simple surprise that was more disturbing than anything he could fabricate.

Travis did a flash assessment of his options, trying to piece it all together. The ferry would reach the landing in a few minutes. He played out the likely outcome of each scenario and tried to think of a way to mitigate the negative aspects of each. He had to make a decision that would allow him to keep his cover with Colonel Reid yet make sense to Sipho. His conscience forced him to deviate from the plan.

CHAPTER 52

I saw his red hair. I yelled, "It's Bubba. He's shouting, '*Hey Craze.
Hey Dog.*'"

Mad Dog raised his binoculars. His jaw slackened; it was indeed
Bubba. He shook his head. "What the fuuuck, Craze?"

We ran to the edge of the water and waved, yelled, arms in the
air. Onlookers gawked, looking from the ferry to us and back. A
knot rose in my throat. *What is he doing here?*

A profane eruption of white and then orange light discharged in
four directions and skyward from the ferry, followed by a blast that
shattered ear drums and knocked our brains against the sides of our
skull. Two heartbeats later came another blast. It ruptured what was
left of the ferry. The fireball changed into a viscous, maelstrom of
burnt orange and black, as if a Bengali tiger was in a blender. The
windstorm delivered a coil of rank odors forged from black oil,
molten iron, corrosive chemicals, and rubber. The aftermath fire
coveted oxygen and sucked it from our space, reversing the wind
flow, leaving us in a vacuum.

Next came parts, raining down: a length of tubular railing, a
headlight, a half-torn basket, the butt of an M-16 rifle, twisted grates,
a bent gear shaft, someone's walking cane, and flesh. A piece of a
hand, half a shin with protruding shards of the tibia and fibula, a
wrist with five brass idzila bracelet rings sticking to burnt, disfigured
flesh.

We hit the ground and covered our heads with our arms. Ten
seconds later, everyone else stood up and ran. Waves created by
the force of the explosion lapped the shore and washed into our

faces. Mad Dog and I stood, chins dripping, staring at the spectacle. The last remnants of the ferry sank into the Zambezi. Scattered oil and fuel continued to burn on the surface. Any wreckage or parts that remained floating would soon be violently cast over the crest of Victoria Falls. My nerves galvanized while cinders of conversations with Bubba crept into my mind. What was he doing here? Who did this?

While others ran, Mad Dog and I scanned the river, seeking any reason for hope. Everything had been liquidated. It was the first time I'd ever seen Mad Dog cry. We stared at each other, bitten by a certainty that swallowed us.

Bubba was dead.

CHAPTER 53

Notions fire-bolted in my head. Exciting ideas, when hatched, go from a silly whim to an impulse, to inclination, and finally to desire. It is natural to embrace the adrenaline, to focus on the promise of gratification, and downplay the immense effort and associated perils. Time, energy, and pitfalls are underestimated or intentionally discounted. And now my bosom had been pillaged and my dear friend had become a barbarous footnote in the Rhodesian Bush War.

"Craze! Mad Dog!" We were still on shore. Jalina and Chris were running down, howling at us, begging us to run to the Pink Panther. Jalina tugged on my arm. "Hurry. Fergus will leave without you."

It felt wrong. To leave this place. This moment. To abandon the air where Bubba just took his last breath. To leave Bubba. *To leave Bubba.* What about his parents? His brother? His sister? We would have to tell them. *Shit.* What do we say? "Sorry, Mr. and Mrs. Brewster, we saw him get blown up, and what was left of him either went over Victoria Falls or was chum for the crocodiles. There was nothing we could do." The thought of this conversation was repugnant.

I recalled a story Bubba had told us. His Peace Corps friend, Jake, had been body surfing. He got roiled in a wave, hit a rock, and injured his spine. He was rescued but couldn't move anything from the neck down. President Carter arrived in Liberia on the same day, and Bubba had a chance to meet him. He chose to do so instead of visiting Jake in the hospital. When he finally got there,

Jake had already been medevacked to Landstuhl Army Hospital in Germany . . . where he died. This choice haunted Bubba so much, he was embarrassed to share it.

Jerry was maniacal. "Guys. Get in the truck. Now! We have to get out of here, eh."

It was the only choice. We didn't know if there would be another attack. Our new friends were hysterical, screaming from the truck. Co-Don stood on the roof of the cab and whistled. Fergus honked the horn and revved the engine, posturing to leave. We ran.

Bernie and Dale waited in the back. They grabbed our belt straps and yanked us over the gate. Fergus shifted into first gear and released the clutch. Jalina asked, "What were you guys doing down there?" Mad Dog was silent. I told them that the guy yelling from the ferry was the friend we'd visited in Liberia, our high school friend. Someone we fished with in Buzzards Bay, drank our first beer with, knew of high school crushes that went untold to anyone else. We knew each other's perversions and deviances, and we trusted each other.

Gears meshed. The engine toiled in the cornmeal sand, muting my voice to the folks in the middle of the truck who were still postulating. "Must have been the Rhodesians." "Must have been ZAPU." "Did you see the red-headed guy?" "A lime hit me in the head."

I flinched with each creak of a suspension spring or thwack of a tree branch. Jalina put her arm around me and pulled me in close enough where I could smell the almond soap she'd showered with that morning. She placed her other hand on my leg, propped herself up on one knee, and whispered in my ear, "You loved him."

I choked *whoop-whoop*, like a person with pertussis. "He was there for me when my mother died; when I had rheumatic fever and had to get around the house by sitting on a flipped-over rug and pulling myself around by grabbing cabinet handles and doorjambs. He introduced us to hiking the Appalachian Trail, rock climbing, and magic mushrooms."

Mad Dog had either heard Jalina's whisper or read her lips. His eyes met mine. He nodded. In that silent exchange he told me that he loved Bubba too. He told me that he knew we were in way over

184

our heads, and he wondered how we could have been so wrong, venturing out like we did. Without speaking he said, "It's you and me, Craze. I've got your back."

Fergus pulled the Pink Panther into our campsite in Kasane. His chin had contracted into his neck, amplifying a bulging set of dark eyes. He was walking the knife edge of Mount Katahdin, fighting the inclination to jump. His first words were to Co-Don, who had already jumped off the truck and was lighting up a joint with Hanna and Jerry. "Put that out or you'll be riding in the back with the rest of the passengers." Fergus was rattled. There was no way to communicate with Marvin in Johannesburg. He tried hard to display the mettle of a leader, but we were now in a state of anarchy.

A veil of dust approached, scuffing along the path that led from the cluster of huts where Mrs. Tonomo lived. He held his arms out as if to apologize for the bother. His eyes sought charity and solace. The left side of his face was rasped as if scoured with a Brillo pad. His gait beveled to one side, and the orange and blue of his jersey were barely visible beneath residues of sweat, smoke, and crud.

Chris gasped inward, taking a sharp slug of air. Words crept from her mouth in a muggy tone of disbelief. "Oh God . . . it's Gary."

Mad Dog and I watched as the emotional amusement ride everyone was on pivoted once again. We'd enjoyed the excitement of moving on with our journey, nearly lost our lives, and now embraced the mystical return of our youngest member. And our friend. But we weren't ready yet to accept any fragments of joy. We listened to the happy exchanges from a distance as Gary gave the others an account of what had happened to him.

They thought he was a Rhodesian agent, possibly a special ops soldier called a Selous Scout. They carted him off in a windowless van to a house in a town that he thought was called Seronga. While his passport was being verified by Gaborone, men in dark attire decided to make their own assessment. "Why did you ask such questions?" they asked. "We have your passport." They stuffed his nostrils with hyena dung, notorious for its stench, a biproduct of digested animal carcasses. With a heavy strip of hide—they called it a sjambok—they beat downward on the top ridge of his kneecaps until the ligament with quad muscles felt like they would cleave. A short man, when left alone with Gary, scratched his face with needles, claiming they were laced with a Bushmen poison that could stop his heart. Finally, the word from Gaborone came and was in Gary's favor. They dropped him off three kilometers from Kasane without an apology.

Jalina and Emilie hugged him. After a brief talk, they pointed at Mad Dog and me, still sitting in the back of the Pink Panther. Gary shuffled over.

"We were listening," I said. "You okay? Did they do anything permanent?"

He reached over the gate and hugged me, and then Mad Dog.

Mad Dog, chin on Gary's shoulder, said, "You gave us a good scare."

Gary pulled back. "I'll be okay. Heard about your friend. Deeply sorry."

"Thanks."

"I forgot to ask. What were you all doing at the ferry landing??"

I stared into his eyes. The innocence was still there. He didn't know.

"We were leaving without you."

CHAPTER 54

Craze: Awkward Grieving

Fergus and Co-Don spent the rest of the day trying to find out what happened at the ferry. They were cautious, afraid to meet the same fate as Gary. An army jeep came by and added to the despondency by telling us that four Botswanan soldiers were killed by hippos last night. "Stay away from the riverbank after dark." Okay.

Speculation fueled new tics, which emerged like weeds from the garden. Doug blinked, like he was hitting a reset button. Jerry twisted his beard. Quinn sucked his tongue between his gum and lip every few words. Veronica hadn't stopped hiccupping since the explosion.

Little circles of three or four people gathered in whispers throughout the afternoon. Private conversations. Firm and varied opinions on what we should do. By suppertime, there had been so many groups and subgroups that the entire cadre of sentiments was exposed. "The company is going to leave us in the lurch—just take our money." "Trindell should have called off the trip. They knew." "Co-Don said Trindell is broke. They'll never help us." "Do you think Gary is a spy?" "I just want to go home."

After supper, Fergus announced that we were going to leave. There was no way for him to contact Marvin from Kasane, and it was best to get the hell out of the area.

"Are we going back to Francistown, our favorite place?" snotted Big-Don.

"It's close to the Rhodesian border and the Botswana Defence Force base there. Could be a target. There's a town called Maun on the southeast fingers of the Okavango Swamps. It has phone service, and there's a place we can stay called Crocodile Camp."

We left at 7:00 a.m. and rolled into Crocodile Camp around six o'clock. The last few hours of the ride toward the Okavango Delta took us through the northern margins of the Kalahari Desert, a breathless landscape of packed silica, sandveld stone, and wavy berms of sand. Splotches of thirsty grass and stubborn camelthorn trees dotted our peripheral vision, but all anyone could talk about was the ferry explosion.

The camp had proper greenery, nata palm trees, and legions of cream-scented lilies showing their swagger. A tightly thatched roof sheltered an outdoor bar that had music, darts, and a barkeep named Peter. It felt like we'd been beamed to a distant planet, and the Kazungula catastrophe was a bad dream. After supper, Quinn taught us how to play darts—games called Killer and Cricket. We deserved to get drunk, and we did.

I felt like my spirit was watching my actions and listening to my words from a distance—or maybe I thought God was watching. My disconnected conscience observed me from the corner of the room, and it was confused. What is the proper way to mourn, and who is judging if the way I am mourning is appropriate? My friend's life ended yesterday, and now I'm drinking and playing darts—even had a laugh or two. Am I supposed to mope? How does one conciliate the forces of grief with the dualism that life goes on? Should I go into our tent, bury my head in a case-hardened box, and grieve? All day? Two days? The Jews sit shiva for a week—at least they spell it out. What am I supposed to do when I grieve? Pray to a God whose form I am uncertain of? My thoughts on God are always in flux. One thing I know for sure: if one of the world's religions has the truth absolutely pegged—they've authorized and certified the truth—it means the rest of the people in the world, the vast majority, are wrong.

I was fifteen years old. Tired from a morning of hauling corn, picking beans, and moving irrigation pipes, I rode my bike home for lunch from my 75¢/hour job at Pushcart Farm. My neighborhood was all six-room capes built on quarter-acre lots after the war. Nine-year-old Nina flagged me down. "Police are at your house."

I bolted home to Nancy Lane, my street. Neighbors were on their lawns and driveways. My next-door neighbor leaned into her handkerchief and bawled. People chatted and pointed. One squeezed her rosary, beseeching Mary. Cruisers and an ambulance fronted my house. My friend's mother called to me, her face harrowed as if she'd had a stroke. She squeezed my wrist and then realized she hadn't drawn up the words she would say. Her lip pulsed, but nothing came out. I was annoyed, wanted to get away. "Something has happened to your mother," she said.

"Something?" It's not a good word. I waited for her to say, "and she is okay." But people don't gather like this if someone is okay. I heard my pulse bang against my eardrum. People overreact, I told myself. Mothers make big deals of nothing. Then I saw Dad's car. *Our* car. Dad was home—in the middle of the day! I peddled around the back door and ran in.

Desperate sobbing—from the opposite end of the house. A policeman reached for my arm. I walked by. Wordless. Gasps, high-pitched and lost, traveled from Mom and Dad's bedroom, down the hall, through the kitchen and into the family room where I stood. I knew it was Dad, and I knew Mom was dead.

She was lying in the hallway, on her back, legs in the bathroom, torso stretched across the hall. Her eyes faced the bedroom at the end of the hall—as if seeking out Dad. I dropped to the floor next to her and sat, nearly touching her, back propped against one wall, muddy sneakers plunked on the opposite. It was my first experience with death. Dad's door was ajar, but for a period I stopped hearing him. Considerations on how she'd died hadn't arrived yet. I should be crying, I thought. Mom would be mad at me if she saw my muddy feet on the wall. No, she won't, I reasoned, then I regretted having had such a thought, that I'm not in trouble.

Instead of crying, I thought of how idiotic and petty we could be to each other; how we could turn something insignificant into a contrived tragedy. Nobody is immune from exhibiting petty behavior, I thought. It's only a matter of severity. I was not an easy kid. I stayed out after dark, spurned authority, and snuck out the bedroom window at night to meet my friends. I had a temper and thought my mother picked on me—common persuasions of a teenage boy. My parents' job was to say Yes or No. I loved them, but never used that word. We didn't say it. It was cultivated in the subtle way that happens in families; helping with homework and science fair projects; being a den mother for Cub Scouts; putting a face cloth on our forehead during bouts with mumps and measles; teaching us to be equally grateful for each birthday present, big or small. When I was eleven, I bought Mom a hideous plastic plant for her birthday with my paper route money. She still displayed it.

I hesitated to touch her, but I reached for her cheek. It was cold and her skin no longer soft. I didn't kiss her, afraid to for some reason. I thought about what a prick I could be to her at times. I don't know how long I sat there before my hearing returned and my heart restarted. *I haven't gone to see Dad yet.* I had to step over Mom to get to the bedroom door. *Jesus!* Dad couldn't look at me, seemingly embarrassed to be crying. He raised his head and our eyes met. I cried. He and Mom were forty-two years old, high school sweethearts, and a cerebral aneurism that yielded to pressure burst and changed his life forever. For us kids, innocence was replaced with rage and then apprehension. There were five of us ranging from five to sixteen years old and Dad barely knew how to boil water.

Each aunt, uncle, and friend that visited evoked a new squall of hysteria, forcing us to relive our grief. Crying brought headaches, fatigue, tears over her loss, her promise, and things she would miss. We cried over our own fate, one wrought from fear and uncertainty. Finally, we had to answer a question we'd never thought to ask. "What does Mom do?"

When Mom died, grief came in waves. Laundry piled up. Nobody was assigned to cook dinner. Six months later, after the flurry of figuring out our cadence, I had my big breakdown. I developed arthritis in my knees, ankles, and elbows as a side effect of a bout with rheumatic fever. And no Mom. Distress came in merciless cycles, each episode with its own fingerprint.

I decided I'd grieve for Bubba on my own terms and ignore whoever the hell was watching me. I'd save my grief for the next hiking trip when he couldn't come; for the next time he wasn't there to give a goofy response; for anytime I smelled limburger cheese. The communications office in Maun was closed until morning. We had to call Bubba's parents . . . and we both knew that was my job. *Shit!* We ended the evening at the bar and had a cordial talk with Fergus. Peter poured us a glass of chibuku, which we raised to Bubba. Gary joined us. He stared into the side of Fergus's face and said, "I never did thank you for leaving without me."

Fergus didn't lift his head. "I'm responsible for everyone. Not just you. And by the way, your cooking partners stepped up for you. Tried to convince me to form our own search team."

Gary brushed his hair from his forehead and looked hard into my eyes. He shifted to Mad Dog and said, "Not surprised."

By the time the sun rose, I'd replayed what I would say a hundred times, keenly aware of my intractable jitters. The phone rang. Mrs. Brewster answered. Her voice frail and barely audible as always, a weaker version of Edith Bunker's tremble. She was surprised. I couldn't bear offering small talk and told her that Bubba was on a ferry and had accidentally died in a cruel attack by one of the political entities of the Rhodesian Bush War. I avoided using words like *killed* or *blown up*, but I didn't want to be vague—which would force me to clarify and then clarify the clarification. I covered my eyes. My nipples hardened like solder, and I pulled my head close to the wall as if it would offer protection. A tear pinched out and slid down my cheek. Then another—*shit!*

Mr. Brewster took the phone from her. A former marine who'd served in the Pacific, his voice was strong. He'd heard what I said. "Craze?" I could hear him helping Mrs. Brewster lie down. I heard a whimper, and then a frank howl. I could barely move air across my vocal cords. Mr. Brewster was a veteran. But he was also a father—proud like all fathers.

"Craze, was Bubba with you? What was he doing so far from Liberia?"

"Sorry. Don't know. We figured he decided to join us. Never got a chance to talk to . . ."

"Did you see him? I mean specifically see him get . . . uh. He's a good swimmer."

"We saw him before the explosion. But. Mr. Brewster. It was immediate. Powerful." I tried hard not to go into detail. He prodded, forced me to tiptoe through events layer by layer. I kept hoping he was satisfied, but Mr. Brewster wanted it all. Finally, I said, "Sir. We were on shore . . . Well. There were pieces, sir. You know." A tiger clawed at my gut. Against my will, my mouth yelled, loudly, like it was angry at him. "Parts, sir! We saw body parts. Pieces of bone and hands and shins. Small pieces."

Mad Dog gawked at me in disbelief. I envisioned Mr. Brewster dropping to the bed. Hugging Agnes. Unable to speak.

"I'm sorry. Didn't mean to yell. Really sorry."

"Craze. His body. How do we get his body?"

Fuck! I held the phone away from my head for ten seconds, wiped my eyes with my upper arm. I heard Mr. Brewster say, "I see." It was the most perverse moment of my life.

"The Zambezi. It's infested with crocs. Hippos. The current is swift. Victoria Falls is down river, sir." Then phone service cut out.

The attendant bit his lower lip and shrugged. "Happens all the time."

The call depleted my will. I desperately wanted to talk to Alex. She was always the one I could turn to. I needed her. Her voice. Her warmth.

"Could be an hour. Could be days," said the attendant. Problem could be anywhere between here and Ghanzi."

A full breath found me, but it only triggered another spate of tears. Mad Dog leaned against the wall frozen, his face paralyzed, eyes empty, devoid of motion or emotion. He found the grace to say, "You did good, Craze."

CHAPTER 55

Travis: Change in Plans

Travis continued to work through the stories in his mind. Sipho expected him to destroy the dolls by sinking the ferry after the Americans boarded it in Botswana. His Weathermen Africa colleagues had insisted that Sipho eliminate all evidence that the technology existed. They would take care of Liberia. Yet, Colonel Reid expected Travis to meet the Americans at the Leopard Spot Campground in Livingstone, Zambia, retrieve the dolls, and bring them to him.

Travis had partially satisfied Sipho. He'd prevented the dolls from getting into the hands of Colonel Reid, and by sinking the ferry, he could maintain his cover with the Selous Scouts. But the dolls weren't destroyed. He'd have to tell Sipho why he deviated from the original plan.

Destroying the ferry was never part of the assignment from Colonel Reid. Travis was simply to meet two tourists who would happily transfer the dolls to him. But if the ferry hadn't sunk, Reid would have expected Travis to meet the Americans and bring him the dolls. Travis reasoned that, if the ferry was at the bottom of the Zambezi, he could explain to Reid why he never retrieved the dolls. It allowed him to maintain his cover—so he thought.

He'd had only had a few moments to make a decision after being shocked at what he saw on the shores of the Zambezi in Botswana. But now he realized that destroying the ferry early was a miscalculation. Reid would figure out that the ferry was going from Zambia to Botswana, not the other way around. He would deduce that neither the pink truck nor the Americans were on the ferry when it blew. They would still be alive. The dolls would be intact. Reid would expect Travis to track down the Americans. A Selous Scout always finishes the job.

Lies were building in Travis's head. He had to keep them to a minimum. When darkness settled, he found the acacia tree where he'd tied up the canoe and paddled across the Zambezi to Zambia. He sought out Sipho's contact, the one that had provided the explosives. The contact had access to a phone. Travis called Reid and told him that the Americans never made it to the Leopard Spot Campground. "The tracker is still working. I'll track them down and get the dolls," he said.

He called Sipho's number at the Wimpy's back office at 12:45 a.m. and told him what he'd seen on the shores of Botswana that forced him to change his plan. He could hear Sipho rap the desk three times with his knuckles. "This is a big risk, Travis. Not good. I thought you could compartmentalize better than that."

"Mm. I don't think we should destroy the dolls before we find out what's in them. We can destroy the information afterwards. But first, let's find out what the other side is trying to do."

"I was told that what's in those dolls is so heinous, they are worried about the world reaction. They don't even want people to know what is possible."

"Let me get the dolls. Let's figure out what's in them. Destroyin' them, sight unseen, ain't the best plan. I mean, what's in them that's so important . . . and what's Rhodesia up to?"

The air hung. Finally, Sipho said, "How are we going to figure out what's in them?"

"I have an idea."

CHAPTER 56

Craze: The Okavango

Fergus had spoken to Marvin in Jo'burg just before I called the Brewsters to tell them that Bubba had been killed. There was nothing in the South African newspapers on who bombed the Kazungula ferry. Marvin was happy that Fergus got us all out of Kasane. He had the main office in London on another line. They wanted the group to stay in Maun for a couple of days while they devised a plan. "Let the good people visit the Okavango swamps."

Mad Dog and I wanted to be alone. Fergus agreed to let us camp overnight in the Okavango. For us, it was a fitting gesture to honor years of camping, hiking, and canoeing with Bubba. For two pula, we rented a mokoro, a canoe hewn from the trunk of a sausage tree, from Mr. Boikanyo, a man whose colorful sign called to us. Mr. Boikanyo frowned when we asked for paddles instead of the typical poles used by locals, who stand upright in the rear of the canoe and pole around the swamp. It was like we'd asked for a fork in a Chinese restaurant.

Mr. Boikanyo's son drove us half an hour north and dropped us at a giant Mashatu tree on the edge of the swamp. "I will be here at 16:00 hours tomorrow to pick you," he said. "Use the tree as your guidepost to get back." He didn't realize that Mad Dog was the ultimate trail sniffer, a guy who headed into the wilds of the Yukon without a map.

Mad Dog still had his own compass. Mulbah in Liberia had mine. The sun was positioned about twenty-five degrees northwest at 1:00 p.m. If we lost sight of the Mashatu tree, we knew we could paddle in the right direction. I pushed us off. Mad Dog fussed with his pack, shifting it, wedging our tent against it so it would ride upright. I started to ask him . . . but then saw him twist Chewbacca into a position where the figurine could see what was going on. I held silent.

We paddled.

The swamp had a primitive yet elegant voice—a maze of channels with frogs plopping, birds crying *weet weet burda burda*, varied whistles and clacks. Parrots with six shades of blue and white-faced ducks. The wood smell of the canoe, the sound of paddles dipping into the water, and the plumage of bee-eaters and hornbills submersed us into thirty minutes of unspoken tranquility before Mad Dog's voice slid into the milieu. "Bubba would love this."

I gasped.

We paddled between a pod of hippos and the shore, respecting their inclination to head for deep water. Sometimes our canoe barely fit into a channel, educating us on the local preference for poling. Four elephants were jumbled on a solid point a few minutes away. We paddled, unable to resist the photo op against the saffron backdrop of the Okavango.

"Hey, Dog, what's that guy who's supposed to meet us in Livingstone thinking right now? Must have been freaked when the ferry went down."

Silence.

"We promised Winston. It's important. I think the guy in Livingstone will wait."

"Too bad you and I couldn't just canoe across. Who says we need to go by ferry?"

We heard clicking sounds ahead to the right. Mad Dog said, "Who knows. The guy in Livingstone might try to get to Kasane somehow. But he'll see that we're gone. Not sure what else we can do."

I'd accepted that the trip to Kilimanjaro was all but lost—and maybe my job at ACORN. Still, ridding the world of malaria, there had to be a way to get there.

"All we can do is hold onto the dolls," Mad Dog said. "Anyway, they're nice. Would make a good souvenir if we never see this guy."

More clicking sounds from the same area.

We wove through a band of water lilies and peered to the right. In a pool tucked behind the reeds, four women were waist-high in the water, each holding a conical basket that looked like a witch's hat made of golden straw with a brim that was four feet wide. Fish traps. One woman wore an eggplant-colored wrap; two wore strapped sundresses. The fourth was bare breasted with short cornrows, tight and pointing skyward. Our passage rendered them silent.

On the shore, behind two fan palms, more clicking. Two men, small in stature, clad in simple white loincloths wrapped around their hips and genitalia, eyed us. The younger, perhaps a teenage son, held a smallish bow on his shoulder and carried a water skin. He seemed to be amused. A blue-and-white beaded headband was wrapped around the older man's brow. We slowed while passing. A third man and then a fourth man appeared.

I said, "Smile, Dog," which we did. I added an unassuming wave.

One of them smiled back. "Hallo," he said, and gestured for us to paddle toward him. The other man, after scanning the contents of our canoe, made a contorted hand gesture to the women, who took it as permission to start giggling again.

I whispered, "Dog. I think these are Bushmen."

"Yup."

"Should we paddle over there? They're supposed to be friendly."

Mad Dog made a draw stroke that turned the canoe in their direction.

The men communicated in tones that mimicked the low whistle you make when you blow across the top of a beer bottle. Succinct clicking and tsk-ing varied with delicate changes in the shape of the lips and positioning of the tongue. The man that said hallo pointed at our packs and then to the beaded headband. He draped an animal skin over his arm, stroked it, and invited us to do the same. It may have been an impala or duiker. He pointed to our packs again.

"I'm pretty sure they want to know if we have anything to trade," I said.

The women laughed and carried on. Mad Dog reminded me we didn't have much. This is extraordinary, was my only thought. The men spoke to each other. With gestures to the mouth, they asked us to eat with them. The "Hallo" man had exhausted his English, but their softened faces and voices, which glided across silica-dusted vocal cords, bred trust and fellowship.

Mad Dog turned his head. "We're going."

Yes. Daylight was nearly finished. Motioning to the men, I patted our tent, placed my hands to my face, and tipped my head. They laughed like we were now long-lost friends. Reports were that the San people were peaceful. Spending even a shred of time with them was an honor.

"They want us to go to with them, probably to their home."

We paddled for five minutes while the men walked along the grassy land adjacent to the channel. At their village, drums thumped and smoke coiled from the end of a long tree that lay in the fire. Intermittent hoots pierced the air. Baskets everywhere. A cluster of low thatched homes were adjoined by fences. Cattle mooed. A man named Sekiewa approached us. He spoke in English. "These are Hambukushu people, the Rainmakers of the Okavango. Some call them the River Bushmen." My spine ignited. All I could think of was Bubba.

Sekiewa invited us to spend the night, offering a one-room hut with two zebra skins covering the floor. They fed us mealie meal and fish, possibly tilapia, that had been charred over the fire. Drums beat. Men wearing multi-rowed anklets of animal teeth stomped and jumped. "A rain dance," Sekiewa said. The Milky Way was bold that evening. I fell asleep thinking of Alex and the nights we'd spent in Zermatt staring at the stars in a sky absent of light pollution.

In the morning, Sekiewa brought us to meet the elder. We removed our shoes and walked across a rock slab that was soaked in goat blood. We had to declare our business, dirt now sticking to the blood on our feet. Sekiewa translated, explaining that we were tourists. The elder asked us to share a gourd of chewable beer. A trading session commenced. Baskets, pelts, beads, and various things you could smoke were offered. Of our cache, they were interested in a couple of T-Shirts and a baseball hat. A man snatched the Matryoshka dolls and brought them to the elder. *Shit.* The elder wanted them. Blood rushed to my brain. *No!* I blurted out, "Sekiewa, the ashes of our dead friend are mixed into the walls of the dolls."

Sekiewa translated. The elder dropped the dolls on his lap. They fell to the floor. Sekiewa picked them up, gave them to Mad Dog. "I see. Do you have something else?"

Mad Dog whispered, "Let's get rid of the transmitter."

He pulled the transmitter that we found in his shoe from his pack. The elder examined it, flipped it over, took the cap off, and saw the wires inside. He certainly didn't know what it was, but it intrigued him. He handed it to Sekiewa and nodded.

We paddled in the direction of the Mashatu tree. I said, "Good thinking, Dog."

By the time we landed at the Mashatu tree, met Mr. Boikanyo's son, and rode back to the camp, it was approaching suppertime.

One fat hen, a couple of ducks, three brown bears, four running hares, five Simple Simons sitting on a stone, six seasick Sicilian sailors sailing the seven seas . . . Doug had scored a bottle of rum, and most of the group was playing a drinking game. We raised our tent and were about to join them when Peter, the bartender, walked up to us. "Is your name Danny?" he asked.

"Yes," I said, surprised that he called me Danny.

"There's a man at the bar. Never seen him before. He'd like to speak with you."

CHAPTER 57

Betsy: Soul of the Mole

Betsy sat at her desk, haunted by a story in the *International Obeserver* about an attack on the Kazungula ferry in Botswana. Sources at Zambian Immigration Control said that eight Zambians, two crew members, a Ndebele woman, and one American were on board. She closed her fists, lowered her forehead to meet them. *Dear mother, please don't let it be Bubba.* The location of the explosion was suspicious. She could picture Bubba's happy face, feel his good soul. And the dolls? Had he found Craze and Mad Dog? Did he tell them not to meet the guy in Livingstone?

She'd seen Winston at the coffee shop that morning while picking up her cup of caffea excelsa. He was marble-faced, curt, and monotone. Cameron, from Weathermen Africa, had told her that Winston was conspiring with an organization that supported Rhodesia in the bush war, a fact that explained the motive behind Winston's miniscule tweak in one of their gene-editing initiatives. She suspected it was the same organization that funneled mountains of money into Winston's research.

Betsy had mapped out several plans on how to stop Winston. All were wretched. There was only one option that would leave her with a morsel of dignity.

CHAPTER 58

Mad Dog came with me. We brushed past the massive bed of lilies that fronted the step-up to the bar area. A lone guy sat at the end of the bar, back to us. He nursed a Lion lager and wore a blue jersey with the name Park and the number 2 on the back. I crossed the floor like I was wading into the cold waters of the Atlantic, warier than I was of the strangers in the Okavango. The hockey jersey made me think he was Canadian or American.

I sidled onto the stool next to him and peeked under his baseball cap. He didn't look up. His beard was full and ungoverned. Fatigued eyelids formed an unconventional squint. Mad Dog moved in beside me. The man lifted his head slowly, looked at me straight on without speaking, and held his gaze. His forearms looked like long bricks with two mulberry veins popping down the middle. I felt an overpowering sense of familiarity. *Who is he?* It was a stare down, some sort of intimidation game.

I looked harder. The eyes. They leaked an uncanny feeling of fellowship. *Oh my. Good Lord.* I scanned the bar to see if anyone else had walked in. I brought my eyes back to his. "Tommy?"

He raised his eyebrows once. I stood to take another look around. When I sat, that big East Boston smile broke across his face. He said, "Hi Danny."

"Holy shit, Tommy, what are you doing here?" It was my cousin. When Dad's brother died, he left my aunt with seven kids to raise. Dad was the only male in the family and became a surrogate father figure, Uncle Dickie. To them he was more than an uncle. Tommy stood. We hugged with a level of affection that seemed to ambush him.

"Jesus, Danny. I been on the run so long . . . forgot what it's like to have family."

His eyes filled. He made no attempt to hide it. I was happy for him, for me, but raspy lumps of despair were evident. Tommy looked at Mad Dog with apprehension.

"He's okay," I said. "We've been friends for life. He knows how to keep quiet." I turned to Mad Dog. "This is my cousin. Tommy. You know, the one I've told you about? The guy who started the United Freedom Front. Been on the FBI's top ten list for years?"

I looked straight into Tommy's eyes. "The guy who is responsible for the FBI visiting our house for a chat every few months. The guy who is the reason our phones have been tapped for years. The guy who is responsible for the FBI standing in the back of the church during family weddings." Tommy was unfazed. Mad Dog absorbed this bizarre event in silence. He extended his hand. Tommy gripped it and nodded.

"What are you doing in Africa?" I asked. "Jesus, when you started doing all that shit with the UFF, I thought I'd never see you again. Last time I saw you was at your mother's place in Maine. You'd just gotten out of MCI-Walpole. You weren't so political then."

"Hmph. Hey, I gotta ask you—please don't call me Tommy no more. Okay? Been going by Travis for three years. Even Norah calls me Travis."

"Sure. Of course." I recalled how Dad told me that Tommy would go to a graveyard and find the stone of a child who was born around the same year as him but died young. Tommy would get a copy of the birth certificate at the town hall and, from there, get a driver's license, social security number, and even a passport.

Mad Dog acknowledged Travis's request with a flip of his hand.

We moved to a table in the corner. Travis told his story. He told us about the raid on his house in the United States, his flight to London with Norah and Jaxon, and how he hooked up with Weathermen Africa and infiltrated the Selous Scouts as a double agent with the help of a guy named Sipho. His account of the assassination attempt on Joshua Nkomo made me jumpy. Mad Dog growled, "Balls."

The more Travis spoke, the more he slid back into his old self—the cousin I knew.

"If the Selous Scouts find out you're helping ZAPU, you're fucked," I said.

"News doesn't reach the States. I watched scouts poison a water hole for an entire village just because they found one gun in a guy's house. Fourteen people died. Two scouts in my unit bombed a church in Salisbury and killed three White people just so they could leave ZAPU pamphlets near the ruins in order to rile up the White fence sitters against ZAPU."

"False flag? Killed their own? Jesus help us."

"They think they're righteous, creating jobs, being the great White heroes. In school they are taught to be paternalistic toward the Africans but are told to 'keep them at arm's length.' A couple of guys referred to them as a flock of subspecies."

Mad Dog tightened his jaw but didn't speak; something he does to mask his anger.

"I seen or heard all this from my own unit in the Scouts. I listened. They bragged about how they changed the voting system so that there were two voter rolls. They made sure most Black people couldn't meet the requirements to be in the A voter roll. It capped the B voter roll at twenty percent, making sure Black representatives would always be a minority."

"You're getting hot," Mad Dog said. "Living with the enemy for too long?"

Travis unleashed. He told us of an episode in Chirundu when one of the Selous Scouts threw a live baby into the river to be eaten by tiger fish after they'd killed his mother; how the Whites would call a Black African a "munt"—a man-cunt. He said the Rhodesians resented South Africans who claimed that they were less racist than Rhodesians. That struck me. How a country that sponsored apartheid and promoted frank degradation of non-White races could feel that Rhodesian racism eclipsed their own?

Mad Dog pulled us back to the original question. "What are you doing here? In Maun? And how did you know Craze was here?"

Travis twitched a smile. "Uh. I'm the guy you are supposed to meet at the Leopard Spot Campground.

"What!"

"I couldn't believe it when I saw you, Danny. I knew you were a traveler, but Africa? I'm trying to play both ends of it here. Colonel Reid wants me to get the dolls and bring them to him. Sipho—at first, he wanted me to get the dolls and destroy them. But we . . ."

Mad Dog stood and glared. "How'd 'you know we were in Maun?"

"When you were in West Africa, a Selous Scout planted a tracking chip in your shoe. I followed you here, but then it seems you left the transmitter somewhere in the swamp."

Mad Dog flipped his arms up. "Damn."

"Yeah, we found it in Mad Dog's shoe," I said". Traded it to an elder in the Okavango."

Travis smiled, shook his head. I stood too. It was a lot to absorb. "We were told the dolls were to be taken to a pharmaceutical in Zambia," I said. "Do you even know Winston Walsh?"

"Don't know him. But I know the story you were told. The malaria story. They were using you. It's true, someone prevented the info from bein' delivered a couple-a-times. But if I brought the dolls to Reid like he asked, the information would be used by Rhodesia."

Mad Dog clenched his hands like he used to when he walked to the line of scrimmage.

Travis's voice sharpened. "Sit, Mad Dog . . . please. Listen. Me and Sipho don't want the dolls destroyed no more. Reid said the dolls have info that will devastate Black Africans in Rhodesia and secure White rule. But he wouldn't tell me exactly what it was. Sipho said there's a scientist with a conscience in Liberia who found out. They arranged the interceptions."

Dog clenched his teeth. "Knew Winston was a prick." He punched the air. "Knew it."

"Bottom line, we gotta figure out what's in the dolls," Travis said. "Where are they?"

"Hold on." I ran to our tent and got the dolls and returned.

"The info is rolled up in the walls of each doll. They put a thin coat of rubber cement on the paper and rolled it up to form a cylinder. Then coated each doll with shellac to seal it."

Mad Dog recited in monotone, like it was fourth-grade show-and-tell. "Shellac: made from the resin of the female lac bug. After she penetrates the tree, she sucks up the sap and chemically changes it into lac, which is then scraped from the bark." Travis's cheeks puffed and his lips tightened to hold back a laugh.

"My father was a painter."

We laughed. The night air seemed to get less dense.

"Winston told us that two things are needed to unroll the dolls," I said. "Pure alcohol to dissolve the outer coating of shellac, and hexane to dissolve the rubber cement—to help unroll the paper. I think we could figure out what Winston's trying to do if we can unravel the dolls. But I might need help. There's a woman on the trip who's got an advanced degree in genetics."

Travis pinched his chin and stared into the courtyard. "We ain't gonna find hexane or pure alcohol around here. Need to get to a bigger town or city."

We talked of family and old stories; of times Travis would visit and we'd sneak off with Dad's BB gun to shoot in the pine grove; of Norah and Jaxon in London and how he missed them. And his mission. "Right now, this is the most important thing I've done in my life. It's real." We agreed to find out what was in the dolls *before* turning them over to Sipho. I told Travis more about Emilie and how we could take advantage of her background.

Before going out to introduce Travis to the rest of the Pink Panther crowd, we told him about our friend Bubba, who was killed on the Kazungula ferry when it exploded. He dropped his head and went silent.

CHAPTER 59

Craze: Where Did It Go?

Emilie nudged Gary and pointed at us as we walked from the bar into camp. Chris, Jerry, and Doug put down their forks. Jalina's tongue poked into her cheek. Heads turned, eyes tapered, lips went pressed and rippled. I don't like secrets, especially big ones. Butterflies, like the first at bat of the season. Keep the lies to a minimum, Travis had said. We'd agreed on a story.

"Hey guys, this . . ."

"I'm Travis. Nice to meet you," he said like he belonged.

Stares.

"Guys, this is unreal. This is my cousin—from home," I said. *True.* "He finished his service with the Peace Corps in Paraguay and decided to backpack around the world. He's going to pick his way across the globe at various harvests." *False.*

Fergus joined. Emilie had already turned to logic. "And you ended up here? In Maun. How did you know Craze was here?"

Travis said he called my father, who knew I was on the Trindell tour from Jo'burg. Africa was a must for him, so he decided to try and find me. The group had already seen Bubba track us down from Liberia, so we thought it was an easy sell.

"Uncle Dickie had the itinerary. I just traced it. A nice woman in Kasane told me the pink truck had gone to Maun. I got a ride with the mail truck."

"You guys sure are popular," noted Emilie, skepticism dripping to her chin.

Quinn squinted. "You must have gotten there the day the ferry went down, yeah?"

"Mm. These guys told me about your close call . . . about their friend."

"Think you can get around the world like that? Picking?" Jerry asked.

"Thailand picks rice March 'til June. New Zealand has apples, and pears in February. Malaysia has durian fruit in April and September. Grapes and olives in Europe. No end." I smiled at Travis. *Who is this guy? Tidbits in his brain.*

"I can see the resemblance in the eyes," Jalina said.

Travis had the family's trademark eyes, a natural squint, long lashes, relaxed glint. Hanna asked him to tell stories, the dirt. He could be truthful, which made it easy. *Minimize the lies.*

I pulled Fergus to the side, asked if Travis could join us on the trip as far as Nairobi, assuming we found our way out of the mess we were in. He didn't say yes, but he didn't say no. I think he was sensitive to the fact that our friend had died. He promised to ask Marvin in the morning—if phones were working.

We slept.

After breakfast, Fergus gathered the group. He'd pulled his self-conscious, evasive mask from his drawer, eyes vacant, typically looking at nobody. "Phones are still down. We're going back to Francistown. Break camp. One hour."

He tried to walk away. Bernie was annoyed. "What's in Francistown?"

Fergus retracted his lip and exposed his canine tooth. "Telephones . . . that work."

"The driver of a delivery truck told us Francistown is safe," Co-Don said. "All we know."

I asked Fergus about Travis. He gave a half-hearted nod and climbed to the top of the cab to secure the tents. We billowed through the scrub all day. Anesthetized faces set up camp in Francistown. Fergus parked the Pink Panther on a gradual downhill.

When we crawled out of our sleeping bags the next morning, Graham and Co-Don were jawing. Graham was in his underpants, face purple, his voice high. "How could he do that? What is wrong with you people?"

Mad Dog got out of the tent first. "What the hell, Craze. The Pink Panther is gone."

Big-Don, Quinn, Bernie, and Jalina joined Graham in his attack. Co-Don half turned away from them. Quinn's Scottish face flushed redder than his hair. He scooted around Co-Don and went nose to nose. Co-Don turned his head, probably to escape the stale cigarette breath. Bitter accents emerged. Quinn's tongue ran heavy and fast, as if he were twelve years old again making trouble with his friends in Plockton.

"Go fuck yourself," Co-Don yelled.

Quinn shoved him backward, over a log onto his ass. "You're lucky I don't kick you in the small of the back."

Mad Dog and I ran over. "Where is it?"

Co-Don rose, spit, told Quinn he was a menace, and walked away. Graham told us that Fergus took the truck and put it on a train in Francistown. The rail line ran from Jo'burg through Botswana, into Rhodesia, up to Zambia. The truck would travel through Rhodesia and north to Victoria Falls. All passengers must disembark before it crossed the Victoria Falls Bridge into Livingstone, Zambia, where they'd unload the truck. Passengers weren't allowed to cross.

"Where's Fergus now?" Mad Dog shouted in Co-Don's direction.

"He's back soon. Talk to *him*." This wasn't Co-Don's doing, but we needed a villain.

Fergus returned. He expected to be the first to tell us the news but learned that Co-Don hadn't kept his trap shut. He pulled off his shirt, surprising us with a chiseled physique.

"I called Marvin. The southbound trip from Nairobi has been canceled, which eliminates the possibility of switching trucks in Lusaka. You've already learned that our truck is on the train." He shot a dagger at Co-Don. "It will be in Livingstone in three days. You have to pay your own airfare from Francistown to Lusaka. End of discussion."

He stormed off. Trindell had just kicked us in the balls and snotted into our coffee. Emilie threw gasoline onto our outrage. "Where's the trailer? The food?"

208

It was a high-handed authoritarian move. What would a bunch of tourists do, far from home, transportation and food taken from them? It was a mentality that seemed to be standard fare in southern Africa, where imposing one's will on another was commonplace, where Europeans imposed their baasskap—White supremacy policies—where White Rhodesians established minority rule while using the 'lesser' races for manual labor. A scout had wholeheartedly told Travis that they "treat the Africans like good pets." We were Trindell's pets.

An additional anvil of humiliation mortified Mad Dog and me. Winston had duped us, sucked us into his plot, and smothered us in an oily coat of self-embarrassment. On top of that, my relationship with Alex was on the knife edge.

Mad Dog was a master of simplification. "Let's fuck him over, Craze. Let's find out exactly what he's trying to do and expose him. Shame him. Shove his Nobel Prize aspirations up his ass."

CHAPTER 60

Winston: Gone Fishing

"I am the orchid mantis," Winston uttered as he drifted through the entrance doors at the airport in Monrovia. He was presenting himself as a pretty flower, irresistible to a butterfly that he intended to eat for lunch. He strolled to the middle of the hall, stopped, looked to the ceiling, and sighed. He wasn't travelling anywhere. He was baiting the mole.

Bobby Diggs idled near the departure control gate. He wore a tattered Firestone cap, horn-rimmed glasses, and a shirt with a Quality First logo adjacent to the flared Firestone *F*. He'd also darkened his skin. Bobby carried a binder that contained headshots of every employee at ACORN, faces he and his team had memorized and been quizzed on. His team, five private investigators and a former MI6 buddy, studied every twitch and head turn at the airport, trying to spot anyone that showed interest in Winston. Two were positioned at the terminal entrance, one at the other side of the departure control line, one near the bathrooms, and one read a book near the bank of pay phones. The sixth ate lunch in his car in the ACORN parking lot, watching to see if anyone followed Winston.

Winston dangled himself like a sand eel on a live line rig for stripers. He yawned, looked at the clock, bought lemonade, studied the departure board, and always made sure the padlock on his briefcase was visible—protecting something important. The plan seemed reasonable. He'd leaked that he was delivering the documents himself, casually mentioning it to some R&D scientists and in a few "just between you and me" conversations. He told

Betsy he'd be gone for a few days. At the Hard Thymes Tavern, Bobby bitched to ACORN workers about Winston's constant badgering and let it slip that he was glad Winston was going away for a few days. Winston and Bobby leaked the date, but not the destination. If the mole wanted to stop Winston, they'd have to follow him to the airport and see which flight he got on.

CHAPTER 61

Craze: Desperation

Emilie, Bernie, and Big-Don composed a letter to Trindell, outlining our grievances. They put our lives in danger. They weren't the experts they claimed to be. They took away our transportation and food and defaulted on the contract which specified they were responsible for "all ferry and river crossings." They needed to pay for our airfare.

Bernie read it to Fergus, who dismissed it. "Useless drivel."

Everybody signed. We walked into Francistown to send it. Fergus was already at the communications office speaking to Marvin. We telexed it to Marvin and to the London office, telling them a signed letter was on the way. Gary knew a lawyer that helped him with his work papers when he moved to South Africa. He called him and asked if he could put pressure on Trindell. Travis searched the town for pure alcohol and hexane. No luck.

Our fate twisted again the following day. The district commissioner of Francistown had received a telex from a counterpart in Kasane. Another ferry had been brought downstream and was moored at the Kazungula ferry landing. Rhodesia and Zambia had agreed to allow a peaceable crossing at 10:30 a.m. the following day. It would go one time and in one direction.

My first thought was, Where the heck is there a telex machine in Kasane? "The Pink Panther will be waiting for us in Livingstone," Fergus said. After intense discussions, we all agreed—let's make a run for the ferry. Let's be done with this god-awful segment of our trip. Let's move on and avoid a pissing match with Trindell. It was the fastest solution.

Co-Don found a driver with an old school bus who was willing to take us to Kazungula. It was a musky, green heap with "Francistown North-East District" barely legible on a body marred by sandstorms, rust, and neglect. We would leave at 2:00 p.m. and drive through the night. It seemed insane, but, like a relief pitcher in baseball, the group chose to forget about our previous outing to Kazungula.

Travis grabbed me by the collar and motioned to Mad Dog. "We can't go with them. We have to get to a bigger city to find the solvents we need."

He was right. But if we went back to Johannesburg, then what? "Travis, I need Emilie," I said. "And she's sticking with the group. I may be able to figure it out on my own. But I really think I'll need help from her. She's the genetics expert."

"You don't even know if she'll help."

"She is a fair and decent person—and a scientist. If I tell her the reason, she'll help. We can get the solvents in Lusaka, Lilongwe, or Dar es Salaam."

The 340-mile trip was a sixteen-hour final exam of grit and ingenuity. Diesel fumes painted our throats; steel skeletons of age-worn seats prodded our bones; engine noise wheezed through a hole in the manifold. We stopped seven times to add engine oil. The sun set and we realized the headlights didn't work. The driver knew of a junkyard in Maposa. He found a light that fit the socket, and he, Dale, and Fergus tied it to the center of the grill and ran wires to the fuse box. One headlight—enough to get there. An hour later, the accelerator cable broke. They rigged a handheld cable and wove it under the dash. One person worked the clutch and steering wheel while another manned the throttle cable. Sleep visited no one, except Travis in the rear and Gary, who slept on the floor. Jalina prayed. She sat beside me and found comfort on my shoulder.

We reached the landing at 6:15 a.m. We saw it—another ferry. The air was quiet. Ghostly glances were exchanged. Leaden eyelids tugged at memories of the last time we were there. The river was peaceful, belying our reflections on mayhem, fear, and death. A blue-and-white waxbill sang. Flurries of black butterflies with a sapphire blue splotch on each wing circled the leaves of jackalberry trees. A pang of buyer's remorse crept onto each face. Emilie whispered, "Oh God, why did we do this?"

After unloading our packs and tents, the driver left, having figured out how to operate the bus solo. Mad Dog, Travis, and I sat under a mukwa tree. Travis eyed the riverbank.

"Do you trust this Sipho guy?" I asked. "Didn't you say he used to be on the other side?"

"Yeah. He's been cool. Got me into the Selous Scouts. Set me up to do things that he wouldn't have done if he still supported the Rhodesian Front, like blowing up the—" Travis stopped in midsentence as if choking on a chicken bone. He redirected the conversation. "We've talked about our families, but not much about you. You ain't married yet. Got a girlfriend?"

Mad Dog snorted. "Got a nice girlfriend . . . and he fucked it all up."

"Thanks, Dog." What could I say? "You met her once, Travis, just before you went underground. Alexandra? Alex? We'd just started dating."

"Her? I liked her. Nice, sweet, funny. You been with her all this time?"

"Mad Dog's right. I've screwed it up. I love her, God I do. It's just that . . . me loving her, her loving me; I guess I haven't let our loves mesh together." I raised my voice to make sure Mad Dog heard me. "But I am going to ask her to marry me."

His eyes popped and his lips pursed like he'd eaten some bad broth. He took on the voice of a Baptist minister. "Praise the Lord. It may be under duress. It may be under the threat of losing her to another guy. It may be because he's been whipped into submission. But Crazy Luke is going to propose."

I laughed. Travis didn't. Something about the discussion seemed to wilt his self-assurance. The morning droop under his eyes opened a canyon of self-reflection. His life carried a heavy weight: the running; the anger that dwelled within him; the sacrifices that come with committing to a cause; his unrealized obsession for human equity. "I miss my family. I miss you guys. Mom. Uncle Dickie. I got Norah and Jaxon, and probably a little one by now.

The guys in the Freedom Front have been my family. But it ain't the same. If you love this girl, you gotta keep her. If you she makes you happy, you gotta marry her."

Mad Dog recognized the temperance of the dialogue. "You have to say something—next chance you get. Let her know. That's what she wants." He lowered his frame to make sure he had eye contact. "It can't wait, Craze. Call. Tell her you want to get married. Leave a voicemail if you have to. It's too late to wait for the right moment. You heard Bubba. You are on the ropes my friend. Don't blow it."

I blinked. My armpits filled with cold sweat.

CHAPTER 62

It was like we'd lost the opener of the World Series and were back for Game Two. Immigration personnel arrived at nine o'clock. Conversations were high-pitched and truncated. It was a private ferry that had been in mothballs. Its owner saw the chance to cash in on the war with his oversized, flat-bottom boat with a deck that rode a few inches above the water.

Bad news came immediately after the officers arrived. "This ferry is only to be used by Zambian nationals—Zambians who have been stuck in Botswana and need to go home."

Fergus talked to them, pleaded. Co-Don hid in the background, still in Fergus's doghouse. Bargaining, threats, overtures, and citations on what we were told by the district commissioner of Francistown fell like stones over a cliff. An offer to pay a "special fee" was dismissed. We weren't going anywhere.

The ferry blurred into the haze with thirteen Zambians aboard. My fellow travelers gazed, open mouthed. I watched the twitch of each face as it grasped the position we were in. No food. No transport. No way to communicate. Edge of a war zone. All we had were our tents. A few of us carried light cooking gear. We camped a few hundred yards from the ferry. Whenever I looked to the river, I thought of Bubba. The only food we could muster from the locals was mealie meal and cabbage. Rumbles and grunts of lions frayed our sleep that night.

Trumping the anger and uncertainty was a turd of embarrassment that had been draped across our shoulders. We'd been gullible. Careless in evaluating information we were given. We were smart people who weren't used to enduring impositions. We'd let blind hope muddle our thinking. Wanting so badly to be able to spin a tale of adventure, we were willing to sacrifice common sense. Even Fergus was angry. Travis never said, "I told you so," but it was in his eyes. In his posture.

Two more days of mealie meal and cabbage passed. Desperation smoldered. Hopes of a stray truck passing went unanswered. More time to think about Winston—profound disappointment and anger scratched at me like a knife on porcelain. For Mad Dog, it was personal. He didn't like being made the fool. "This guy could use his smarts to help people . . . like my sister. Instead . . ." Mad Dog wanted the wrath of the scientific world, the press, and the law to pummel Winston into a heap of manure.

A guy in a land rover arrived at our camp and identified himself as the high commissioner of Zambia to Botswana. He'd received a telex with official word that the ferry would run again tomorrow, and we could be on it. News of our plight had reached the right ears, *hallelujah*. Again, I thought, where's the telex in Kasane?

We were the only passengers at the checkpoint the next morning. Immigration officers plunked a big stamp in our passports:

DEPART KAZUNGULA FERRY REPUBLIC OF BOTSWANA

It felt like we'd just passed a board exam.

We walked to the top of the landing and stood on the same soil as before. Mad Dog sat on the ground, knees up, staring at the spot where the ferry blew. My heart hammered like it was going to batter its way out of my throat. Thoughts of Bubba overwhelmed. The loss, his horrific fate, the call to his parents. He must have found out about Winston and was coming to warn us. Winston was responsible for his death. Mad Dog had a flattened stare. I asked if he was okay. Twice, his mouth gestured and faltered. Finally, he said, "I'm impossibly sad."

The owner of the ferry waved at us to come down. Jalina and Emilie were the first to get there. They turned to us before stepping on the gangplank, held their arms in the air and hooted, "Yahoo," extending their pose for a photo op. Travis was squinting upriver. Jalina and Emilie stepped on the gangplank. Travis yelled, "Wait." They didn't hear. He yelled louder. They stopped.

First came the percussive staccato of rotor blades from upstream. A helicopter with quilted beaver brown panels and rectangular doors on each side swept along the riverbank. The doors were open. Men in fatigues sat on the landing rails outside of the helicopter, feet dangling, two men on each side. It flew low and reached the ferry in an instant. Jalina and Emilie dashed up the landing, away from the river. The brassy rat-a-tat-tat of machine gun fire shellacked the ferry. Noxious whiffs of gunpowder. We ran.

"Gotta to be shitting me," I cried in full sprint. We turned to see the soldiers howling, jeering, waving their guns as the helicopter clacked down the river and bore right. A second copter followed, strafing the ferry again and taking out a flagpole that flew the flag of Botswana.

"Rhodesian, Alouette 3 chopper, a hyena cleaning up scraps," Travis mumbled.

The ferry owner shook his fist. Jumped. Screamed. Immigration officers hid. The attack settled one thing: we were never going to try to cross the river again. We had to get out of there—for good. Three days went by. Ten days since the day we woke up and found that the Pink Panther was gone. We were limited to mealie meal, cabbage, and an occasional desert melon. Two soldiers in a jeep visited. It took them several trips, but they moved us back to our old campsite, in Kasane, six miles away. They told us the ferry wasn't running anymore. Gee.

The campsite had been completely abandoned, but the water spigot at the outside bar worked. A full week went by, and then another before a Honda Gold Wing motorcycle roared into camp. A British guy named Charles and his French girlfriend, Violetta, were on their way to the Linyanti Game Reserve, where they intended to camp for a month. "We met in Mexico six years ago. Been camping around the world ever since," he said. He told us that there had been attacks in Lusaka. "There aren't any phones in Linyanti, but I'll let them know of your plight," he said.

More days passed. Ribs protruded on shirtless men. Bernie and Jerry's skin stretched tighter on their cheeks. Mad Dog's shorts fell below his hip bones. Dale's beer belly dissolved, and Quinn's fair skin blotched purple. The plumpness of the women's butts tapered. Cup sizes waned, spurring some to forsake their bras. A local killed a deer and brought us some venison—transient relief for our cravings. Gary crawled into the stockroom behind the bar, found six cans of beans and two cooking pots. We heard gunfire regularly.

Another week passed—thirty-one days since the Pink Panther vanished. The every-other-week mail truck never came. Piss-and-vinegar conversations reigned, and boredom incited lunacy. Dale manufactured a monkey trap from a trash barrel and a discarded radiator but couldn't articulate what he'd do if he caught one. Quinn told nighttime stories of gore and treachery in Dhofar. Jerry's backgammon board exposed new levels of derangement. Emilie read.

We picked at the dolls to see if we could unravel them, but the shellac coating and rubber cement were too firm to do it without damage. Travis said he could sneak across the river, but we'd agreed that we'd figure out what was in the dolls first. And we needed Emilie.

I wanted to find out what drove Tommy/Travis to such extremes. One evening we were by ourselves, sitting on a fallen tree trunk. Dad had told me that Tommy hated the Communist Party. I always suspected he and Dad had been in contact while he was on the run. I asked straight out, "When did you get so political? The last time I saw you, you said that you weren't guilty of the crime you were imprisoned for, but it made up for things you got away with. When did the social consciousness hit you?"

"While I was in prison—in MCI-Walpole."

"Uh-huh. And?"

"Tension between Blacks and Whites—it was wicked inside. I seen a White guy get shanked by a Black guy in the yard with dozens of guys around—twice in the neck, twice in the gut. Two seconds. Then there was payback, which was always worse. Endless cycle of racist hate brought in from the outside. They didn't learn it on the inside. It's just more concentrated in the big house. Nobody wanted it to get better. When Martin Luther King got assassinated, it really cooked me. I started readin.' Talkin.' It evolved rapidly in my heart."

I thought, How sucky, to live every minute worrying about each corner you turn, who was behind you, whether you looked at someone the wrong way. I couldn't think of what to say. *Gee, Tommy, that must have been awful.* Yuk.

"You know what it was like for me growin' up in Eastie and Dorchester. You fight for every penny, for your neighborhood. I earned respect in prison. We had a brotherhood. Curtis LaDuke mentored me. Helped me understand *why* the scales are slanted against us—against anyone who isn't in the elite. I read Che, Mao, Malcolm. I decided I ain't gonna sit back and do nothin'. If I do that, nothin' happens. It'll never get better."

"I got out. Me and Curtis started a bookstore. I learned more. We sold Langston Hughes, James Baldwin, Che, Fanon, Amiri Baraka—people burning with it. You know, fervor. Purpose. It became like a calling. I don't know, like a priest gets a calling. When you just can't help it. We decided we had to be more aggressive. It became a duty. First, we hit the statehouse. Then the courthouse in Boston. And we realized we could *do* this. It got bigger . . ." He looked at me. "I wasn't gonna suck you into it, Danny. Hell, you got a real life—the first one to graduate from college. Let's hope your fancy degree can figure out what that asshole Winston is doing."

"But why the violence? When you guys blew up the Suffolk Courthouse, Mike's friend was in there. His lower leg was blown off."

Tommy swallowed and stared straight ahead. "I didn't know. Tell your brother I'm sorry. Truly sorry. But I can't let it bother me. It might bother me, but I can't change what I'm doing. People in power have no sense of justice. They're arrogant. You see what they are doing with apartheid? With White rule in Rhodesia? How they slant education? Even at home, police target you if you are Black or Hispanic. Prejudicial hiring. Lower pay for the same job."

My father always said that Tommy was a "great kid but has a short fuse." I stayed quiet.

"I killed all them people in Vietnam . . . for what? I'm ashamed. I was s'posedly helping the warmonger generals expand our so-called democracy. But our government only serves those at the top. We don't have a democracy. We have a bunch of fat, dangerous cronies engaged in a constant power grab. I hate them and their lopsided wealth. Not any different than Rhodesia."

Well, I asked. I didn't have an issue with what he said, but I didn't want to imply that I condoned his methods. My cousin Bobby, Travis's brother, had similar views but chose to go the peace, love, and protest route. I'd heard enough, told him I had to take a piss.

The next morning, a guy named Allen showed up at the camp. He was the proprietor of Hunter's Africa, an outfit that took people on hunting trips before the war scared customers away. He told us that the rondavel we encountered when looking for Gary was his. He had a Siemens T-37 telex machine inside, powered by a kerosene generator. Allen's telex was about to make us famous.

CHAPTER 63

Craze: Contacts and Confusions

Allen received a telex. Two Air Botswana pilots were arrested as spies in Lusaka. All flights between Botswana and Lusaka were canceled. This eliminated the option of flying from Francistown to Lusaka—if we could ever get to Francistown.

We learned that Zambia's president, Kenneth Kaunda, was walking a fine line by allowing Nkomo and ZAPU to operate within its borders. He didn't want to go to war with Rhodesia, but his tacit support drew the ire of Ian Smith. ZAPU criticized Kaunda and demanded he provide more food and ammunition, threatening to overthrow the government if he didn't.

Mad Dog and I sent telexes to the US embassies in Zambia, South Africa, England, and Botswana. Jalina and Chris sent the same telex to the British Embassy in Zambia. Doug, Jerry, Gary, and Emilie sent one to the Canadian Embassies in Zambia and South Africa.

```
TOURISTS ON OVERLAND TRIP SOUTH AFRICAN
PLATE 213NJL TO LONDON STRANDED IN
BOTSWANA 5 WEEKS
KAZUNGULA FERRY GONE. VEHICLE SENT VIA
RAIL TO LIVINGSTONE NOW ALL FLTS TO
LUSAKA CANCELED COMPANY TRINDELL TRAVEL
EXPED.LONDON(TELEX 122860 METMAK)
TAKING NO RESPONSIBILITY. CAN YOU AID
OR ADVISE
```

Fergus used Allen's telex to communicate with Marvin. He refused to tell us anything, saying, "It's none of your business," a phrase that

ignited a strombolian fire within each of us. The next day he walked
the six miles to the ferry. When he returned, he told us that two
soldiers would take him to Francistown the next day.

That night a villager brought us a cauldron of locally brewed
beer and an old guitar that had been left behind years before.
Morning hangovers were wretched and deserved. The early rat-a-
tat of machine gun fire crushed any mirth that may have lingered.
It went on for ten minutes, straining our mood and focusing our
acuity.

We checked with Allen. The British Embassy had replied to
Jalina and Chris. They were trying to find transport that could come
to Kasane and take us to Francistown. From there they'd convey us
by rail to Johannesburg. None of the US embassies replied.
Another round of gunfire began. Fergus left for Francistown with
the soldiers.

When the sun set that night, I picked up the guitar, found a spot
out of earshot, and started picking out Neil Diamond's song, "Play
Me." Alex loved the message in that song—two people finding each
other, different people with different things to offer. Jalina
wandered over and slid next to me. Without speaking, she wrapped
her arm around my waist. My eyes welled. She squeezed. Tears
leaked. The events of the past months were caving in.

One emotion triggered another completely unrelated emotion.
I liked Jalina and by now felt some affection for her. She was a
friend, not just someone I was friendly with. That affection made
me think of Alex and how I'd screwed that up. Somehow that led
to thinking of Bubba and then to the stress of carrying the
Matryoshka dolls, the dangerous spot we were in, running into my
revolutionary cousin, and now feeling a moral obligation to find out
what Winston Walsh and the Rhodesians were up to. Meeting
Travis made me feel I was deficient in some way. He had passions
that I never had. He was committed to something. I didn't know if
I truly had a vacuum in my heart, or if I was normal and he was the
freak.

Jalina didn't ask. She seemed to understand my need for self-
examination. She kissed my cheek. Softly, a bit more than a peck.
Then did so again. I turned my head intending to thank her for

offering comfort. But my lips reached for hers. They were salty from the tears. She paid no heed. It was nice. She pressed harder. Her tongue parted my lips. She went deep. I felt ashamed for liking it. I wilted. I convinced myself that I deserved a mental furlough, that the concoction of circumstance allowed for irregular conduct. I kissed her back. Her mouth was wet and soft. Moral pretense perished, and I succumbed for an accusable duration. Calling whatever force influenced my spirit, I pulled back and throttled to a tender hug.

The next day, telexes from the Australian and Canadian embassies came in. Both were making inquiries on transport. The Canadian embassy looked into arranging a helicopter but was discouraged from doing so given the recent attacks at the border. Mad Dog and I were pissed off at the US embassies. Four embassies. No response.

Co-Don heard from Fergus. The Pink Panther was in Livingstone waiting for us. We had to get out of Kasane. No shit! Marvin would pay for a train from Francistown to Johannesburg. From there we would have to pay for a flight to Malawi and then hitchhike, yes *hitchhike*, three hundred miles to Chipata on the Zambian frontier border. Fergus would retrieve the truck in Livingstone and pick us up in Chipata. "Go fuck a duck," Big-Don said. Swears were strung together in combinations that I'd never heard. Bernie sent a response:

```
THIS IS NOT A HITCHHIKING TOUR.
WHERE IS OUR TRANSPORT?
ARE YOU WILLING TO LEAVE US STRANDED
HERE?
```

Marvin must have misread the telex or thought it came from Co-Don. He replied,

```
YES, LEAVE THEM STRANDED THERE
```

We seethed. Bernie briefed everyone when we got back to camp. Civility vanquished. "We could kill him," Quinn suggested.

Next day breakfast, Big-Don was perched on a rock, smirking like a boy who'd licked the candles on the cake. "You should be at the front of the class fuming," I said. "Where's the caustic Don? Where's the vitriol? Where's the bombastic acrimony?"

Big-Don waited . . . enough time for all heads to turn his way. He spoke. "I sent a telex to Reuters yesterday afternoon. They've picked up our story. They are going to follow up with Trindell before they release it to print."

"What do you mean?" Emilie asked. "You contacted Reuters? *The* Reuters?"

Big-Don made a poor attempt to be coy. He was the oldest in the group, and his inner cockiness was now unharnessed. Going forward, he would be our kingpin. "Yes, Reuters international news agency. The biggest news agency in the world."

CHAPTER 64

"Nothing, Gus. Still don't know who the mole is. Bobby Diggs had enough men in position to cover the entire airport. If a tsetse fly was following me, they'd have spotted it."

Winston heard Gus spit into a cup, freeing the white, ropey buildup of saliva from the chaw in his cheek. "Gunge, Winston. Your Americans never met Ron's guy at the Leopard Spot. The ferry blew before they got there. They're still mucking around in Botswana somewhere."

"Well aware, Gus. Saw the ferry news in the *International Herald*. Who did it?"

"Reid doesn't know. He heard from his scout after the ferry, but not since. We assume he's chasing your pals down. If this guy can't find the dolls, you'll have to—

"Not possible. Doctor gave me an absolute *No* to flying. Last time I flew, the blood clot almost killed me. If Ron's guy doesn't find them, I'll go overland. Deliver them myself."

"Hmph. You'll figure it out. I remember when you were nine years old, still living in Rhodesia. You'd taught yourself basic concepts of aerodynamics and took some membrane material that your parents used to process nickel. You cut it into synthetic wings and glued them onto the smaller wings of wasps you'd trapped. Thought they'd be able to fly faster."

"Ha. My killer wasp force. Father had a good laugh at that one."

CHAPTER 65

Craze: Wayward Wheels

The telex at Hunter's Africa became our universe. Reuters sent a telex to Dave (Mad Dog) Hill. Big-Don had told Mad Dog to expect it. They wanted to hear the story from a second source. Ten of us gawked at the telex machine like we were watching a launch at Cape Kennedy. A real conversation, back and forth. Mad Dog replied:

MANY THANKS. FERRY NO GO. NO TRANSPORT. EXPECTED TO HITCHHIKE TO FRANCISTOWN. PROPOSAL UNZEEE UNACCEPTABLE. DRIVER LEFT. CO-DRIVER TOLD TO LEAVE US BEHIND IF WE CAN GET OUT. ADVICE?

HOW ARE YOU FARING FOR FOOD?

ADEQUATE, BUT DIMINISHING

ANY ILL HEALTH

NO JUST STRANDED

IS THE ENTIRE GROUP STILL IN KASANE?

YES WE WANT TO GET TO FRANCIXTOWN

CBC TORONTO HAS PICKED UP STORY. ANY MESSAGES FROM THE CANADIANS

PLS STRANDED BUT OKAY IN GOOD HEALTH

PLEASURE. IS THEIR POSITION THAT YOU NOW HVE TO HITCH TO FRANCISTOWN?

YES

WHEN DO YOU THINK YOU WILL START?

AS SOON AS ANY TRANSPORT IS AVAILABLE. RIDES FROM LODGE GUESTS HEADING SOUTH?

```
NO  LODGE  GUESTS.  SORRY.  HOPING  LOCAL
TRANSPORT TRUCKS WILL COME BY.

OK THTS ABOUT IT. HOPE ALL GOES WELL.
WILL KEEP UP PRESSURE HERE.

END
```

Daily telexes followed. Marvin's reply of, "Yes, leave them stranded there," was like red meat to Reuters. The *Toronto Globe* and CBC Radio Canada reported the story, as did newspapers in South Africa, the USA, Australia, and the UK. Allen heard it on the Air Gaborone radio.

Travis scowled. "We don't want this kind of attention."

"If they help us get out of here, we'll probably end up back in Johannesburg. We can surely find the solvents there. I was thinking of telling Emilie what's going on. If I wait 'til we get to Jo'burg, she might skip away from us. I think I'm going to need her help."

"Not yet. The less time she has to keep a secret, the better."

Three more days passed. At last, a tired savior dropped into our lap. A DAF flatbed truck with "Coley Hall" lettering on the grill pulled into Kasane. It was a supply truck that had been sitting idle in the Linyanti Game Reserve due to the lack of tourism. "Heard about you folks from Charles and Violetta. I'm on my way to Francistown, thought I'd swing by. It'll be uncomfortable, but you can ride in the back."

"Glory be. I may reform my ways," exalted Hanna, who still wore makeup after being stranded for six weeks. It was a green ten-wheeler. Removable, rusted, two-foot panels surrounded the bed. Tires were bare, windshield cracked, and the cab smelled like a marathoner's underwear. To us, it was Noah's Ark.

We left the next afternoon. The ride was painfully slow, but we were moving. With no covering over the bed, the all-too-familiar dust choked us, caked our hair. Quinn took a pair of his black underwear, yanked his head through a leg hole, and used it a mask. He swore they were clean. We knew better. The metal bed dug into our sit bones, forcing cycles of shifting from one uncomfortable position to another. The driver lasted until late afternoon before the sweltering cab forced him to stop. We were so tired we rolled out our sleeping bags on the ground, not bothering to set up tents.

The next day we slogged into Francistown at five o'clock. We never thought we'd be so happy to see our old campsite. The one where the truck had disappeared.

Co-Don went to the train station and returned with tickets for the seventeen-hour ride to Mafikeng on the South African border. It left at 6:00 p.m. the next day. We looked at the tickets. Fourth class. Cars that carry cages with small livestock, exposed to billowing black smoke from the coal-fired engines. Big-Don sent a telex to Reuters, telling them about the fourth-class tickets. Continued wrongful conduct. We spent a few extra Pula and upgraded to second class, but Big-Don didn't tell Reuters. "Let them print the truth. They bought us fourth-class tickets."

Gary, Mad Dog, and I cooked a magnificent breakfast of eggs, ham, toast, and potatoes for breakfast. The locals laughed. We were like kids who kept running away and returning. Hanna noticed that Co-Don was missing. Gary dismissively said, "Yeah, he found a ride to Mafikeng and is going ahead of us—to prime the immigration officers for our arrival."

Big-Don cockled his lips. A nostril flared. "You didn't think to tell us this until now?"

It was already in the news. Bernie picked up the afternoon issue of the *Rhodesia Chronicle*, which read, "The second driver left the group of tourists alone without a leader."

"This is fucked," Travis said. "Reid thinks I'm trying to find you guys. With all this press, I won't have any excuses."

He was right. People in the shops and restaurants asked us if we were okay. Local officials expressed concern for our well-being. As a courtesy, they sectioned off an area of the train for us. The ride to the border took twenty hours. Doug, Jerry, Graham, and Cathy had visa problems and couldn't get back into South Africa. Co-Don was nowhere to be seen. The border police called Trindell Travel. Trindell refused to accept the charges. We agreed not to continue without them. We wanted the group to meet Marvin in force—with all of us there. Locals offered to let us stay in their homes. The people of Mafikeng rocked.

I swallowed a train-station-grade grilled cheese and tomato for breakfast. The entry visa problems were resolved by four o'clock.

By then, Emilie had been interviewed by CBC for a fifteen-minute special, and the *Daily Mail* in London put the story on the front page. Australian ABC National TV gave daily reports. Reuters had become our advocate for some reason. Big-Don said they may even offer legal assistance.

Marvin had gone to the train station in Johannesburg that morning, expecting us to arrive. Had the driver or co-driver of the trip been with us, he would have known we weren't on the train. Had Marvin accepted charges for the phone call from the border police, he would have known there were visa problems and we weren't on the train.

But now we were together again. United. We caught the 11:55 p.m. train for the ten-hour trip to Johannesburg.

Part III
Bigotry

Convoy meeting point, Bulawayo, Rhodesia

CHAPTER 66

Craze: The Siege of Rissik Street

Marvin stood on the platform looking rakish in a blue blazer, red-and-black striped tie, and glossy brown monk shoes, double-buckled. His hair was perfect, toffee blond covering his ears, slicked back, and incandescent. "Look at him, all spiffed up for the press," Quinn carped.

Jalina turned her head. "Ew. You'd think he had a date with Sophia Loren."

Big-Don had asked us to put on a ragged look for the cameras, which we were happy to do given all the bullshit Trindell had pulled: parking the truck on a down slope and secretly hushing it away; stranding us in remote Botswana for six weeks without food or transport; telling us to fly to Malawi and hitchhike three hundred miles to meet the Pink Panther. I'd rubbed a T-shirt against the side of the train and put it on. Mad Dog put on a shirt that hadn't been washed since the Ivory Coast. We conspired to don cheerless faces for the press.

A punctilious version of Co-Don stood next to Marvin. Someone must have told him to wash his hair and button up. Fergus was absent, probably on his way to Zambia to pick up the Pink Panther. When we stepped off the train, Marvin held out his hand. Nobody acknowledged. Six photographers jockeyed and flashed. Twice as many reporters scurried, thrusting microphones in our faces. Big-Don spoke for us, underscoring our shameful treatment and citing our rawboned cheeks and scraggy attire. We gathered for a group shot. Photographers insisted on angry faces. Front page.

It was a mile to the Trindell office on Rissik Street. Marvin had arranged for two vans to take us there. Before going into the building, I talked to Travis, who was busy formulating a story to explain to both Sipho and Colonel Reid why he was delayed.

"Tell him this," I said. "You came after us after the ferry blew. You crossed the river, went to Kasane, but by the time you got there we were gone—and there was no transport for a couple of days. You followed the signal to the Okavango, but it was transmitting from the middle of the swamps."

Travis flushed his torso to within an inch of mine and said, "Mm. All true."

"Yeah. You canoed out to the signal. Found the Rainmaker village. They told you that the elder traded an eland pelt and a blow pipe for the dolls and a mysterious chip. But the next day the elder traded the dolls to someone else."

Travis was barely audible. "And I've been running around the swamps trying to find the dolls. One story. One lie that works for both Sipho and Reid. Reid will have seen the signal go to the middle of the swamp. It gives me an open-ended timeline. Hm, I could tell Sipho the truth, but I want to find out what's in the dolls first. I trust Sipho, but still, I don't trust anyone now."

Travis closed his eyes. That smile crawled back onto his face. "You're learnin', Craze."

I beamed, like I'd earned my tenderfoot badge in spy school . . . and he called me Craze.

At the Trindell office, Marvin said he'd booked rooms at the Alendene Hotel in the nearby Hillbrow neighborhood. "Your tasks are to check into the Alendene and book your flight to Malawi. Payment for the hotel is your responsibility. When you get to Malawi, you have to find a way to get to Chapata. Fergus will be waiting for you at the border."

Bernie pulled at his goatee. "'Find a way.' Is that what they call hitchhiking now?"

"That is the plan. It's the only plan," Marvin said, playing dumb, deflecting. His fallback line was, "You'll have to take it up with London," knowing we were in no position to do so.

We had planned for this event on the train. Big-Don's lips broke their normally rounded form. He smiled, strode over to Marvin, got into his space and calmly unwrapped our game plan. "We have already paid you to take us from Johannesburg to London. That included transport, food, and accommodation. You now expect us to pay for it again. We aren't leaving this office until you honor your contract."

Marvin's Ken doll face turned to quartz; threads of his dapper attire unfastened. He hadn't grasped the color of Big-Don's words yet. Big-Don rephrased, enunciating one word at a time. "We are going to stay in this office until you provide us with accommodations and transport." Co-Don threw back his long hair and grinned. He'd seen the ferry explode. He knew our friend was killed. He saw us eat mealie meal and cabbage for weeks. He knew that stealing the truck away was an odious ploy. He understood—we were staging an old fashion sit-in.

Marvin scanned the room to see who was on board. Eyes pierced through him. It was a sanctioned act. He placed both palms on his desk and leaned. "Aw. You can't stay here."

Veronica, Bernie's normally quiet wife, lifted her tiny frame and dragged a chair over to Marvin. She stood on the chair so she could be nose to nose with Marvin. Her face was red. "We've been sleeping outside on the edge of the Kalahari. We've been sleeping in dust bowls and swamps. We've been bombed, shot at, had our truck and food taken from us, and have eaten more dirt than an earthworm. If we can do that, we can certainly sleep on the floor of your bloody office." She hesitated, arms straight down, fists squeezed, and added, "You fucking Pommy prick!" The room erupted. I'd never laughed so hard. This tiny woman undressed Marvin and exposed the sock in his pants. Veronica sat.

Marvin snaked to the corner of the room and motioned for Co-Don to join him. They talked. We reveled in his ashes. He returned to his desk, sat, and continuously rapped his fingers, seemingly intent on annoying us. "He thinks we're bluffing," Jalina whispered. An hour passed. Marvin smoked. Did a crossword puzzle. Another hour. He put his hand on the phone, said he was calling the police. We shrugged. He removed his hand. Police meant more press.

Twenty more minutes. He tried again, this time lifting the phone to his ear, surveying the room for a reaction. He dialed. Slow learner, I thought. The police answered. There was a discussion, but Marvin told them it wasn't necessary to come. He hung up, said he'd lock the doors on anyone who left the room to go to one of the hallway lavatories. We stayed. The sun set. Droopy rays cast by the mercury vapor of the fluorescent lights replaced natural light.

We decided to send Big-Don and Dale out of the office, knowing they wouldn't get back in. Big-Don had the Reuters contacts, and Dale would be a mature, effective partner. People sat on rolled-out sleeping bags and played cards. Big-Don called Reuters. They sent a reporter right away. Dale called the police. When they arrived, he showed them several newspaper articles. They knew who we were. Reporters from the *Sunday Express* and the *Star* arrived, expecting us to be arrested.

The police knocked on the office door and asked Marvin to join them in the lobby, where Big-Don and Dale waited, along with full-dress policemen who stood erect, chins up, in their shiny brimmed service caps. Big-Don told us later that much of the conversation was about public perception. This kind of thing didn't happen in South Africa. But we were international tourists—and we were White. South Africa struggled with its image and didn't want to get into the muck with a story that the press had already spun in our favor. According to Big-Don, the police asked Marvin why the company was trying to screw us.

The sergeant said, "They're not breaking any laws. Haven't done anything wrong." He suggested Marvin call Trindell's headquarters in London. Marvin returned to the office to make the call. He asked us to wait in the hallway. The police assured us they'd let us back in after the call. Everyone ran to the bathrooms. From the hallway, we could hear Stephen Williams, the chief executive of Trindell, yelling through the phone at Marvin. Marvin hung up.

"If you don't leave the office by 10:30, the trip will be abolished," Marvin told us. We sat, stone-faced. We asked what abolished meant. He was evasive—probably didn't know himself. Gary stood. He was pale and his lower jaw shimmied. I could barely hear him say it. "I've had enough. Good luck, guys." He left.

Hours passed before Stephen Williams called Marvin back. He said that the tour was now "withdrawn," and "there won't be any refunds." I swear he wanted us to beg our way back onto the tour. Co-Don came back. Marvin wouldn't let him in. He tossed a rope to Doug and told us to go to the window. We did. The press wanted a photo. Doug dropped the rope out the window. Dale attached two bags of sandwiches, fruit, chips, and soda to the end of the rope.

At 1:30 a.m., Marvin said he was leaving and was going to padlock the door behind him. "You'll have no food or lavatory for the entire weekend."

Mad Dog said, "We can haul up food. And below that side window is a roof we can crap on." A cheer erupted in the office.

Twice Marvin bluffed like he was leaving. Then he went with Co-Don to the lobby to meet with the police and told them he wasn't pressing charges. When we exited the building, flashbulbs popped. Travis was across the street, collar up, brim of his hat pulled low. "Now you've done it," he said, hackles frozen on his neck.

We slept at the Alendene Hotel that night on Trindell's dime. The next morning the front page of the *Sunday Express* read: "The Siege of Rissik Street." There was an edge-to-edge photo of Marvin, Co-Don, and three policemen meeting in the lobby, and another photo with an arrow pointing to the sixth-floor window.

CHAPTER 67

Travis: Weathermen Unite

Travis called Sipho and told him he'd tracked the signal to the Okavango, only to find out that the Americans had traded the dolls to an elder, who, in turn, traded them to someone else.

"Damn it, Travis. I don't like it."

"Trading is how the Rainmakers live. Don't worry. I've got a bead on the dolls. I'll hunt them down. You have to trust me."

Sipho grumbled, "That's exactly what I've been doing. Those dolls better not get into the wrong hands. You better find them."

"Yep."

Sipho said he'd spoken to Cameron, the head of Weathermen Africa in London. "I told him about the change in plans, that we're going to find out what is hidden in the walls of the dolls before destroying them. He agreed. I promised the dolls will never reach the pharmaceutical firm in Rhodesia."

"What about stopping this Winston Walsh guy in Liberia?" asked Travis.

"We have someone inside there. They've worked with us on a plan to stop him. Not an easy decision for her. Bold. We're going to destroy all sources of the information in Liberia. Will also destroy the weekly backup tapes that are sent to Switzerland. By the time we're through, the only place the genetic and manufacturing information will exist will be within the walls of those dolls. Understood?"

"Completely."

CHAPTER 68

Craze: Gemsbok

We squeezed into Jalina's room and spent the morning deciding who would talk to the next reporter. They smelled a story of chicanery and wanted exclusive information on danger and death, the ferry explosion, helicopter attack, and the siege of Rissik Street.

"You guys are relentless," said a camel-haired charmer with a shamefaced grin who plunked a bag of Dutch donuts on the table. Heads turned, and at first were scorn-filled. "I'm back in if you'll have me," he said. Jalina looked to the ceiling. Chris sighed. It was hard to stay mad at Gary.

"Who's that with you?" Mad Dog asked, referring to a woman standing in the hallway.

He called us out to meet her. "This is Jayne Lamont. From the *Rand Daily Mail*. Wants to write about my arrest and the loss of your friend, Bubba."

"Human interest angles. Anger, fear, loss," she said.

My head dropped. I realized I hadn't thought about Bubba for a couple of days.

"Yes," Mad Dog said, loud and without equivocation.

I asked Gary and Jayne to give us a moment. He and Jayne stepped down the hall.

"You sure, Dog? Travis won't be happy."

"He gave his life trying to warn us. It's our chance to honor him. We can make the story about *him*. His character. Mr. and Mrs. Brewster didn't even get to bury their son. We can at least make them proud. Say what good friends say. Let them know . . ." Mad Dog's voice parched. ". . . what he meant to us."

A cloud of sorrow engulfed me. We went to our room to grab our jackets. Travis was there, sitting on my bed. "Going out to find a pharmacy that has 100 percent alcohol. You comin'?"

"Um. Can't now. Maybe later." I didn't dare tell him we were going to talk to a reporter, even if we planned to keep it generic. "I think it's time to bring Emilie into this," I said. "She could decide to leave at any time. Things are skittish. Look what Gary did last night." He nodded.

I slid a note under Emilie's door, asking her to meet us at the Gemsbok Coffee Shop at three o'clock. I told her to come alone.

During our walk to the *Rand Daily Mail*, Mad Dog asked Gary why he left the Trindell office early. "I choked," he said. "The police. Threats from Trindell. The arrest in Kasane made me jumpy." So much had happened, I'd forgotten that he was arrested and detained in Kasane.

A picture of Steve Biko, an anti-apartheid activist with a group called the Black Consciousness, greeted us in the lobby. Jayne told us that "the *Mail*" broke the story of his death in 1977. The government had banned him from speaking in public. He couldn't talk to more than one person at a time. They claimed he incited racial confrontations. While on a trip to Cape Town, Biko was arrested at a traffic stop, jailed, stripped, and later severely beaten and died.

Jayne drilled us with questions and typed amber-colored letters onto a CRT screen. She was able to erase words, fix spelling, and move sentences around using something called a Lynolex system. "He loved his parents very much," Mad Dog said. "They taught him honesty and respect." The Dog can be a master, I thought. Says so much with so few words. At the deadline, the room turned into a tornado. Jayne hastily confirmed our names and addresses.

Gary gave me an odd look. "Did you say you're from Massachusetts?"

"Yes, a small town called Norwell." His cheek puffed. He muttered a line or two of the Bee Gees song "Massachusetts." He looked at his watch and said he was off to meet Big-Don and Bernie. They were going to meet with his lawyer friend.

Nearly everyone was interviewed that day, generating headlines: "Tourist Group Stranded in Remote Botswana," "Stranded Tourists Will Seek Court Hearing," "The Siege of Rissik Street," "Crackdown Leaves Tourists Stranded," "Norwellians in Hairy African Adventure," "Holiday of a Lifetime Goes Bust," "Irate Clients Locked in Tour Office."

Emilie walked into the Gemsbok Coffee Shop at exactly three o'clock and sat down with Mad Dog, Travis, and me. A travel agent in Canada had offered to pay the Canadians' airfare to Malawi, but Emilie told them she was sticking with the group.

I raised my eyebrows and said to Travis, "See?"

Mad Dog opened. "Emilie, we have something to run by you . . . it's confidential."

She snickered and looked at me as if to say, *What are you guys up to now?*

We'd intended to be vague, but Emilie lived in science. Besides, I needed to talk to someone of her ilk, and holding it in was making me crazy. I told her about the research center in Liberia; about Winston Walsh and his gene-editing technology, and how he'd wrapped the manufacturing instructions into the walls of a set of Matryoshka-like nesting dolls we were carrying; how delivery of the protocols to a pharmaceutical in Zambia had been thwarted three times—probably by an insider.

Travis cut in. "Emilie . . . These dolls were never supposed to go to a pharmaceutical company in Zambia. They were supposed to go to a pharmaceutical in Rhodesia."

"What? You have something to do with this, Travis? But you just . . ."

"Showed up in Maun. Yes." Travis said.

I could almost see her brain churning behind her mahogany irises.

Her voice softened. "What do you mean when you say gene editing? You can't exchange one nucleotide in a gene sequence for another. That's silly."

"That's exactly what I'm saying. They can find a specific gene by looking at repeating sequences of the nucleotides." I looked at Mad Dog. "The ATCGs." He nodded. "They know how to find a specific nucleotide—adenine, thymine, guanine, or cytosine—and replace it with another. They can cut out thymine and replace it with guanine, or cut out adenine and replace it with cytosine."

Her eyelids dropped. "Robert Holley and Fred Sanger tried to do gene sequencing in the mid-'60s. That was on yeast and E. coli. The first complete sequencing of a gene wasn't reported until seven years ago, around 1972. And that was sequencing, not editing."

"I'm telling you; this place is decades ahead of mainstream science. They seem to have endless funding and have assembled a team of the best scientists in genetics and nanotechnology."

"Nanotechnology? For what? To deliver the active components?"

Travis's eyes flitted with each volley. He stared at me like I was a stranger.

"But if they edit just one nucleotide, the DNA will code for a different amino acid. The gene will produce a different protein.

"Protein. A string of amino acids linked together," Mad Dog droned.

"Like the lac bug," Travis laughed, referring to Dog's previous discourse on shellac.

"Exactly," I said. "And since it's being changed in the DNA, it's forever."

Emilie's voice faltered. Creepiness was setting in. "Oh, Craze. I don't know."

"The details are over my head. In general, if you know which nucleotide you want to edit, and you know the hundred or two hundred nucleotides on either side of it, the sequence is unique enough to identify the specific one you want to cut out and replace."

"Hm. Finding it is one thing, but replacing it with another?"

"Winston said something about using a protein attached to an RNA strand that is a mirror image of the A's, T's, C's, and G's in the DNA."

Travis's blue eyes looked like he'd met a ghost. "This is like a bad movie," he said.

"Correct," Mad Dog said.

I explained how Winston told us that his intent was to rid the world of malaria by making mosquitoes resistant to the malarial parasite. Then it hit Emilie in the same way it hit me when Winston explained it in Liberia. "It's brilliant, you know. So much could be done . . ."

I stopped her. Travis signaled that it was okay to tell her more. I told her about Travis being embedded in the Selous Scouts, that it was how he'd learned that the instructions were really intended go to a pharmaceutical in Rhodesia.

She thought for a moment. "Does it matter? As long as malaria is eliminated . . ."

"That's the thing," Travis said. It's not about malaria. They're going to use it to harm the native peoples in Rhodesia. To help them win the war and maintain White rule in Rhodesia."

Emilie pushed on her long hair. "Mother Madonna. What are they going to do?"

"We don't know . . . exactly," Travis said. "That's what we need help with. I don't know what you two are talkin' about with all the nucleo bullshit, but I know what I seen in the eyes of Colonel Reid. Sounds like it will devastate the Black people in Rhodesia."

"The answer is in the dolls," I said. "Help me interpret the information. Will you do it?"

Travis reached under the table and pulled a bottle out of his pack. "Martinis anyone?" He'd found 100 percent alcohol and bought three liters of it.

Mad Dog pumped his fist and leaned into the center of the table. "Could this be used to change the genes that can make someone's eyes blue?"

Emilie grimaced, unwilling to answer.

Travis followed with, "What about hair color? And ain't color blindness genetic? Or how about them dwarfs or the Down's syndrome people?"

I was about to say yes, but Travis took it one step further. "Emilie, is there a gene that makes you smart? Or—or can you change genes that make you age?"

Emilie rubbed her face with the heels of her palms, and then locked her hands behind her neck. She muttered a French word she never used. *"Putain!"*

CHAPTER 69

Sausage, eggs, and chips for breakfast. "You're scarfing down your food like a seagull on amphetamines," Mad Dog said. "And your earlobes look dry."

"My earlobes look dry?" Sometimes he just tries to irritate me. I hate how he can always read me. "Travis doesn't know," I said.

Mad Dog put down his fork, picked a chunk of gristle from his teeth, and folded his arms.

"The lawsuit. I didn't tell him we were joining."

"We have to. First, we are going to fuck over this company. Then we are going to fuck over Winston. I don't like being the chump—the border guys in the Ivory Coast, Winston, Trindell. We should just give Travis the dolls and be done with it. Let them figure it out."

"Sure. Then how do we fuck over Winston? No. Emilie and I have to figure it out first. Besides, now I want to know what's in the dolls. His handler, this guy Sipho? He used to be in bed with the White Rhodesians. Could change sides with the wind."

"Yeah."

"With the media attention, we have a better chance to expose Winston to the scientific community, to the world. And the media will be all over this lawsuit."

We piled into the office of Bowfillan, Gilman & Blackdock in the United Towers building on Main Street to meet with Andrew Dunard. Andrew had read the newspapers. He knew of our plight before he met with Gary, Big-Don, Dale, and Bernie. He impressed, with his pressed woolen trousers and fitted Coofandy waistcoat that dovetailed over his athletic frame. His suit jacket hung on a mahogany oxford valet in the corner. Andrew welcomed us with a bourbon-coated voice, professional, with an aggressive edge that suggested it could unleash if necessary.

Jalina sat beside me wearing a short, burnt-orange cord skirt with a front zipper and a cheetah-print blouse that barely reached her waistline.

"You look nice," I said.

"Stutterford's," she said. She crossed her legs and pulsed her foot up and down to the rhythm of the Howard Miller clock on the wall. The outside of her dancer's thigh brushed against mine.

Andrew paced and rubbed his thumb on the tip of his pointer and middle finger as he spoke. "The arrogance and lack of concern from this company has stirred my mothering instincts. Your case is unusual because you are peregrines—the Roman term for foreigners who are free citizens from another country. Trindell is a UK firm. You are foreigners suing another foreigner for a breach of contract that occurred in a foreign land—Botswana. South African courts can only exercise jurisdiction of such a request in two circumstances: First, if the latter were arrested. Second, if the latter had its assets attached by the court. By attached, I mean either the sheriff seizes their assets, or the bank freezes their accounts. Questions?

Mad Dog flashed at Jalina's legs and skipped his eyes aside, as if looking at the sun. He whispered, "Craze, did you call Alex yet?"

Andrew noticed and addressed Mad Dog. "Yes. A question?"

"Where is the nearest place to make a phone call home—to the United States?" Andrew, froze, perplexed by the irrelevance of the question. After a pause he said there was an office next to American Express on Joubert Street.

What are you doing? I don't need you to remind me. You know I'm in a panic about Alex already. We'd been in South Africa for three days, and I hadn't called her yet. Mad Dog was being a friend whether I liked it or not. He'd seen the tension between Jalina and me sharpening. To be honest, I was scared. The phone call would change the direction of my life, regardless of her answer to my proposal. I was afraid because I wasn't worthy of the answer I wanted. I tried to pinpoint why I felt that way but had trouble shaping my specific failings. Should I spend energy searching for something without knowing what I was looking for? I didn't know whether those last few tangibles were buried so deep in the rubble they couldn't be reached, or if I was shielding them so forcefully, I couldn't see them. She deserved more—I knew that. She was the jewel, but for some reason she loved me.

A couple of months had passed since Bubba died. Time can prey on emotions. Not like a bluefish that takes a single, violent, chomp from a poagie; more like a cod that nibbles at a clam on your beak hook, making you question if it's really there. Every time I laced up my boots, or looked at those dolls, or listened to Gary talk like a goofball, I thought of Bubba. I missed him. Once or twice he told me he loved me, but I didn't say it back. We didn't talk like that in my family. When he said it, I felt warm inside, surprised, but touched. Still, my body went ew all over. Not knowing what to do, my mouth would respond with a hapless quip.

Of course, I wanted to hear Alex say yes. When I left for Africa that morning, she still wanted to marry me. Go with that—call her, you chicken shit.

Andrew talked. "Unfortunately, this company doesn't have much to attach in the Transvaal. Some office furniture, brochures, small equipment—worth very little. "

"I thought they had another truck in South Africa," Gary said.

"Possibly. But they've either hidden it or gotten it out of South Africa. I reviewed your case with a colleague who is an experienced junior advocate. In his opinion, Trindell's meager assets are enough for now. If we attach anything, regardless of its value, we can establish jurisdiction. Once we establish jurisdiction, the court can hear us on the breach of contract case."

"How long will this take?" Emilie asked. Heads bobbed.

"I specialize in applications to the court to enforce rights and obligations. It's a path for quick justice, done by submitting an affidavit—provided the evidence isn't in dispute. Marvin is being served a subpoena as we speak. This afternoon, Bernie, Dale, and Don will finish the affidavit we started yesterday. Bernie will be what we call the first applicant—technically he will tell the story and you will review it and attest to its truth. Don will bring you copies of the final affidavit this evening. You will sign at 8:00 a.m. tomorrow. I asked for an emergency hearing. The court understands that you are international tourists and can't just hang around. We go to court tomorrow afternoon.

"Jesus Christmas, tomorrow?" Jalina expressed our happy astonishment.

"Yes, 14:15. Come to this office at 8:00 a.m. to be sworn in before you sign the affidavit. We will include other documents along with the affidavit: a copy of their brochure, a copy of the letter you sent them from Francistown, their booking form, contract terms, and receipts."

Andrew addressed Mad Dog and me. "I understand you have the original telexes sent from Kasane. I'll need to make a copy."

"What should we wear? To court." Hanna seemed eager to brandish the best possible combination of tight pants and blouse. Andrew laughed.

"Come as you are." He sobered his delivery. "Most importantly, be on time. You won't have to speak. We will submit three motions. We'll ask for a full refund, what you paid for the trip. Second, we will ask for an attachment of all Trindell's bank accounts, trucks, office furniture, equipment, and anything else of value in South Africa. Third, we will ask that they pay your legal fees. I intend to apply as much pressure on these buggers as possible."

CHAPTER 70

Travis: Swamp Talk

"I've been running all over the swamps trying to track down the dolls, Colonel. The Bushmen are a close-mouthed group. And it's hard to find one that speaks English. I want to hunt down the Americans and kill them just for being idiots."

"They traded the dolls for a fucking deer pelt and a blowgun? I didn't like it when I saw that signal go into the swamps and never come out," Reid said.

"Sir, I may need a few guys to help. Do a systematic comb of the villages in the Okavango to find the dolls." *He'll never go for that. Needs his men to fight the bush war.*

"This was a simple mission, Travis."

"Seemed so. You didn't tell me the ferry was going blow up, sir."

There was a pause. Finally, Reid said, "The ferry. Mm. You heard anything about that? I've checked around. It wasn't us."

"I was just waiting around the campground, sir. Nothing suspicious there."

"Hm . . . all right."

Travis didn't like the probing trills and elongation of words hidden in Reid's tone. He'd only met Reid twice, but it was enough to recognize his normal cadence.

"How do you know this Boesman is telling the truth?" Reid asked. "Ever think of that? Maybe the Americans still have the dolls."

The blister of Reid's *Boesman* slur lit Travis. "He's a Hambukushu elder, sir. Respected head of the Rainmakers of the Okavango." *Shouldn't have said that!*

"How's that?"

"I know one thing, sir. The Americans were there, with the elder. He had the transmitter from the shoe. Not sure when the Americans found it, but they left it with the elder. Probably wanted to throw off whoever planted it."

"Which means, they might still have the dolls. Have you seen the news?"

He lied. "Just got out of the swamps an hour ago. I'm in Maun."

"Well, the Americans are in Johannesburg—along with the whole crew from that trip. They are all over the newspapers, TV, radio. My bet is they still have the dolls. Get your ass to Johannesburg."

CHAPTER 71

Craze: Court Supreme

We packed into Andrew's office, were sworn in, and took an oath that the statements in the affidavit were true. We signed. The header of the affidavit read: "The Supreme Court of South Africa, Witwatersrand: Case 79–9189."

What? The Supreme Court!

Neither Mad Dog nor I had been involved in any court case before, yet, that afternoon we found ourselves walking down Pritchard Street to the Supreme Court of South Africa. Directly in front of the courtroom gate, a taxi stand sign read: "Staanplek Vir Blankes" (Taxi Stand for Whites). Next to it was a bench you could sit on—if you were White. "Whites Only." Two blocks away was a bench for "Non-Europeans Only." White people weren't allowed to sit there. It was for Africans, Coloreds, and Asians.

"What did you eat in Botswana?" "How close were you to the ferry when it exploded?" "Anything to say to Trindell in London?" We ignored reporters as we walked through the iron gates, up the granite steps, and through a Victorian archway to the court. The texture inside was dark and wooden. Somber russet tones stained the benches and walls, but the "Whites Only" rectangular signs on the benches of the Supreme Court were gleaming. Andrew, Big-Don, Dale, Gary, Bernie, and Veronica were already in front of the public section on the right side of the court. The rest of us took residence behind them. Barristers sat in the middle benches, all White men wearing white wigs that hung to the shoulders. It looked like a fistful of tampons had been neatly glued to a drapery that clung to their heads. Andrew would not speak. He had briefed the barrister on the case. The barrister would present to the court.

The clerk called our case. Neither Marvin nor any representative from Trindell showed up to honor the subpoena, an act of disrespect that made Supreme Court Justice Preiss sneer and disparage Trindell's integrity. Our barrister showed his talents. Tissues and tears flowed as he projected theatrical tones of disgust and disbelief, that anyone could treat such wonderful young adventurers like this. His eloquence would induce anyone to sympathize with the poor souls that were forced to endure such a heinous affair. Reporter's notepads smoked with contempt.

The first words from Justice Preiss's mouth were, "You people have been through a pretty rough time already. I don't understand how any company can be so irresponsible." He granted all our requests but allowed Trindell eight days to defend themselves. He suggested we sue for personal damages, such as plane fares home, additional food, and expenses for staying in Johannesburg. He was angry at their treatment of us, even angrier that they'd slighted the court.

The solemnity of the court bridled our instinct to high-five. Andrew was ready to burst, proud of his work and of the result. But something else had infected him. He liked us. We held our composure until we reached the steps of the court.

Handshakes, hugs, kisses, and a hoot from Jerry lionized the moment. A moment that felt like it would bind us for life. It was more than a bond sprouted from unsought duress. The words of the Justice made us feel important and valued, but admittedly, the smell of retribution brought the greatest joy. I hugged Mad Dog and pivoted directly into Jalina. She wrapped her arms around my neck and kissed me briefly on the lips. Her hold was long and tender. I found it hard to let go. When I did, she placed her lips such that the moisture and heat of her breath coated my ear. She whispered, "Good on ya, Craze."

I didn't know what that meant, but the message was not in the words. Embers glowed . . . hotter. I feared they might flare if given more oxygen. It confused me. How could I feel this way? Alex is the one. You know that. Is it possible to feel this way about Jalina if I am about to propose to the woman I've loved for years? Feelings for Jalina did not diminish my love for Alex, but I wondered how it could happen, whether it meant the roots were not deep enough. But they were! Still, it shouldn't happen if your love is strong and true. Right? What's going on? These relationships are at different places—use your head you idiot. You know you want to marry Alex. Is this a sick cosmic test? Even if this is just infatuation, you can't give into sensuality. It was like fighting gravity. I had to accept that gravitational forces exist and learn how to grapple with them with integrity.

Doug gave me a chest bump. Andrew shook my hand. He reminded us all that this was just the first round. Trindell would have their say next week. It also meant we had a week to kill. It struck me as odd that I could piously scoff at the site of the "Whites Only" signs, yet swim comfortably in the same pool where redemption as granted by the same people who administered the laws that substantiate those signs. I fought to reconcile these disunioned thoughts.

That same afternoon, we received a typewritten court order, signed by W.P. Van Oudtshoorn, Registrar:

1) Directing that the respondent refund forthwith the sums paid by the applicants [for the tour]
2) Granting applicants leave to attach certain trucks, tents, camping equipment, office equipment, and shares issued in Trindell Travel (Propriety) Limited; which assets belong to the Respondent and/or their proprietors ad fundandam (or ad confirmandam) jurisdictium in Witwatersrand local Division of the Supreme Court of South Africa; authorizing Applicants to seek relief by way of edictal citation served on the Respondent's registered office in London. That the above be executed with immediate effect.
3) Ordering respondent to pay the costs of this application—legal fees.

In the late afternoon, the sheriff went to the Trindell office to remove everything from it. Marvin was there. He wouldn't let them in. The sheriff headed back to the court, seeking a writ to break the door down.

CHAPTER 72

It was 2:00 a.m. The blast that ramrodded Winston Walsh's dreams burned a hot wire into his heart, drove him upright from his bed, and pressed him into a dash for the window. By the time he raised the sash, the burn overlayed the roof of his mouth and webbed into his jaw. His mind clicked through the possible causes. The core of a power transformer overheated; a spark ignited a vapor cloud from a leaky LNG tanker; a rubber compounding plant exploded. The thunder of a second explosion blew through the fronds of the palm trees. *Probably a transformer. Chemical and gas explosions are usually a single blast.*

He saw it. A diffused corona of orange-and-yellow light hovering above trees that lay between him and ACORN. His face mummified. He ran to his jeep, befit with despair, trying not to let conjecture overwhelm him. But his fear was black and certain. He wheezed.

Winston sped toward the center, the place he devoted his life to, the place where he used his ingenuity to advance genetic research to a point yet to be conceived by the cleverest minds. The tires of the jeep spewed mud like a Mozambique spitting cobra. As he drove, he gathered his hair and banded it into his trademark ponytail. His charcoal eyes bled with rage.

The center was ablaze. Fire apparatus hadn't arrived. Save the key data, he thought. *My office safe!* He skirted along the service road to the rear of the administrative wing and approached the emergency exit. He swiped his card. Nothing. Joggled the handle. A mattock lay in the dirt, near a trench the ground crew had been digging. He picked it up and swung at the window. A third explosion seemed to come directly from the middle of the wing, from exactly where his office was. He fell. The temperature slingshot to an unbearable degree. The unlit cigarette fell from his lips. He ran. A fourth explosion. Despair.

The sabotage was encyclopedic, meticulously destroying the genetics, administrative, and computer system areas, while sparing the live primate domicile. It looked like steps were taken to protect the chimps and orangutans by turning on water sprinklers. Dark heat and smoke shunned would-be rescuers. A shrill that mushroomed from Winston's mouth was inaudible above the fury. Sirens now wailed. Too late. *This is personal.*

Prototype experiments gone; millions of dollars of avant-garde equipment destroyed; painstaking details of his work in ashes— along with his place in history alongside Mendel, Watson and Crick, and Marie Curie. The band of the world's greatest scientists at ACORN would disperse. How could he ever pull them together again?

And what of Gus Cooper and the New Pioneer Column? Confidence and funding would dry up. The Column was barely interested in the medical benefits of his research. Their primary concern was its impact on the fate of Rhodesia, White rule, and their personal stake in diamond, gold, and other mines. It was *their* country—they reasoned—and they loved it. *Wait! Backup tapes of the mainframe are sent to a warehouse in Switzerland each week.* By the end of the day, Winston would learn that the warehouse with the backup tapes had also been destroyed.

The anguish caused Winston to retrace his path in life. Raised in Matabeleland, the southwestern part of Rhodesia, his parents were tireless, managing three gold mines and one nickel mine. Attending schools—all White—was his joy. He couldn't imagine why anyone would spend their spare time on anything that wasn't academic. His gift, an ability to combine academics with imagination, was recognized early by his parents and teachers.

Winston learned from his parents that hard work was rewarded, and that the superior intellect of the White race on the evolutionary scale was God's design. It was an axiom—an established, self-evident truth. His mother once told him, "It is better for the oxen to be given work and to be fed than to allow them to ineffectually subsist amid the whims of nature."

At the age of eleven, Winston's parents arranged for special oversight. He moved to Bristol, England, with his mother and took on a rigorous course load at the Stonar School. An elite tutor helped him trim up his didactic work and taught him how to apply his knowledge. Even at a young age, he grasped the love and sacrifices his parents made for him. At sixteen, he was off to Rice University in Houston, and then on to MIT and Oxford.

His mother moved back to Rhodesia to be with his father before Winston finished his bachelor's degree at Rice. He completed his PhD at MIT and post doc work at Oxford and went on to earn the chief research officer position at the center in Liberia, where he used his charm and imagination to lure a team of scientists that refused to define limits.

In 1971, during his second year in Liberia, Winston received a box the size of a small cooler. It contained two oversized pickle jars, the kind you see in a general store. In each jar floated an eyeless shroud of dermis and hair—faces preserved in formaldehyde—the faces of his parents. He was confused, amazed at how anyone could fashion such detailed replicas. An envelope was at the bottom of the box. It was from the Patriotic Front.

```
We have taken back the land and mines
that your parents and their descendants
stole from our people. We will retrieve
all land that has been stolen. If you try
to reclaim your property, you will meet
the same fate as your parents. LAND IS
THE ECONOMY AND THE ECONOMY IS THE LAND.
```

The lilac coloration of a lump on the lower left eyelid of his father's face was a perfect match to a cancerous growth that had been treated years before. The discolored birthmark in front of his mother's right ear was something he'd stared at for years when she held him. He sobbed. But the war was going well—his parents had told him so. He dialed 2-6-3, the country code for Rhodesia, and added his parents' phone number. A boggy voice answered. Winston was stupefied. "I'd like to speak to Joel Walsh," he said.

Gravel pressed through the phone lines and rattled the hair cells of Winston's inner ear. "Mr. Walsh and his wife have gone to meet the Devil."

His neck hairs rose. Nerves fired from his abdomen to his toes. He'd been wronged. Wronged in a way that is irreversible, in a way that has set off sparks throughout history. Overreaction is a course that the wronged find most comfort in. It is the haven for ex-lovers, neighbors, governments, and those duped in bad business deals, who think that disproportionate revenge will bring justice and pleasure. Winston's anger consumed him. He vowed to get revenge in his own way, using his own set of rules, manifesting in a manner that would be undetected and disproportionately inhumane. The fact that few people would understand how it was done made him smile.

His thoughts returned to the explosion. The concepts of his gene-editing technology were still sound, but the secretive, self-contained nature of ACORN was a careless miscalculation. Details, algorithms, and documentation of gene sequences were lost. Precise protocols for manufacturing were gone, now residing only in the heads of the scientists. Reconstructing the details would require mountains of time and effort.

Science can work both ways, he thought. The dolls contain information on how to manufacture the end products—enough information to reverse engineer the critical details.

CHAPTER 73

A reporter from the *Beeld* took Mad Dog and I to Norman's Grill for dinner on the evening of our court ruling. We were the only Americans. Our friend Bubba was dead. It was nectar for the media. But we learned more from them than they learned from us.

He'd just come from the Trindell office, where the sheriff used an apparatus called the Big Red Key—a battering ram. It splintered the jamb and snapped the latch in a single thrust. The office had been emptied. Still, they seized a few brochures, a desk, and four chairs—enough to establish our right to sue and to send a message from the court, comply with subpoenas.

"Think you'll get your money back?" asked the hard-hitting reporter. Mad Dog stuffed another dinner roll into his mouth.

On the way back to the Alendene, a set of fingers wrapped around my collar and pulled me into the recessed entryway of a nail salon that was closed for the day. "Mad Dog!" I yelled. The assailant spun me around and pinned me to the door. A purple vein ballooned like a mole tunnel the length of his neck.

"What are you doing?" Travis's sockets looked ready to cave into his skull."

"You're choking me."

"Let him go, Travis." Mad Dog held a rusted masonry chisel he found on the sidewalk.

Travis released me, put his palms on the door, elbows on either side of my head. He glared at Mad Dog. "Put that thing down."

"I know what you're going to say." I was embarrassed.

"Damn it. You couldn't just let it go? You're putting the star of Bethlehem over your head and saying, 'Hey. I'm right over here.'"

I had to choose between opposing forces, and I chose both—an impossibility. Retribution against Trindell had sidetracked us into an elixir of fame and notoriety. Exposing Winston called for subtlety and thought—requirements clouded by the breath of vengeance.

"Winston knows we were on this trip," Mad Dog said. "He reads. Reid and Sipho know you never found the dolls. It's no secret that we're in Jo'burg, Travis."

Still nose to nose. "Posing for the papers in *I was stranded in Botswana* T-shirts? Talking to reporters?"

I yelled, loud enough to loosen the bricks. "You're right." Travis took his hands off the door. "But it's done. If we unravel the dolls and figure out what Winston and the Rhodesians are up to, we can use our notoriety. Reporters will listen to us."

"Uh-huh. Well, there's one little catch, Craze. I tried your little story on Reid. But he thinks you still have the dolls. Told me to come to Jo'burg and find you."

Overnight, Mad Dog and I both took ill. Fever, headache, joints ripped in pain. Late morning, Emilie and Jalina stopped by our room. They offered us rubdowns with Vicks VapoRub and Tiger Balm, a potent, camphor-laden ointment. It was a heartfelt gesture. We'd become friends to the bone, and their concern was natural and rooted.

"Andrew and the barrister met with Trindell's lawyer this morning," Emilie said. "Andrew threatened to send a truck to Marvin's house and clean it out, force him to prove which furniture was his and which belonged to Trindell."

"Good," I said. The court date was still a week away. Enough time to work on the dolls and find out the truth while we still had all the attention.

Without knocking, Travis slipped into our room. He scoffed. "What? Oh." I laughed, told him it was okay. He dropped his rucksack. A blue pail hung from his hand. He looked at Jalina, then back at me, and said, "I thought we could, uh, you know, maybe work on the . . ."

His awkwardness led Jalina to think that an inside joke or private exchange was going on. Emilie shifted her glance between me and Mad Dog, and then cupped her hands to her face and shot me an eyeball. Jalina caught the exchange. She resisted an impulse to up and leave. Instead, she prosecuted. "What's going on, mates?" It sounded sexy in a Mae West sort of way. *That's it. I am officially a boneheaded ass.*

"I'm telling her," I said to Travis. "I trust her."

Travis wiggled his ears. It was a signal we used as kids that came in handy when playing cards or talking to parents. Wiggling the ears meant no. Raising the eyebrows meant yes. I raised my eyebrows. He wiggled his ears again. I volleyed with a triple eyebrow raise.

"You ain't thinkin' straight. You know that?"

Mad Dog's head rose from his pillow, exposing one sleepy eye. "I vouch for her," he sniveled and resumed staring at the wall.

Travis closed the door. "I swiped this bucket from housekeeping. Let's get the first part done, remove the shellac."

I told Jalina about ACORN, about Winston and our task to deliver the dolls and how it progressed from an innocent favor to a clusterfuck. I told her how we had to remove the shellac that coated each nested doll with alcohol and then use hexane to dissolve contact cement that bound the paper walls together. She listened and barely flinched, surprising us with her lack of wonderment. An accusation rang from her lips. "Craze and Mad Dog . . . masters of international intrigue. I knew something was up with you two. Simple American tourists out on a romp." She shucked a look to Emilie. "Seems you're in on this too." So sexy, I thought.

"Jalina, we aren't part of this . . . plot," I said. "Okay, we are now. But it wasn't our doing. We thought we were helping a good cause. We told Emilie because she can help us."

Travis plunked the alcohol from his rucksack onto the night table. He walked over to my pack, reached in, and pulled out the dolls. Jalina gasped. "They're lovely." She picked them up and held them to the light. "Mm, delicious."

Travis poured alcohol into the pail.

Jalina choked. "What are you doing?"

He gave her a *Who the hell are you* look. "I'm dissolvin' the shellac off the dolls."

She picked up the dolls and mimicked Travis, putting on a dismal Boston accent. "Well, you ain't doin' it right, mistah. Not like that." Assertive, even cocky.

Contemptuous glares.

She persisted. "It ain't gonna work if you dunk the whole friggin' doll in theyah. You gotta get a spray bottle, like the kind you clean yah cah windows with." She tired of the accent. "And you need something like a cafeteria tray. And rags. Plenty of soft rags."

We laughed. Travis sneered.

"We should do the smallest doll first. It would help if . . ."

I stopped her. "Jalina. Do you have any idea . . .?"

"What? I told you what I do for a living. I can help. From what I see, you need it."

"You work in publishing. Reviewing old books?"

She pretended to be indignant. "Men don't listen. Yes, I work for a publisher. With rare and antique books. We restore them for resale, sometimes for museums. If you don't handle these dolls properly, you'll ruin them."

Mad Dog muffed, "You go, Jalina." Face still in pillow.

Travis said, "Holy mother of Jesus."

Jalina lectured. "Find some bottle caps and put them face down on the tray. One at a time, stand a doll on top of the bottle caps and spray alcohol on it. Give the shellac ten minutes to soak in. The excess will drip off the dolls into the tray. Wipe the doll clean and do it again until all the shellac is gone. Use a clean rag each time."

After a pause, she asked, "Where are you going to get hexane, Travis?"

"Ain't figured that out yet."

By now, Jalina had fully launched herself into our predicament. "Sometimes we use hexane at work. To remove certain types of grease from manuscripts. When we need it, we get it from the shoe factory next door. They use it to make glue for their soles. Something like that."

"A shoe factory?"

"They use heaps of it. I've seen two places in Jo'burg. One called Jozine Shoes—off Park Drive—another just past the train station on De Beer Street. It has a weird name, but you can't miss it if you walk up De Beer."

She glanced at Travis.

"When it's time to unravel the paper from the contact cement, we'll need a similar set up, but we'll also need an ironing board and an iron. And a few plastic knives. Can you get all that?"

Travis grinned. "Yes, ma'am." Then he flapped his fingers, tips up. "Craze, gimme the dolls. With all the stink you guys created, someone might come looking for you."

I handed them over. "Be kind."

Jalina said, "I almost forgot—tweezers—two pairs of tweezers." Travis winked.

Jalina noticed the incredulous bearing of my face and raised her voice. "You need more Tiger Balm on your shoulders. Roll over."

CHAPTER 74

Gus: Where's the Guy?

Gus wanted to crane his neck through the phone and let Ron Reid smell the cloud of compost in his breath. "Where's the guy you sent to get the dolls, Ron? 'Perfect for the job.' 'Duck soup,' you said."

"Didn't count on someone blowing up the ferry. That screwed up everything. My scout tracked down the signal, but it took him into the heart of the Okavango. By the time he got to it, the Americans had traded the dolls to a Bushmen elder, who then traded them to someone else. He's been in the swamps going village to village trying to find them."

"So, he never met up with the Americans? Been on a one-man scavenger hunt around the swamps?" Gus nearly swallowed his chaw. "This is bullshit, Ron. Did you hear? Segregationist land laws have been repealed. We had a ruse election for God's sake. In the rural areas, insurgents are converting people. We have to win this war outright. Send more guys to help him for God's sake. Ticktock, Ron."

"Guys are fighting in the bush. I think these jokers left the transmitter with the elder on purpose. I think they still have the dolls. I told Travis—he's my scout—I told him to drop the search and get his ass to Jo'burg and confront the Americans."

Gus spit. "You trust this guy? The question was a low blow to Ron. Trust was paramount in the Selous Scouts. "I know you like Americans, Ron. I know you like this guy. Have you given him enough scrutiny?"

"He's proven himself."

"Don't care. Find someone else. Send him to Jo'burg too. There's too much to lose." The distended draft of Reid's inhalation whooshed over the phone line.

Reid was smart, knew where the money came from, but didn't like being a subordinate. Still, he said, "A guy got released from hospital today. Was going to put him back in the field, but . . ."

"Good. Have him check out those guys and Travis in Jo'burg. You see the stunt these Americans and their tourist buddies have pulled? Like bloody celebrities."

Gus told Ron about the attack on ACORN. How the Liberian research center was destroyed in a highly organized attack—which included destroying the storage building in Zurich where the backup tapes were kept.

"The dolls are the only source of the original information left, Ron. Understand?"

The low, metallic *zeet zeet* of an African dusky flycatcher sitting in the hollow of a tree outside Ron's window chafed his eardrums.

CHAPTER 75

Craze: Double Dancing

"Reporter's downstairs. Who wants to talk to him?" Gary asked. Mad Dog fiddled with his Swiss Army knife. I took my sneaker off and inspected for a pebble. Enough already.

Encounter Overland Tours, a competitor of Trindell, was cashing in on the disproportionate ballyhoo of our case. Good versus evil in big, bad South Africa. They took us to the weekly tribal dances at a circular arena with a pea gravel ground cover and fifteen rows of bleachers at a gold mine on the outskirts of Johannesburg. The workers provided their own entertainment, a distraction from missing loved ones in distant provinces. Usually Whites weren't allowed, but Encounter had a long-standing connection. Travis stayed in Johannesburg, intent on calling Norah and Jaxon.

Fifteen hundred spectators swayed to the a cappella chants of low, pulsating voices. Troupes danced, each with a specialty, like stick wielding, hoop jumping, gum boot thumping, and resolute foot stomping, which, when done in unison, shimmied our seats. A man sitting next to me said, out of the blue, "My brother was killed in Sharpeville. Protesting the pass laws." I stuck my tongue into my upper lip and raised one shoulder. "It's why we carry these things around."

He handed me a tattered 3½ x 5-inch booklet with more than ninety pages. The main page included his photo, fingerprints, and his "Group," which was Zulu. Inside were details of his birth, lineage, where he worked, education certificates, results of X-rays, and other identifying info. In the back was a folded piece of paper that outlined how designations were made.

> "A White person is one who is in appearance obviously white—and not generally accepted as Coloured—or who is generally accepted as White—and is not obviously Non-White, provided that a person shall not be classified as a White person if one of his natural parents has been classified as a Coloured person or a Bantu. A Bantu is a person who is, or is generally accepted as, a member of any aboriginal race or tribe of Africa. A Coloured is a person who is not a White person or a Bantu."

"My 'Book of Life.' Restricts where I can live, work, socialize. Must always carry."

Mad Dog peeked over my forearm. "I see it," he said, red cheeks popping behind the black of his beard. I nodded to the man, swallowed, handed him his passbook, unsure if my face showed humiliation, sympathy, or was just plain goofy. I felt like a fucking idiot.

On the ride back to Johannesburg, Mad Dog put down the hammer on my procrastination. "It's time, Craze." Head down, I raised my eyes to meet his. "Time to call Alex."

I swear my vision blurred. I was going to propose—over the phone. No ring. No hugs or kisses. I'd thought about preparing bullet points, like I would for a presentation. Ridiculous.

Alex said hello. She knew it was me. Nobody else called at 6:15 a.m. She was cheery.

"Alex, hi. Wow. Um. How are you? Sorry, we haven't had access to telephones. I wanted to call and let you know what's going on." *That's not the reason you called, you pinhead—sidetracked already.*

"How am I? I'm fine . . ."

Of course she is. She's always fine. I am not fine. What am I? I am not an unsalable man. A romantic, yes, but what good is that? I listen—most of the time. Go out of my way to make things special for our friends, for her. Who is this other guy? Is he muscular? Does he have a wild shock of hair and a mustache that curls over his top lip? What does he say and do to make her feel loved? Has she surrendered herself to his thoughts? My next thought made me sick. *Does she love him?*

Mad Dog gnawed on a stick of biltong.

". . .but what about you?" Her tone was sincere and emotional. "A reporter from Reuters called your dad last week and let him know you were all right. Are you? We heard about Bubba. Horrible. I'm so sorry." I couldn't speak.

She added, "My roommate showed me an article in the *New York Times.* There was a blurb in *Newsweek.* A local reporter is writing a bigger piece. Are you safe? How is Mad Dog?"

I told her about the ferry and the lawsuit and that we'd probably be in Johannesburg for a couple of weeks, staying at the Alendene. For some reason, I told her about the morning the six lions sniffed around our tent. She started asking more questions. I blurted, "Alex, I miss you."

The line went silent. Five seconds. Six. Seemed like a lifetime. I heard her tenuous curtain drop from eight thousand miles away. "I miss you too. I do. I . . . love you." Something about hearing another's voice destroys any preliminary analysis or independent reasoning. It was happening to her. To me.

"Alex, the reason I called is to tell you how humbled I am that you have loved me for all these years. I can still see you in the beautiful dress you wore to the prom. I remember how unworthy I felt when I asked you to go with me; how happy I was that you said yes; and how our relationship deepened with each year. I've always known you were a better person than me and loved how you made *me* a better person."

She stopped me, sniffling now, and said, "You think I'm a better person than you?"

The question shocked me. Could she not know that I felt that way? To me it was like the difference in light cast by the sun or the moon. A shameful notion battered my conscience: Is she trying to justify a decision she already made?

"Always. I admired you as a person long before I loved you."

I heard gasps. She was crying.

"Alex, I still feel the same. Nothing has waned. But now I'm asking you a different question. I don't want to spend another day without you by my side. I would be honored, so happy, and fulfilled if you would spend the rest of your life with me. I promise I'll let your mother beat me at hearts and . . . uh, Alex, will you marry me?"

I heard her choke then sob without constraint. Gravity pulled a tear from my duct. Mad Dog took off his sock, did a mock wipe of his eyes, and offered it to me as a handkerchief. But I swear I saw a real tear. I blew my nose in it and threw the sock in his face.

"I don't believe it," she said. *Just say yes, Alex.* "I have to tell you." She drew in a waft of air like she was about to jump off the Border Street Bridge in Cohasset into the Atlantic. "I met someone. On my three-week trip with my roommate. I met him in Seattle, but he's from Vancouver. We've been calling and seeing each other off and on. When we can. Bubba never said anything to you?"

I didn't want to tell the truth and say he told me all about it while we were sitting on a rug at the Liberian border. That would taint my intentions, and she may think it was the only reason I proposed. But I wasn't going to lie. I'd just proposed. Though my dark side reminded me that Bubba couldn't contradict me—a fleeting, distasteful thought—I didn't answer. I asked, "What do you mean you've been seeing him? Like a real relationship?"

She blubbered. "Yes, he's been away lately, but he called and proposed to me . . ." She paused for a few seconds. ". . . yesterday. I don't believe it. I've been proposed to twice in two days."

How could this guy propose? They barely know each other. "He asked you to marry him? I'm stunned. God, you just met. Is this some sort of crush?"

"I didn't say yes, but . . ." She paused. "I've been thinking about it. I've also been worried about all of you in Botswana and have been trying to find any scrap of news I can.

"You are considering it? Saying yes? You're seriously considering it? Marriage?"

"Yes. Considering it." She was more assertive and had reined in the sobbing. She asked, "When did you decide to you were going to propose to me?"

"I had an epiphany one evening. We were in Botswana. One of the couples on the trip was so in love . . . I missed you so much. At every corner of the trip, I've thought about you, wanted to share it with you. Well, not the ferry explosion."

She laughed.

"I want you for life. My experiences in Africa are lessened because you aren't here." Mad Dog pulled up his sleeve and tried to stick his armpit into my nose. "I was going to propose to you in Nairobi if you could come—make it something magical, you know? But I couldn't wait. You have always been the one, never a doubt. I'll say it again. I want to marry you, Alex. Please marry me. I'll let you name our kids. I love you. I love your family. We are time-tested. I get excited each day I see you. I know you feel the same."

"That's why this is so hard." Her strength withered. She sniveled. "Now what am I supposed to do? I love you. But I feel like I got over a hurdle and can't cross back."

I reeled. She's dead serious. *What balls this guy has!* I thought asking her to marry me would flatten any infatuation she had with this guy. "Alex, you are the strongest person I know. You can do whatever you want; there's no hurdle. No rules." *What else? Think.* "When I left, you asked if I'd marry you when I got back. You wanted me to say yes. My mind was a mess that morning. I was surprised and stupid. I wanted to be the one to ask you. To give you the choice. But now I'm telling you that the answer is yes."

"But . . . you didn't say yes then. You didn't leap in the air. And it took, what? Weeks, months before you decided? On that day, after all these years, you weren't ready to answer."

"I've always known, Alex. It was never *if.* Never."

She paused. "I am going to hang up and think about everything you said. I'm overwhelmed. Please call me in a few days?"

We walked back to the Alendene. Mad Dog put his arm on my shoulder. "Sorry, Craze."

The trim ring of our room lock was on the floor. The door was open. Shorts, sandals, and T-shirts had been tossed against the window, some torn. The air smelled of honey-laced tobacco and rotted cabbage. My camera was on the end of the bed, back flap ripped off, 300 mm zoom lens smashed on the bathroom tile. Chewbacca was face down under the heater.

Mad Dog whispered, "Do you think?"

Footfall, soft and determined, whooshed up the hallway like a ghost. It crept louder to our door. Travis stepped in, skin covered with the shine of sweat, left eye puffed, and the webs of both palms bleeding. Gashes extended across his hands. He was out of breath and amped, eyes hovering as if hanging from the ceiling like a disco ball. He whispered, "Sweet Jesus."

I stared at his hands. He looked up, exposing an abrasion under his chin. He reached into his pocket and threw an octagonal dog tag on the bed, holes drilled on each end, knotted with braided twine. An osprey insignia was stamped on the back. He raised his eyebrows once.

CHAPTER 76

Craze: Unraveled

I sat on the bed dazed, watching the others. Between the call with Alex and the break-in, sleep was impossible. Talking to Alex had inflamed my insecurities. Strong morning coffee didn't help. Depression had been an infrequent guest for me, but it now roosted in a corner of my mental real estate. Anxiety, self-doubt, and obtuse panic tugged at my spirit. I stared at the legs of the ironing board.

Emilie waved a small towel to shoo volatile vapors of alcohol and disbanded shellac out the window. Travis had gathered everything on Jalina's list. He "found" some hexane and brought the other items she'd asked for, including the ironing board, iron, plastic knives, and tweezers. She had won his respect, and he gladly accepted his next assignment, to wipe each doll with the light touch of an archeologist after she de-shellacked them.

"That's the last one," she reported in a businesslike fashion. The eight dolls were free of shellac and stood drying on the night table. Step one was done. I hadn't helped at all. I'd told Travis about my call with Alex but hadn't mentioned it to anyone else. Still, Jalina picked up on my fog of detachment.

"What's wrong, friend? Out of sorts? I thought I rubbed that terrible flu out of you."

I'm not sure if I didn't want to burden her or if I was calling on a need for privacy, but it wasn't the right time. "Things at home. Sorry."

She knew enough not to push. I liked that about her. She picked up one of the dolls and admired it. It bore a female image. "We should let these dry this afternoon," she said. "Tonight, we can use the hexane and start unraveling them. I hate to do it. They're so beautiful. "

Mad Dog agreed. "That doll is an Ashanti queen. The woman's clan is the most important to them, not the man's. They follow their family lineage on the woman's side. When they get married, the man's family pays the woman's family, like a dowry."

Jalina flicked her hair back. "Oh, I like that." I stared at Mad Dog like he was an alien. He shrugged.

Emilie had grown uneasy. "You know, guys, I can't guarantee I'll be able to understand the information in these dolls. I hope it's not beyond me."

"None of us knows shit," Mad Dog said. "The more I see in this part of Africa, the more pissed off I get. Gotta try our best. Maybe between all of us we can do this."

While the dolls dried, we went on a guided bus tour of Soweto. The black Africans called it the whitewash tour because it was the only way for a White person to see Soweto. The narrator never mentioned a protest where twenty thousand high school students rebelled against a mandate that said certain subjects could only be taught in Afrikaans, a version of Dutch that most of them didn't speak. Hundreds were killed in the protest, unwilling to bend their will to another White minority scheme.

The tour showed that everything was grand and wonderful. The exact words were, "These people don't know how lucky they are. We treat them so well." The tour guide repeatedly pointed out houses and boasted, "See that wire? It means the house has electricity." One block from the paved streets lay muddied lanes with box houses packed so tight, one neighbor could hear the other snoring. A woman walked barefoot through puddled squalor into her yellow ten-by-ten-foot shack. Horizontal sheets of corrugated tin were pieced together by crudely cut interlocking slots. Electrical wires had not found those shanties.

Jalina spoke for us all. "Who are they trying to kid?"

After the tour, we ate fish and chips at the Guildhall Pub and returned to the Alendene to work on the dolls. Travis went to his hotel for a shower and said he'd join us shortly. Jalina sharpened a plastic knife by scraping it on the brick wall until the serrated teeth were gone. She set the iron on low and put a towel over the ironing board.

"Okay, Craze," she said. "See the seam here? When I get the edge loose, grab the corner with your tweezers. I'll hold the other corner and tease the paper apart with the knife. Mad Dog, once the entire doll is unrolled, lay it on the towel on the ironing board and put another towel on top. Run the warm iron over it, lightly, low heat. The excess cement and hexane will dissolve under low heat. Clean the residue with a towel."

"Yes, ma'am."

Jalina laid a doll horizontally in the tray, sprayed hexane on the seam, and waited. My heart banged with delayed thumps. This was the moment we'd either ruin the dolls or expose their secrets. Drafts of hexane fumes irritated our nostrils and throats. The seam of the first doll loosened at the corners, and then along the furrow. I latched onto the corner with my tweezers. Jalina pinched the other corner and ran the plastic knife down the furrow, teasing it apart. Alternately, she would spray hexane into the seam, wait, tease with knife, and unroll. "This is fascinating," she said. "It's made of thin, waterproof paper. Expensive."

The skin around my nipples crinkled when I saw the formulas, writings, diagrams, and genetic annotations reveal themselves, one inch at a time. The doll unraveled evenly without trauma, tears, or scuffs. Emilie stretched her neck to see. Jalina handed the scroll to Mad Dog. She was running this show. "Emilie, hold onto one end of the scroll while Mad Dog irons it out."

"Happy to."

Jalina sighed and wiped her forehead. I giggled. "That's one," she said.

The brown pigment in Emilie's eyes darkened. "They printed on both sides," she said.

Excitement recast itself as unease. We were witnessing serious stuff. Historic. My thoughts turned to Winston, that prick, with his faux pompous altruism to save the world from malaria. The weight of the next step pressed on me. Emilie and I had to read, had to figure out what we were looking at. She looked at me, jaw pulsing and said, "Craze. What if we can't?"

While Mad Dog and Emilie cleaned up the first doll, Jalina and I continued unraveling the others. Open windows allowed vapors to escape, but all I could smell while leaning over the tray was Jalina's wint-o-green breath and lavender talc. Our ears and cheeks unavoidably brushed. My head raced in knots from Alex to Winston to Bubba to Dad to Jalina to my genetics professor to Travis. *What is wrong with me?* I'd just proposed to Alex, and I was allowing myself these stupid dalliances. Maybe it was stroking my ego. Maybe I thought this thing with Jalina was real. Or both. Having proposed, did I now need to know someone else could be attracted to me? That would be the embodiment of insecurity. If I pledged my love to another, was I supposed to be immune to attraction? *Just handle it. Why is her breath so damn hot?*

After a few dolls, we took a break. Travis was outside the door telling someone he'd come by later when he was done. He entered and I blocked the door with my foot before he could close it. "I need some fresh air," I said, sticking my head out the door. Hanna was sashaying her ass down the hall. She turned, smiled, slowly lifted her blouse to expose her naval, and gave me the finger. Then she cupped her hand around the cheek of her round ass and walked. I went into the room, glared at Travis, and wiggled my ears. He raised his eyebrows—twice.

By nine o'clock we'd unraveled the last doll. Scrolls were stretched across the bed. Emilie pulled her hair back. Her eyes flitted from one scroll to another. I knew she felt the same as me. Undressed. Everybody looking at you. It was up to us now.

Fumes from the hexane burned my throat, Jalina was dizzy, and we all had headaches. We escaped to the Blue Croc Pub for a well-earned beer. Quinn, Big-Don, Dale, Bernie, Veronica, and Hanna joined us. Jerry, Doug, Gary, and Chris were spending the night at Gary's uncle's place about twenty miles outside Jo'burg. Chris was Jalina's lifelong friend, so I worried that Jalina had told her about the dolls. She promised me she hadn't and then whispered, her lower lip clipping the tragus of my ear, "I don't have a roommate tonight." My eyelids slipped down. I swallowed.

Travis bought us a round. While we were unraveling the dolls, the others had hatched a crazy idea. They'd spent the day looking into the possibility of travelling north through Rhodesia to Victoria Falls. We collectively bemoaned the thought that we'd never seen the falls, despite having spent all those weeks just a few miles upriver. Still, the idea was nuts.

"It's not that wild," Bernie said. "People still go about their lives in Rhodesia. We've got six days to kill before we go back to court. Look." He opened a piece of paper with an itinerary. "We can catch the 12:10 a.m. train to Beitbridge on the border and then rent a car and join the 1:00 p.m. convoy from Beitbridge to Bulawayo. From there, we can join a convoy the next morning to Vic Falls."

"You're leaving this coming morning at 12:10 a.m.?"

"Yeah. Not tonight. Tomorrow night. Doug, Jerry, Quinn, Dale, Hanna, Veronica, and Chris are coming. Cathy and Graham haven't decided. Big-Don is staying in Jo'burg in case Andrew needs his help."

"What about Gary?"

"He's staying behind. Wants to catch up with a couple of friends."

"Humph, Chris is going to Rhodesia? Nice of her to tell me," Jalina said.

A man wandered to our table and, without asking, snapped a photo. His camera bag had a Rhodesian Herald patch on it. Veronica gave him a kindergarten teacher scolding. "That was rude, sir. You should ask. We are not animals." I thought of all the stealth pictures I'd taken of the colorful African people.

He nodded but didn't care, same as a child. "Zach Reynolds from the *Herald.* You're the group that was stranded on the border, yeah? Anything new on the court case?"

Quinn sneered. Travis was red with rage. Mad Dog ignored.

"Did I hear you say you're going to Vic Falls? Anything you want the public to know?"

Big-Don answered, highbrow politician voice fully activated. "We're doing just fine. Looking forward to returning to court next week. Now piss off."

"Can I get your names?" He asked. His sidekick pulled at his sleeve and whispered something to him.

Veronica sang in a soprano voice, "Nooooo, cheeky bloke."

They left in a hurry. Quinn scowled. "Bloody press."

Bernie reined the conversation back to visiting the falls. "Jalina, Chris asked me to tell you that she was going to Rhodesia. Said you were off somewhere. Never came back to your room."

I was intrigued by their gumption. But we'd just unraveled the dolls into eight scrolls. Dissecting the information was critical. Then Mad Dog said, "I want to see the falls."

I was incredulous. What was he thinking? He knew what was going on. He insisted that Travis, Emilie, and I join him at the pool table for a private conversation.

I said, "This is ridiculous, Dog. We can't go. We have to work on the scrolls."

"Yes. And you're going to need a lot of time to study them."

"Exactly."

He drilled through the cue ball, pulverizing the racked balls loud enough to turn heads. "These scrolls are ruining what we came to Africa for. You're the one who is so wrapped up in this. Besides, who do you think you're helping anyway?"

"What's that supposed to mean?"

"From what we've learned, the Rhodesians are capitalists. But Nkomo and Mugabe are both socialists, supported by Russia and China. Why should we care about them? How does that help the United States?" Pent up acrimony lived in a drizzle of moisture that occupied the corner of Mad Dog's lip. "This isn't what we came here for. We came to see the jungle, the desert, the animals, Vic Falls, Kilimanjaro, the Nile. Not to get mixed up in this shit."

My earlobes turned red. I'd consulted with Mad Dog on every step. Every decision. He'd been supportive, even helpful. Was this what he really thought? I barely parted my teeth. "Mad Dog. Maybe we shouldn't have done this. But we did. We are in it. You are right. There are two sides here. Neither is perfect. But we've been made painfully aware that Winston's objectives are fundamentally hateful to fellow humans. I won't walk away knowing that I may be able to prevent a horrific event."

"Sure, Craze. Evil genius, right?"

Travis jumped in, quelling his confrontational nature. "Mad Dog, this isn't for malaria. You know that. Reid told me it wasn't. It will devastate Black Africans. I've seen your integrity. Remember who you are. Are you going to turn your head?"

Mad Dog blunted his stance. He leaned over the table, thought for a moment. "We can do both. Travis and I can do all the driving. You and Emilie can sit in the back and look things over. We'll get our own car: me, you, Emilie, and Travis."

"And Jalina." It was a reflex—just came out of my mouth.

Dog stared at me. Pure ice. He held it for a long time before acquiescing. "And Jalina."

Of course I wanted to see the falls. I started thinking. It's several hours on the train to Beitbridge. Several hours to Bulawayo and another five or six hours to Victoria Falls. If we can't figure it out in that amount of time, we probably never will. I said to Travis, "If we do figure it out, you can tell your guy Sigfo. Hell, you can give him the scrolls if that's what we decide."

"It's Sipho. S-i-p-h-o. I've seen Vic Falls already. It's a spectacle. I say let's go."

He'd been with us for so long, I'd forgotten that Travis had been in Rhodesia. "What's it like? I mean, how dangerous is it?"

"Bernie's right. People go about their business. It's a bush war. Ain't World War II. Places are safe, but there's always a chance something could happen. For me, not a problem."

Emilie hesitated, stroking her hair with both hands. "So, you think it's safe?"

"Safe enough. Craze is right. You'll have plenty of time to look at the scrolls."

Mad Dog looked at me and Emilie and asked, "Are you in?"

CHAPTER 77

Craze: It's Complicated

I wish I could say that Jalina lured me to her room with a scorch of sensuality that would thwart any man's wall of resistance. It was worse. I wanted to be there. I had feelings for her and allowed myself to be there despite knowing that parallel worlds don't exist. You can't pretend that, while living one life, the other isn't hanging above you, living within, listening, judging.

I don't know if being eight thousand miles from Alex affected my thinking. I knew it shouldn't. The news of this guy proposing forced me to look inward. Initially I saw the faces of shock, anger, and doubt sitting next to a bushel of self-condemnation. Then came an awakening. Bubba said they slept together. *She* cheated on *me*. A fact I considered while concocting a justification for going to Jalina's room—an attempt to account for my failings. She cheated on me, asked me to marry her, and then continued her relationship with this guy. I could spend energy lamenting my plight. Analyzing. Figuring out what I did wrong. Or I could get pissed off.

We seldom fought and were never plagued by a stale love. It was still undeniable. I was mad at her for not telling me that her timeline was near a breaking point. But I was angrier at myself, that my sensitivity was so obtuse I didn't, couldn't, recognize her current view on life. I agonized over my lack of empathy and feared I was fundamentally unkind.

It was tender but awkward, non-award-winning sex. I'd never been with anyone other than Alex, and it was different—the kissing, the contours, the pace, the amount of pressure. It was quirky and fun, but I couldn't get my mind off Alex. It felt like I was in a movie.

I watched myself move from frame to frame, each time stopping, thinking, and consciously stepping into the next frame. It was on me. The conflict affected my concentration. I didn't love Jalina. In another place and time I could have, but I didn't. I was in *like* with her, forced to grapple with unprocessed affection. I'd never cheated on Alex. I'd had opportunities—a couple that tested how tightly my gravel was bound—but despite enjoying the attraction, I kept my distance. I was human, but also faithful.

It was no longer a spontaneous kiss or flirtation with Jalina. We had an easy understanding between us. But physicality consumed us that night, perhaps nourished by months of shared peril. She subdued me with her dancer's thighs, inciting me to walk a forbidden path. Her strength and delicacy built steadily, driving us to a showdown of who would please who more. In the end, the dogfight in my mind took hold, and when the bright blush rose in her face, I found myself thinking of Alex—unfulfilled, contrite, and drained of my dignity.

The next night, we packed and went to the station for the 4:00 a.m. train to Beitbridge. Cathy and Graham didn't join us. They withdrew from the lawsuit and were flying to Malawi. Travis had bought a cardboard shipping cylinder at an office supply store, perfect for storing the rolled-up scrolls. Mad Dog, Emilie, Jalina, Travis, and I found and defended a train compartment that had six seats and a foldout table. Travis drew the curtains.

Emilie and I had already started examining the scrolls and had outlined segments of the manufacturing process. Multiple components had to be synthesized in order to make the gene editing work. Sophisticated equipment was cited. Specific temperatures, pHs, dwell times, raw materials, solutions, pipet tip calibrations, isolation and extraction procedures, harvesting, and storage were detailed. We found instructions for producing two different nanoparticles, which would be used to deliver the components once inside the host.

There was no mention of mosquitoes anywhere. No mention of malaria. In a programmatic textual paragraph titled "Delivery," a plan was outlined that used a government-sponsored milk program as an artifice to distribute the gene-editing solutions into the Black population. We saw numerous references to Hemoglobin S, the type found in sickle cells.

"It's strange, these references to sickle cells," I said. They were mentioned so often I'd dreamt that sickle cells were chasing me through the Callahan Tunnel. "Is it possible that the genes being edited do, in fact, have something to do with preventing malaria? Winston sold this to us as a remedy to stomp out malaria, and now we see these sickle references throughout."

That irked Mad Dog. "The guy is scum. Didn't like him the minute we met. Besides, what's sickle cell got to do with malaria?"

Emilie grinned. We started to talk at the same time, but she nodded for me to go ahead.

"It's been shown that people who have sickle cell have resistance to malaria. You remember when we were with Winston, and he went over what DNA really does?"

"Yeah, sure . . . some of it," Mad Dog said.

"Hemoglobin is a protein," I said. "Red blood cells use it to carry oxygen around your body. In sickle cell, there is a single change to the DNA sequence of hemoglobin."

"You mean in one of the ATCGs?"

"Right. Hemoglobin has two alpha and two beta protein chains." I stopped, looked at Travis and Jalina, and stepped it back in order to give a quick primer. "Okay, guys. Follow the bouncing ball here. Proteins are made of strings of amino acids linked together. Humans have only twenty different amino acids. The chains can be short or long. They are three-dimensional, twisted, a fact that is very important. Think of them as a key that must fit a lock in order to work properly."

"You mean all proteins, like muscles and shit, are just different combinations of these twenty amino acids?" Travis asked.

"Yes. So, the next question is: How is the order of the amino acids in the protein string determined? DNA. It's the boss. You've seen diagrams, right? The double helix with a strand of letters. Well, there are only four letters, A, T, C, and G. Those are called nucleotides." I drew out a long strand of twenty-one ATCGs in random order on a piece of paper. I circled the first three letters, then circled the following three letters, and went down the line.

"When this strand of twenty-one nucleotides is processed by your cells, it will make seven amino acids that will be linked together. Each group of three codes for one amino acid. If the first three are GGT, one amino acid is made. If the next three nucleotides are ATC, a different one is made."

Mad Dog was annoyed. "What's sickle cell got to do with malaria?"

"When a mosquito bites you," I glanced at the women, "I might mention that only female mosquitoes can infect you with malaria." Without a thought, Emilie bit Mad Dog in the shoulder.

"The mosquito injects the malarial parasite into your blood," I said. "It goes to the liver cells, reproduces, and releases more malaria into your blood, infecting more red blood cells. The membrane of a red blood cell has a protein called actin. Malaria steals the actin and uses it to form a bridge across the cell, which becomes its home before it returns to the liver.

"Here's the thing. If you change a single letter in the chain, it will make a different amino acid. In the case of the hemoglobin found in sickle cells, one of the ATCGs is different, causing the sixth amino acid in the protein to be valine instead of glutamic acid. It sounds small, but valine is less polar than glutamic acid. It's less water soluble, which makes the cell sticky."

Mad Dog appealed. "How do you remember this shit? Again, English please."

"I worked in hematology at BU Medical Center. We did malarial studies there. Anyway, it turns out that the same change that causes cells to sickle also prevents the malarial parasite from stealing the actin, which, in turn, blocks it from attaching to the red cell membrane. It creates a dead end to the life cycle of malaria. The bad news is that the stiff fibers stick together, causing the cell to curl up and sickle, especially if oxygen is low—like if you exert yourself or if you have pneumonia. Sickle cells can't squeeze through your capillaries and clog them up. Leads to pain and even death, especially if you got a sickle gene from both of your parents."

"That's all great and interestin'," Travis said. "But what's he trying to do?"

Emilie and I exchanged glances. She said, "It's hard to say. Maybe he found a way to use the good part of this sickle cell defense to prevent malaria but not harm the person."

"Or could this be a *cure* for people who already have sickle cell disease?" I asked Emilie. "His whole shtick is gene editing. He might be editing the genes that cause sickle cell, enabling them to make normal hemoglobin. That would be extraordinary."

Travis smirked. I stared at him and said, "What?"

"So, what you're sayin' is, in people who have sickle cell, he wants to switch out one of the nucleotides that code for the sixth amino acid in hemoglobin so it will make glutamic acid instead of valine?" A grin stretched across his face. He flipped a hand. One by one we broke into a belly laugh, shook our heads, and savored the twinkle in his eye.

But Mad Dog didn't laugh. He was unfazed by our rosy postulation. "If that were the case—if he developed a cure for sickle cell—why wouldn't he just tell us that?" The high pitch of our cheeks dropped to our chins like a landslide.

CHAPTER 78

Ron: Selous Smellous

Ron Reid was in his office enjoying his morning coffee and Marmite on toast. He scanned the *Rhodesian Herald* and spotted a two-inch blurb at the bottom of page three: "Stranded Tourists to Visit Vic Falls." The two-sentence article wasn't important, but the photo of the tourists sitting in a Johannesburg bar nearly sucked his eyeballs into his puffy cheeks. He squinted to bring the picture into focus, and his heart drowned in disappointment. Hot air fluttered across his vocals, barely loud enough for a dog to hear. "Travis."

There he was, in the bar, in Johannesburg, guzzling a pint with the Americans when he should be yanking them into a dark basement and encouraging them to be truthful, making them fear for their family's safety. If they didn't have the dolls, he should've dragged them back to the swamps to find them. The smell was foul.

Reid's disposition turned to that of a rhino with a sore head. His nostrils spread. The hair in them burned. His initial trust in Travis had been resolute. But there he was, in the photo, with his own agenda—sly, uncommunicative, and hairy at the heel. Selous Scouts were supposed to improvise, blend in, become friends, disarm their prey. But they were to be scrupulous with their superiors. From Jo'burg, Travis could have easily called him. He hadn't.

And where was the scout he'd sent to Johannesburg to team up with Travis, confront the Americans, raid their room? He should have reported back by now. Reid returned to the photo and the box article. No byline. He called the *Herald* and asked to talk to the reporter who wrote the article. He wanted to know when the tourists were traveling to Victoria Falls. Travis had betrayed him. This was personal.

CHAPTER 79

Craze: Hippocratic Yuck

Our train arrived in Beitbridge, South Africa, and ambled across the border to Beitbridge, Rhodesia. Rhodesian immigration wanted us to have plane tickets to our home of origin before they'd let us in. An officer recognized us from the press coverage. He conferred with one, two, three other officers. Opinions were exchanged. They called superiors in Salisbury, the capital. When the honchos heard who we were, they tempered their bluster. "The boss asked me to apologize to you folks for all the trouble we've caused—you know, with the helicopters at the ferry. Hope you understand. Welcome to Rhodesia."

We walked, found a car rental place run by a guy named Leo. He outfitted us with a 1972 Fiat Giardiniera station wagon: a boxy white bust-up loaded with scars of abuse but had enough room for us to spread out scrolls. The others went for a 1970 VW bus: a two-toned red-and-white classic. The delay caused us to miss the one o'clock convoy to Bulawayo. The next one was at 7:30 a.m. Leo warned us to never travel without a convoy. His friend's brother and parents were killed in an ambush when they tried to go it alone.

An immigration officer popped into Leo's shop and invited us to sleep on the floor of a private club he belonged to. We took him up on it. That evening, he introduced us to several soldiers who were winding down at the club. One guy had used his own private plane to fight in the war: rigged the landing gear to carry bombs made from pipes, TNT, nuts, and bolts. They brought us chocolate pudding bars and asked the chef to cook us some gem squash. A woman gave us camouflage bandanas. Soldiers sang, pleading with us to join them. "*I don't mind dying for a Rhodesian cause, but I'll never die in a misguided war.*" Their exaggerated hospitality added complexity to my internal conflict. People with bad ideologies weren't always fang-toothed ogres dripping with venom. I shuddered when I asked myself how they'd treat me if they knew I was trying to throw a stick into their war. But my skin color alone accounted for the rush of goodwill, and they probably had few opportunities to be hospitable in war.

In the morning, a sergeant gave an orientation speech for the 7:30 a.m. convoy. "The sides of the road are cleared for thirty meters on both sides to discourage an ambush from the terrorists." I noticed he called them terrorists, not guerillas. "We will travel fast, as fast as the slowest car in the convoy can go. If you are attacked, floor it and get the hell out there. If you get hit, get out of your car and lie low in the ditch on the side of the road. We'll come get you. Do *not* stay in your car." Our adrenals released epinephrine, which bound itself to receptors that dilated our pupils. Travis nodded as if to say, It's okay.

Three Mazda pickup trucks with upright, cylindrical, bulletproof gun turrets bolted to the beds were spaced at the beginning, middle, and end of the convoy. A swivel seat for the gunner was in the center of the iron mesh cylinder. The lead vehicle was a mine detector that looked like a triangular bug with eyes. Tires were extended on long axles, and a barrel-like chamber protected the driver. Our car was behind the middle gun turret, which was manned by one of the soldiers we drank beer with. Every car had guns—except ours. Several people came over and welcomed us to Rhodesia, wished us a good trip, assured us everything was going to be all right.

Travis drove. The pace settled at 120 km/h, around 75 mph. Nothing happened. Emilie and I had pored over the scrolls on the train and made an outline of the manufacturing process. But we were stuck. Neither of us knew which codons coded for which amino acids. If you wrote out every possible three-letter combination of ATCG, there were sixty-four combinations. Each combination was a codon. Humans only have twenty amino acids, because sometimes two or three codons, groups of three nucleotides, will code for the same amino acid. And a few codons are used to start and stop translation. Unless you worked with it every day, you needed a table to know which codons code for which amino acids. We needed a genetics or cell biology textbook.

Soldiers offered us good wishes when we arrived in Bulawayo at around noon. A one-dollar-a-day hostel was our resting place. Travis pulled the hood of his sweatshirt over his head. He'd been at the base in Bulawayo before he was whisked off to train for the mission to kill Nkomo. He might run into a Selous Scout. He was also worried that he might need Sipho's help at some point. We agreed that he should contact Sipho while we were there and let him know that he'd found us, and we were close to figuring out what's in the dolls. Sipho's office at Wimpy's was just a mile away.

Travis and I went to the National University of Science and Technology, NUST, to search for a genetics textbook. Mad Dog and Emilie went to look for one at the Bulawayo Polytechnic, which was closer to town. But the NUST library was still under construction. By the time we got back to the hostel, Mad Dog was sitting outside at a picnic table writing in his journal. When he saw us, he bobbed his head and said, "Found one." He shot his thumb toward the hostel.

Emilie sat on the bed, humming, squinting over a section of the scrolls, shifting her eyes between the scroll and a textbook. She held her hand up, head still down. Finally, she looked up. "This is fascinating. I admit, I was skeptical. But it looks like gene editing probably works. It's one of the greatest advances in science in all of womankind." Smirk.

"What's with all the sickle cell references?" I asked. "Are they after malaria at all?"

"Haven't gotten that far. I started at the top just to rebuild my foundation. Now that I have a solid understanding of how it works, I'm working on the detail."

Chris popped her head in, looked at the scrolls, and rolled her eyes. "A sorry bunch of dags you are. A bloody nerd game you picked up in Jo'burg?" She told us they were going out to dinner at 6:30—two hours.

Damn, I'd planned to call Alex, and the telecom office closed at five. I ran out, past Mad Dog, and yelled, "On my way to call Alex." He straightened, jumped from his seat, said he was coming. I asked myself how I could be so lucky. The phone rang. A cassette tape clicked. "Hi, this is Alex." *Damn, it's mid-morning there. She's at work. How could I be so stupid?* "I'm away for two weeks and will return your call when I return." *You shouldn't say that on the phone, Alex.* "Please leave a message at the beep." *Wait. Two weeks? Where did she go for two weeks?*

That was a dagger. *Maybe the glow will wear off in two weeks. They will quarrel. She will come to her senses. He'll say something bad about her roommate. Don't hang up. Say something. No mumbling.*

"Alex, this is Craze. Sorry I missed you. I love you. I said I'd call back in a few days but missed the time zones . . . We were on the road midday. I'm sure you've been thinking about our lives together and the love that has filled them, how it has held us together. The thought of moving into a new episode makes me happy and whole." *God, that's cheesy.* "I want to marry you, Alex. Um . . . okay, I was sad, uh, upset to hear about this guy you mentioned. That you're . . . interested in. I've thought about it. A lot. About my imperfections. My . . . selfishness. I want to, no, I will be better. For you. I'll grow for you. With you." *What else? Say more.* "Oh, don't feel awkward about coming back to me. I can overcome what happened." Voice drop. "I can even understand it." *Perk up, you idiot.* "It's not a matter of learning. I have to do a better job expressing what I already know. I'm committed to you. Getting through the hard times. I'm not going to quit on you." *That was good. Cliché, but sincere.* "I want to have kids with you. I'll teach them to love travel, to love hiking, and to love the Doors. I'll even take a shot at teaching them to be charitable and kind." I paused again. I hadn't prepared for an answering machine. "Oh. We decided to travel through Rhodesia—to see Victoria Falls. The court date is next week. I'll call you when you get back . . . from wherever you are. I love you."

The cheerfulness of my voice faded. Tears leaked, found my chin before I thought to wipe them. My nose dripped. Mad Dog put his hands on my shoulders and looked at me straight on. "It's not over, Craze. I'd kiss you, but you're too ugly." Snot shot onto my upper lip. Mad Dog made a joke. Bad timing, but Mad Dog made a joke.

Dinner was merry. We filled the corner of a steak house and ate fine Rhodesian beef with an array of salads, vegetables, bread, and dessert for $2.90. I saw a behavior I'd noted in Beitbridge too. The Black waiters—or any service people—served us with hands shaking, afraid to do anything wrong, like a sense of inferiority had been drummed into their essence. If they spilled a drop of coffee or fumbled your change, they trembled. They flinched, while soldiers drank tequila and sang depraved lyrics, words said without fear of reprisal or castigation. *"He has foreskin hanging to his knees,"* and, *"He has pulled the clitoris, the gland. Pull, Pull, he has pulled the testicle, the gland. The drum of the vulva is beating."*

Still, I thanked one soldier for the hospitality we'd received. He said Rhodesia needed all the friends it could get. Another asked, "What will you tell people about Rhodesia after you leave?" I wondered whether their friendliness was born from a concern for their international image or if it was possible they were conscious of their flaws. Yes, they controlled the country, but had a life where men, woman, and children carried guns to the grocery store, to church. A woman told me she had a gun hidden in every room, worried that she'd be attacked while sipping tea.

I went to bed with fitful ruminations that I'd screwed things up with Alex and had frightful visions of men with foreskin that fell to their knees.

CHAPTER 80

Craze: Give Don't Take

The route from Bulawayo to Victoria Falls was the most hotly contested stretch of road in the war. The 7:00 a.m. convoy included six pickup trucks with gun turrets and two minesweepers. If one was hit, there was a backup. Jalina noted that once again we were the only ones without guns. "Feels like we're traveling naked," she said.

Travis yanked a pistol from his back belt. "Not completely naked. Compliments of Sipho, a Beretta M92. I only got two nine-millimeter clips with ten rounds in each. It's something."

Emilie already had the scrolls out. We agreed that she'd study the DNA editing section while I examined the section on nanoparticles. After a half hour she elbowed me, her cheeks brushed gray with confusion. She pointed to the genetics book.

"See this?" I leaned in. She pointed at a scroll that had a long string of ATCGs sequenced, more than six hundred, with a hundred forty-six highlighted in red. She'd taken a pencil and drawn a line between every third letter at the end of the red area. "Look here. This string of letters codes for the amino acids in the beta chain of hemoglobin. But look at the sixth amino acid. It's CTC, cytosine-thymine-cytosine. When I look at the table, it says CTC is the three-letter code for glutamic acid."

I looked at her, wondering what the problem was. "Well, that's normal. It's supposed to be glutamic acid."

"But look here." She underlined another string of letters. "This is what they are changing the DNA strand *to*. They are changing CTC to CAC. They're changing the middle nucleotide from thymine to adenine. CAC is the DNA code for making valine."

I had to engineer in my head around what Winston was trying to do. Her discovery was so heinous I searched for reasons to think she was mistaken, had gotten it wrong. But it was unambiguous. Travis, who'd been listening intently blurted out, "You gotta be shitting me. He ain't trying to cure malaria. He ain't trying to cure sickle cell." He paused, as if he were doing the same thing as me, trying to find a different interpretation. Perhaps he was recalling what Ron Reid had said, that it would guarantee that White rule was preserved in Rhodesia. "He's trying to change the hemoglobin of normal people into sickle cell hemoglobin. He's planning to *give* sickle cell to the Black Africans."

Emilie swore. "Jesus Christ, Craze. Travis."

Jalina whispered, "Crap on a cracker. I'm going to be ill."

Mad Dog sat silent. Deliberate.

I struggled, finally saying the first words that came to me. "That would be . . . genocide." I thought for a moment. "Not everyone with sickle cell disease dies, but a lot do, especially if they have limited access to healthcare. And those who don't die, suffer. This change in their DNA would give them the full sickle cell disease, not just the trait. Homozygous. Like they inherited a sickle cell gene from both of their parents. It's either death or a painful life."

Jalina tilted her head back and called out loud, "The milk program."

"Huh? What about it?"

"You told me that one of the scrolls said they were going to use the milk program. Can they spread it that way?"

I found the scroll and reexamined it. It made sense. "They plan to use lipid nanoparticles to deliver the editing components to endothelial cells in the bone marrow, where red blood cells are made. These lipids are designed to have an affinity for bone marrow. That's it. They want to give people sickle cell via the milk program."

Jalina was indignant. "And the milk program is for Black Rhodesians only. The Whites have their own supply."

Travis cut in. "When I was on patrol with the scouts, the guys told me that the men in Black families usually drink the milk. You'd think the kids would get it. But the men, the providers, they take it to be strong."

"And the White Rhodesians know that," I said. "They'll make sure the milk gets delivered to the right villages."

"This is insane," Travis said. "Reid was right. Once the Black population is weakened with sickle cell, they'll be scared shitless. They won't understand it. won't have the will to fight no more. Wicked. Guerillas trained in Tanzania will think they'll catch sickle cell if they come. The revolution will die."

Jalina's lips puffed. Her nose bled from a rise in blood pressure. "The message is not lost on me. They couldn't make a more supremacist statement. Everyone knows sickle cell afflicts more Black people than White. This guy Winston could have picked any disease. He's trying to tell Black Africans that they are genetically inferior."

"It's strictly a genetic disease," I said. "They'll never suspect milk—won't know how it happened. If it were an infection, maybe. But nobody will tie sickle cell disease to bad milk."

Mad Dog turned his neck and faced us in the back seat. "Craze, if this happened and these people all get sickle cell, what will happen to their babies?"

I bit the webbing between my thumb and pointer.

"You know, like if it's changing their DNA, will it also change the DNA in their sperm and eggs? Will all their future kids automatically get the sickle cell gene, and will they pass it on to the next generation?"

Emilie cried, "Putain de merde."

CHAPTER 81

Craze: Unspent Revelations

As we pulled into the town of Victoria Falls, clouds of mist swirled above the trees—a result of the Zambezi River throwing itself over the precipitous cliffs of the riverbed, where its waters plummet 350 feet into a chasm and crash into the basalt bedrock that formed 180 million years ago. The collision at the base is violent. Water rebuffs and drives back to the sky, befogging the airspace above the First Gorge. Dubbed Mosi-oa-Tunya, "the smoke that thunders," by locals, it is more than twice the height of Niagara and is over a mile wide—the largest curtain of water in the world.

We pitched our tents on the lower apron of the Victoria Falls Hotel, whose white, swanlike wingspan stretched around grounds that lay a thousand feet from the oxbow bend in the Zambezi River—a point where the second gorge hairpins into the third. The bush war had turned a magnificent jewel, with its reflection pool, mango trees, gardens, and manicured lawns, into a monument of bygone glory, now desperate for business. The town's population had fallen from 11,000 to 168 in the past year, the cruelty of war impacting every man, woman, child, and enterprise. I assembled Mad Dog, Travis, Jalina, and Emilie for a final ratification of a decision we'd reached in the car. Mad Dog carried the mailing tube with the scrolls under his arm.

"Second thoughts? Anyone?" Jalina, Emilie, and Travis nodded. Mad Dog grunted and said he'd tell the others that we were going down to see the falls.

We followed a gravel path through a few scrub and acacia trees and past the Big Tree, a colossal baobab that was said to be two thousand years old. Beetroot scents from geosmin and the redolence of wet vulcanized rock wrapped around us as we approached the Devil's Pool, an absurd spot reachable from an island on the Zambian side, where adventurists can sit in a pool that is fronted by a bulwark of rocks perched on the edge of the falls. The path had no people or fences, creating a spectral stillness that coexisted with the unrest of the falls. Our clothes flapped like a loose sail in a squall. We walked along the rim of the First Gorge and were at eye level with the waters of the Zambezi, which flowed directly at us and tossed itself over the opposite cliff into the gorge in front of us. We tracked along the rocky path that ran parallel to the falls.

Its power reminded me of how helpless and wide-eyed I'd been. When faced with an urge to be part of something flashy, a turning point in science that I had nothing to do with, I'd been typically impulsive, never considering what would become of our caper. Instead, I indulged in the anticipation of regalement and ignored plausible peril. My friend was dead, my relationship with Alex teetered, and we were about to heave a brilliant cornerstone of technology into the raging waters of Queen Victoria. I'd convinced myself that I did these things for many reasons: for the adventure, for the audacity, and yes, for my interest in people and cultures. I must have thought it brought me happiness, but happiness was further from me than it was before I left; before I set foot in Liberia; before I set off on this latest whim, fantasy, urge, whatever you want to call it; before I clumsily avoided Alex's parting question.

"Craze, there's something I should tell you."

I stared at Travis, as did the others. *No more surprises Travis, please.*

"You know when I seen Sipho in Bulawayo?" I nodded. "It ain't no big deal. Well, it is a big deal. In a way. No, it is . . . a big deal. You got this background, you know, with this genetics biology and stuff. It's a good thing, but you know, it ain't light—what you're about to do. I mean, what you're about to do ain't a light thing. In the long run. It's just that . . ."

Jalina shouted, "For God's sake, get the thorn out of your backside. Spit it out, mate!"

293

He wove his fingers together, flipped them around, and stretched. "Okay. That there." He pointed at Mad Dog. "Them scrolls in Mad Dog's hands. That's it. That's all that's left. At least it's all that's left in writing. Sipho talked to the guys at Weathermen Africa. They destroyed the research center in Liberia. It's gone—completely. The backup tapes for the computer were in Switzerland. They're gone too."

He inhaled, tilted his head imperceptibly.

"When you throw the scrolls into Victoria Falls, it will take years to reassemble all the pieces of research. The scientists have already scattered. They ain't happy with Winston."

"Grâce à Dieu! Thank God," Emilie said.

I was dumbstruck. "What do you mean it's gone?"

He flicked all ten fingers in the air. "Blown up. The entire center."

I understood why Travis wanted to tell me, why he fumbled in his speech. Despite his malicious intentions, Winston had mapped out a technology that could truly help the world. We were about to destroy it. Travis had gained an appreciation of the good that gene editing could do if guided by the right hands.

While driving to the falls, we'd debated what to do, and agreed we wanted to destroy the scrolls. The Weathermen were right. Winston's goals were so hateful, it was dangerous to let the world know about it, that it was even possible. Weathermen Africa didn't want to put ideas into bad people's heads. Mad Dog thought it would be fitting to throw the scrolls into the vortex of the falls, an homage to Bubba, whose remains went over the falls weeks earlier.

Mad Dog and Chewbacca stared at a tourist map. He said, "Let's walk to the Rainbow Falls section—at the junction of the Second Gorge. The outlet there flows under the Vic Falls Bridge, and off toward the Indian Ocean. The scrolls will get bashed to bits at the bottom of the falls and then be pulverized by rocks in the whitewater."

We walked.

Travis whistled. Jalina twirled, showing off a dance move. When we reached Horseshoe Falls, which was halfway to Rainbow Falls, a rainbow stretched across the sky and begged us to take a photo. I huddled the group, set the timer on my camera, and propped it on a rock for a group picture. Mad Dog held up the mailing tube for the shot.

I asked one more time: "The whole center . . . destroyed? You're sure?"

I was about to press the timer on the camera and run back to the group when a dainty voice, barely audible over the roar of the falls, emerged from a side path in the brush.

"I can take the picture for you, Crazy Luke."

Spikes shot up my spine. I turned. There she was, standing in the mist with the sun illuminating her left cheek. My instinct was to run and hug her. For some reason this instinct is common when you see someone in a different setting than usual, in a place that is out of context. It can even happen with people you are neutral with, but the circumstance spawns a feeling of kinship. I stepped toward her, but my happiness impulse succumbed to logic. I stopped. Questions replaced my goodwill. *What is she doing here? How did she find us?*

I looked in every direction, wondering if she was alone. Mad Dog stepped forward, walked toward us, peering at her through the colored mist. He slipped the mailing tube behind his back and joined in my disbelief. He stuck out his neck and uttered, "Betsy?"

"Hello, Mad Dog. Long time since Old Man George paddled you to the airport in Liberia."

I was fearful of the answer to my next question. "What are you doing here?"

Betsy approached, hands at her side, no one in sight. Her smile was soft, lips partially parted like a proud mother. But her eyes held a secret. She glanced at Travis, Emilie, and Jalina, still standing at the photo spot. "Don't get too close to the edge," she yelled. "The rocks are slippery." She waved them up. They came and formed a semicircle.

"Craze, Mad Dog. You know that Winston suspected that someone at ACORN was sabotaging the delivery of our technology?" We nodded. "And then he arranged for you to deliver it—and did so without my knowledge I might add." Her voice was broken with contempt. Mad Dog and I shared a distrustful glance but held our silence. "I was responsible. I was the insider. 'The mole,' if you wish. It broke my heart. I began to suspect Winston was hiding something. A change in the tone of our dialogue, words or concepts left unfinished in our discussions, understated shifts of his eyes, a clever response that emitted a stench of avoidance. When you work with someone for so long . . ."

It made sense, but I was still wary.

"Why didn't you confront him? You're the CEO," I said.

Betsy's cheeks caved as if someone had extracted a scoop of ice cream. She leaned against a bolder. "Because I wasn't sure. He made a subtle change to one of our research lines. It was so miniscule it took me months of sneaking around his office; studying logs stored on lab equipment; eavesdropping on phone calls, to figure it out. Then I found comprehensive documents in his safe. I collaborated with my colleagues at Weathermen Africa to prevent the protocols from reaching their destination until I was certain."

Travis broke in. "You found out he changed it so you were givin' people sickle cell instead of curing malaria. Right? Like that kind of subtle?"

Betsy was shocked. "How do you know that? How could you possibly . . .?"

Mad Dog opened the mail container, unrolled one of the scrolls, and then rolled it up and put it back into the container. Betsy's jaw fell to her chest. She reached her arms toward the scrolls. Mad Dog stepped back.

"You are certainly industrious. You not only unraveled the dolls but you deciphered what's in them. Impressive. Before I ask what you plan to do with the scrolls, I want you to know that the research center in Liberia is gone." Her sweet voice was tainted with an acrid syrup, face muscles flattened and unmoving.

"I arranged for ACORN to be destroyed. I asked Weathermen Africa to do it. I told them where the backup tapes were stored in Switzerland." She started to tremble in what looked like self-disgust. "The center was my life. The chimpanzees . . . a life with meaning, with gratification. We did things that have an infinite capacity for good. But if Winston showed me one thing, it's that the world is not ready for gene editing. If guided by the wrong hands, the harm can be incalculable. That so many humans have an innate calling to be destructive has made me weep. The ACORN scientists, it could be decades before a team of their caliber reassembles. When they do, I hope they find a way to put people in a just state of mind."

Her skin turned ashen and tight. Drops of water bounced off her face.

"Now. What do you intend to do with the scrolls?"

"We're feeding them to the falls," Mad Dog said. "Food for the crocodile gods."

Color crept into her cheeks. She smiled, lifting an air that had become tentative.

"Happy to hear that, Mad Dog."

"What are *you* doing here?" Travis asked. "How'd you know we were here?"

"I followed Winston here. Once the center was destroyed, I knew he'd try to hunt down the dolls. They are the only written remains of his work. Ah. And with all the press you've gotten, it hasn't been hard to figure out where you are. Winston is staying at the Kingdom Hotel. It's a small town. It won't be hard to find the famous tourists."

"Then let's go," Mad Dog said. "It's two more minutes to the Rainbow Falls. That's where we're tossing them." Then he asked, "Betsy, did you know Bubba was on the Kazungula ferry?"

She staggered. Her voice was disturbed, laden with regret. "Yes. I suspected as much. He was coming to warn you. He felt responsible for hooking you up with Winston. We agreed that he'd go to warn you while I made plans with Weathermen Africa."

"I don't get it. What's your connection to Weathermen Africa?" I asked.

"I was in the SDS in College. The Weather Underground grew out of that group—too violent for my tastes. But I still had friends and kept in touch, especially when they branched into Africa and focused on fighting apartheid." Betsy looked at Travis, hesitated, seemingly in need of sharing guilt for Bubba's death. "Have you told them, Travis?"

Travis pinched his lips between his thumb and forefinger. Chains pulled his shoulders toward the center of the earth. His eyes fidgeted. They fixed on mine, then shifted to Betsy, to Mad Dog, to the falls, and finally to the ground. "Craze, Mad Dog. I'm sorry." He paused, but guilt never penetrated his face. "It was me. I blew up the ferry." He raised his eyes to mine. He was not going to look away.

It took a moment to grasp what he'd said. He'd just admitted to killing our friend. Our best friend. Rage engulfed me. I charged and knocked Travis to the ground. We wrestled like we did when we were kids. The rocky ledges were wet. I turned to punching— punches he deflected with ease. He didn't fight back. I was never a match for him, and he knew it. He just took it. I landed a blow to his temple, another to his lip, reached for his balls and squeezed. That was enough. He stabbed a forearm to my head and threw me off like I was a beach towel. I tumbled toward the edge. Jalina shrieked. I stuck my leg out and thwap, stopped rolling. I stood. Another charge was in me, and I started at him, sneakers slipping on the rocks like a kid in the snow. I looked foolish. When I reached Travis I dropped to my knees, curled my head down, and cried.

"Listen . . . Craze." He looked at Mad Dog. "Mad Dog. This is hollow . . . and it sucks." He spoke like he was in the back of a church. "But . . . but I'm an agent. Embedded in the Selous Scouts. I was supposed to blow up the ferry with you guys on it and sink them dolls along with it. The only reason I didn't is because I saw you standin' there on the shore in Botswana. I was like, 'What the hell is he doin' here?' Then I realized you were the two guys I was looking for." Travis bent, placed his hands on his knees, and brought his head close to mine. I could smell his biltong breath. "How could I blow up the ferry with you on it?"

His words stank like a bucket of chum after three days in the sun. "Why'd you have to blow it up at all?" I was shouting now. "Why didn't you say it was a dud? Say the bombs didn't ignite? Jesus, Travis, you could have said anything."

His head cocked, he'd fallen to his knees and was holding onto his balls. "If that ferry doesn't blow, Ron Reid is expecting me to bring him the dolls. By sinking the ferry, I could tell him the dolls went down with it."

I screamed, "Fuck you, Tommy!" My viscera flamed. I wasn't interested in his post-game commentary and self-justification. Linkages in my head wanted more answers. "Why were you going to sink it with us on it? What good would that do?"

"Look, the information was in two places: at ACORN and in those dolls. Sipho wanted me to get rid of the dolls at first. Cameron from Weathermen Africa was going to take care of destroying the research center." He looked at Betsy. "Apparently in collaboration with her. Sinkin' the ferry allowed me to get rid of the dolls and keep my cover." He waited for me to respond. I had nothing. "Now that we know what Winston was up to, it's a good thing we succeeded. You succeeded. You figured it out." Travis looked around and swept his hand in the air. "All of you."

Mad Dog caught Travis in an inconsistency. "Your story doesn't add up. After you blew up the ferry, you didn't go back to Reid and tell him the dolls went down with it."

The changes in the countenance of one's face when caught in a lie are easy to spot: a twitch in the lower eyelid, a cornea glazed and unguided, a false smile. "I had no time to think. I needed an excuse for Reid and thought sinking the ferry was the right thing to do. But I realized he would find out that the ferry was going in the wrong direction when it sunk. He'd know you weren't on it. So, I told Reid I was going after you guys to get the dolls. In any case, if the ferry didn't go down, I'd have had no excuse for not getting the dolls and bringing them to him. At least not right away."

"This is convoluted. Either way, killing a few people is just fine with you, right Travis?" My disposition needle was pinned on disgust. His willingness to hurt people for a cause finally sunk in. The altruistic armor of his Robin Hood life: a man fighting for the people, the elusive warrior for righteousness. It peeled off me like a bad sunburn. Hearing and reading about him over the years, even talking to him about it since we met at the bar in Maun, was twisted. But it was no longer distant. Now he had killed my friend.

"I don't know what to say." By now mist had penetrated everyone's clothes and hair. Drops of water trickled from a set of rosary beads Jalina had pulled from her pocket. Travis was somber but said, "Sometimes it is . . . fine. Not fine, but necessary—when you imagine the alternative. Your friend Bubba is a hero. He was coming to warn you. He dropped everything to make sure those dolls didn't get into the wrong hands. And they didn't."

"You're a dick. And a murderer." It was a nice try, but the gratuitous pep talk didn't resonate with me. I had some understanding of his thought process, but it gave me little comfort. I realized how much our lives had diverged in the past few years. Travis waited for me to respond. When I didn't, he tried again.

"Craze, we did it. You, Mad Dog, Jalina, Betsy, Emilie. We did it. We destroyed this guy, Winston, and his plans."

The barrel of a Lee-Enfield L1A1 semi-automatic rifle poked from behind a thicket of red milkwood trees and approached us. Attached to it was a fibrous man wearing a brown beret that edged across his forehead an inch above the eyebrow, the excess felt draped over his right ear. An osprey insignia was conspicuous over the left eye. His gravelly voice penetrated the rumble of the falls, enough for us to hear his declaration. "Not yet."

CHAPTER 82

Craze: Convergence

Colonel Reid approached Travis with the punitive face of a proud father whose son was caught stealing lobsters from his neighbor's pots. A father whose disappointment trampled his pride, fueled partially by anger but more so by his own misjudgment and blindness. He'd been hoodwinked and had allowed his fondness for Travis to supplant his objectivity.

"Brutus! Working with the floppies. Remove the pistol from your belt, Travis. Put it on the ground." Travis did as asked.

"Step away and show your hands."

A shadow emerged from the milkwood trees: tall, long blond hair unkempt and flowing, wet cigarette behind his ear. A green-and-white Rhodesia rugby shirt with a white lion insignia clung to his torso. Mad Dog gnarled with contempt, "Asshole."

I was prepared to stare Winston down, but his eyes were fixed on the mailing tube in Mad Dog's hands. Reid grinned. I wanted to rant, but Winston spoke before I got started. His voice was calm, measured, and rehearsed. He'd surely justified his ideology in his mind many times.

"It is not simply our place to live among nature," he began, staring at the falls, one of nature's most beautiful creations. "It is our place to guide nature, to live *with* her, not *beside* her." He paused, eerily loitering within himself, preparing to dispense the sagacity that was his gift to the world. "If man wants to use his power and intellect to divert these falls and turn them into electricity, he can do so. Tourists won't like it, but the evolution of our species incudes intellect. It is not to be squandered." His eyes locked on mine. "I'm sure you agree."

Emilie threw her arms up. Reid jerked his rifle at her but restrained his impulse to squeeze the trigger. She was steaming. "You think that being smart gives you privilege? Gives you a license to destroy and debilitate noble people? Your *mind* is the disease. Barbarism is not a substitute for intellect. Fuck you and your attempts to dignify racist application of science in the guise of evolution."

Reid interrupted. "Noble people? You call them noble people? There is an order to this world, young lady." Reid had turned professorial, as if we were his pupils. "An order that is progressive, an order that has purpose. Mankind has an order. As Saint Thomas Aquinas said, 'There are possible and necessary beings.' These 'noble people' as you call them are not part of *man*kind. They don't live like us. They don't behave like us. They don't eat like us, and they certainly don't think like us. Oh, there are bohemians who want to elevate them. But you can't change nature. Their place is to serve as we allow. We can treat them well, and we do, but it's not our responsibility to cultivate them into something they are not."

Jalina twisted rosary beads around her fingers. The acrimony behind Reid's rhetoric seemed to coat the back of her tongue. She'd seen the squalid conditions in Soweto, the trembling waiters in Beitbridge, the "whites only" signs everywhere. But it was different to hear it verbalized so bluntly from a supremacist's heart. She blurted, "Thomas Aquinas said God was the only necessary being. You left that part out. What's that make you?"

I forgot about our situation for a moment and drifted. I thought, Are we that stupid, even when it is so plainly in our face? Or is it easier for us—and by us, I mean White people—to put our antennae of racism aside, only to pontificate against it when it is convenient? When it serves our moral high ground? When we want to portray that we are culturally enlightened?

Winston picked up where he left off, more animated, each word crisp with intent. "These—animals—stole—my—home. Killed—my—parents. Took—everything—from—me."

"They decapitated his parents, ripped their faces off, and sent them to him in a box. Is that something noble people do?" Reid asked. He glared at Emilie.

Winston approached Mad Dog and put his hand on the mailing tube. Dog squeezed his fingers, refusing to surrender.

"Give it to him," Reid grizzled. He raised the Lee-Enfield to his eye and pointed it at Mad Dog.

Winston's eyes turned to cold steel, piercing through Mad Dog, but he spoke softly, as a parent to a child. "C'mon, Mad Dog . . . let go."

Mad Dog let out a howl that bounced off the gorge walls. He brought his football karate chop down on Winston's forearm, dislodging it from the mailing tube. He cocked his arm, intent on throwing the scrolls into the chasm of the falls, but Winston dove toward him and hit his arm before it came forward. The scrolls fell to the wet rocks and bounced a few feet away. Reid repositioned, rifle trained on Mad Dog, and yelled at Winston to clear so he could take the shot. Jalina screamed. She ran toward the scrolls. Travis picked up his gun and fired two shots at Reid. They missed. Jalina swiped her leg at the scrolls, trying to kick them into the gorge. She slipped, fell on her butt, and whacked the back of her head on the rocks. Reid swiveled his rifle toward Travis. Travis dropped to the ground flat on his back, legs spread wide in the direction of Reid, head up, chin tucked tight to his chest. Reid darted. Travis straight-armed the Beretta, steadied his hands above his crotch, and fired twice. Burnt powder filled my nose. Travis fired again—miss.

Reid positioned himself behind Emilie, using her as a screen. He advanced toward Travis, keeping Emilie between them. Winston bent to pick up the scrolls, but Mad Dog tackled him. Emilie shouted, "Travis," and dropped to the ground. Travis got off two clean shots, the second one catching Reid in the arm. He fired again. The grainy thud of the bullet hitting Reid's sternum made me throw up in my mouth. Reid's rifle fell to the ground. The force drove him into a crevice that slanted away from the falls and formed a back chute. Emilie ran to the chute and watched Reid slide forty meters into a kidney-shaped pool. She kicked Reid's rifle away like it was a rat carrying the plague. It slid along the wet rocks. Travis ran to the top of the chute. A ledge obscured the front third of the pool. He emptied his final round into the water at the bottom of the chute and reached to his back pocket for the second clip. It was gone, possibly dislodged, out on the rocks somewhere.

Winston broke from Mad Dog and ran, but not toward the scrolls. He bent over, picked up Reid's Lee-Enfield, and shot into the air to get the feel. Nobody moved. Travis shuffled toward Mad Dog and me. Winston tossed his hair back and launched into a soliloquy.

"In the fifth century there was a town in Sicily called Camarina." He took a dry cigarette out of a pack in his pocket and lit it. "The Carthaginians were their enemy, but a great marsh, the marsh of Camarina, stood between them." Winston smiled. He had an audience. He had his cigarette. He had the gun. "A great plague afflicted Camarina, spreading an illness that scared them terribly. The town leaders were sure the marsh was the source of the sickness. They wanted to drain it, but the oracles advised against it. Despite the warning, they drained the marsh."

It was shocking to witness the intoxication of Winston listening to his own voice.

"Of course, as soon as they drained the marsh, the Carthaginians marched across the dry swamp and killed every person in town. History, my friends. Man and nature working together. Intellect ruling over the lesser." Winston scanned his audience.

"You're not smart," Jalina said "You're a bully. I know third graders smarter than you." Travis looked amused by her matter-of-fact manner.

Winston bounced his eyes along the horizon and bore his pupils into Jalina's. Well, dear. The problem is that you five . . ." He stopped and looked at Betsy. "Six. You six have drained the marsh of its goodwill. Curiosity. Dangerous, my friends. Sadly, given what you know, I can't allow you to carry on. Now, can I? Time to join your friend Bubba in the Zambezi. Maybe you'll catch up to him at the Kariba Dam."

Betsy spoke up with the lilt of a kind grandmother, appealing to both shame and dignity. "Winston. You've been wronged. Look at me. Winston . . . please look at me." He did. "You are better than this. I know this. I've worked with you. Years of good work. Not meant for something like this. I've loved you as a colleague and a friend. We can still work together—save the world from horrible diseases. Like we talked about. Malaria, cystic fibrosis." She faltered when she started to say, "Sickle ce—"

His face went bloodless; a citadel of malice invaded each muscle. "You! Your eminence is abrogated here. You destroyed the center. Now you beg for my charity?"

Winston raised the barrel and pointed it at Mad Dog. Two shots rang out. One bullet scraped the edge of Winston's neck. Mad Dog let out a roar that came from his ankles. He charged and drove Winston ten yards like he was hitting a tackling dummy. He released and we watched Winston's momentum carry him over the ledge into the First Gorge, falling three hundred feet into the lethal rips, rocks, and unflinching churn. A churn that shredded objects that were inferior to its natural might. Adrenaline overpowered Mad Dog, forced him to his knees. He'd just killed a man. In time, he stood, came to me, and draped his arms over my shoulders, barely able to stand.

A rattle came from the direction of the gunshot. We turned. Gary and his waves of camel hair marched out from the stand of milkwood trees, a worn Weatherby Vanguard hunting rifle strapped to his shoulder. He smiled. It was not a boastful smile. There were other things on his mind. Behind him a girl, a woman, walked cautiously into the open, onto the rocks. She was looking down, mindful of her steps, and then raised her head, said, "Hi," and laughed.

CHAPTER 83

Craze: Yes

Mad Dog gaped like the day he pulled in his striper rig off the coast of Martha's Vineyard and found he'd hooked into a short-nosed sturgeon. He knew that laugh. Everyone in our hometown knew that laugh. Alex peeked from under her bangs, sheepish, waiting for a reaction. In the brightness of her smile, I detected a sadness, which I assumed was a battle between the impropriety of being happy and the graveness of what had just happened. Shots fired. People killed.

Screw that, Alex came! She waited for me to run to her. I pushed Mad Dog and his angst aside and went to her thinking, Is this is how she envisioned this moment when she decided to surprise me? This is the ultimate gesture. Who's the romantic now? I was moved, happy to accept the defeat of knowing she had out-romanticized me.

I called, "Alex," and was surprised that the bloom in my voice perfectly expressed the affection I was feeling. I walked slowly, hugged her, picked her up, spun her into a twirl that induced another laugh.

"I can't believe it, Alex. You're here. All this way. And you guys came up through Rhodesia. Amazing." I looked over to Gary, who guardedly watched with keen curiosity while scanning the margins of our surroundings for activity. I waited for his eyes to land on mine. "Gary, my God. You are the man sir—a good man. Thank you for bringing her here." A wave of humility dropped into my heart and weakened my voice. "It was very kind of you, my friend."

". . . Pray for our sinners, now and at the hour of our death. Amen." Jalina's voice rose from its whisper. "Not to mention, thanks for saving our lives, mate."

Emilie's cheeks were now high and pink, "Dieu merci, merci Gary. You are full of surprises."

Mad Dog gave Gary a fist pump. Jalina's brown eyes shoveled through my irises without judgment, acknowledging a mischance of time, telling me with tenderness that she understood. My lips tightened and curled up, but my eyelids loosened in apology and admiration of her. She shuffled her gaze to the ground and stepped away. Travis stared at me, arms crossed, head shaking, with a facial pucker that was scolding and empathetic.

"But what? How? When did you decide to come, Alex? How did you know where I was?"

Another laugh. She hooked her thumbs into my belt loops and pulled me close. "Geez, you're not hard to find. You told me you'd be in Johannesburg for a couple of weeks to finish the court case. I knew who your lawyer was. I knew what hotel you were at. And you guys are still in the news, even at home. 'Stranded Tourists Going to Victoria Falls,' 'Tourists Party with Soldiers in Rhodesia,' 'Botswana Travelers Eat at Steak House in Bulawayo.' Seriously!"

I kissed her. Her lips were firm and cool at first., she seemed conscious of the audience, but muscle memory melted her self-awareness and they parted, years of comfort, intimacy, and friendship fueling a presage that was wonton and fierce. It crossed my mind to ask her the question. *The* question. She had answered it by flying to Africa, hunting me down, and braving the Rhodesian convoys. Still, I wanted to hear it. More importantly, I wanted to make sure we shared the special moment that comes after the word, "Yes." I despised public proposals, spectacles that fail to be as bold, momentous, or charming as intended, forcing the woman into an awkward position. Give me mushy. Give me purpose. Give me eloquence.

Betsy's stare was cold, seemingly uninterested in the sentiment. She focused on the mailing tube that still lay on the ground. She picked it up and caressed it in her arms like a baby. It was the only remnant of years of research and toil. She found a spot on the ledge of the First Gorge, near the place where Winston went over. Her face was bleak and hopeless, aware of what she was about to do. She squatted, arms down like a standing long jumper. She lowered the scrolls to the wet ground, and exploded upward, thrusting her arms out, and hurled the scrolls into the chasm of "the Smoke that Thunders." Both feet landed firmly on the ground, arms still extending skyward. Her heart was empty. She collapsed. Spray spattered her face. She wept. A forecast of hope escaped her lips. "We'll be ready someday."

A thought struck me. "But Gary, how did you know we were in trouble?"

"I didn't. But I wasn't foolish enough to come to Rhodesia without a gun, like you guys. That would be insane."

Travis scoffed. "Call me a biscuit."

"We found your campsite at the Vic Hotel. The other guys said you came down to take a gander at the falls. Just stumbled into your little predicament, which I hope you are going to fill me in on. That kook was ranting, and I saw he meant business. What did you do to him? Anyway, it looked like he was going to pop you, so I popped him first."

Mad Dog put his arm on Gary's shoulder. "We'll tell you everything."

The rainbow was still there, buffing its colors across the sky, playing the seductress and whispering one word in my ear: "Now." I took Alex's hand and pulled away from the others, down a path to a spot where a few boulders had created a recessed nook. My heart raced. Alex was nervous, having figured out what was happening. I dropped to my knee.

"I know I proposed over the phone, but I want this occasion to be special." I stammered. "I guess you've done that already. Special. Made it special. A special occasion. You coming here is a statement, and I am humbled by it—by the statement, by you. Alex, I am humbled by you."

She interrupted, bashful, but with love in her eyes. "I want to say something first."

I was happy to have my lack of eloquence interrupted.

"I love you. It is deep and permanent. The past few months have been a lot to bear. I am sorry to have caused us this pain." Her words were gentle and tender, and I was relieved to get a few seconds to regroup my thoughts. "I decided I had to come to Africa because . . ."

I couldn't stand it. I blurted out, "For God's sake Alex, will you marry me?"

She pulled back, opened her arms to the wind, looked to the rainbow and said, "You idiot. Don't you see? I've already said yes."

"I know. I understand that," I said. "But I still wanted to hear you say it. I wanted us to share the moment that comes after the question."

"I said yes . . ." She faltered, looked to the heavens for help. ". . . but. But not to you."

The love I'd seen in her eyes was that of love gone by. A love that still existed, but had been willingly parked, not to be diminished but to be honorably abandoned.

"I said yes to the man I told you about. The man I met on my trip. I have thought it over . . . and over and over . . ." Her back stiffened. ". . . carefully. I am happy with the place I've come to in my heart. But I'm not happy to do this. Not at all."

Until that point, I'd never thought about what I feared. Bosses and friends had called me fearless because I climbed mountains, took on impossible projects, and bought plane tickets to places they'd never heard of. It was a misinterpretation. For a moment I thought I feared the loss of those challenges and the obligations that might pare away my choices. But now I knew what I feared, and it was peering at me, for I could see my own reflection in her eyes. I saw someone who wasn't good enough. Someone who was almost good enough, but not quite so. A person with enough integrity and virtue to gain some love and affection with an occasional ovation. But still not good enough.

It was like I was living a riddle. I knew Alex. I could see she was in pain. I also knew, and could see, that she had untangled her feelings and slogged through the shapeless density of her decision. Yet, I thought if I talked, if I made her do one more examination of her soul, maybe even make her laugh, the emotion of considering our life together would bring her to pause. I fought the instinct to brood. *Did she come all this way just to say no?*

"Alex, think about what compelled you to come to Africa to see me. That act alone is a profound expression of love, a level of affection that is rare for any couple. I'm ready, Alex." I took both her hands into mine. "I'm ready. You wouldn't come all this way just to say no."

Travis coughed. They had wandered down to our nook, figuring we'd had enough time. The moisture in Alex's eyes spilled onto her cheeks. She squeezed my hands, but her eyes were looking over my shoulder. Gary was the first to step into the imaginary circle that surrounded us. He brushed his hand on my upper arm and squeezed it as he walked by. The anticipation of this exact moment, this precise turning point in Alex's life overwhelmed her. A deluge of tears fell, this time with unbound sobbing. She took a step backward. Two. Gary wrapped his arms around her, and she clutched him with unusual familiarity. Then she jumped up, wrapped her legs around his waist, locked her ankles behind his back, and held on. She pulled her head back and kissed him. Not a kiss of friendship.

Are you shitting me? Gary? From Vancouver? Bubba told me the guy was from Vancouver, but really? Gary? Blood rushed to my ankles. My heart popped with anarchist rhythm. Alex dropped to her feet.

Mad Dog said, "Holy shit."

Travis supplicated the spirits of Jesus, Mary, and Joseph. Gary put his arm around her shoulder, and they started walking on the path toward the town of Victoria Falls. She looked back at me, once. Her eyes, lips, and cheeks had patched together a message of compassionate certitude. Gary glanced back and said, "She told me about visiting your friend Bubba in Oregon. And then in the newsroom . . . it clicked when you told me you were from were from Norwell, Massachusetts." He walked.

CHAPTER 84

Fallout

An FDR quote that had been hibernating in my head since the tenth grade took a seat. "Courage is not the absence of fear but rather the assessment that something else is more important." Alex and Gary held hands as they walked. *Does that quote apply if you fear yourself? Am I supposed to withdraw and let another man step forward and take her? Should I scream and holler despite knowing her well enough to admit that the fight is over?* They disappeared around the bend.

If I create havoc, make her hate me, it will be easier for her, put a stamp on her decision. No, I want to inflict maximum guilt. I swayed, like a boxer blinded by a left hook, shaken by how quickly it happened. No more time than it took to see Bubba part with life.

"Nothing that close," is what Gary said in Kasane when I asked him if he had marriage in his sights. He said it after I'd told him I was going to propose to my girlfriend. He decided to propose after he figured out the connection! I hollered, "He's a shiny bauble. He wasn't going to propose." My words bounced off the mist and dissipated into the gorge.

Travis looked upon me with pity. Deadness forged on my face, distilling contradictions as I conversed with myself. I thought, I am unhappy and therefore I want her to be unhappy. It doesn't mean I never loved her. But the brief time it took for scorn to replace love alarmed me. I wanted to find my friends, cry to them, and have them brand her as vile and uncaring. Is love so fragile—or is it pride and insecurity that cause a mind to change course so easily? Her character did not change in those few seconds. She didn't suddenly lose the effervescence and decency that I loved her for yesterday. Yet I wanted to despise her. I was not prepared to be rational. I was not willing to accept the wise notion that time would heal, that there would be another. Beware anyone who offered me the adage, "When one door closes . . ." If they said it, I might strangle them. I could not bear the injury to my pride—an infirmity that made me more loathsome.

I did not want to be happy with myself or accept the foolish idea that being happy with oneself is enough. I wanted to be angry. Devastated. I wanted to think that happiness had been torn from me forever. I wanted to be pitied. I felt pitiful, therefore it is fitting. She cheated on me, and in a relationship, cheating is a form of lying. So why did I feel such an absence of rectitude?

That night I penned some self-serving lyrics, intending to find notes for them on the guitar at some point. It made me feel better— for around ten minutes.

```
I didn't think I'd ever know what it was
like to be this low, stripped of all I
came to know in myself. I wonder what
it's like to lie, to let affection
calcify, as the seeds of your evolution
die away. What will ever happen to the
clothing I have sewn? Weighed so less,
to the best, sorter of the stones. Had I
been a lesser man and lied those tears
away; had I been a lesser man, she'd
still love me today. I didn't think she'd
ever find such a simple state of mind,
to leave me for a blind autumn fire.
```

Selfish thoughts, unwilling to accept my part or acknowledge my flaws, but an apt reflection of my post-devastation bankruptcy. While the bogeyman steam shoveled boulders of shit from one part of my head to another, Betsy sat on the edge of the gorge, alone, still crying; and in the diffuse battlefield of armed conflict and world opinion, Robert Mugabe and Joshua Nkomo were winning the Rhodesian Bush War.

CHAPTER 85

Craze: Editing Everything

"They seized his car, furniture, TV, stereo, and silverware. It was the Bentley Gold golf clubs that made him cry." Andrew Dunard's silk voice spiraled though a carvery of tawny burnt ribs, seared ostrich steaks, and chicken peri peri, at our breakup dinner at the Thunder Gun Steakhouse outside Johannesburg. Twice we'd gone back to the Supreme Court to see the men with the tampon wigs and curly eyebrows. Andrew argued that, in South Africa, Marvin was Trindell Travel and Trindell Travel was Marvin. They ruled in our favor both times, levying an abundance of anguish on Marvin which brought us a victory devoid of bliss.

Tireless jokes on the virtues of mealie meal and cabbage bounced off the beamed ceiling. Doug and Jerry stood atop their chairs.

"But you saw the ferry get blown to bits yesterday," Doug said.

Jerry replied, "Yes. Let's go back tomorrow."

"Men shooting from helicopters. Another fine mess you got us into."

"But the waterfall. I want to see the waterfall."

"That's silly. We'll have to go through the war zone in convoys."

Jerry looked down, as if drawing inspiration from the teak charcuterie board. "Precisely."

Doug cut his next line short after catching a glimpse of Mad Dog's confused look, one that said, "My friend died amid that mayhem." The dinner ended with hugs, kisses, and promises of correspondence. Mad Dog, Travis, Betsy, Jalina, Emilie, and I relocated to an adjacent pub.

"What's that?" Emilie asked Travis of a wrapped newspaper with a twine bow.

"Not more genetic code, I hope." Betsy's temple twitched, troubled by her own humor.

He peeled open the package. It was a red stone carving of a mother and child, arms encircled and joined as if they were one, entirely without angles. "I love it," Jalina said. She leaned her head onto Emilie's shoulder.

"We're naming our new baby Tinashe. A Shona name. Means We Are with God.

His cover blown, Travis was heading for London to unite with Norah, Jaxon, and their new baby. He offered to visit the Trindell office in London with a brick of C4. We declined. He laughed, but his squinty eyes penetrated the levity and found me. In them I saw an apology, an application for absolution as if I were Father McGann at Most Holy Redeemer on Maverick Street in Eastie. Travis had killed my friend, and he was my blood. DNA. I dropped my head to my folded hands and raised my eyebrows once.

"Come," he said, and pulled me to the end of bar. "I have a midnight flight. Tell Mad Dog and the others I said bye. I ain't going through it with each of them."

"You going to stay in London?"

He wrapped his fingers behind my neck and leaned into my ear. "Can't." He flicked his head toward the table. "They know about London. I'm goin' to the States to regroup the United Freedom Front. Work to be done." He squeezed the back of my neck, said, "Craze, you'll never see me again," and walked out.

Mad Dog was talking about a Kansas TV station that dropped subliminal messages into a news report in an attempt to catch the BTK serial killer. Betsy's feet were drawn beneath her chair, ankles locked, neck twisted toward two guys playing Space Invaders. Her burdens were heavy and many. She'd lost a friend in Bubba. Her colleague had allowed gargoyles in his head to distort decency and expose a racist heart that rejected all mantles of shame. "How could I not know?" she said, barely audible, chilled that her friend was able to hide it from her. "The money. He'd won so many awards. I just assumed."

"You were colleagues. Friends," I said. "Why would you question?"

"How many organizations like the New Pioneer Column are out there? White supremacists with money." She pointed her knees forward and looked at us one by one as she spoke. She wondered how long supremacist groups would endure. Asked us what we thought would make them surface. "They see brotherhood as validation," she said. Winston had betrayed the spirit of their work and contorted his genius into atrocity. So much so, she was willing to sacrifice her research center—a decision that ate at her life force. After hearing his speech on the ledges of the falls, she blanched at his choice to use sickle cell as a means of perverting gene editing.

"Technology isn't the problem," she said. "It's born from raw science."

Mad Dog said, "Not your fault, but it's an ethical sac of bile. People will always screw things up. Needs to be in good hands . . . used for a good purpose." Dog's earlobes turned purple with pain. I know he was thinking of his sister.

The problems were absurdly difficult. For what purposes should gene editing be used? How should it be regulated—and by whom? Used for diseases, of course, though some would claim that was solely God's realm. But, once the technology was out there, rogue groups or countries would misuse it. If it could cure Alzheimer's, then yes. If genes were found that fostered intelligence, the zone was grayer. Engineering blond, brunette, light or dark skin, blue or brown eyes, carried an Aryan stench. What of aging? Could it be arrested or reversed? Where would the additional food, air, land, and water come from? Were there genes that predisposed someone to be kind, angry, or patient? Did a misplaced A, T, C, or G incline someone toward bigotry?

"What will you do?" Jalina asked.

Betsy sucked a deep breath of dry Transvaal air. "The chimps are still alive. Gravity pulled on the lines of face. "The workers have cared for them. I'm going back. Will rebuild enough to finish our hepatitis work. We were close to a vaccine. I can do that with modest financial support."

Jalina and Emilie decided to call it a night. As they stood, Emilie asked Betsy what the second nanoparticle was for. She said something about stopping and starting transcription and proliferation of unipotent stem cells. Emilie laughed, shook her head, and dropped a peace sign as she and Jalina walked out the door.

Betsy stood to say goodbye. We embraced with a firmness and finality wrought from shared ordeal and respect. Mad Dog took her by the hand, odd I thought. "Take this," he said.

A roll of film was in his hand. Mad Dog's left cheek twitched.

"I took pictures of all the scrolls," he said.

Her breath drew sharp, and her chin poked out like a Hapsburg jaw. Mad Dog faced Betsy, but his eyes turned to me. He pursed his lips, something he does when he digs in. Betsy pinched the tail of the film and drew it from its cartridge. It coiled and hung from her fingertips like a strand of DNA. She dipped the end into the candle jar and watched the flame crawl up the coil, spine straight, one eye on Mad Dog. She winked and walked out the door without a word.

Mad Dog and I talked about the convoluted path of our African ramble. How, in White suburbia, it was decidedly easy to grow up apathetic to racism; to give passing acknowledgement to it; discuss it in school; maybe even march in a protest or two—and then move on—lives unaffected. Apathy provided no relief for those of color. They didn't have the option to put it aside. We'd seen sectarianism at its core: White ideologists that champion apartheid in South Africa and minority rule in Rhodesia. They set the tone for the everyday Joe to scoot along in idle acceptance. Easy if the advantages were on your side. Were they bad people at birth? They grew up in a domain that benefited them. First, they were innocent, then they were taught, then they accepted, and finally they believed and defended—with all their heart. "We've been here for three hundred fifty years. There's nothing I can do," they told us. It was bigotry breeding bigotry to a point where it persisted, dominated, and, with repetition, became engrained within the individual who eventually held it as truth.

"You think it's hypocritical that we see all this, but still drink in the pubs, laugh with the soldiers, ride past rattled slums, and walk freely past the signs that say 'Non-Europeans' or 'Beware of Natives'?" I asked. "We've seen the fright in their eyes, the way their labor is exploited. Yet we used the White courts, shopped in the Whites-only stores."

"What are you saying? You saying we're racist?"

"Huh? No. I mean we're . . . not. Right?"

"Just because we came here? Don't call me that."

"Maybe we're oblivious to where the line is. Maybe we don't want to know where the line is."

I didn't know what I was feeling. I thought, Does a willingness to visit these countries make me complicit in supporting them? Does spending my tourist dollars imply a morsel of legitimacy? Or am I grossly ignorant? Still, I was better armed and able to speak with credibility. I applauded those who were all-in with their credo without having seen or touched the injustice. Not everyone gets to stick their fingers into the wound. There are those like Travis who empathized so completely that they went to extremes and even violence. Perhaps our character suffered because we—White suburbanites—had the option to insulate ourselves, to seclude and compartmentalize racism as needed. You tell yourself you will carry what you've learned when you return home and apply it with conviction, hoping not to make self-promises that you forget—in the same way I forgot about my promise to help the next poor person after I saw the starving woman in Bobo.

"You think we'll be more vocal when we get home, Dog? I'm afraid we might go back into our cocoon. Because it's easy."

"I know what I saw. What's in my heart. That's enough."

There it is, I thought. Essentially saying that casting our vote was enough. We didn't have to campaign. Leave the fight for social justice to people like Travis. In lieu of developing my own backbone, I thought. "Or maybe don't normalize it by staying quiet when we hear it," I said.

Dog took a sip of beer, raised his eyebrows once. We talked about what we would say to our Caper Crew friends when we got home—without Bubba. We could never articulate what we'd seen and felt. Talk would turn to stories of elephants and lions and things that were still ahead for us: Kilimanjaro, Ngorongoro, sailing on a dhow up the Nile through the Sudan and Egypt. I would go back to a job in the Boston Medical Area, and Mad Dog would seek something that satisfied his interest in the environmental sciences.

After Gary and Alex left Victoria Falls, they disappeared. I continued to be hurt—so bitter I was swollen with it, fueled by disappointment with Alex and anger that blazed within myself. Immensely broken-hearted, the experience didn't make me stronger as some would suggest, another adage that deserved its own pyre.

The morning after the breakup dinner, I sat on my mattress and took a final survey of my room at the Alendene. Mad Dog loomed in the doorway, pack secured, holding hands with Emilie. His expression bore an artful carriage. He said, "Let's go, Craze."

Jalina stepped through the door, sat on the bed next to me, and locked her arm in mine. She held our plane tickets to Malawi in her hand and gave me an order. "C'mon, mate. Flight's in two hours. Let's get on with it."

NOTE FROM THE AUTHOR

I thought I was going to transcribe a journal I wrote during a 1979-1980 trip to Africa. I'd quit my job in the Hematology Laboratory at Boston University Medical Center Hospital, and, along with my friend Mad Dog, bought a one-way ticket to Africa. I quickly learned that it was more fun to fictionalize our journey while using experiences in my journal to capture the physical, emotional, and political atmosphere of an important time in African history, a time we naively stumbled into.

As a student, I was fascinated with the fact that a change in a single nucleotide of a DNA strand, essentially a hiccup of nature, could change a fully functional hemoglobin molecule into one that sickles. To top that, the new hemoglobin offered some protection from malaria . . . but could also kill you. Inserting this concept into our travels hatched a plot that spawned a sticky note assault on my kitchen wall. Despite the use of several real names and events, I assure you that all other elements of the story, characters, dialogue, and events were drawn from my imagination.

I hope you enjoyed reading this book as much as I enjoyed writing it. Reviews are important to independent authors. A one sentence review on Amazon or your favorite book website can make a huge difference.

ACKNOWLEDGEMENTS

Let's start with my editors who deserve a mountain of praise for taking on a greenhorn and finding a way to dispense large doses of candor with grace.

My story editor, Steve Parolini, turned my kitchen wall into a mosaic of notes by dealing out tough love, POV wisdom, and storyline guru-ness, while laying a hammer to any inconsistencies.

Sincere thanks to Sara DeGonia, from DeGonia editing, for taking a backhoe to my semicolons, inflating my self-worth when needed, and keeping me focused on the North Star.

My Caper Crew friends for life, Dave (Mad Dog) Hill and Paul (Bubba) Brewster, helped me paint authentic settings and characterizations of Africa by sharing their journals, photos, reminiscences, confessions, and recollections of our travels.

Most of all, I must thank my wife, Marie, who endlessly humbles me by living a life of selfless compassion for those whose fate has been diverted by one of life's landmines. If she had made a promise to help the next needy person after seeing the woman at the market in Bobo-Dioulasso, she'd have kept it. And brought them cookies. And soup. And cornbread. Her unconditional support and encouragement are constant reminders of how life should be lived. Not to mention her mad beta reading and proofreading skills.

A shout out to my beta readers, Jenn, Lisa, Lindsey, Lilli, Marie, Nancy, and Roberta, for generously offering their time, feedback, and encouragement.

Special thanks to Andrew Duncan, who schooled me on the legalities and terminology of 1979 law in South Africa.